# Courage

# to

# Change

*Grant Us Grace Book Two*

*By Elizabeth Maddrey*

With gratitude and love for birth parents

everywhere.

"Come open the door. It's cold out here and I'm freezing my you-know-what off."

"Brandi." Phil sighed into the phone and sank onto the foot of his bed. "What are you doing here?"

"I figured it had been a while since we partied, so I brought a six pack over to share with my husband."

"*Ex*-husband."

Her voice lost the playful tone and took on a hard, bitter edge. "It's not my fault you decided to get sober. Find Jesus. All that crap. What a drag."

The pounding on his front door echoed up the two flights of stairs.

"I came by to give you another chance to see what you're missing. Let me in."

"I'm sorry, but no." Phil rubbed his temples as a migraine began to build. "Go home…please." He should just hang up. Of course, the last time he'd done that she'd made such a scene the neighbors had called the police. At least after that his mother had finally understood why he hadn't wanted Brandi to have his new address. If he didn't love this historic little town on the river that was still an easy commute to his job in downtown D.C., he might consider moving again and just not tell anyone. He realized Brandi had been wailing into the phone and he'd missed it. "Back up. What?"

"I said I've got nowhere else to go, Phil. Let me in."

The rational side of his mind argued against the tug of guilt. Steeling himself against the inevitable tirade, he took a deep breath. "You don't have a place here, either. Now, you need to leave before the neighbors get concerned."

He flinched and held the phone away from his head at the string of threats and epithets she unleashed. When she was finally quiet he put the phone back to his ear. "I'm hanging up now. Good night, Brandi." He clicked the phone off as she started in again. The phone rang almost immediately. Phil cradled his head in his hands and ignored it. When his answering machine picked up she started ranting right where she'd left off. He groaned and went to the bathroom for some aspirin.

He'd never expected things to turn out this way. He'd been filled with such joy when he understood and accepted what Christ offered; he'd assumed Brandi would share in his excitement. Boy, had that been a miscalculation.

Phil shook two aspirin into his hand. He wouldn't trade his relationship with God for anything. If only he'd been more willing to hear God calling him before he made the mistake of marrying Brandi in the first place. Of course, he wasn't listening to anything about God at that point. What was it everyone always said about hindsight? The phone was ringing again and more vicious banging echoed up from the front door. He crawled into bed fully clothed and buried his head under a pillow.

**ꝏ3ꝏ**

Phil woke when the sun streamed through the wall of glass that made up the back side of his bedroom. The last vestiges of his headache hovered, leaving his brain foggy and his eyes sore. Grimacing, he threw an arm over his eyes. After several minutes he pushed himself out of bed, grumbling. He squinted resentfully at the cheerful sunlight as he stumbled to the bathroom. "Fine. I'm up."

Grabbing the bottle of aspirin, he angled toward the elevator. *Lazy. Take the stairs and quit whining.* With a mental shake, Phil propelled himself down two flights of stairs to the kitchen. He peeked out the sidelight window by the front door, relieved when he didn't see Brandi curled up on the porch. *Maybe she has enough sense to go somewhere else in the cold.*

He eyed the thick layer of frost on the small plot of grass that served as his front yard and noted the absence of footprints. Hopefully she'd left soon after she'd quit calling back. Phil poured coffee and gulped the first mug to chase another dose of aspirin, barely tasting it as it burned down his throat. He poured himself a refill and glared at the furiously blinking light on his answering machine. With a sigh, he sat at the little table he'd centered in the bay window at the front of the house and reached for the phone. Punching in the familiar number, he sipped his coffee and watched his neighbors leaving for work.

The phone picked up after the first ring. "Grant Sommersby."

"Hi Grant, it's Phillip Reid."

"Morning, Phil. I don't imagine you're calling this early to reschedule the golf match you owe me?"

"Sadly, no. She came over last night. Filled up my entire answering machine tape spewing venom and hammering on the door." He groaned and rubbed at his throbbing temples. "I haven't heard from the neighbors yet, but I won't be surprised when I do."

The sound of shuffling papers crackled across the line. "Okay. We've got the police report your neighbors filed last time. You still have the messages?"

"Yeah." Phil scrubbed his hand over his face. "She's the only reason I keep that old tape machine instead of switching to voice mail."

"Well, if there are threats on the tape and we can get a neighbor's statement we can probably get a temporary restraining order."

"I don't know…"

"Phil, she's harassing you. Don't you think it would be a wakeup call for her?"

"I guess. It just seems weird for a guy to be the one requesting a TRO. You know?"

Grant gave a sardonic laugh. "I know what you're saying, but you'd be surprised how many men are the victims in relationships. Not saying you're a victim, not in the traditional sense, clearly. But Brandi needs help. And more than that, as your attorney and as your friend, I just want to see you free of her."

Was this really the right thing to do? "Yeah, all right. I'll be in a little after ten at this point. Can you just leave anything I need to sign with Sam at the front desk? I'll run them across the street to you when I get in."

"Sure thing. Did you choose me as your attorney just for office proximity?"

Phil laughed. "It didn't hurt."

With a chuckle, Grant said goodbye.

Phil popped the tape out of the answering machine and set it on top of his laptop bag. Filling a third cup of coffee, he headed upstairs to get ready for the day.

∝Ǝ℞Ọ

Phil didn't make it to his desk until almost eleven. He'd taken the answering machine and signed papers to Grant. Now it was just a waiting game. He still wasn't convinced this was the right thing to do, but he needed

Brandi to move on. He'd spent four of the past five years praying they could reconcile and remarry. But she had no intention of changing her lifestyle, and regardless of the shame he felt from being divorced, it was past time to let her go. Unfortunately, now she didn't seem to want to leave. He pushed those thoughts aside. There were still a few minutes before his new clients arrived and it was time to focus on their problems rather than his own.

Allison scrubbed her hands vigorously at the sink, trying to avoid splashing soap down the front of her suit. The black silk and wool blend had been a splurge and she wanted to keep it looking new for as long as she could. She rinsed and looked for a paper towel. Both dispensers were empty again. Was she the only one who let Sam know when they used the last paper towel?

Allison shook her hands over the sink, catching herself just before she wiped them on her skirt. She let out an exasperated groan and smoothed her hair before taking a quick inventory of herself in the mirror. *Good enough.* She squared her shoulders, fixed a smile on her face and glanced at her watch. Her new client would be here soon and she wanted to review his case file one more time.

A muffled sob echoed from the farthest stall. Allison paused, her hand on the door handle, and she angled her head to see if there were feet visible. "Everything okay?"

A sniffle was the only response. Allison frowned. The shoes didn't look familiar. She probably shouldn't know her co-worker's shoes quite that well. Crossing the room, she tapped lightly on the stall door.

"Can I get someone, or something, for you?"

More sniffling. "No." The person in the stall cleared her throat. "I'm okay. Thanks."

Allison pursed her lips. Should she push? Even though she was in a hurry, she hated the idea of leaving someone crying in the bathroom without at least trying to help. "Who are you meeting with? I can stop by their office and let them know everything's all right, or send them in to talk to you."

"I'm here with my dad. He's," she blew her nose, "He's the one meeting with an attorney."

Flipping through what she knew of the other cases in the firm, Allison couldn't place who this woman was. "Do you remember the attorney's name? They're probably getting worried, even if you're not the primary person in the meeting."

"Dad's not going to miss me. He's on a mission." The stall door unlocked and swung in, revealing an obviously pregnant young woman dressed in khakis with a man's white dress shirt buttoned over a red tank top. The tank looked like it had been snug before the girl's pregnancy and was now close to popping its seams. She offered a wan smile, dimples appearing in her blotchy red cheeks, and swiped at the drips of mascara running down her cheeks. "I'm Lindsey."

Allison smiled back and extended a hand in greeting. "Hi, Lindsey. I'm Allison." The girl had to be in her mid-teens. That probably meant the pregnancy factored in to her dad's meeting with an attorney. She could only imagine the drama that must be unfolding in that office. Still, Lindsey looked so forlorn. "Let's get you cleaned up and see if we can't figure out where you should be. I'm guessing they've noticed you're not there."

Lindsey scoffed but moved toward the sinks with a defeated sigh. "Might as well. I think I remember where the office is."

"Come on, I'll…oops." Allison stopped and lifted a finger. "We're out of paper towels. Let me go get some. I'll be right back."

Lindsey nodded.

Allison dashed from the bathroom and hurried down the hall to the reception desk. She caught the eye of the assistant and waited until she'd disconnected her call. "Sam, we're out of paper towels in the ladies' room again. Also," she turned and looked down the hall to make sure Lindsey hadn't followed her out, "there's a young woman in there. Has anyone been reported AWOL?"

"That's Phil's client's daughter." The older woman shook her head, deep furrows forming in her forehead. "They just called and said to make sure she didn't leave the offices. I'll walk her back to Phil's."

Allison started to object. Any excuse to stop by Phil's office was worth the inconvenience. His blue eyes could warm her from the tips of her toes to the top of her head with the briefest contact. She glanced at her watch. *Dang it, there isn't time.* "Thanks. That'll keep me from being late for a new client meeting. Take paper towels, would you? She's pretty unhappy."

Sam nodded and pressed a few buttons on the phone to transfer incoming calls to the backup receptionist. She grabbed the keys to the supply cabinet. "I can only imagine. I don't have all the details, but he said enough when he made the appointment that," she pushed back from her desk, "well, it's a tough situation."

Allison opened her mouth to press for details. Something about the girl tugged at her heart. Plus, she might be able to contrive a way to stop by Phil's and talk to him about it if she knew more about the case. Another look at her watch had her simply nodding. "Let me just run in and let her know you're on the way." At Sam's look she shrugged. "I said I'd be back. I get the feeling many people don't follow through with her the way she wishes they would."

❦

At the knock on her doorframe, Allison looked up. Phil leaned against the jamb. His laptop bag was slung over one shoulder, the jacket to his suit draped over it. He'd loosened his black, silver, and pink striped tie and opened the top button of his white shirt. Reminding herself not to stare, she couldn't stop her eyes from drifting over his long, lean form. Her pulse drummed in her ears. Was he talking? She looked at his face. His lips weren't moving. *Phew. Don't stare. You're being obvious.* She offered a polite smile.

"Working late?"

Allison checked the clock on her monitor and laughed. "I guess so. That hadn't been my intention, but I got caught up." She paused and narrowed her eyes. Now that the drumming in her ears had quieted some, she could focus on the shadows under his gorgeous eyes. "You okay? You look pale."

"Had a migraine last night, barely slept, you know how it is. Tack on the challenges of the day." He shrugged and swung his head to look down the hall then returned his gaze to Allison. "Anyway, I hear I owe you thanks for finding and returning my lost sheep?"

"Who? Oh." The corner of her mouth twitched up. "Lindsey? Right place, right time is all. But you're welcome. Is she going to be okay?"

Phil tucked his hands in his pockets. "Yeah, though I don't think her father actually cares one way or another…I try, I really try, to see the best in my clients, but sometimes…While I agree with his lawsuit in principle, I'm not sure it's really the right thing when you take into consideration everyone it's going to impact."

"I've had cases like that. You can always have him find another attorney." Poor Lindsey. And poor Phil.

"I could. But at this point, I think I'd rather see what, if anything, I can do to make this easier on the girl."

Phil's compassion and empathy for others impressed her, as it always did. "Is the case related to her pregnancy?"

Phil nodded. "Actually, if you have time tomorrow, I wouldn't mind talking about a few aspects of the situation with you, get your take."

"Sure, hang on." Allison minimized the document she'd been working on and opened her calendar. Looking at the next day's full schedule, she chewed her lower lip. There had to be time somewhere. "Pretty much the only time I've got is lunch." She looked up and raised her eyebrows in query.

"That works. Brown bag?"

"Why not. I've probably got some leftovers languishing in my fridge that haven't completely turned into a science experiment." Allison typed the appointment into her calendar, ignoring the butterflies that danced in her belly.

"You can always order in if that's what you want to do. But I'm not sharing my PB&J, so don't even think it."

She sent a reminder to Phil's email and wrinkled her nose. "No problem on that score, I can't stand PB&J."

Phil's eyes widened. "How…what…?" He gaped at her. "That's un-American."

"You're getting it confused with apple pie. Which I like. All this talk of food has reminded me that it's well past dinner time. So I think it's time I head home. See you tomorrow." *Smooth. Real smooth. Though I guess it's better than obvious drooling.*

He smiled as she gathered her things, slipped past him, and started down the hall. Just before she turned the corner, Phil called out, "Nice suit, by the way."

Allison floated on cloud nine the whole way home.

ﾂﾂﾂﾂ

Despite the chill in the air, Phil propped his feet on the railing of the balcony outside his fourth floor bedroom and looked out over the Occoquan River. He had an email from Grant waiting for him, but couldn't quite work up the nerve to get to it. Every encounter with Brandi left days of cleanup in its wake. He was so sick of it. He stuffed his hands into the pockets of his coat and wished he had a beer. His fingers found his AA chip and traced the Roman numeral six that was prominent in the center. He forced his thoughts away from the feeling of a cold, foamy beer sliding down his throat. *This, too, shall pass.* At least now it was easier to resist the urge to drink, even if the desire for alcohol was still there.

The meeting with Marcus and Lindsey had been harder than expected. He was able to empathize with a father's need to defend the honor of his daughter. But it seemed like it was just making Lindsey suffer even more. *I'm not convinced legal action isn't just going to make things even worse. For everyone. Maybe Allison will have some insights.*

He smiled and pictured Allison behind her desk, her chestnut hair tucked behind her ears as she focused her gray-green eyes on the screen in front of her. *Why is that so alluring? What am I thinking? I had my chance at marriage and blew it. I really should keep my distance.* Still, a chance to be alone with her, even if it was just a quick working lunch, had his pulse pumping in anticipation. *Even though nothing can ever come from it…she has to eat, and so do I. Why couldn't I have met her before it was too late?*

The morning sped by. Allison started the day five minutes behind schedule and had worked her way up to a full twenty. She frowned at the knock on her rarely-closed door and kept typing. When the knock repeated, she growled low in her throat and saved the file.

"What?"

Phil poked his head around the door. "Bad time?"

The quiet hum that filled her brain when Phil was nearby picked up, keeping time to the drumming of her heartbeat. Was it time for lunch already? "No. Sorry. Come in. I'm just behind today."

He didn't move. "We can reschedule."

She pushed her hair behind her ears. "No. A break is probably the best thing for me right now. This," she gestured at her computer, "isn't going anywhere." If nothing else, once lunch with Phil was over, she might have more concentration than a flea. *Who am I kidding? I'll just be thinking about what he said instead of what he might say.*

Phil eased into the room, clicking the door shut behind him. "Um. Where?"

Allison followed his gaze to the small round table surrounded by four chairs that was crammed into a corner. Heat stole across her cheeks. Fat books, some open, others stacked, completely hid the tabletop. Nearly all of them looked like porcupines, their pages bristling with multi-colored sticky notes. *He must think I'm a slob.*

"Just push them out of the way to clear a spot. I'll go get my lunch from the break room."

By the time Allison returned with a handful of paper towels and a brown paper sack dripping liquid from one corner, Phil had carefully stacked the books into taller piles, clearing two places at the table. Wrinkling her nose, she spread the towels over her eating space and set the bag down.

"What happened to your lunch?"

Allison grumbled. "Some moron wasn't paying attention when they jammed their plastic container of soup into the fridge. The container that was, apparently, not sealed properly. It leaked all over the lunches that happened to be sharing the shelf." She pulled an assortment of plastic bags from the lunch sack. "Sadly, or I guess thankfully, depending on how you look at it, I've encountered this phenomenon before and come prepared."

Phil chuckled. "You even wrap whole fruit in a bag?"

Allison pulled an apple out of its protective shield. "Have you ever had chicken noodle flavored apple? It's not pleasant."

"Wouldn't it just wash off?"

"Sure. But the taint lingers. At least to me." She glanced down at his sandwich. "You actually brought peanut butter and jelly? I thought you were joking."

He shrugged and took a bite. "Some things are classics for a reason. And it'll always go together. Unlike," he squinted at the array of assorted leftovers in front of her, "what is that, fried mozzarella and lo mein?"

"What's not to love? Leftovers are like chocolate, they go with anything." First the messy table, then the lunch of a teenager. So much for making a great impression. "So, what's up?"

Phil wiped his mouth. "The gist of it is that Lindsey is sixteen, going on seventeen, and the man responsible for her current state is almost twenty-seven."

She gasped and revised her thoughts about Lindsey's dad to give him a little more credit.

Phil nodded. "In a nutshell, yes. Marcus is, as you'd imagine, livid. The problem is that multiple people have notified the authorities, but no one is motivated to do anything. The police told him that while it's technically statutory rape, it's not worth pursuing since the father of the baby isn't in a position of authority and Lindsey insists it was consensual."

"But if he presses charges, they have to act."
Dumbfounded, Allison zipped through various solutions,
but none felt right. Sympathy for Lindsey clouded each
picture. Was it even possible for her to come out of this
mess whole?

"Yeah, but they've told him no judge is going to
give the man more than a slap on the wrist, if it even gets
that far. So, he figures he has a better shot with a civil
suit. Thus our appointment."

"And Lindsey's feelings on the matter?"

"Aren't relevant, as far as Marcus is concerned.
But I'd say she's completely opposed, thinks they're
madly in love, and is lobbying for dad to give permission
for them to marry." He straightened the wax paper that
had held his sandwich and began peeling his orange onto
it. "She has a vivid 'happily ever after' fantasy in place.
Despite the fact the boyfriend has already stopped
returning her calls."

Given those facts, happily ever after didn't seem
very likely. How did you overcome that big of an age
difference in the long run? It was possible, but it stacked
the deck against them. Maybe him leaving was better,
even if it was terrible right now. *Unless he's just lying low,
hoping Marcus' anger will dissipate.* "Is the disappearing
boyfriend dad-related or pregnancy-related?"

"Pregnancy, from what I gather. Seems like his
desertion is actually the majority of the push behind dad's
lawsuit. It's bad enough his baby girl is pregnant, but now
the guy's not even willing to stand beside her." He balled

up the orange peel and wax paper and pulled a candy bar from his lunch bag.

"So what is Marcus hoping to accomplish?" Allison eyed Phil's candy bar. Would it be totally out of line to ask for a piece? Probably.

"On the surface, he just wants to make sure the baby is provided for financially. But I get the feeling it's really about punishing the guy and maybe, to a degree, his daughter."

"No chance she'll place the baby for adoption, then?" It was the best option she'd come up with for Lindsey's future. Even then it would be a tough road.

"Not at this point. She's pretty adamant that they're going to be a family. I don't think she understands what goes into parenting. That's one of the things I wanted to talk to you about. You've mentioned the Pregnancy Resource Center a few times. Do you know someone there?"

"Sure. You remember Kevin from the Christmas party?"

Phil nodded.

Allison smiled. Maybe taking Kevin to the Christmas party hadn't been a terrible idea after all. Though she still wasn't sure if Kevin's comment, the one he guaranteed would let Phil know Allison was interested without making her look desperate, had helped or hurt things as far as a future between her and Phil. "His fiancée is working there now."

"Could you get in touch with her and see if they have recommendations for parenting classes or an education program? Something that might help her realize what the reality of life with a child is going to be? The one positive I can see in this situation is that Marcus understands his daughter needs to know what she'll be dealing with before the baby comes. I think he might be hoping she'll change her mind about adoption, but at least he's smart enough not to force the issue at this point."

"Sure. I'll give Lydia a call tonight and let you know what I find out."

"Thanks." Phil looked down at his watch. "Guess I'd best get back to my desk. I have a client call scheduled in a few minutes." He cleaned up his lunch trash and started to pull the books and files back to where they'd been.

Allison waved her hand at the pile dismissively. "Leave that. I've been meaning to tidy this table up for a week. We can't all be obsessively neat, you know."

Phil's laugh lingered in the room after he left.

*Why does watching him eat a sandwich leave my heart all aflutter?*

*Get a grip, Al.* She pushed her hair back behind her ear. *And get that haircut scheduled. Soon.* There was no reason to have turned a single question about the PRC into a lunch meeting. A flicker of hope sprang to life in her heart. *Don't get carried away.* It was possible she was the only one he knew with a connection to the PRC, though he could have just called on his own. It wasn't as if you had to have an introduction to talk to someone there.

How did you send a hint that you were interested in someone without appearing forward? She grabbed the candy money she kept in the pencil rail of her desk. At least chocolate was uncomplicated.

CS&O

Allison stepped into her condo and laughed when her black cat languidly raised his head from the off-limits coffee table and gazed at her. "Pippin, you know better." Allison strode across the plush carpet to scoop him up and nuzzle his head with her chin. He tolerated the caress, even managing a short burst of purring, before twisting and leaping neatly from her arms, stalking off into the kitchen.

Glancing at the inviting overstuffed sofa, Allison almost plopped down in front of the TV. *No, change first. Then you can vegetate longer.* She stroked the sofa's velvety aqua upholstery and ran her hand along the top of one of her deep purple chairs as she made her way to the bedroom. When she'd pulled on pajama pants and a sweatshirt, she headed back to the kitchen. Pippin scolded her from his perch on the counter.

"I know, I know. Dinner time." Allison measured some dry food into his bowl and set it on the floor. Scratching his head, she plunked him next to his dinner. "You know better than to be up there."

The cat ignored her, turning to munch his food. Allison laughed and poked through the refrigerator for her own dinner. Placing three mostly empty takeout containers on the counter, she hopped onto a stool. It probably wasn't too late to call Kevin. She grabbed the phone and punched in his number.

"Hello?"

"Hey Kevin. It's Allison."

"What's up?"

"I wondered if I could get Lydia's number from you. I thought I had it from last spring, but can't seem to put my fingers on it."

Kevin guffawed. "Not surprising. I know how organized you're not."

"Hey. I can find what I need when I need it." She glanced around at her semi-orderly kitchen. *Most of the time.*

"All evidence to the contrary."

"Are you going to help me out or not? I can call the Browns."

"You need their number too?"

"Have you always been this irritating?"

With a laugh, Kevin rattled off ten digits.

Allison snagged a piece of junk mail off the pile on the counter and scribbled the number across the back of the envelope. "Thanks…will she think it's weird if I call her? I haven't really talked to her since the whole…"

"Rehab thing? I guess it depends on why you're calling."

"I have a work-related question. Can't really go into the details, with you or her, but I'm hopeful she can provide some insight."

"Then I definitely don't think she'll mind. She really does like you, you know?"

Allison scoffed. "Sure. Everyone likes the person who sees them at their worst and, oh yeah, makes a play for their fiancé."

"I wasn't her fiancé at the time. Besides, unless you've mentioned that to her, she doesn't know about it. We went to dinner once. We're friends. We can do that."

"I'm just so embarrassed by the whole thing. Especially with the Phil situation…"

"Any movement on that front?"

Allison propped her elbows on the counter. "Not sure. We had lunch today. Ostensibly to discuss a case, but really, he could've sent me an email. Or looked it up for himself."

"Hmm. Are you praying about it?"

"Not really. It seems silly to bother God with something like this."

"Al." Kevin's voice was stern. "You know better than that. Pray about it. I will too, if you like."

"Deal." She frowned. "Can I ask you something?"

"Apparently."

Allison groaned. "I'm serious."

"You know you can. What's going on?"

"Didn't it ever bother you? Being single?"

Silence stretched across the line. "Yeah, yeah it did. Even knowing, or at least thinking I knew, God was going to bring me and Lydia together."

"Sometimes I just get so frustrated. I mean, I'm reasonably certain I don't have the gift of celibacy. I want to get married. I want everything that goes with it. And the older I get and more of my friends get married...I just wonder sometimes if God forgot about me."

"Been there." Kevin cleared his throat. "Look, I know it's probably not as useful coming from yet another friend who's engaged, but I always thought King David said it best. 'I've never seen the righteous forsaken.' God hasn't forgotten you, Al. He couldn't. You're inscribed on the palms of His hands. Hang in there, okay?"

"Sure. Not a lot of other options."

Kevin's laugh made her smile. "You know what I mean. Go call Lydia. I'll talk to you later."

She put the phone back in its cradle. What was it going to take to get Phil to notice her as more than a coworker and friend? Or should she be content with that? Was she so in love with the idea of being in love with someone that she'd set her sights on Phil and was missing out on the person God had for her? *I really do need to pray about it.*

After tossing the empty takeout containers in the trash and a quick, but useful conversation with Lydia, she settled on the couch and flipped on the TV. The channel guide led her to her favorite Tracy/Hepburn classic, *Desk Set.* Pippin padded over and jumped up, snuggling into the crook of her knees. She reached over to scratch his ears. There really wasn't *anything* better than a purring cat. A vision of Phil on the couch with her flitted through her mind. Okay, there wasn't *much* that was better than a purring cat.

It had been an exhausting day. Allison had hoped to have time to go over the notes she'd taken for Phil during her phone conversation with Lydia the night before, but she'd barely had time to drop the file on his desk between meetings. When she dragged herself home, she set her laptop bag by the door and gave herself a night off to read.

A knock at her door startled her out of the web of fantasy her book created. Glancing over at the clock, she frowned. Who on earth was coming by at almost nine at night? Whoever it was, they could deal with her pajamas. Allison shuffled to the door and peered through the peephole.

Allison opened the door a crack and gaped at the young woman standing in the hall. "Lindsey? What are you doing here?"

"I wasn't sure what else to do." Lindsey twisted her fingers together and shifted her weight from one foot to the other. "Please...can I come in?"

Allison opened the door wider and stepped aside. "How did you find me?"

"Google, mostly."

"Have a seat. Can I get you something to drink before you explain that?" She shut the door.

Lindsey shook her head. "I'm fine, thanks." She settled into one of the purple chairs and looked around.

Allison resumed her spot on the couch. "So, Google?"

"Your firm's website...you all have head shots? And there aren't a ton of Vasak's in the phone book. I took a chance that A. Vasak was you and followed someone in. I got your apartment number off the mailboxes."

Allison winced. What if 'A. Vasak' had been some sicko? Lindsey didn't seem to spend much time considering consequences before she acted. *That's unfair...who does at that age?* Still. It might not be a bad idea to completely unlist her phone number. As a criminal defense attorney, she'd had clients in the past that she had no desire to run into in her hallway. "I guess you're lucky I have an unusual last name. So...what prompted your bout of Internet sleuthing?"

Lindsey wet her lips and stared at the floor for a long moment. "My dad. He's kinda gone off the deep end. I get that this isn't what he planned...but I can't seem to get him to understand that I don't want Ben to get in trouble." Her voice broke. "Even if he really is finished with me. Us. Me."

"Okay. But why come to me? Why not call Phil— or better yet, why didn't you speak up when you were in the office?"

"I tried. But Dad's beyond ticked. And Mr. Reid...I don't know, he just doesn't strike me as someone who understands what it's like to be a sixteen year old girl."

"He's more sympathetic than you'd expect. But I can see how you'd think that." She drummed her fingers on her knee. Should she even get involved in this? "Here's the thing, Lindsey. I'm not really sure what I can do. I can talk to Phil, if you want. But ultimately you're going to have to work this out with your dad."

Lindsey's whole body seemed to deflate as she nodded. "I know. I just..." Her eyes filled with tears as she met Allison's gaze. "I thought Ben and I would get married and be a family...but he's made it pretty clear that's off the table. So now I don't know what to do. I...how do I raise a baby by myself?"

"Won't your parents help you?"

"Mom died two years ago in a big wreck on the Beltway. Dad's been in a tailspin ever since. He's doing the best he can, but neither of us has really figured out how to live without her. I can't imagine putting a baby into the mix."

"Oh, Lindsey. I'm so sorry." Allison blew out a breath before tentatively asking, "Have you considered adoption?"

"I hadn't. Now…I guess I need to. But I don't even know where to start…and what if I can't? Giving up my baby…I just don't know."

"I don't really think I can help you there. But I do know someone who might be able to. Have you been to a Pregnancy Resource Center at all?"

Lindsey shook her head.

It was good she'd been able to connect with Lydia last night. At least now she knew in more detail how a PRC could help. "Okay. Basically, the PRCs are around to help women who find themselves in exactly the situation you're dealing with. They have all kinds of educational programs—they can help you figure out if parenting is possible and what that would look like. They can also help you investigate adoption and see if it's the right choice for you. I think they'll even work with your dad to help him…adjust."

"Really?"

"Really. Let me get their number for you." She rose and flipped through the pile of mail she never seemed to finish sorting. She knew there was a newsletter from the Center in there somewhere. "Here. This is a few months old, but the contact information is certainly accurate."

Lindsey took the paper and studied it. "Thanks. You really think they can help?"

"I really do." Allison plopped back onto the sofa. What now? "Does your dad know where you are?"

Lindsey shook her head.

How did that happen? Her parents had always known where she was and when she'd be back. "You need to call him and tell him you're okay. Did you drive here?"

"Bus. And some walking."

"You definitely need to call your dad. He can come get you, or I can take you home if it's all right with him for you to ride with me."

Lindsey pulled out her cell phone and had a quick conversation with her father. Allison was relieved there was no obvious shouting.

"He'd like to talk to you." Lindsey offered the phone.

*Oh boy.* "Good evening, this is Allison Vasak." One corner of her mouth twitched up as Marcus started in with a frantic apology. "No, sir. It's not a problem...yes, we met briefly at the firm." She gave Marcus her address and handed the phone back to Lindsey who said goodbye and hung up. "Now. Are you sure I can't offer you a soda or something to eat while we wait?"

C≥≈∂

Allison held open the door of the Pregnancy Resource Center for Lindsey and her dad. Lindsey shot her a grateful smile. "Thanks for coming with us, Allison."

"Not a problem. Let's go check in. I don't think we'll actually be meeting with my friend. But Lydia says everyone here is great."

When they'd signed in, the three took a seat. Awkward silence filled the waiting area. Allison stood and walked around to read the titles of some of the brochures that were displayed throughout the lobby. She made her way to the shelf that displayed adoption information and collected several different pamphlets for Lindsey. "Here. Why not do a little reading while you wait?"

"Oh. Um, sure." Lindsey gave her dad a sidelong glance then looked back at Allison.

"Never hurts to be informed." Allison patted Lindsey's shoulder and handed another brochure to Marcus. Neither of them looked comfortable, but she felt certain this was the right place for them to be. She brightened her tone. "Right?"

"Right. Sure." Marcus accepted the paper and looked at the title. Clearly startled, he glanced at his daughter then back to Allison. He drew his eyebrows together and looked more closely at the paper in his hand. "Are you really considering this, Linds?"

Lindsey chewed her lip and shrugged.

"Okay." He slipped an arm around her shoulders.

Allison felt some of her tension drain away. Maybe Marcus would be able to help Lindsey after all. At least it looked like he was starting to understand how miserable the whole situation was making her.

The door by the reception desk opened, revealing a smiling, fairy-like older woman. "Lindsey?" Her smile spread as she crossed the room and extended her hand. "It's so nice to meet you. I'm Maureen." She turned her smile on Marcus. "You must be Lindsey's dad."

"Marcus. Hi." He inclined his head toward Allison. "This is Ms. Vasak. She's the one who told us about your office."

"Please call me Allison. We've never met, actually, but I've been a supporter of the Center for quite a while. It's lovely to have a chance to see your place in person."

"I recognize your name from the mailing list. You know you don't have to bring a client with you in order to get a tour, right?" Maureen's eyes twinkled.

Allison chuckled. "It's been on my to-do list for years. I just never seem to manage it."

"Well, I'm glad you found the time to at least stop by today." Maureen turned her attention to Lindsey and Marcus. "What I'd like to do is split you two up. One of our peer counselors, Catherine, is getting a room ready. Lindsey, she has a bunch of information that she'd like to share with you—but most of all, she'd just like a chance to chat and get to know you. We don't want to overwhelm you right out of the gate."

"Okay." Lindsey cast a nervous smile at Allison.

"Marcus, I'd like to meet with you myself. I've been exactly where you are, and I know the tumultuous waters you're facing. Is your wife unable to be here today?"

Marcus looked down and cleared his throat. "She died a few years ago."

"I'm so sorry." Maureen closed her eyes briefly. "If it would make you more comfortable, I can see if my husband is able to join us. He can provide a dad's perspective."

"You don't need to trouble him. Though maybe I could connect with him down the line?"

"Absolutely. He'd love that. Let me just get Catherine and we'll get things rolling." Maureen flitted back through the door. Murmured conversation drifted down the hall. She reappeared with a tall, slender redhead at her heels. "Catherine, this is Lindsey. Lindsey, Catherine. Your dad and I'll be upstairs if you need anything."

Lindsey stood, clutching the brochures, and followed Catherine through the door into the counseling area. Allison offered a silent prayer for this to be a productive meeting.

"Thanks for smoothing the way, Allison. It's always good to have someone along when you're doing something new."

"My pleasure." Allison could recognize a dismissal when she heard one. Though she hadn't expected to stay the entire time, she'd thought she might be able to sit with Lindsey until the girl felt more comfortable. Hopefully she'd be all right on her own.

Allison turned to Marcus. "Let me know if there's anything else I can help with. Or tell Phil. And, pass that along to Lindsey, please?"

"I will." Marcus offered a tight smile. "I appreciate this."

⚜

Outside, Allison took a deep breath of the brisk January air. She needed coffee. The mermaid on the sign across the street beckoned. The jazzy strains of *Fly Me to the Moon* poured from her bag. Her pulse rocketed as she dug out her cell phone. Giving Phil his own ringtone had been a late night whim. She should probably change it back to the default before he found out what song made her think of him. On the other hand, why would he be calling if he was close enough to hear?

"Hey, Phil."

"Hey. How'd it go at the PRC?"

"You must have a spy camera somewhere. I just left. Seemed like they were in good hands."

"That's a relief. No problems with anything?"

Allison checked for traffic and darted across the street. "Not one. And it seemed to me that Marcus might be slightly more open to the idea of adoption than any of us originally thought."

"Huh."

She chuckled. "Anything interesting happening at the office?"

"Did you forget where you work? Well, actually…"

"Oooh, what?"

"Sam brought in a delicious chocolate cake for the break room. Sadly, it's pretty much gone."

"Seriously? Why would you mention it if there's no chance of having any? That's just mean."

Phil laughed. "I might have saved you a piece. On the other hand, if I'm such a mean person…I guess I just have an extra piece for myself stashed away."

"You're a prince among men." She glanced at her watch. "Tell you what. I'm going to grab us both a coffee and you can meet me in the park across from the building in, say, fifteen minutes. If you bring two forks, I'll share."

"Deal…you really think you can walk back here that quickly?"

"It's only five blocks." She pursed her lips. She wasn't really wearing the right shoes for running. Or even walking crazy fast. "Okay, make it twenty."

"See ya."

Allison tucked the phone back in her bag. There was a coffee place next door to the firm's building. She'd pop in there instead.

⚮

*What am I doing?* Phil set the phone back in its cradle. He peeked at the thick slab of cake he'd stashed in his insulated lunch bag. It was definitely large enough to share. He closed the lid and checked the time. It was close enough to the end of the day that he could head home after cake and coffee.

In fact, despite how much he wanted to see Allison, maybe it would be better if he just dropped off the cake and ran. It wasn't fair to give her the wrong idea. He'd made a colossal mess out of one marriage already. Didn't Jesus say He hated divorce? And if that wasn't enough, Brandi had made it clear many times that sharing him with God wasn't something she was willing to do. *But not every woman is like Brandi. Especially not Allison.* If he was listing differences, he could start with Allison's heart for God and go from there. What would it be like to be in a relationship with someone who understood what being a Christian meant? *Not that I have any right to even think that way. Especially not about someone as wonderful as Allison. No matter how much I want to.*

Still arguing with himself, he grabbed two plastic forks from the basket by the fridge in the break room and headed for the elevator.

As he stepped out onto the sidewalk, Phil saw Allison leaving the coffee shop in the building next door and stopped at the corner to wait for her. "Need a hand?"

Allison shook her head. "I got it. You look like you've got just as much. Going home from here?"

"Figured I might as well."

"That's my plan, too. I only came back this way for cake. Well, and to get my car."

He laughed and cupped her elbow to steady her as the coffee cups wobbled when she stepped down off the curb. "Careful. It's chilly enough to need that coffee if we're sitting out here."

"That's January in D.C. One day it'll be sixty and gorgeous. The next we'll have snow." She spotted a bench under a bare tree. "How about over there?"

"Sure." He kept his hand under her elbow as they crossed the lawn, enjoying the tingle the contact sent through him. "So everything went well with the Bowers?"

"Seemed to. I guess we'll see. But Maureen, she runs the Center, really seemed to put them at ease. I'm hopeful they'll get the help they need. Even if I did just cost the firm a client."

"I hadn't thought of it from that standpoint. On the other hand, the partners are always harping about doing what's right for the client. And a trial, no matter how much better it might make Marcus feel initially, is just not the right solution." Phil pulled the cake from his lunch bag and the two forks from his breast pocket. "*Voila.*"

"Oooh. That looks heavenly. Did Sam make it?" Allison took a big bite, avoiding the frosting, and rolled her eyes in exaggerated pleasure. "Never mind. It's clearly homemade."

Phil chuckled and took a sip of his coffee. She looked so cute with the little dab of chocolate just above her upper lip. He fought the urge to lean over and wipe it off with his thumb. Or better yet, kiss it off. *Whoa. Where did that come from?*

"Aren't you having some?"

"I already had a piece. I'd hate to deprive you."

Allison shot him a quizzical look. "This is too big for me to eat by myself. Besides, I thought you said we were sharing."

He stared across the park, watching the cars stack up at the traffic lights. He wanted to share the cake and then ask her to dinner. But no work excuse came to mind. And he didn't want dinner to be work related. *This isn't fair to either of us.* "I can't do this."

"Eat cake?" Her forehead wrinkled and she shot him a clear look of confusion.

Phil frowned. "No. Look, Allison. I…you know I'm divorced. I just can't do this. It isn't right." He stood and collected his things. "Thanks for the coffee…I'll see you around." *Stupid, stupid, stupid.* He strode across the park toward the parking garage, a metallic taste in the back of his throat. It was foolish to think he could be friends with Allison and not want more.

Allison parked in front of the strip mall that held her Tae Kwon Do dojang. On the way from work, she'd made a quick detour by her apartment to change. She hadn't planned on making it to class today and hadn't brought her gear to work with her like she normally would have. But the encounter with Phil at the park had left her unsettled and desperate for activity. Maybe an hour of sweating would help her understand what was so repugnant about her company that the prospect of sharing a piece of cake—cake he saved for her, mind you—sent him running for his car. Sure, she'd hoped that she and Phil could translate cake-in-the-park into a real dinner date, but it's not as if she was asking him to marry her. Yet. She blew out a breath. Even if it was what she wanted. After Phil's abrupt departure, the cake turned to dust in her mouth and she'd handed it to a homeless man hovering near the parking garage. At least he'd seemed excited about it.

Annoyed with herself, she grabbed her water bottle and slammed the car door. A good sparring session was just what she needed. Hopefully Sarah would be at class tonight. Maybe they could go for dinner afterward. Better yet, skip dinner and just get a truly decadent dessert. Cheered by the prospect, she pulled open the door and lifted her hand in greeting to the people already stretching on the mats. She stowed her bag and water and joined them.

When class was over, Allison plopped onto the mat next to Sarah. "You were late again. How do you always manage to miss the warm ups?"

Sarah shrugged. "We can't all be perpetually on time. Besides, if I didn't run late, we probably would never have met."

"And that would be a tragedy of epic proportions. At least for me."

"Smart aleck."

Allison grinned. "Me?"

Sarah guzzled her water and stood, offering a hand to Allison. "I thought you weren't coming tonight. Didn't you say you'd probably be working?"

"Yeah. Turned out I wasn't needed past initial introductions. And then…" Allison looked around as students started to trickle in for the next class. "You have time to grab something to eat?"

"Sure. What did you have in mind?"

"Melting Pot?"

"Uh oh. Are we just having dessert?"

One corner of Allison's mouth quirked up. "That okay?"

"Oh, why not? We just worked out, right? I'll meet you over there." Sarah headed toward her car.

Traffic was light. They were seated just a few minutes later, with dark chocolate Oreo fondue on order.

"So, what's up?"

Allison recounted the cake-in-the-park incident with Phil. "I just don't understand it. It was cake. And okay, sure, I was already trying to figure out how to casually turn it into dinner. But even if I had, so what? It's not like I actually said, 'Hey, let's go out on a date, Phil.' We're friends, I thought…what's wrong with hanging out now and then?"

Sarah pursed her lips. "Do you know anything about his divorce? Sounds like there's some kind of baggage there."

"Well, yeah, of course there's baggage. He's divorced." She paused as the server brought their fondue and explained the tray of dippers.

"But no, I don't have a ton of details. Just that she kicked him out because she was tired of being married. Or something to that effect. I can't imagine he was doing anything that made her the injured party in the deal."

"I don't know, Al. This sounds like a little more than 'once bitten.' He hasn't said anything else?"

"He mentioned once, like almost two years ago, that he didn't think you could ever remarry after a divorce. But he'd just been talking about how depressed he'd been after the split and how she still popped up every now and then and made life tough. I figured it probably had to do with that…I get that divorce isn't ideal, particularly for Christians, but it seems awfully rigid to think that means you can't remarry at some point. Especially if you're not the one who broke up the marriage in the first place."

Sarah twirled a banana slice around in the chocolate. "Changing his mind seems like a lot of work when it's not like the two of you are even close to dating. You have a little crush on him. Why not chalk it up to that and move on?"

Allison used a spoon to douse a marshmallow and tried to keep the bitterness out of her voice. "Sure. Move on to one of the thousands clamoring at my door."

"Well, they might be, if you'd loosen up a little and be willing to play the field."

"You know that's not what I'm looking for, Sarah. Besides, I've never figured out where the Bible says abstinence isn't important once you're finished with college." Allison frowned and waved a hand in front of her face. "We don't have to get into that again, sorry."

She bit her lip to keep from mentioning the feeling she kept getting that there was supposed to be more between her and Phil. She knew Sarah didn't believe that God still spoke directly to people, or that He got involved in their daily lives. And she just wasn't in the mood to get into that discussion again, either. She forced her tone to be cheery. "What's new with you?"

Phil pulled into the driveway of his sister's townhouse. The fact that there were lights on inside was a good sign. He'd swung through a Boston Market to pick up meatloaf and creamed spinach to share. Karin always told him she loved it when he dropped in, but he didn't want her to think he took his baby sister for granted. He winced as he remembered her response the last time he'd called her his baby sister. At twenty-seven, she was three years his junior, and very much a grown woman. But she'd always be about fourteen in his mind. He rang the bell and pasted on a smile that didn't quite reach his eyes.

She opened the door, grinning widely when she saw his takeout bag. "Dinner. You're a life saver. How'd you know?"

"Older brother intuition."

She glanced down at her wrinkled pink scrubs. "Come on in. I just got home. Let me run up and change.

I don't think I have anything ooky on these things, but really, who wants to chance it. You know where the plates and such are."

Phil nodded and went into the kitchen. He bypassed the paper plates Karin always had stacked next to her actual dishes and dug around for some serving dishes. He slid the meatloaf onto a platter and the sides into bowls then set the table. It was homier that way. More like a family dinner. Or so he imagined. Their family had never been big on eating together. With the string of step-dads they'd had after their father had walked out, he wasn't sure if he would've considered sitting down for a meal an indicator of being a 'family' anyway. For all intents and purposes, it had been just him and Karin since he was fifteen.

"Ooh, fancy." Karin planted a quick kiss on his cheek. "What can I get you to drink? I have water. Anything else is iffy."

With a laugh, Phil said, "Water is great. Got ice?"

"How you can drink ice water in January is beyond me. But yes." She waved him off as he moved to help. "I'll get it. You sit down and tell me what brings you this way."

"Can't I just want to see my sister?"

Karin set his water down by his plate and took her seat. She reached for the meatloaf. "Sure. But you usually bring hamburgers when you're just swinging by on a whim. Meatloaf and creamed spinach? That's conversation food."

Phil scooped spinach onto his plate. "Conversation food. I'll have to remember that. As it happens, I mostly just wanted to see a friendly, familiar, and uncomplicated face."

"Uncomplicated, hm? What's her name?"

Phil shook his head and took a bite.

"Oh come on. It's obviously a woman. You're the one who made the whole 'I'm not perpetuating this cycle. Clearly no one in our family can handle marriage' speech after Brandi left you. So whenever you start to think about another woman like a single, attractive, thirty-year-old male should, you come over here with conversation food. Thus I repeat myself: what's her name?"

Sometimes baby sisters were more trouble than they were worth. "Allison."

"Allison, the attorney at your firm, Allison?"

He nodded.

"Oooh. Office romance. A tad cliché, but still promising. Tell me about her."

"There's no romance. I don't understand how you keep missing that when you can vividly recall that the Brandi fiasco proved I'm not fit for marriage."

Karin's face betrayed her irritation. "She did no such thing. She certainly proved that *she's* not fit for marriage. But what did you do? You made changes in your life so that you could be a better husband. She repaid you by kicking you to the curb. She'd rather have someone to party with who is hung over and constantly in danger of losing his job than someone responsible who is actually on the partner track at his new law firm." She stabbed her meatloaf viciously, her voice taking on a sarcastic edge. "You think that proves that you're the one who has issues. Get a grip, Phil."

He set his fork down and tented his fingers. "If you look at it that way, okay, fine. But the fact of the matter is I drastically changed who I was after I'd made a commitment to someone. Didn't she have a right to expect me to stay the person she married?"

"No one stays the same unless they die overnight. You may not see it, but she changed too…just in the opposite direction as you."

"Either way, it's too big a risk. I'm not going down that road again."

She shrugged and forked up another bite. "All right. So, why the food then?"

"Because I really *want* to go down that road again. Against my better judgment. I thought dinner with my kid sister might help me remember why remarriage isn't the best idea."

Karin rested her fork on her plate and closed her eyes. After a moment, she resumed eating. "First, thankfully, you and Brandi never had kids. So you're not like Mom, bringing someone into a house where they can do harm to your child while you're in la-la land. Second, you're not Mom. You're not out looking for someone to make you feel whole. You know who you are already. Anyone you date, or marry, down the line is going to complement that, not give you the mistaken idea that now you're complete."

"I'm so sorry, Karin."

She waved off his apology. "We're not going down that road tonight. You weren't very old when she brought that man home. What were you supposed to do? You know mom would never have believed either of us. Not over him." She managed a weak smile. "Besides, I'm seeing a therapist now through work…it's helping some."

"I wish you'd talk to my pastor."

She scowled. "Don't push your luck. I know you've got the God thing going and it's working for you. Maybe I'll get to that point someday. I have to admit, watching you makes me wonder. But for now? I'm good." She scraped the last bit of gravy off her plate. "I've got ice cream in the freezer. If I share it with you, will you at least tell me more about Allison and let me decide if I should push you into getting over yourself?"

"What kind of ice cream?"

"Moose Tracks."

Phil groaned. She knew him too well. "All right. But don't be skimpy with the scoop."

Allison pushed back from her desk and stretched. It was just after one p.m. and she'd already put in close to eight hours. At least it was Friday. That was a definite silver lining. Even if it didn't look likely that she'd be able to sneak out early after all. She made a check mark on the top phone message and filed it with that client's paperwork. She glanced at the next message on the stack and rubbed her temples. She'd call Lindsey back in a minute.

She spun her chair so she could look out over the park. Her gaze flitted to the bench where she and Phil had almost shared cake yesterday. *Best not to dwell on that.* She forced her eyes away from the bench and tracked the progress of a group of tourists riding Segways down the D.C. sidewalks. The phone rang.

She swiveled to grab the handset. "Allison Vasak."

"You're there, thank goodness. Oh, um, this is Lindsey."

"Hi Lindsey. I just saw your message, you were next on my list. What's up?"

"He's still at it. I really thought his time at the Center made a difference. Last night we had a good conversation and…"

"Slow down. Who's still at what?"

Lindsey's impatient sigh blew through the earpiece. "My dad. He still thinks we need to press charges against Ben."

Allison flipped to a clean sheet of paper on her ever present legal pad. "Lindsey, your dad's working with Mr. Reid. I'm not sure I can, or should, get involved. If he and Phil decide that bringing some kind of suit is the right course of action, well…I'm not really sure where you think I fit in."

"Then I want to hire you."

"Hire me to do what?"

"I…I guess I want to file for emancipation."

Allison closed her eyes and leaned back in her chair. This had the possibility of turning into a huge mess. "First, I'm not that kind of attorney. Second, that's really a drastic step. You'd be completely on your own and I'm not sure your relationship with your dad would ever recover."

"He's got to stop this. I'm going to do whatever it takes to make that happen. Whether you'll help me or not." Lindsey's voice caught.

"Lindsey." Allison let out her breath slowly. There had to be some way to diffuse the situation. Marcus clearly didn't understand what he was doing to Lindsey. She just couldn't believe he'd keep pushing if he did. "Let me talk to Phil. Maybe he and I can sit down with your dad."

"It's not going to make a difference. Even that lady, Maureen, couldn't talk him out of it."

"Unless he told you, we don't even know what he and Maureen talked about yesterday. They could have spent the whole time getting to know one another. Give me a couple of days to look into it, okay?"

"You'll help me?"

"I'll try." The first priority was to get Marcus and Lindsey communicating with one another. Both had her sympathy. There had to be some way to help them through the situation and maybe find a way for everyone to come out better for it.

Lindsey sniffled. "Thanks. Do you think...could I maybe come and stay with you for the weekend?" Her voice was small, pleading.

Allison squeezed the bridge of her nose. Compassion was one thing, but she didn't want to choose a side or get caught in the middle. "Let me talk to Phil. I'll call you back before the end of the day, okay? Just hang tight."

She ended the call and stared at the phone, hoping for a solution. The minutes ticked by. She didn't want to talk to Phil. The thought of seeing him again had knots forming around the butterflies in her stomach.

She'd spent the bulk of the night figuring out how they could both still work at the firm with only minimal contact. Step one would be to quit the Wednesday Bible study he led at the office. Step two, distance herself from the Bowers case. *So much for the best laid plans.* Allison tapped the receiver. She could send an email. At least then she wouldn't have to deal with looking at him. Or she could call his office. Or just grow up and deal with the embarrassment of having been so obvious that she scared him off. *Get a grip. You're a professional. He's a professional. Just go get it over with.* The little pep talk spurred her to her feet. Clutching the legal pad and message slip as armor, she headed down the hall. Just outside his door, Allison paused and smoothed her skirt. She could do this. She straightened her shoulders and, before she could talk herself out of it, rapped twice.

"Yeah, come in." He sounded distracted.

Allison pushed the door open and gave him a tight smile. "Have a minute?"

"Sure." He gestured to his guest chair. "Take a seat?"

Allison stayed rooted to her spot just inside the door. "I just got off the phone with Lindsey. Have you heard from Marcus today?"

"Not that I'm aware of. But my voicemail light has been blinking for the last two hours. I've been swamped and haven't gotten to it."

Allison forced herself to stop fiddling with the edges of her notepad. She was here about Lindsey. She needed to put her personal discomfort aside. "From what Lindsey said, Marcus is still planning on getting Ben into court. She's pretty upset."

"Understandable." He steepled his fingers and tapped them together. "Do you mind waiting for a minute while I zip through those messages and see if he left anything detailed?"

She shook her head and moved to a chair while he picked up his handset. He skipped quickly through several messages before grabbing a pen and legal pad. "Aha. Here he is." He scribbled a few notes then set the phone back down. "Well. The long and short of it seems to be that Ben showed up at their door again last night. He still isn't interested in standing by Lindsey and the baby. Now Ben's pushing hard for an abortion. My guess is someone reminded him that if she decides to raise the baby he's going to be legally obligated to eighteen years of child support. And he's panicked."

"Poor Lindsey." The explanation made sense. Why hadn't Lindsey explained all of that? Though the take away was still that Lindsey didn't want legal action and was willing to take drastic measures to get Marcus to see that.

"I can't imagine a discussion of abortion went over particularly well with Lindsey…and I suspect her reaction is what's behind Marcus' desire to punish Ben."

"Even if it's not what she needs or wants?"

Phil shrugged. "That's not really our call. I can help Marcus bring a civil suit if he's determined to do it.

And I can't blame him if he is." He met her gaze. "What?"

Allison rubbed the back of her neck. This is exactly the position she hadn't wanted to be in. Especially now that things were weird with Phil. Still, Marcus deserved some kind of warning that his thoughts about what was best were pushing his daughter away. "If he really starts to push, he's going to ruin his relationship with his daughter. She asked about hiring me to help her with an emancipation proceeding."

Phil's eyebrows shot up.

"Yeah. My thoughts exactly. I told her that's not the kind of law I practice. And I bought a little time saying I'd talk to you…but lawyers who deal with that kind of filing are easy to find if she decides to try to go through with it. I'm not convinced she'll be able to get a judge to sign off…but even trying to get the ball rolling is likely to damage her relationship with Marcus beyond repair."

Phil glanced at his watch and shifted some papers to look at his desk calendar. "All right. Let me call Marcus."

"Just don't…don't mention what Lindsey said. She didn't say I couldn't share it with you, but I'm reasonably sure she doesn't want her dad to know where her thoughts are heading. Or if you need to mention it, maybe do it as an abstract possibility?"

Phil scowled. "I'll see what I can do. But he is her father. Don't you think he has a right to know?"

Allison stared past Phil to the window. "Sometimes it really is better not to know all the details. It leaves more room for hope."

Allison would do anything to go back to not knowing exactly how much Phil didn't want to date her. She figured the feelings probably translated to most situations. She rose to leave. Pausing at the door, she turned back to Phil. "Keep me posted, would you?"

Back in her office, Allison closed her door and tapped her fingers against the desk. She'd really like to talk to the counselor Lindsey met with at the PRC. There were all kinds of confidentiality issues involved in that, though she supposed she could take Lindsey on as a pro bono case. Then she'd just need Lindsey's permission to talk to the staff at the Center. That was probably the best step. Allison set those wheels in motion with a few quick phone calls then got back work on her pending paying cases.

CRRR

Phil spotted Marcus in a corner booth toward the back of the busy steakhouse. He wound his way to the table and shrugged out of his suit jacket. "Thanks for meeting me after hours. I just couldn't make it work any earlier today."

"Not a problem. It's kind of nice to get out of the house and not be headed for work." Marcus peered around Phil toward the door. "Is Allison not coming?"

Phil frowned and shook his head. He hadn't even thought of inviting her along. After all, he was Marcus' attorney. Lindsey seemed to have involved her because they bonded in the bathroom. He wasn't convinced she wanted to be involved. Especially not after yesterday. *And that's entirely your fault.* "No. I didn't invite her. Civil suits aren't her specialty."

"Ah. She's just been so helpful, especially with understanding Lindsey." Marcus lifted a shoulder. "I just assumed. Then again, it's Friday. She probably has a date."

"To my knowledge she's not seeing anyone right now."

Marcus hummed quietly.

Phil squashed a stab of jealousy. He wasn't even eligible for the market anymore, let alone in it. If Allison wanted to date, she was certainly allowed to do so. The same freedom applied to Marcus. Even if his heart sank at the vision of the two of them together.

He was about to bring the conversation back around to the business at hand when the server appeared. Both men ordered a soda and placed their food orders as well. When the perky young waitress left, Phil spoke. "How did your conversation with the woman at the Pregnancy Center go? What's her name again?"

"Maureen. She was very helpful, though she seems focused on finding out what Lindsey thinks is the right course of action and doing that." Marcus shook his head. "I don't necessarily think that Linds is capable of knowing what's right for her. After all, if she did, we wouldn't be in this situation."

Several retorts came to mind, but none were very professional. He bit his tongue.

"Anyway, she gave me a book they use with parents. And I'll go back and meet with her again. But I don't think she understands how important it is that Ben be punished."

"I take it, then, she didn't encourage pressing charges?"

Marcus' expression was one of disgust. "No. She said they've had a number of girls in the same situation who reported it to the police and the result was the same. Unless the man is in a position of authority, no one wants to do anything. Especially since he wasn't violent or coercive, at least according to the law. But I ask you, how did he get her into bed if he wasn't coercive?"

Phil noticed the patrons at nearby tables turning in their direction and gestured for Marcus to calm down and lower his voice. "I can understand how hard this is."

"You have a daughter?"

"No. But…"

Marcus snapped. "Then you can't understand. You can try. You can perhaps empathize. But you don't truly understand."

"Fair enough."

Phil sat back and folded his arms while their drinks and food were delivered.

"But I do think you need to consider Lindsey's point of view here. There's a very real possibility that you could irreparably damage your relationship with her if you insist on pushing this lawsuit. I don't think that's what you want."

"What can she do? She's my daughter. And a minor."

"She could always look into emancipation. If she did that, you could no longer sue on her behalf. And I don't think either of you would recover from the damage to your relationship. At least, not any time soon."

Marcus narrowed his eyes as he sawed into his steak. "I don't think she'd even think of something like that. Unless someone put her up to it."

"I'm not saying she knows about it. I'm just saying she does have options and if she feels trapped, she may start investigating them. Don't you think it would be better for the two of you to work together? She's got enough upheaval in her life right now."

Marcus sighed and set his fork and knife down. "I get so angry every time I think about it. This man gets her pregnant. Puts these dreams of family in her head. Then runs. He's a coward and a manipulator. I want him to pay like she's paying and will be paying for the rest of her life."

"Don't make her pay even more than she already is."

Marcus lowered his head to his hands. "I'll think about it."

The morning light streamed through the open blinds of Allison's bedroom window. She was curled up with Pippin drinking coffee and reading when her phone rang. The desire to stay immersed in the fantasy world of her book warred with her need to see who was on the other end of the phone. She glanced over, too lazy to move. Plus, it really wasn't fair to dislodge the cat. Satisfied with her excuse, she adjusted slightly and resumed reading her book. Then her cell phone began to ring.

She stabbed a bookmark into her place and snatched her cell phone off her windowsill. "Hello?"

"Hey Allison, it's Laura. Where are you? Your car's in your spot, we thought you'd be home."

"Laura? Wait, who's we?"

"Oh. Lydia and me. Matt's giving me the day off from the kids and Lydia roped me into going wedding dress shopping with her." There was a muffled denial in the background. "She didn't have to press too hard. It's fun. You have to come with us."

Allison stifled a groan. Watching other people try on wedding dresses was really not what she wanted to do today. Or any day. Especially when it was so they could marry someone she'd had a crush on. Though that wasn't entirely fair since she'd never actually thought it would work out between them anyway. She'd really wanted it to though. But Kevin had always been for Lydia. Thankfully, Lydia had finally figured out that she was for him, as well. *If only Phil would change his mind about me.* Laura had continued talking. "Sorry, missed that. What?"

"Where are you? We'll come pick you up."

"I'm at home, but I hadn't planned on going anywhere today."

"So buzz us in. We'll wait while you get dressed."

Allison groaned. "I really don't think…"

"Stop being such a wuss." Lydia yelled into the phone.

Laura laughed and Allison heard a scuffle over the phone before Laura was back on the line. "She's not wrong, you're being a wuss. Buzz us up or we'll have to start randomly pushing buttons down here. Maybe one of your neighbors will have pity."

"Fine." Snarling, Allison ended the call and went to the security pad, buzzing the main security door open. She unlocked her condo door and stood in the hall, arms crossed, to wait for them. When she saw them giggling down the hallway toward her, she felt her spirit lighten.

"Hey, Al." Laura grinned and threw an arm around Allison's neck. "Thanks for hanging out with us today. With the new baby, I don't get a ton of kid-free time right now. It's good to spend it with both my girl friends."

Lydia's smile was slightly more reserved.

"You're sure you're okay with me tagging along?" Allison tilted her head at Lydia.

"Of course I am…unless you're going to whine the whole time. Then I'll figure out a way to make Laura leave you here."

Allison waved them into the apartment. "Come on in."

Lydia glanced around the apartment. "I'm not sure I would have pegged you as having colors like this."

"Hey, the black and navy suits are just lawyer wear." She glanced down at her pajama pants. "I will, however, go throw on something a little more respectable for bridal boutique hopping. Give me a few minutes. There's coffee in the kitchen. Make yourself at home. And pet Pippin. You're stealing his cuddle time." As if summoned, Pippin stalked into the room and eyed the newcomers as Allison hurried back to her bedroom to change.

Five minutes later, Allison reemerged in jeans and a teal sweater. She'd taken a few extra seconds to apply a light dusting of makeup. She smiled when she saw Lydia and Laura settled on the sofa, each with a mug of coffee. "Does that mean I have time for another cup?"

Lydia glanced at her watch. "Sure. Our first appointment isn't for another hour and it'll only take about twenty minutes from here."

Allison refilled her mug and settled into one of her armchairs. "So have you set a date yet? Last time I talked to Kevin you were still trying to figure that out."

"Not yet, though I'm thinking maybe September."

"Wow. That far off? I figured you'd aim for the spring. Do the whole June Bride thing."

Lydia shook her head. "With all upheaval of last year...I just want him to be sure he knows what he's taking on. And, well, I feel like I need a little more time to be really, truly healed in here." She tapped her chest. "I think Kevin would prefer June, but he also understands my point. Honestly, September is a compromise. I was pushing for June next year."

Laura leaned forward. "That's much too long. Long engagements are hard. Especially when you're committed to staying pure until you're married."

Allison winced and glanced at Lydia out of the side of her eye. Had she felt the dig?

Lydia chuckled. "You don't have to tell me. Brad never managed to actually propose and I still let him use our 'engaged' status to wear down my resolve."

Laura blushed and stammered, "That's not how I meant..."

Lydia waved it away. "Don't worry about it. We all know the sordid details of my life at this point. I'm learning to live with it and grow from it. And I'm starting to be more comfortable talking about it. Working at the Pregnancy Resource Center has helped with that."

"Are you counseling now, too?" Allison swung her legs over the arm of the chair and settled deeper into the cushion.

"I'm not *that* comfortable. Though I think Maureen would like it if I did." Lydia shrugged. "We'll see. I may get there yet."

"Speaking of the Center," Allison took the last swallow of her coffee and set the empty mug on the coffee table, "if one of your clients gives you written permission to talk to me about her case, would that be all you need from a confidentiality standpoint?"

"I think so, but you'd be better off asking Maureen. Is this about the girl you brought over this week?"

Allison nodded. She'd call Maureen first thing on Monday.

Laura looked between the two of them, clearly confused.

"Sorry, Laura. I have a client. Well, Phil has a client who has a daughter who needs the services of the Center. I played middleman. Middlewoman. Whatever." Allison flicked a dismissive hand. "There's more to it, and I really wish I could get feedback from both of you, but between Center confidentiality and attorney-client confidentiality…I've probably already said more than I strictly should have." She stood and smoothed her jeans, wishing her confusion about Phil could be wiped away as easily as the wrinkles. "Should we get going, ladies?"

Lydia laughed. "Let's go. My wedding dress is out there somewhere."

⚜

"We're flying to Vegas and eloping." Lydia rested her head on the table they'd managed to snag in the crowded restaurant. Laura and Allison chuckled.

"Oh, now, it wasn't that bad." Laura bumped Lydia's arm, trying to nudge her back up.

Allison shot Laura an incredulous look. "It wasn't? Four bridal shops and," she glanced at her watch, "seven hours later...I lost track of how many tacky dresses they tried to foist on her. At this point, I'll cover the airfare if it means I never have to set foot in a bridal boutique again."

Laura and Lydia both burst out laughing.

Allison continued, "Can you believe some of those dresses? I just want to find the designer and ask what was going through their brain. If you can make someone whose figure is as close to perfect as hers," she gestured at Lydia, "look dumpy and fat, you seriously need remedial design school."

Lydia grinned. "I had that thought about several of the bridesmaid dresses they managed to get you to try on. How did they manage that?"

Allison buried her head in her hands, moaning. "I have no idea. Temporary insanity, I guess." She looked up and fixed her eyes on Lydia. "I will not be in your wedding. I've already been a bridesmaid twice. There are no more available opportunities for me in the bridesmaid department." The chant about three times a bridesmaid echoed in her ears. "Though given the way things are going in my world, it's not likely that I'll ever actually be a bride...so in that case, if you need a tenth bridesmaid, just let me know."

Laura widened her eyes. "How did you get up to ten? I thought it was just going to be your sisters."

Laughing, Lydia shook her head. "It is just going to be my sisters. Someone," she tilted her head at Allison, "is a tad prone to exaggeration."

"Phew." Laura swiped a hand across her forehead in mock relief before turning to Allison. "Now, what's this about you never being a bride? I thought Kevin said there was a guy at work?"

"Kevin has a big mouth." Allison shrunk into herself. She'd clearly made a mistake asking Kevin's advice about Phil. But who else was she supposed to ask? Kevin was pretty much it for male friends, and she'd wanted a man's perspective on the situation.

"Oooh. Spill. I hadn't heard about this." Lydia frowned at Laura. "How come Kevin's talking to you about this and not me?"

"This was before you and he were speaking again."

"Ah." Lydia paused. "Wait. Was this the guy at the party for work?"

Allison nodded. Apparently everyone knew all the details already. She'd have to find a way to get back at Kevin. "Phil."

"Right. Phil. So?" Lydia looked at Allison. "Let's go. Details."

"There are no details. In a purely friendly gesture, I brought him coffee and offered to share the cake that he snagged for me out of the break room. He then explained in no uncertain terms that, being divorced, he was not interested in me and never would be. Period. End of scene. Exit stage left, chased by a bear. Except that he was fleeing a park in the city. And there were no bears."

Laura and Lydia exchanged a fleeting look.

Laura reached across to pat Allison's hand. "I'm sorry. That seems…like he really likes you and is terrified."

"I agree." Lydia's vigorous nod set her ponytail bobbing.

"What are we, six? He likes me so he kicks me and runs away?"

Laura shrugged. "You've met Matt. Do you actually think boys ever really grow up?"

"Kevin's a grown-up." Allison looked at Lydia. "Isn't he?"

"Most of the time, but he has his moments." Lydia quirked one corner of her mouth up. "I think Laura might be on to something."

"Great. Just great. I avoid dating all through high school…and most of college…in an attempt to escape the juvenile rituals of the teenage boy, only to find out that there is no escape."

"Pretty much." Laura gave Allison's hand another pat. "So what are you going to do about it?"

"Nothing. He made his position clear and, from what I can gather, he thinks he has a Biblical basis for it. I'm not going to try and convince him to act against his conscience. Or God. And besides that, I was raised not to chase boys." No matter how much she wanted to. Allison craned her neck around. "Do they actually have wait staff here?"

"I'll go up front and see what I can find out." Lydia pointed at Laura as she started toward the hostess stand. "Explain the male of the species to Allison while I'm gone."

"I really do think he's acting like he's interested. Too interested, in his mind. And that's why he's running scared." Laura narrowed her eyes. "Something must have happened to make him think that you're also interested?"

Allison frowned. "I can't think of any...Oh...Kevin."

"Kevin?"

"Kevin. At the holiday party, Kevin said something to Phil about how he'd heard a lot about him. Then he tells me that's a guy signal that I'm interested and Phil will understand."

She'd hoped Phil would understand the hint. Of course, she'd hoped that his reaction would be positive. Now he was running in the opposite direction, all because she'd gone against her instinct and let someone signal her interest. "This is exactly why I don't think women should make the first move in a relationship. Kevin opened his big mouth and now I have even less than the no chance I had before. Do you think Lydia will mind if I damage her groom if I promise he'll be recovered before their wedding?"

Laura snickered. "That might be part of it. But that was what, a month ago? Two? What else?"

"No idea. Honestly. I brought him coffee because he saved me cake. And, in the spirit of appreciating a kind gesture, offered to share said cake with him." Allison sighed. "Unless he can read minds, that's it. I'll admit that I had been hoping to turn cake into dinner, but I hadn't gotten past thinking that it would be fun to do. Anyway, doesn't matter. Like I said, I'm not pushing this. I've decided my best course of action is to be as polite and professional as I can be in the office, and beyond any required interaction, just leave him alone. Which means, I guess, that I'll be bailing on the office Bible study. But I miss a lot anyway, depending on court dates."

Lydia returned to her seat and slid a huge piece of cake covered with glistening strawberries into the center of the table. "This is compliments of the manager, who is very apologetic for the delay in our service. And yes, that's how he talks. It was all I could do not to laugh. Anyway, someone should be with us shortly."

Laura grabbed a fork and took a bite. "Oh, wow. They can be slow any time if this is the reward. She,"

Laura stabbed the fork in Allison's direction, "thinks that the best thing to do is just forget about Phil."

"Ah, the playing it cool angle? That can backfire." Lydia took a bite of the cake.

"No. No angle. Just moving on." Allison carefully dug some of the cake away from the icing and ate it. Moving on was best for everyone. Now she just had to convince her heart. And figure out what she was moving on to.

"But he likes you. You need to show him you're not easily scared off." Lydia scooped up the icing Allison left behind. "Or do you not really think he's that special?"

"I am easily scared off...but he is special."

Laura licked her finger and patted up the chocolate crumbs around the edge of the cake. "What makes him special?"

Allison forked more icing away from the cake before spearing a bite. "He's genuine. He's been through so much, and yet he's let God use it in his life to make him a better person." She set down her fork. "He's incredibly easy to talk to and he gets my sometimes-snarky humor."

"Sometimes?" Laura shook her head.

"Fine. Strike 'sometimes' from the record. And it doesn't hurt that I find him more attractive than anyone I've ever known." Allison got tingles just picturing him sitting at his desk reading an email. She'd never given much credence to the idea of chemistry...until she'd met Phil.

Their server appeared, apologized for the delay and took their order, promising to have it out as quickly as possible.

Allison buried her head in her hands. "I don't want him to feel like I'm chasing him. Women chasing men never ends up going well."

Lydia chewed on her lower lip. "I can see that. But you can still remind him of the possibilities for a fuller, richer life if he would just find the courage to change his position. Isn't that what lawyers do?"

Allison stood in the foyer of the small neighborhood church she attended. Lindsey had left a message the previous night asking if she and her dad could come to church with Allison in the morning. She was glad they were interested and hoped they'd follow through. She loved her church. Where were they? Should she call? Reaching for the cell phone in her purse, she glimpsed them making their way through the parking lot.

"I'm so glad you made it." Allison held the door open as Lindsey hurried in from the cold. Marcus took the door and gestured for Allison to proceed him.

Lindsey grinned. "It's been a while since we've made the effort to get up on a Sunday morning." She hesitated, a hint of sorrow clouding her face. "Mom always made sure we were on time."

"I should have kept us involved. The people at our old church tried...but I was so angry. They finally gave up." Marcus sighed.

Allison's heart broke for them. They'd had so many difficulties come at them lately, it was no wonder their relationship with each other was struggling. Maybe getting plugged back into a church, even if not this one, would help with some of that. "Why don't we go get seats. They'll be starting soon and the worship time is something you don't want to miss."

Lindsey slid her arm through Allison's and grabbed her dad by the hand. "Thanks for letting us come with you, Allison."

Patting Lindsey's hand, Allison led the group into the sanctuary, scanning for empty seats. "My pleasure."

CS&O

When the service was over, Allison turned to Lindsey. "What did you think?"

"I enjoyed it. I'd like to come back again. What about you, Dad?"

Marcus stood and glanced toward the front of the church. "I'd like that, too. Could you excuse me a moment?"

"Sure." Allison watched Marcus make his way to the front of the room where the pastor stood surrounded by congregants. The pastor turned at Marcus' approach and extended his hand. That was promising. Maybe some more outside counsel would help. It certainly wouldn't hurt. Still, she didn't want to just stand around with

Lindsey, that would get boring very quickly. "If the pastor gets to talking, your dad could be a while. Let's go out to the foyer. Maybe I can find the youth pastor and introduce you. There are a number of kids your age in the youth group."

Lindsey looked down at her obviously pregnant belly. "Do you really think that's a good idea?"

Allison patted the girl's shoulder. "Of course it is. Everyone's made bad choices in their lifetime at one point or another. There'll be some, I'm sure, who are quick to judge. But there'll be others who'll give you a chance. Haven't you found that's the case at school?"

Lindsey grimaced. "At least some of them knew me before all this."

"True." It was a valid point, but Allison knew many of the kids in the church and had always been impressed with their ability to exemplify Christ. It was one of the major reasons she stayed at the church, even though she didn't have a huge group of friends her own age. "We can wait here if you'd rather. But I think you'll be surprised. My experience with the folks at this church, including the kids, is that they're good people."

Lindsey looked toward the front where her dad and the pastor were sitting, deep in conversation. With a heavy sigh she nodded at Allison. "All right."

"Come on. When your dad's done, maybe the three of us can go get lunch."

"That'd be great. I'm starving."

Allison threaded her way through the crowd toward the youth room with Lindsey in her wake. She found the youth pastor and his wife stacking chairs. "Jared."

"Allison." Jared's eyes lit and he set down the chair he'd been lifting. "Come to help? We miss you around here."

Chuckling, Allison shook her head. "Maybe in the spring. Life has been a little too crazy to add working with the teens back in. But I can help stack chairs after I introduce my friend." She turned and spotted Lindsey hanging back in the hallway. Rolling her eyes, Allison waved her into the room. "Lindsey, this is Jared Templeton. Jared, Lindsey Bowers."

Lindsey offered a shy smile. "Nice to meet you, Mr. Templeton."

"Jared, please." He nodded toward his wife who was still working across the room. "That's my lovely bride, Anne. Hey, Annie, come and meet Lindsey."

Anne shoved the stack of chairs against the wall and swiped a hand across her forehead as she crossed the room. "We've got to figure out a way to rope the boys into doing this for us." She grinned at Lindsey. "Nice to meet you. Will you be joining us, I hope?"

"I think so." She glanced at Allison, nerves visible on her face. "If it's all right?"

"Why wouldn't it be?" Anne smiled warmly.

"Um." Lindsey rubbed her stomach. "I wasn't sure if…"

Anne waved away her objection. "Please. You're not the first pregnant girl we've had in our class and, unfortunately, I doubt you'll be the last. People sin. Sometimes the consequences are more obvious than others." She offered a gentle smile. "I can't promise people won't talk, but I can promise that most of the kids are going to welcome you. We have an unusually good group of kids around here."

Jared nodded. "It's true. Usually youth groups aren't much different from a secular gathering. But these kids, most of them at least, really love the Lord. There are a few cliques, and we're working on that. But this is as close to perfect as I think you're going to get this side of heaven." He stopped and studied her face, chuckling. "I wouldn't believe me either, but I promise you, I'm not making it up."

"I can vouch for it, too. I help out when I can. These are good kids, Lindsey." Allison gave her shoulders a quick squeeze. She was pleased to feel some of the tenseness loosen. "Give them a chance."

"We're all getting together at our house tonight to watch a movie, if you'd like to join us." Anne hurried to the small platform at the front of the room. She dug through the canvas bag that was propped against the podium and returned with a bright pink flyer. "This has all the info. We'd love it if you came."

Lindsey took the flyer, folded it without looking, and tucked it into her purse. "I'll think about it."

"We should probably go see if your dad's done talking to the pastor. We don't want him to think I spirited you away." The last thing she wanted to do was make Marcus worry. He had enough of that without adding to it. "Plus, Jared, you've still got quite a few chairs to stack, so we won't keep you."

Jared laughed. "You always know just how to get out of helping."

"It's a gift. It's really good to see you two, though. I'll try and get my schedule back under control so I can help out again."

Allison and Lindsey found Marcus standing in the foyer looking concerned.

"Sorry, Marcus. I dragged Lindsey off to meet the youth pastor and his wife. I thought you'd be a while. Sometimes when the pastor gets going…I hope we didn't worry you?"

"No, no. I just got out here." He glanced at Lindsey. "Ready to go?"

"Allison thought maybe we could grab lunch?"

Marcus' face brightened. "I'd like that. You're not busy this afternoon?"

"I try to keep Sundays as open as I can. You burn out quickly without a day to rest. There are several good restaurants near here. What are you hungry for, Lindsey?"

❧❦

When they were settled with sodas at a Mexican restaurant, Allison looked at Lindsey. "Have you thought about the movie night at all?"

"What movie night?" Marcus shot his daughter a confused look.

Lindsey pulled the flyer out of her purse and passed it to her dad. "Not really. Though," she frowned and took a long drink, "I actually kind of had other plans for tonight. I was going to see if you'd maybe go with me to a teen single moms group the Center offers. Please, Allison?"

"Are you sure they'd be okay with me going with you?" It sounded about as fun as walking over hot coals. How much further involved was she going to end up getting? On the other hand, it was clear Lindsey missed her mom. She needed some kind of female role model in her life.

Lindsey nodded. "I asked Catherine if that was something you could come to. I was disappointed they wouldn't let you stay with me during that first appointment, though I guess I understand their reasoning now. But she said it wouldn't be a problem since this is a group anyway."

Allison wanted to help Lindsey; it was why she'd invited them to church. But this still felt like something that would be more suited to a real family member. Or at least a close friend. "You wouldn't rather have your dad go? Sounds like maybe they're going to have information that he should hear, too."

"I don't think being the lone male in a group of teenaged single moms is really how I need to spend my Sunday night." Marcus cast a somewhat desperate smile at Allison. "If you'd go, that would be great."

Cornered, Allison nodded. "All right. But if you change your mind, it won't hurt my feelings."

Lindsey's eyes shone with gratitude. "Thank you so much. I really want to go, even though I'm not sure about being a single mom. I didn't want to go by myself." She sent an apologetic look in her dad's direction. "Um, Allison? Do you think you could pick me up?"

*In for a penny.* "Sure. What time?"

Lindsey and Allison arrived at the Pregnancy Center five minutes late. They followed the sound of voices down the hall to the large conference room at the back of the building. Several small groups of three or four teenagers were chatting quietly together. Some of the girls were hugely pregnant, others much less so, and the rest looked well on their way to reclaiming their pre-pregnancy figures. A larger group of older women stood in a half-circle on one end of the room. They were talking, but also watching the girls.

Maureen detached herself from the group of adults as Allison and Lindsey entered the room. "Lindsey, you made it. I'm so glad." She grinned and took Lindsey's hand in hers. "Allison, it's lovely of you to come with her. Why don't you go introduce yourself to the moms and I'll introduce Lindsey to some of the girls."

Allison's smile stiffened. She wasn't here as a mom. Was she already too involved? Too late to do anything about it tonight, but she'd have to spend some time going over alternatives later. She turned toward the women while Maureen tugged Lindsey away.

"Hi." Allison lifted a hand in greeting. "I'm Allison Vasak."

Catherine, the volunteer counselor Lindsey had seen, grinned. "I'm so glad Lindsey got you to come. She's really missing her mom right now."

Allison winced.

"I don't know if that came out right. She just needs a female friend, and she felt like she connected with you." She gestured to the other ladies. "We're not all moms. Maureen seems to forget that every now and then." She pointed to a few of the women, said their names, and explained the relationship to the teens in the room.

"Thanks. That makes me feel better. I want to help, but I don't want to overstep."

Catherine chuckled. "It's a fine line. Working at the Center has taught me that more than once. Let's all get a seat. Looks like we're about to start."

The women who were there as support for the teen moms sat in chairs toward the back of the room, while the girls all took seats at three tables arranged in a U at the front.

"Good evening, ladies. I'm so glad you're all here. I look forward to our monthly meeting and the chance to see how you're doing with your upcoming parenting plans or how the implementation of those plans is going now that your babies are here. Let's open with a word of prayer." Maureen bowed her head. Around the room, the girls slowly lowered their heads. Some rolled their eyes while others looked as though they were expecting a personal and immediate benediction of the Spirit.

"Heavenly Father, we thank you for bringing each of these young ladies here tonight. We're grateful for the women who came with them to offer support. Help this time to be comforting and encouraging. Reveal your plans for these young women and their babies. Help them to see it and step out in faith on the path You would have them walk. Amen."

Maureen looked up and smiled. "Tonight we're focusing on a housing plan. Obviously you need to figure out where you and your baby are going to live. For some of you, that's an easy answer because your parents have agreed to help you out. So you'll live at home. Raise your hand if that's your current plan."

About half of the hands went up. Lindsey kept her hand down, though she appeared to be waggling her fingers indecisively. Did that mean Marcus was telling her she couldn't live at home with the baby? Maybe Lindsey just wasn't sure how well that would actually work. Maybe Phil knew...but she wasn't going out of her way to talk to Phil. She'd have to ask Lindsey later.

"Great." Maureen turned her attention to a petite brunette sitting at the far end of the table. "Chloe, when did you change your mind about living at home?"

The girl cleared her throat. "Mom and I talked. A lot. She was worried if I lived at home that she'd be stuck with the baby all the time. She's got a pretty busy social life and doesn't want to be saddled with a baby anymore...she was lookin' forward to me bein' out of the house next year when I hit eighteen. But I found out I can graduate this May if I take a few night classes. And my job says they can take me full time when school's done. So mom figured with me payin' rent and payin' her for a few hours of babysitting, she could maybe drop a few hours on her job and end up havin' more time." She lifted a shoulder. "We're gonna give it a try. If it doesn't work, then I have a friend who'll take me in for a little bit, 'til I can figure somethin' out."

"Sounds like you and your mom are making progress. I'm sorry she couldn't make it tonight though." Maureen's glance was sympathetic. Chloe shrugged.

Allison wanted to find and throttle the girl's mother. How did parents get so selfish they could turn their back on a child in need? At least it seemed like the girl was trying to do the best by everyone involved, even though she clearly wasn't happy at home. From a financial standpoint, what she described seemed like a good option though. Maybe something like that would work for Lindsey?

"Tanya, I thought your parents had agreed to let you stay home. What happened?"

Tanya snapped her gum. "When I have my baby, the state has to give me Welfare and an apartment. Why would I stay with them and my five brothers if I don't have to?"

Maureen's eyebrows lifted. "Where did you get the idea that the state will give you housing?"

"Saw it on a TV show." Tanya nodded emphatically.

"Catherine?" Maureen glanced toward the back. "Could you go get the housing book? While she's doing that, let's think about some of the pros and cons of having your own place. Everyone, jump in." Maureen wheeled a whiteboard closer to the tables. She set up two columns, Pros down one side and Cons down the other. The girls called out things like paying rent, the freedom of your own space, not having a curfew and other rules, and not having someone right there to help at any time of day or night. Allison watched Lindsey. She might as well have been a statue. What was she thinking about?

Catherine came back with a fat binder and set it on the table in front of Tanya.

"What's this?" Tanya nudged the book and blew a large pink bubble.

Maureen flipped a few pages before tapping the photos on the page where she stopped. "These are some of the local Section Eight housing options."

Tanya wrinkled her nose. "Those places are dumps. I ain't living there."

"That's what the state will give you, if you manage to qualify and get a spot. When I last checked, and that was only about two months ago, there was a four year waiting list to get on the waiting list for the next available spot."

Tanya shoved the book, nearly sending it flying off the table. "Nuh-uh. The state has to take care of me. It's a law."

Allison schooled her features as she listened to Maureen calmly explain the realities of the overcrowded and underfunded housing subsidy system. She'd never realized how much legal information someone in social work needed to understand. Maureen clearly knew her stuff. Even though it didn't seem to be making an impact on Tanya. The girl continued in her hard-headed insistence that she and her baby would be living like royalty on the state's dime just as soon as she gave birth. After several minutes of conversation, Maureen sent Catherine out for a welfare and housing office contact sheet so Tanya could take it home and do some firsthand research. Maybe talking to the overworked state employees would help the realities of the situation sink in. Then again, Allison saw clients every day who never figured reality applied to them.

They spent the rest of the hour discussing how to set up a contract with their parents for living at home. What expectations were reasonable and what was not. The moms in the back often interjected with thoughts and comments. It was obvious that many of the young women had started to grasp the reality of single parenting. Maureen was incredibly even-handed about the various options, never pushing one over the other. Instead, there was quite a bit of discussion on how to make the choices that would work best for them and their babies in the long run. It really wasn't much different than how Allison had seen the family law attorneys in the firm approach their clients. Lindsey remained silent throughout the discussion. How much was she taking in?

⚜

Lindsey stared pensively out the window on the way home.

"What'd you think?" Allison glanced over, but Lindsey's face betrayed very little information.

Lindsey sighed and shifted in her seat. "There are so many decisions…and I can't just think about myself. I have to think about the baby and what's best for her…or him." She moistened her lips. "Thinking about where to live…I mean, what's dad going to do with a baby in the house? He has to get up early for work. He works crazy hours and travels some. He's not going to be able to help out. Not really. Plus, I can't graduate this year. I could probably get my GED, I guess I need to look into that. But then what? If I get a job, anything I make will probably go straight into childcare. It's not like I'll be able to save up for anything. And I won't be the one raising my baby on top of it…she'll be in daycare all day." She wiped a tear from her cheek. "What kind of life is that?"

Allison measured her words carefully. She didn't want to dismiss how Lindsey felt, but nothing in that scenario was overtly bad. "It's the kind of life lots of kids have. Even with older, married parents. It's not necessarily a bad thing."

"It is to me. I want to give my baby what I had. My mom," her voice broke, "my mom was always there. We played. She read to me. She was a constant part of my life."

"If you lived with your dad, would you need to work? Could you stay home and focus on raising the baby?"

Lindsey sniffled. "Maybe. I guess I need to talk to Dad about it. We've been discussing the situation like it's not real, just a 'what if'. I think we both need to accept the fact that this is happening." She turned her face to the side.

Allison saw Lindsey's shoulders shaking as she silently cried. She gently rested a hand on Lindsey's knee. "You've got a little time yet."

Lindsey nodded.

When Allison stopped the car in front of the Bowers' house, Lindsey wiped her eyes and smiled awkwardly. "Thanks for going with me."

"You're welcome. I want to help if I can."

"Thanks."

Allison watched until Lindsey closed the house door behind her and the porch light turned off. She wanted to talk to Phil. Not just because she wanted to discuss Lindsey...she missed him. He'd probably have suggestions of how Allison could help without getting too entangled. If it wasn't already too late for that. But her resolution to keep their relationship strictly business meant no after-hours calls. She'd see him in the office tomorrow. *No. No going out of your way to see him.* She'd send him an email in the morning.

11

"Who will buy my sweet red roses?" Sam sang as she poked her head in Allison's office, peering above a vase containing two dozen tightly closed red buds.

Allison glanced up from her screen and her mouth dropped open. "Those are gorgeous. Who sent them to you?"

"I wish." Sam shook her head. "The day my husband thinks to send me flowers when it isn't our anniversary is the day I realize I've passed away and not bothered to notice."

Laughing, Allison gawked at the blooms. "Then who are they for? I need some scoop, obviously."

Sam eyed Allison. "You're really not playing dumb, are you? Hmmm. The plot thickens." She arranged the vase on Allison's desk and checked the angle to the door. "Yep, right there will ensure they're seen by just about anyone passing by."

"Wait. They're for me?" *Who on earth had sent these?* She leaned in to sniff. "Oooh, they even smell good. Is there a card?"

Sam pointed to the small envelope hiding behind a fern and Allison plucked it out of the arrangement. "It helps to open it. Get a move on, girlie, enquiring minds want to know."

Sliding her finger along the flap, Allison opened the envelope and pulled out the card. She drew her brows together as she read. What did this mean?

"Well? Who're they from?" Sam gave her an impatient look and started to reach for the card.

Allison pulled it to her chest, dazed. "Just a friend."

"Honey." Sam stared down her nose at Allison. "No 'friend' is sending two dozen roses this gorgeous unless you saved his life." She gestured for Allison to hand the card over.

Hesitantly, Allison complied. "Only because we're friends. You can *not* tell anyone."

Sam's studied the card. "Is this Marcus who I think it is?"

With a single nod, Allison reached for the card again. She still didn't understand how this had happened. "I've been helping Lindsey out some. I feel for her. She doesn't really seem to have any other mature female influences in her life." She chewed on her lip. "I certainly didn't anticipate this."

"Hmmm." Sam tilted her head to the side. "Will you call him?"

"I should at least say thank you." She hunched her shoulders. "What?"

"You know what."

"I don't know…I'll have to think about it."

"Keep me posted." Sam looked at her sternly. "Seriously. I don't want to have to wait on the grapevine."

Allison tossed a flippant salute at Sam's retreating form.

"Don't think I didn't see that." Sam called over her shoulder as she disappeared.

Allison reread the card. Saying thank you was definitely something she'd need to do sooner than later. But she wasn't sure how to answer the question he'd posed. Well, that wasn't entirely true. She did, in fact, know that she was free Friday. She just wasn't sure if she should let him know that. He wasn't her client. Which removed at least one complication. But he was Phil's. And that made the whole situation with Phil even stickier. Even if it shouldn't. After all, Phil didn't want her and she wasn't going to chase him. *Now what do I do?* She sighed and tucked the card in her pencil drawer, forcing her attention back to her computer. *Worry about it later, that's what.*

Allison glanced at her watch. It was close enough to noon to take a break. She shut the door to her office and picked up the phone. She needed advice from someone with nothing at stake in this whole mess.

"Hello?" Laura answered after several rings.

She angled so she could see the roses on her desk and smiled. "Hey Laura, have a minute?"

The baby was squalling in the background and Jennie was chanting something that Allison couldn't quite make out, but Laura just chuckled. "Of course I do. What's up?"

"Okay, I have a hypothetical situation for you."

"Yay. I love those. Shoot." Laura spoke away from the phone and the background noise dissipated.

"Say you have a crush on someone that you work with."

Laura laughed. "Check. I know how that is exactly."

"Okay, so, again, hypothetically, you help this coworker out with a client in the office at the coworker's request and then continue to help the client in an unofficial capacity."

"Okay. I'm a really nice person to do that on my own time, aren't I?"

"You are. You are." Allison leaned forward to sniff the roses. "If the hypothetical client sent you flowers and asked you on a date, how would you respond?"

"Hmm. I need a few details to correctly formulate my hypothetical response. First, what kind of flowers."

"Roses."

"Mmm. Red?"

"Yes."

"How many?"

"Two dozen."

"Two dozen? Seriously? Do you have any idea how much that must have cost? You've got better clients than I do."

"He's not my client. Hypothetically he's the client of the coworker I have a crush on."

"Oh. Right. I forgot that little detail."

"Yeah." Allison spun her chair to look out the window. Staring at the roses made this feel more complicated than it should be.

"But didn't Phil pretty much tell you there was no chance?"

"Are we totally giving up on the hypothetical ruse? 'Cause it was making me feel a little better."

"Fine, fine. Didn't your coworker, hypothetically, tell you he wasn't interested in dating ever again? Wait...I don't think I put the hypothetical in the right place." She groaned. "Can we please just acknowledge that we're not eleven and use names? I'm trying to nurse an infant and keep a toddler from getting jealous of all the one-on-one mommy time her sister is getting while we're doing this. I can only multi-task so much."

"All right. You're right." Allison sighed. "But to answer the question, yes. Phil made it pretty clear in the Cake Incident that there was no hope. But then you and Lydia convinced me that I should just get him to change his mind…which I don't think I'm going to do by dating his client." She lowered her head to her hands. "This sounds like a bad soap opera."

"Soap opera, sure. But it actually sounds like a pretty good plot. Maybe you can write it up and sell it when you're done using it."

"Laura." She hated the whine in her voice but was powerless to stop it. "What do I do?"

"Well…unless there is a firm rule about dating clients of other staff, I don't know that you need to worry about Phil and his involvement. This man, what was his name?"

"Marcus."

"Marcus isn't your client. So if it's not going to be seen as unprofessional or bad conduct or whatever lawyers call it, all I think you really need to worry about is this: are you interested in him?"

Allison huffed out a breath. "I don't know. I'm interested in Phil. Who is not interested in me. Or he is interested in me but doesn't want to be. Or whatever his deal is. And I'm worried that I'm so interested in simply being with someone that I can't make a sane decision about this." She sounded pathetic, even to her own ears. It was a good thing Laura was preoccupied with the baby or she'd likely get a swift verbal kick in the tail. Which was maybe what she needed, but she wasn't ready to admit that yet. "So. Marcus. He's a lot older than me…his daughter is sixteen. He's got to be at least forty. And he's a widower. Though I don't know if, or how much, that matters…I called you for advice. Advise me."

"I'm trying to. But I'm not going to just tell you what to do. That's a strict violation of the Hairdresser's Code."

Allison let out a short laugh.

"Next question, is he a Christian?"

"Think so. He and his daughter came to church with me yesterday. She mentioned that her mom used to be sure they went every week. I got the feeling it wasn't a foot dragging thing on his part though. And he spent twenty minutes talking to the pastor after the service."

"So probably a checkmark in that column. You should nail that down before too many dates, but we don't have to rule him out automatically. Next question then is how much do the age difference, daughter, and widower status bother you?"

"Honestly? I'm more bothered by the 'client of the man I've got a crush on' thing than any of those. And I know the crush is not really something to fixate on, since it's in that weird one-sided nebulous state." Even saying that, she couldn't stop herself from picturing Phil writing the card for the flowers instead of Marcus.

Laura chuckled. There was more rustling and a loud burp echoed over the line. "Excuse us. Lunch was yummy, apparently. Back to business…Jennie's starting to get restless so I'll have to go soon. Back to the first question. Are you interested in him? Enough to go out and see what, if anything, is there?"

Allison hesitated. She quickly sorted through her conversations with Marcus. He was easy to talk to and she'd enjoyed the brief times they'd spent together, though she'd been more focused on Lindsey than anything. "I'm not *uninterested*. But I just don't know. Phil..."

"Yes, Phil." Allison heard more rustling and a tapping sound before Laura continued. "I'm not usually a fan of the jealousy angle. But maybe if Phil realized that you were taking him at face value he'd be motivated to reevaluate his position on dating and possible remarriage. And if he isn't, then, at least you're getting out there and having fun instead of pining over someone who doesn't reciprocate."

"I'm not pining." Allison glared at the phone's base. "Pining. Honestly..."

"Defensive much?" Laura laughed. "As for the wanting to find love thing...I've been there. And yeah, it's tough to wait for God to bring you the right man, but Al, when a man asks you out, unless God makes it really clear you should say no, you probably have to explore the prospect if you're going to find out if he's the one." A wail erupted in the background. "Look, that's my thought. Think it over and keep me posted, okay? I need to run before chaos ensues. Love you, bye." The phone clicked in Allison's ear.

"Yeah. Bye." Allison set the phone back in its cradle and frowned at the roses. She drummed her fingers on her desk. Why couldn't God just put a big flashing arrow over the head of the man He had for her? Then she'd be sure not to miss out. It'd be so much easier.

After several minutes, she took a deep breath, pulled the card from the drawer, and picked up the phone again.

"Hi, Marcus? It's Allison...Yeah, hi. I got the roses you sent, they're lovely. Thank you so much...no. No, I'm not busy Friday...I'd like that...Sure, seven is great. See you then."

CRThis

On Friday, Allison dressed a little nicer than usual. She was meeting Marcus at a restaurant and wanted to go straight there from work rather than drive home and then back into the city. She couldn't remember being this nervous about a date in a long time. Even her ill-fated date with Kevin, after years of admiring him under the radar, hadn't put this many butterflies in her stomach. Of course, it had been a while since she'd been on a date with anyone who wasn't already a friend. Maybe that was the problem. *Worry about that later.* She had several court dates coming up and needed to put in more prep time.

Phil appeared door of her office and leaned on the frame. "Hey, thanks for the email Monday keeping me in the loop with Lindsey and Marcus." He had a steaming cup of coffee in his hand and was dressed in the more usual Friday 'uniform' of slacks and a polo. His gaze landed on the dozen roses she'd left at work.

She'd taken half of them home and left half here. There were so many of them. Besides, she was at work more than home most days. She might as well have some in both locations.

His eyes widened. "Whoa. Those are nice."

Allison could feel the heat rush to her cheeks. "Yeah, they've held up pretty well."

Phil's gaze took on an air of scrutiny. "You're all dressed up." He glanced back at the flowers. "Big date tonight?"

She lifted a shoulder. "First date. Not sure if it's big or not yet."

He straightened. "Oh. Great. Well," he glanced down the hallway then back at Allison, "have a nice time. And a good weekend."

"Thanks. You too." *What just happened?* He'd looked disappointed. But he'd made it clear he wasn't interested. Hadn't he? Or had she just torpedoed what little chance she did have with him?

Allison craned her neck to see through the crowded seating area of the trendy tapas restaurant Marcus had selected. She should have suggested meeting outside. Even with the cold, it would have been easier to find each other. She didn't have his cell phone number, either. From what she could tell, she'd gotten there ahead of him so she fought her way to the side of the foyer and tried to position herself where she could see the door.

After several minutes of being jostled every ten seconds, Allison finally caught a glimpse of Marcus. She wove through the crowd and tapped on his elbow. "Hey. Found you." She grinned as he started and turned. "I hope you haven't been waiting long. I was over there." She pointed to the spot she'd occupied, now filled with an overly demonstrative duo. The couple looked like they'd be better off with privacy, at least for the comfort of the other patrons.

"Nope, just got here. Sorry to be late." He leaned back and gave her a friendly once over. "You look amazing."

Pink stained her cheeks as she smiled. "Thanks. So do you."

Marcus slipped his hand under her elbow and guided her to the hostess stand. "Good evening, I have a reservation. Bowers?"

The harried hostess glanced at her book and nodded before smiling and offering a pager. "It should only be a minute or two. But this way I can make sure you actually get your table."

Marcus took the pager and stepped to the side.

"I've never been here before." Allison glanced at the throng of people waiting the sixty-five minutes the hostess was quoting to people who arrived with no reservation. "Is it really that good?"

"I've only been here twice. Never on a weekend though. I had no idea it got this crazy. Still, yes. The food's great...You like Spanish food, I hope? I didn't even think to ask. We can go somewhere else."

"Oh no, I love just about any kind of food. The only thing I've tried and not really loved has been Ethiopian. I just can't get past that spongy bread they serve." She shuddered. "My roommate in college though, she loved it. Of course, she grew up in Africa where her parents were missionaries, so that might explain it."

Marcus chuckled. "I've never tried Ethiopian. I will admit to being, by and large, a meat and potatoes guy.

Steakhouses are really more my speed. But I thought this might be a fun change of pace." The pager in his hand began to buzz and flash. He waved it to catch the hostess' attention, keeping his hand under Allison's elbow as they zigzagged their way to their table.

After they were seated, Allison glanced around and let out a relieved sigh. "I'm pleasantly surprised that the glass walls block so much of the noise. I was worried I'd be straining for every word through dinner."

"That thought crossed my mind as well." Marcus smiled and picked up his menu. "Have you done tapas before?"

Allison shook her head.

"Basically, it's like appetizers. Each item has a small portion, a good size for two or three to share, but you only get a few bites each. So the best way, really, to have a meal is to agree on what you want to eat and order a variety."

"Fun. Though I suppose it's good that I don't have any issues sharing food." She laughed at Marcus' expression.

"That hadn't occurred to me, either. I'm a little out of practice."

"Well, you're in luck. I'm also pretty easy to please, though I don't care for shrimp. Beyond that I'm game for whatever. Since you've been here before, why don't you choose?"

Their server appeared with water and rattled off the specials. After a brief consultation, Marcus ordered several different dishes and the server disappeared.

Allison took a sip of water. Now came the potentially awkward small talk. This was her least favorite part of every date. And it always seemed worse when you didn't really know the person yet. She'd stick to what she did know. Maybe that would help it be less stilted. "So how's Lindsey doing? I haven't had a chance to get in touch with her this week."

"She seems to be doing a lot better, actually. I think that's due, in large part, to you. So thank you." He paused and lined up his silverware. "You didn't agree to come to dinner just because of her, did you? It's okay, if you did, but I'd really like to know. I didn't ask because of how helpful you've been with Lindsey." He gave her a half smile and gently tapped his spoon on the table. "And now I've made things awkward. Or more awkward, if that's possible."

"I didn't mean to give that impression, I'm sorry. No. If it was just because I enjoyed spending time with Lindsey, I would've asked if she could join us. Or maybe asked her if she wanted to hang out, just us girls."

Of course, she wasn't sure exactly why she'd agreed to the date. Hopefully he wouldn't press on that score. She thought he was nice. That seemed like a good enough place to start. Laura's comment about stepping out in faith echoed in her mind. *Dear God, please make it clear. Even if it's not a flashing sign...could it be something?*

Marcus' face relaxed into a wide smile.

It was the first real, stress-free smile she'd seen from him. With the worry erased from his features,

Allison noticed how deep his brown eyes were. He really was rather handsome. She didn't feel any tingles, but the nerves that had kept her on edge all day began to dissipate. "Would you rather I not talk about Lindsey? The single mom support group on Sunday seemed to have given her lots to think about, and since I hadn't had a chance to check in with her...I've just been curious and concerned."

"There was definitely some reality therapy Sunday night. She and I have talked about the various ways it might work for her to live at home with the baby. And we're starting to explore other options more thoroughly. As much as I hate the idea of my first grandchild being adopted...I'm beginning to see how it may well be the best solution for everyone."

Allison reached across the table to touch his hand. "I'm sorry. It's a difficult situation for everyone involved." She gave his fingers a quick squeeze and pulled her hand back, clasping her fingers together. "We'll change the subject. Tell me who Marcus Bowers is."

He laughed and checked his watch. "Well, handily it's early yet. Once upon a time..."

∞

Allison crawled into bed just after midnight. She turned out the light and flipped to her side so she could stare out her bedroom window. The lights of DC glowed on the horizon. She'd had a surprisingly good time on her date with Marcus. He was a great conversationalist, his dry humor often understated and sometimes biting. He'd been candid about his wife. They'd met in college and that had been it for both of them.

Allison sighed. That was always how she'd pictured her life. Being twenty-seven and still single had never been in her plans. She'd never felt she was particularly adept at being alone. Even now, when she could easily afford her condo, she was frequently tempted to find a roommate just for the sake of companionship. For now Pippin was enough company, but what she longed for was the kind of connection Marcus had clearly had with his late wife. It was obvious he still missed her, and that he probably would for the rest of his life.

She admired his resilience and his willingness to step back into the world of dating, having realized that he needed the companionship and balance a mate provided. Allison shifted and fluffed her pillow, trying to get comfortable. They'd discussed Christianity only enough for her to be satisfied that yes, he believed. Beyond that, it was clear he'd been angry at God since his wife died and was only now beginning to mend those fences. How much of the reconciliation had to do with Lindsey's situation? Even if that was the motivator, it was good that it hadn't pushed him into even more anger instead. Still, she'd have to pray about starting any kind of serious relationship with him until he had his spiritual feet back under him. That had always been her first priority, and she didn't see any reason to change it now.

After dinner they'd hopped on the Metro to the Smithsonian station and walked around the monuments on The Mall. They were always so beautiful at night. Since it was colder than either of them had anticipated, with the wind whipping around them, they'd cut their walk short. He'd walked her back to her car. She wasn't sure if he'd wanted to kiss her good night, but she'd done everything she could to make it clear that wasn't on the agenda for the evening and there hadn't been any awkwardness.

As she drifted off to sleep, she replayed her favorite pieces of the evening, only partially realizing she'd replaced Marcus' image with Phil.

Phil sat on the deck outside his bedroom and stared into his coffee. Allison's date was a good development. She was moving on, so she'd heard what he said in the park. He just hadn't expected her to move on so quickly. What if he'd totally misread her interest? That whole incident in the park…he must've looked like a fool. But hadn't her date to the Christmas party all but said she was interested in him? Surely he hadn't been that far off. Either way, going on a date was a good thing for her. And for him. Right?

His little pep talk wasn't having the desired effect. With a sigh, he sipped his coffee. He'd bailed on his weekly poker game with the guys from church. He wasn't in the mood to hang out and listen to them trash their ex-wives. He understood the desire—after Brandi's reappearance last week, boy, did he understand it. But he also felt the best way to move on was to push past it. He knew if he went to the game, he'd not only lose his $2 stake, but he'd talk too much about either Brandi or Allison. Or both. None of the other guys had an issue with getting remarried. In fact, it seemed like most of them were planning on it, and didn't understand why their dates always went so poorly. Phil figured it was because they talked about their exes the whole time. Since he'd been pretty vocal about his decision to stay single, he really didn't need any ribbing about Allison.

He woke up grumpy and dissatisfied on Saturday morning. Lying in bed, he looked out over the river waiting for the view to soothe him. How had Allison's date gone? Who had she gone out with?

He threw off the covers and dragged on workout clothes. The garage for his town house had room for two cars and a large storage space in front of the parking area. He'd converted his into a home gym, complete with Nautilus machine, a collection of free weights, an elliptical and a stationary bike. Wanting to keep his mind from straying, he opted for the concentration required to lift weights with good form.

His muscles were quivering from exertion when he set the weights back in their racks. He decided to throw in some cardio as well. He'd just mounted the elliptical when his cell phone rang. *That's what voicemail is for. Oh, who am I kidding?* It might be important.

"Hello?"

"Phil, baby. Why aren't you home?" Brandi's voice was slurred. Something crashed in the background.

"Oops. Sorry about that, what is that thing? Anyway, where are you?"

"Where are you, Brandi?"

"Looking for you. Thought you'd be home. Oooh." He heard rustling across the line. "You got a new mattress. Comfy."

"Are you in my house?" He looked up at the beams of the first floor. How did she get in?

"Well, you've never invited me in. Thought I'd see where you ended up after you let me keep our condo. Seen the outside plenty, decided it was time. Anyway, we need to talk about this restraining order, honey."

Phil gritted his teeth and quietly moved toward the garage door. She'd crossed the line. He'd tried, really tried, to give her the benefit of the doubt with all her antics. But this was too much. "It's pretty self explanatory. Now please, get out of my house and go home."

"Well now, that's part of the problem. I don't have any place to go." Her voice took on a faint whine.

"The condo?"

"Marshall's living there. He kicked me out when I checked out of rehab after two days."

Phil closed his eyes and rested his forehead against the window of the garage door. "It's legally yours. He can't kick you out. Call the police and go home."

"It's more complicated than that. Rehab costs money, so I signed the condo over and he covered the fees. Look, we can talk about this when you get home. The point is, I realize I've handled this badly. All of it.

You're the only one I've ever loved, Phil. Come home and let's talk."

"I'm on my way home now. But Brandi? Don't be there when I get there." Phil ended the call. He didn't want to call the police, but what choice did he have? Going upstairs and trying to talk with her would just make things worse. At least he'd learned that much when he tried to save their marriage. At this point, it was time for her to move on and he'd have to be strong enough to do what it took. He'd deal with the guilt somehow. He dialed the police and reported an intruder. He assured the dispatcher he was safe and would wait in the garage for someone to arrive and disconnected the call. He hesitated, hating to ruin Grant's Saturday. On the other hand, since Grant was his friend as well as his attorney, he'd probably be annoyed if Phil didn't call.

"Morning, Grant."

"Phil. Missed you at poker last night."

"What, you only got to win $8, instead of $10?"

"Something like that. How am I supposed to afford a delicious McDonald's combo for lunch if you skip out?"

"Fire up your clock, you get paid for this call."

"Uh oh. Brandi?"

"Yeah. She's in my house. I've called the police, but figured I should give you a heads up as well."

"The ink on the TRO is barely dry. Does she have no sense?"

Phil saw the police car pull into his driveway. "Apparently not. Look, the cops are here. I'll get you all the details. You free for dinner tonight?"

"Sorry, man. I got suckered into helping a friend of a friend move. Fax over what you've got, maybe we can hit lunch after church tomorrow."

"Will do. Later." Phil hit end and raised the garage door. He greeted the officers and explained about the restraining order he had against Brandi. "Before I hung up on her and called you, she was talking about how nice my mattress is. That's on the fourth floor, if you count this level. There's an elevator, if you want." He pointed to the call button. "Otherwise, we can go up the stairs."

"We'll take the stairs. Don't want to alert her with the elevator noise. But sir, you should just wait here." The two men climbed the stairs, hands on the butts of their pistols.

Phil grabbed the camping chair he stored in the garage and tugged it out of its cover. He didn't want to wait down here. Though he'd probably be in the way upstairs. Still, she was in his house and he wanted to help get her out so she understood this wasn't ok. He opened the chair and sat, propping his feet on the bumper of his car. *Might as well catch up on my email. Ah the joys of a smart phone.*

Nearly half an hour later, the two policemen returned. Brandi, hands cuffed behind her back, walked between them. She alternated between spitting insults and wailing. When she saw Phil, she began to scream. "How could you do this to me? How dare you!"

"Sir," one of the officers stopped to talk to Phil while the other escorted Brandi to the back of their car. "She claims she lives here and that she is, in fact, your wife."

"Ex-wife. She's never lived here. I got a restraining order last week because she keeps showing up and has started making threats. This is the first time she's broken in. I have the paperwork for the TRO upstairs."

The cop nodded. "We'll need to see that. You'll want to have your front door looked at." He offered a slight smile. "She couldn't explain how it got that damaged when she came into her legal residence with her key."

Great. More clean up. Would she ever stop causing problems? Did he even deserve for her to? "Thank you, Officer. Give me just a second and I'll go get that paperwork." He darted upstairs, grabbed the restraining order and a business card and hurried back down to the garage. "Could you please get me a copy of the report? I'll need it for my attorney. His information is on the back of the business card on top."

The officer scanned the paperwork and handed it back then tucked the business card into his pocket. "We'll be in touch."

When they'd driven off, Phil closed the garage door and headed upstairs. The oval etched glass that had been in the center of the door was now shattered in the foyer. It was one of the Victorian elements that had drawn him to the home in the first place. He should probably get something sturdier as a replacement. If he could find something with the same charm.

He trudged upstairs and into the shower. When he was dressed, he found some cardboard to temporarily close the house. It wouldn't keep anyone out, but it was better than issuing an invitation to thieves. After sweeping up the broken glass from the door he picked up the shards of his grandmother's antique vase. *Sorry, grandma. I know it was your favorite.* He'd see if he could fix it later. The first order of business was a new front door.

Phil stepped back and surveyed the new door. It was nearly identical, though the salesman had assured him the glass in the center was strong enough to withstand some serious whacks with a flowerpot. He hoped so. Since there'd been no damage to the door frame, it had been a fairly simple matter to remove the hinges, pull off the old door, and hang the new one. He'd gone ahead and changed the locks while he was at it. He hadn't looked to see if Brandi had helped herself to his spare key, but he wouldn't put it past her. The last thing he wanted was to wake up some night and find that she'd come with a key this time.

The anger he thought he'd dealt with was beginning to simmer in his heart again. Why couldn't she just leave him alone? She'd been the one who wanted the divorce. She was the one who wouldn't even try marriage counseling, though he'd gone by himself for several months hoping she'd decide to tag along.

He stored his tools and looked around. He didn't feel like just puttering around the house anymore. He could almost feel Brandi's taint on his things. Hopefully that would pass quickly. He loved this house and really didn't want to move. Rubbing the back of his neck, he dug through the fridge, emerging with a cold soda. He popped the top and sat at the kitchen table. The drink did nothing to soothe the turmoil bubbling under his skin. With a sigh, he reached for his cell.

CR80

Pastor Paul Brown opened the door and smiled warmly. "Phil. It's good to see you again."

"Thanks for seeing me on such short notice."

"I'm glad you called. Come on in." Paul stepped back and gestured for Phil to precede him into the small home office just off the foyer. "Can I get you a drink? Water or soda? Or tea? I think we have some iced tea."

"I'm good, thanks." Phil stuffed his hands in his pockets and looked at the tidy bookshelves that lined the far office wall. Was he really so incapable of dealing with things that he needed to be back here? If he was honest, the answer was yes. Wasn't honesty supposed to make you feel better?

Paul pulled the double doors shut and angled the guest chair to face a short leather sofa against the far wall of the office. "How have you been doing?"

Phil sat on the couch facing Paul and frowned. "Until last week, I would have said great. You were a big help before and during the divorce. When all was said and done, I felt like God was working through the situation, and maybe, down the road, Brandi would look back and see Him reaching out to her. I hang out with a few other divorced guys, and they're always trashing their exes, or bragging about their incessant dating, or both." He shrugged. "I've never felt the need to do either. The anger wasn't there. And dating...well, I don't think it's in the cards."

"So what happened?"

"Brandi happened. My mother means well, but she's never been overly happy about our divorce. She figures that even if I'm unhappily married I'm closer to giving her grandchildren than if I'm single."

Paul laughed. "There is logic there."

"Yeah, I guess. Still. She shouldn't have given Brandi my new address. But she did, and then Brandi showed up last week, making threats and trying to get me to let her in. She and her latest, I don't even know if they got married or were just hooking up long term, are, apparently, history. And somehow she's managed to get kicked out of the condo she owns—the one we used to live in." Phil reached up to rub his temples. How was anything this convoluted and dramatic part of his life? "Anyway, between that and the messages on my answering machine, my attorney was able to get a temporary restraining order. I feel bad about going that route, but she's just not taking a hint."

When Phil paused, Paul nodded and gestured for him to continue.

"Then today she broke the glass in the front door so she could let herself in. She broke a few other things while she was in there as well. I was in the garage working out. She didn't realize I was home. Long story short, the police came and she was carted off. And all the anger is back."

"Seems to me the anger is reasonable given the circumstances. What else is going on?"

"You really can see everything, can't you?" Phil let out a short laugh. "For the first time since the divorce, I'm attracted to someone. And I think she's interested in me, too. But I'm just not sure remarriage is okay...I want to say from a Biblical standpoint, but really, I think it's probably more fear. I mean, look at my track record. I'm not winning any awards in the marriage game."

"That's a bit harsh. You put a lot of effort into your marriage with Brandi. Even what ended up sparking the divorce was an attempt to make things better. You saw the damage alcohol was doing to your relationship, and you made a change. She just didn't want to make that change with you. You're not responsible for the divorce, Phil."

Phil scrubbed a hand through his hair. "I know that up here." He touched his temple. "But..."

Paul smiled. "It's always easier on this side of the room." He tapped his lower lip with his pen. "Let's do this. You and I will commit to praying about both of the situations. Brandi clearly needs to get some help. But she's going to have to want it, and I think that's the first thing we need to pray for. Next, let's pray that you'd have clear direction about changing your stance on dating and remarriage. And that you and I would be given the same word from the Lord, so that you'll know it's from Him and not just a reflection of your desires."

"Okay. But…what if we don't agree?" Phil wasn't certain he'd recognize a true word from the Lord. His desires were pretty strong, and getting stronger. Even if there was no chance now with Allison, he couldn't stop thinking about her.

"Then we keep praying until we're in unity. But keep in mind that it'll take courage to change your mind, even if that's what you hear God telling you to do."

"Finding Jesus was the best thing that ever happened to me. Even with all the upheaval that came from that decision. I'll follow where He leads."

Paul grinned. "Why don't we plan to meet again next week?"

"Sounds good."

"Can I convince you to stay to dinner? My daughter and her fiancé are going to be joining us. They're about your age. And it seems to me that maybe you could use some more friends in your age group. I love counseling, and I'm so glad you came to me now and during your divorce. But sometimes a friend's ear is even better."

"Yeah. That's a lack I've been noticing myself. I initially came to you for counseling because I wanted someone who didn't know me or Brandi. I thought it might make her more comfortable." He shrugged. "That didn't pan out. But I've been thinking of coming to your church for a while. There aren't many older single people at my church, so friends my age are few and far between."

Paul stood and jerked his head toward the doors. "Let's go see what my wife's got cooking and if Lydia and Kevin have gotten back from cake tasting yet."

As they stepped into the hallway, the savory smell of spicy chili permeated the air. Both men took appreciative sniffs. The front door opened.

"Phil?" Kevin offered a quizzical smile as he held the door for Lydia.

Phil nodded, not quite able to place Kevin, though he looked very familiar.

"We met at Allison Vasak's Christmas party?"

"That's it...Kevin, right?" Phil offered his hand and turned to Lydia. "Which means you must be Lydia. I hear congratulations are in order?"

Lydia nodded, her glance clearly speculative. "Thanks. I didn't know you knew my dad."

What did she mean by that? She must be better friends with Allison than he realized. He'd thought they were just acquaintances, though it could always be the phenomenon of coupledom kicking in…what one person knows, the other soon discovers.

Paul spoke into the silence before it could get awkward. "I worked with him several years back and he was able to stop by to catch up today. I invited him to supper."

Phil smothered a smile at the implicit warning to be nice that he heard in the Pastor's words. "I came to Pastor Brown for counseling before and during my divorce. Some things have cropped up lately that made me realize it might be a good idea to come back." He rested his hand briefly on Paul's shoulder. "I appreciate the attempt at privacy, but presumably they both know I'm divorced. And really, I don't have a problem admitting I need counsel. Before the divorce?" Phil lifted a shoulder. "Totally different story. I don't want to intrude on a family dinner though. How about a rain check?"

"Nonsense." Lydia stepped forward and slipped her arm through his with a glance at Kevin. "Come on, let's go see how we can help Mom get that chili on the table. Knowing her, there'll also be fresh baked cornbread."

Kevin shook his head at Phil's wordless plea for help. "You don't want to miss Mary's cornbread. Or her chili. Might as well just give in."

With a laugh, Paul shooed everyone down the hall toward the kitchen.

Phil let them lead him along. It really smelled too good to miss. And Lydia had quite a grip on his arm. *It's almost like she's determined to keep me here. Why?* His train of thought derailed when he spied the platter of fluffy, golden cornbread on the counter.

"Hi, Mrs. Brown. The Pastor invited me to stay. I hope that's all right?" Phil's stomach rumbled.

The tinkle of Mary's laugh filled the room. "Of course, Phil, it's delightful to see you again. I'd be disappointed if you didn't stay for dinner. There's always plenty. Though with Kevin around, you might have to fight a little harder for the cornbread."

"Come on, let's get the table set so we can eat. All that cake tasting has made me hungry for real food." Kevin grinned.

They busied themselves grabbing piles of bowls and spoons.

"How can I help?" Phil tucked his hands in his pockets and looked around the kitchen.

"You can take the cornbread in. Just through there." Mary nodded at the doorway into the dining room. "But no snitching. I've counted those pieces. Then just take a seat anywhere, we're ready."

Everyone trailed behind Phil and swiftly set the table. Phil waited to see where everyone would sit before sliding into the chair next to Mary and across from Kevin. Paul said a blessing and the food was quickly passed around. The only sounds for several moments were spoons scraping bowls as they started in on the fiery no-bean chili and airy cornbread. Phil couldn't remember the last time he'd eaten so well.

Mary looked across the table at Lydia. "So, honey, did you find a cake you like?"

Kevin groaned.

Lydia elbowed him. "Poor baby, having to eat cake all afternoon. I think we did."

Phil watched Kevin shake his head.

Lydia frowned. "Fine. Yes. We did. It was a tough choice though."

"Well, why don't you run me through your favorites and I'll see if I can guess the one you're leaning toward." Mary grinned. "That way I can imagine all the flavors without actually having the extra calories."

Lydia laughed and launched into a bite-by-bite retelling of the afternoon. Kevin listened for a minute before scooting his chair slightly in the other direction and looking across at Phil. "How are things in the world of attorneys?"

Phil scooted his chair a bit as well so the conversations had less overlap. "Can't complain." He paused. Things actually weren't going all that great with two of his clients. Throw in Marcus as an on-again, off-again client and it looked even less exciting. "Well, I could, but really, why? Clients are good things, even if their problems aren't."

Kevin chuckled. "Sounds like the software world."

Would Kevin know about Allison's date? They were friends, so he might. Did single women tell engaged friends about stuff like that? Even if she did, what would it look like if he brought it up…and how quickly would it get back to her? He didn't care. The idea of Allison on a date had the chili churning in his stomach. Phil cleared his throat. "Heard from Allison lately? We've been so busy at work I haven't really seen her."

Lydia glanced at Kevin without interrupting her description of a strawberry cake with chocolate mousse filling.

Kevin shook his head almost imperceptibly at her. "We called her last night to see if she wanted to hit a movie with us and the Stephensons. She knows Matt and Laura from college, too, so we'll all hang out now and then. She had a date though. A guy named Marcus, I think? She's been helping his daughter, or something." Kevin shrugged. "Haven't heard how it went, but since she didn't call at eight asking where to meet us, it can't have been all bad."

Phil's mouth went dry and his pulse thrummed in his ears. He fought the urge to clear his throat again. "That's a good sign." He'd told her he wasn't interested. She'd moved on. That's what he wanted. And Marcus seemed like a nice enough person, even if he had an awful lot going on in his world right now. Allison was a single adult. So was Marcus. And Phil had had his chance. He just hadn't realized he'd only get the one.

As soon as dinner was over, Phil excused himself and headed home.

Allison spent Saturday tidying up her apartment. She'd fallen behind, again, in her cleaning schedule. She'd tentatively invited Marcus and Lindsey over for lunch after church the next day, though she couldn't figure out why. The words had slipped out and, before she'd realized what she said, he'd accepted. So now it was a day of mad cleaning. And self-flagellation. *Why are you so worried about this? They were both here when Lindsey came over, and it wasn't pristine then…it's not an uninhabitable mess now, either. You live here.* She paused in her attempts to scrub imperceptible mildew out of the grout lines in her bathroom floor. *What, exactly, is the problem?*

"It's the date." She muttered, scowling at the floor and renewing her efforts to scour the grout. "Now I'm just not sure where things stand." She scrubbed harder until her hand slipped off the handle of the brush and her knuckles rammed into the corner of a tile, ripping the skin. "Dang it."

She sucked on her knuckle before spitting it out and gagging repeatedly as the floor cleaner hit her tongue. Rushing to the sink, she rinsed her mouth until she could no longer taste the bleach, then cleaned her oozing knuckles with soap. She'd need bandages on two of the scrapes…which meant no more heavy cleaning. She didn't need to flex her fingers more than necessary. Everything was sparkling already anyway.

As if sensing that the cleaning binge was over, Pippin emerged from his hiding place under the bed and trailed behind her to the kitchen. The phone rang as she grabbed a prepackaged meal out of the microwave. She pulled off the top to let the steam escape as she answered. "Hello?"

"Hey Al, it's Kevin. Hang on a second, I want to put you on speaker." The call took on the echoing quality of a speakerphone. "Okay, can you hear me?"

"Yeah. Who else is there?"

"Lydia."

Lydia chimed in, "Hey, Allison."

"Okay. So what brings us to this party line?" Allison stirred the gravy into the dried out mashed potatoes, ignoring her throbbing knuckles.

"You'll never guess who joined us for dinner at the Brown's tonight."

"Kevin. If I'm never going to guess, why can't you just tell me? Honestly, Lydia, can't you keep him from being ridiculous? I thought that was the sole purpose of being engaged."

Lydia laughed. "Not so much, no. But I'll put you out of your misery. Phil."

"Phil? What about Phil?"

"He ate with us this evening." Kevin's voice took on a teasing air. "And he was very curious about your date last night."

"Oh, no." As her heart plummeted to her knees, Allison poked the gray lump that was, supposedly, Salisbury steak. "You didn't tell him who I was out with, did you?"

"Was I not supposed to? You didn't say no one could know."

"Lydia, why didn't you stop him?"

"Well, honestly I didn't hear much of the conversation. I was talking wedding cake with my mom. Which reminds me, I need you and Laura to come and taste what I think we've decided on. I just want to be sure."

"I can eat cake. But just remember I'm not in this wedding." She'd had a date, there might actually be hope for her to one day be the bride and not the bridesmaid. Allison pictured herself in a white gown heading down the aisle. The groom in the distance was fuzzy. Concentrating, she put Marcus' face on him, but with each step down the petal-strewn path, the features morphed into Phil's. She shoved the meal to the center of the table. So much for being hungry. "About Phil. I guess I can't be too mad. Even if I'd really like to be. I didn't say not to tell anyone because, really, who would've thought you'd be talking to Phil? Why was he there, anyway?"

"Hmm. Lydia?"

"I don't see why we can't tell her. He was open about it. Apparently he saw my dad for counseling during and after his divorce and came back today for the same. Not sure what's going on though."

"Huh." Allison tapped her lip with her finger. Had she sent him back to counseling? If so, what did that mean? She squashed the tiny flutter in her stomach. Could he be reconciling with his ex? "I guess I'll decide not to be vain and assume it has anything to do with me. From what I gather in the break room, he's got some pretty stressful clients right now. Way worse than Lindsey and her dad."

"Speaking of Lindsey's dad." Kevin cleared his throat. "I admire your attempt to deflect the conversation away from your date last night but let's hear it. How did it go?"

Allison filled them in on the restaurant and the easy conversation. Then she sighed. "I'm still not sure what to do. Marcus is nice, and fun. But he's quite a bit older. And I'm worried that he's only interested in me because I'm helping his daughter and that I might only be interested in him because I want someone in my life. Plus, despite the Cake Incident and all of his protests to the contrary…I wonder if I shouldn't hold out for Phil."

Kevin hummed. "No words of advice from me. I always knew who I was holding out for. Even when she wasn't interested or I tried to give up and move on. Lydia, maybe you can provide some thoughts? Besides, this is more a conversation for girlfriends, so I'm leaving. I'm glad you had a good time though, Al. You deserve a good man. Whoever he is."

The echoing ended and Allison assumed the phone had been taken off speaker. She heard Kevin speaking to Lydia and a door shut before Lydia came on the line. "Sorry about that. He's headed home. I can let you go if this is awkward. I know we're not best friends...though if you have room for someone you know way too much about, I'd be game."

Allison laughed. "A year ago, I would have told you exactly what you could do with that suggestion. But seeing how good you and Kevin are together...I'd like that. I've got a rather pathetic lack of girlfriends in my life right now."

"Ha. If you ever want to find out who your real friends are, try ending up in rehab. It was amazing, though not that surprising if you really stop to think about it, how many people were mysteriously too busy to reconnect when I got back. On the other hand, the friends that stuck? They're the best. And I'll just put this out there so it's understood, I appreciate all you did for me last year."

"I'm glad it worked out." Allison stood, stretching and moved into the living room, dumping her uneaten dinner in the trash to keep Pippin out of it. She still didn't know what to do with the information about Phil. If he really wasn't interested, why would he care who she was dating? Was it just curiosity? "Do you have any thoughts about the whole Phil/Marcus thing?"

"Just two. First, I know how it is to let wanting to be married turn into taking the first person that shows interest. It's tough to be single once you're out of college, especially in the church. It's like some unspoken condemnation that you've missed God's will, even though no one would say it to your face. Don't be like me though, okay? Hang in there—God's faithful." She paused and Allison heard Lydia take a swallow of something. "Second is probably the one thing you don't want to hear. You need to pray about it."

"Yeah. I really do. I haven't been doing as much of that as I should be." *Why is that?* Allison frowned as she rubbed Pippin behind the ears. "Thanks, Lydia. Now, tell me about the cake. Sitting and sampling different cakes sounds like the perfect way to spend an afternoon."

Lydia chuckled. "I thought so too. Until about the eighth piece. After that, no matter how good they are, they all start to blur together in a sugar high."

16

"Will you go to the single mom's group again tonight, Lindsey?" Allison looked across the booth at the young woman. Marcus had suggested they eat out rather than imposing on her hospitality. Even after spending the bulk of her Saturday cleaning and stressing over a menu, it seemed like a good idea to Allison. Something about them coming over had kept her on edge all through church. As soon as they agreed to go out she calmed. The local hamburger chain Lindsey suggested was popular with the after church crowd. They'd been lucky to snag a booth, even if Lindsey was getting large enough that fitting between the table and bench was challenging.

Lindsey glanced over at her dad. "I'm not sure. I've been going in and talking to Catherine almost every day this week…I need to figure out what makes the most sense for both of us." She rubbed her belly. "I have nearly eleven weeks left, and I don't have any definite plans. It feels like I should."

Marcus reached over and squeezed Lindsey's hand. "That's still plenty of time. You're making plans now...we're making plans now. We'll get it sorted out."

It was good to see that father and daughter had found some sort of happy middle ground. The strain between them had eaten away at Allison and she'd been praying something would happen to heal the growing rift. They needed each other right now, whether they realized it or not. No one had mentioned legal proceedings lately either. She hoped they were off the table for good. Better not to ask and ruin the conversation though. Maybe she could ask Phil tomorrow at work. Or would it be even more awkward now that he knew she'd been out with Marcus?

"You all right?" Marcus was peering at her, visibly concerned.

"Yeah, sorry. Got distracted." Allison took a sip of her soda. *Worry about Phil later.* "What types of things have you been doing at the Center?"

Lindsey poked at her hamburger. "The most helpful has been looking at the expense of raising a child. I've been pricing diapers and formula and all those things. Who knew it was so expensive?"

Marcus raised his hand, causing both women to laugh.

"Thanks, Dad. Anyway, even without rent, looking at basic needs like those and child care...I just don't know how I'd earn enough to do this on my own."

"You know you don't have to do it alone." Marcus patted his daughter's hand.

"I know Dad, I do. But it makes sense to think it through as if I did. Because at some point down the road, if I choose to parent, I *will* be doing it alone. I can't live with you, mooch off you, forever."

Allison's brows lifted. "That's a pretty forward thinking plan though. Shouldn't you be focusing on the next six months or so?"

Lindsey hunched her shoulders. "Parenting is a long term decision…so I need to think long term. I still have dreams of my own. I want to graduate from high school, not get a GED. I want to go to college, and maybe even grad school. The more doctor's appointments I go to, the more I realize that I think I want to be a nurse. Maybe a nurse practitioner someday. I'm not sure how I get to that point as a single mom at sixteen."

"It would be challenging…but it's not impossible, Linds." Marcus folded his hands in his lap. "Adoption is just as long term a decision as parenting, just in different ways."

"I know, Dad. But I'm trying to do the right thing and really think this through. One of the things Catherine keeps reminding me is that doing what's best for the baby also means taking into account the kind of mom I want to be. I don't know if I can give up my dreams, or postpone them, and not have it influence the way I parent. I don't want to be a mom who resents her child."

"That's some heavy thinking, Lindsey." Allison took another sip of her drink. "I hope you're doing some praying along with it?"

"I'm trying to...but I guess I don't really know if I'm doing it right."

"There's not really a way to do it wrong." Allison paused. She didn't want to sound preachy. At the same time, prayer without the right foundation wasn't going to help the situation either. "You do need to make sure you're on the right footing first."

Lindsey looked confused.

*Help me, Lord. This has never been my strong suit.* "You need to know that your relationship with God is on track. That should take precedence over anything else."

One corner of Lindsey's mouth curved up. "Catherine said the same thing. She helped me ask Jesus to forgive me and live in my heart. I knew having sex was wrong." She flashed an apologetic smile at her dad. "But I've been so angry at God since mom died, I didn't really care. But now that I'm working on my relationship with Him, it's made me seriously start to consider an adoption plan, to be willing to put the baby ahead of anything else. I know it's not probably what you want, Dad, but..."

Marcus slid his arm around Lindsey's shoulders and pulled her close. He dropped a kiss on her head. "I wish your mother was here to help us with this. She was always the wise one in our family...though it sounds like you're stepping into her shoes. We'll both pray about it."

When they finished eating, Lindsey excused herself to go to the restroom, adding a self-deprecating joke about the perils of pregnancy as she levered herself out of the booth. Marcus and Allison watched her squeeze through the crowded tables until she was out of sight.

Returning his gaze to Allison, Marcus cleared his throat. "I had fun on Friday."

"I did too. Thanks, again, for dinner. It was nice to try someplace new." Allison met his gaze and tried to come up with something to say that wouldn't sound overly flirtatious.

Marcus searched her face, a frown tugging the corners of his mouth. "I was wondering, hoping really, that you might want to go out again this Friday?"

Allison chewed her lip as her thoughts raced. She'd had fun. Marcus was a nice man and he was comfortable to be around. He didn't make her heart leap when she saw him like Phil did, but she knew from watching her parent's steady and comfortable marriage that sometimes that could be enough. She'd always wanted more than that for herself, but maybe that was a pipe dream. Watching Marcus, she realized some of her conflict must be visible on her face. With a wan smile she nodded. "Sure."

"Not exactly the eager response I was hoping for, but I'll take it."

"I'm sorry, Marcus. I…I had fun. And I like you, and Lindsey. I just…" She didn't know how to finish the sentence. How much plain speaking was too much in a new…what was this? Friendship? Relationship?

"Don't worry about it. But if you're only saying yes to be polite, please don't. I'd rather you said no if you're just not interested."

"I'm not uninterested." She huffed out a breath. "I know how horrible that sounds. I'm not trying to be coy or heartless." Allison closed her eyes. Maybe there was no such thing as being too plain. She'd certainly prefer it if the tables were turned. Even as much as Phil's speech in the park hard hurt, she'd rather know how he felt than continue to wonder. "In the vein of honesty being the best policy and so forth, I've been attracted to someone else for a while. I thought things might be starting to work out, that he might feel the same. Then," she lifted a shoulder, "he said some things that made it pretty clear that he'd noticed my interest and didn't return it. But he's not always acting like that's really the case…and saying it out loud just now made me realize how very high school that sounds. So…I'd like to get to know you better. Can we start from there?"

"Of course. That's the only place to start, the beginning."

Allison noticed the crinkles at the corners of his eyes as Marcus smiled. Her mother had always said etched-in laugh lines showed a person with a good sense of humor and a firm grasp of reality. Looking at Marcus, she understood her mom's words better.

"Can I pick you up around seven?"

"I should be able to make it home by then, sure."

"Dress comfortably, I have something fun in mind."

"No information other than that?"

"Nope." Marcus' eyes held a mischievous glint.

Lindsey appeared back at the table and glanced at her seat. "Do I need to wedge myself back in there or are you ready to go, Dad?"

Marcus laughed and slid to the end of the booth. "I'm set." He waited for Allison to slide out of her side and held her coat so she could slip her arms in. "Thanks for having lunch with us. I'll see you Friday."

"See you then." Allison caught Lindsey's startled exclamation as she headed toward her car. Didn't Lindsey know she and Marcus had been out? Allison had assumed Marcus would clear it with his daughter before asking anyone out. It's what she would've done. Lindsey had seemed surprised though. It was definitely something she needed to check on before Friday. She didn't want to damage the newly healing relationship between father and daughter. Or hurt her young new friend.

## 17

Phil shifted the bag of takeout to his other hand and leaned on the doorbell. He grinned as the sound buzzed through his sister's house much longer than necessary. Several minutes passed. As he was contemplating another long buzz, he heard shuffling footsteps coming toward the door.

"Afternoon." Phil nudged the door open farther than the crack Karin had opened it and stepped in. He took in his sister's fluffy pink bathrobe and tousled hair before heading back to the kitchen. "I see you made the early service this morning."

"Just like every Sunday. Up at the crack of dawn and then back to bed as soon as church is over." She shut the door and shuffled sleepily after him. "You know Sundays are my day to sleep in." Sniffing, she eyed the plain white bag. "Barbecue?"

"I was in the mood. It wasn't too far out of the way." He shrugged and set out two place settings before opening the containers and arranging them so they were easy to reach from both seats. "Have any soda? This would go well with a Coke."

"I don't know. Probably. Check the fridge." Rubbing her eyes, Karin dropped into a seat and scooped a large helping of shredded pork onto her plate.

Phil returned with two sodas. He popped the tab on one and set it in front of her before doing the same for himself. He ignored her curious gaze and began scooping pork, Southern style green beans, fried okra, and corn onto his plate. "What?"

"I could ask you the same thing." Karin gestured to the food. "What's going on, Phil? Not that I don't love spending time with you. Seriously. But you haven't brought this much food over since things started getting bad with Brandi."

Phil blanched. Between Brandi and Allison, he had entirely too many women to think about. Was he really that transparent?

Karin set down her fork. "Please tell me she's not back in your life."

"Not like you mean, no." He puffed out his cheeks and let the air out with a quiet pop. "She broke into my house yesterday. I had her arrested." He stabbed some of the pork. "I feel okay about that though. Last time she called and caused a scene on the porch I almost called the police. She's got to get it through her head that she can't keep doing this."

Karin watched him, lips pursed. "All right. You seem considerably less annoyed than I'd expect. So it's probably not Brandi." One corner of her mouth quirked into a smile. "Care to tell me what emotions I am helping you eat?"

"I am not having emotional eating troubles. That's something women do, not men. I simply came to visit my sister with a meal. An expensive meal, I might add, for which you have not yet thanked me."

Karin made her voice high and prissy. "For which you have not yet thanked me." She laughed. "Do you hear yourself?" She took a bite and dramatically chewed and swallowed. "Thank you, oh dearest brother, for this delightful repast." Rolling her eyes she grabbed a cornbread muffin from the container. "Better?"

He turned a chuckle into a cough and sipped his soda. "Much."

"Heard that." She laughed. "So come on, spill."

"Allison went on a date with one of my clients. Well, former client. He decided to drop his suit."

"Allison? Didn't we just do the 'I like Allison but can't admit it to myself' meal?"

"Do I need to find someone else to be my sounding board?"

"Depends. Are you going to stop bringing me food if you do?"

"Absolutely."

"Then no." She grinned and took another bite.

"Good grief. I'm pathetic, aren't I?"

"Nah. Lonely. Confused. Quite possibly in love. But not pathetic."

He furrowed his forehead. "I'm not in love with her."

"Okay. You'd know, of course."

"Don't humor me. I would know. And I'm not." *Can't be. Won't be.*

"Of course." She smiled at him, her face the picture of innocence. "So it's the former client thing that's the problem?"

"No. Even if he was still my client I don't think there'd be anything wrong with it, at least from an ethical standpoint."

"Let me see if I understand. You don't want to date her, because you're not dating anyone ever again, but she can't realize that and move on?"

Phil narrowed his eyes. "I don't think I'd put it exactly like that, no."

"How would you put it?"

How would he put it? He wasn't sure, but certainly not like that. *Oh, who are you kidding?* "Okay, yes, maybe that's how I'd put it. That doesn't mean I'm in love with her. Maybe I think she could do better."

"Ah. There's something wrong with him that you're privy to because he was your client." She shot him a knowing look. "Wife beater? Child predator?"

"You know that's not the kind of law I practice. No. He seems like a nice, normal man."

"Married, then, and hiding it?"

Phil shook his head. Karin suggested numerous off the wall problems before he held up his hands in surrender. "Okay, okay, okay. Maybe I just think she'd be better off with me."

"She would be…but I thought you didn't want her, or anyone."

He frowned and looked down at his empty plate. Reaching across the table, he collected her dishes and stood, muttering as he took them into the kitchen, "Maybe, just maybe, it might be time to consider changing my stance."

Another week raced by. Allison had three new clients to deal with, as well as the final court dates for two other clients. She spent her days running at top speed, starting at four thirty when her alarm went off and rarely crawling into bed before one a.m. By Friday afternoon, she was exhausted and looking forward to a quiet weekend spent, primarily, asleep.

"Knock knock."

Allison glanced up from putting the final touches on a closing argument she expected to deliver on Tuesday or Wednesday of the next week. "Marcus?" She checked her watch. "You weren't picking me up until seven, right?"

"Right. I was in the area meeting with a client and thought I'd stop by to see how you were. You never returned my texts...you look tired."

Great. Allison knew the long days had been leaving their mark, but she'd thought she was keeping the physical evidence at bay. She bit back a snotty reply and tried to smile. "It's been a long, busy week. Honestly, I'm not sure I remember getting any texts." She grabbed her phone to check. "But here they are. Still unread, actually." She turned the phone so he could see. "Sorry. I've been averaging three hours of sleep a night. My energy's been focused on keeping my head above water."

Concern flashed across his face. "Do you need to reschedule?"

It was tempting. She briefly allowed herself the fantasy of going home and crawling into bed, not to emerge until Sunday. She pushed it aside. She'd always disliked people who didn't keep their commitments, even if they had valid reasons. "No, we don't need to do that. Realistically I've had so much coffee today that even if I went home and tried to crash, my body would be buzzing too much to allow sleep."

"All right. But you can change your mind at any time. I had something semi-active planned. Should I change that to something more low key? We could go see a movie or something if you'd rather?"

"Active is good. I can't promise I wouldn't fall asleep at a movie. I'm sorry. I have a few weeks like this a year, I just never seem to know when they're coming. I suspect if I was just slightly better at planning I'd be able to predict somewhat, but..." she shrugged, "nature of the beast."

"It's really not a problem. I just don't want you to feel like you have to go out if you need to go home. If you decide you'll be better off rescheduling, give me a call." He stood and collected his briefcase.

"Oh. I almost forgot." Grinning, he dug around in the case, finally emerging with a bag of dark chocolate almond bark. A sparkling bow tied the clear cellophane package shut. "I saw this yesterday and thought of you. Plus, it's a clue for what we're doing tonight. See you at seven."

"See you then. Thanks." She tugged at the bow as he left. The first bite confirmed that this was first-rate dark chocolate. There was just the right amount of bitterness to complement the almonds. Mmmm. Allison broke off another piece and reclosed the bag. There was something to be said for a man who showed up unexpectedly bearing chocolate. It wasn't a flashing arrow, but it might be a sign. Of course, the cake Phil had saved for her had turned out to be a sign, too. Just the wrong kind of sign. *Why can't I just admit that Phil's out of the picture? Marcus is in the picture now, and he's turning out to be pretty great.*

She savored the treat and let her mind drift. *I should've asked about Lindsey. I don't want to keep going out with Marcus if she's not okay with it. Has he even thought to ask her?* It was something that really needed to be settled sooner than later. She'd take a few minutes to call Lindsey and find out for herself.

Allison had five minutes to change before Marcus was due. He'd never given her any indication that he habitually ran late, so she rushed through changing into jeans and a sweater. She wasn't sure it was appropriate, but he'd said active and casual. And if he wasn't going to give her more information, she wasn't going to stress about it. Besides, it was cold out there. Since they'd ended up walking around after dinner last time, she wanted to be better prepared in case that was again on the menu.

Marcus rang her apartment at exactly seven. She buzzed him into the building and gathered her coat and purse while she waited for him to arrive at her door.

"Ready?" He was wearing jeans and a dark green sweater. The worn leather jacket she'd noticed several times completed his outfit.

"All set. Do I get a hint now?"

Marcus shook his head, eyes glinting with mischief. "You'll find out soon enough."

Laughing, she checked to be sure her door was locked. "Lead on."

It was a short drive into Old Town Alexandria, though they hit some traffic on their way down I95 to King Street. Marcus found a parking garage then tucked her arm through his as they exited onto the cobblestone street. "Just down here, about a block." He glanced at his watch. "We should be right on time."

They turned the corner and Allison scanned the shop names, hoping to recognize something. She didn't make it to Old Town as often as she would have liked.

She loved the feel of the historic area and the glimpses of the Potomac River you could catch between buildings.

"Here we are." Marcus held the door for her.

She glanced up at the sign that hung above the door. The shop's name, *In the Kitchen*, didn't mean anything to her. She assumed it was a new restaurant. Things were coming and going in Old Town all the time. Looking around while Marcus let the hostess know they had arrived, she saw four rows of countertops, each one set up like two miniature kitchens. Each end of the counter held two place settings and two stools that tucked under the outcropping. It didn't look Japanese...but could it be some kind of new Hibachi style place? Several other couples were milling around, each keeping close to one of the kitchen areas. She and Marcus followed the hostess to the front row, taking the last available spot.

The hostess stepped to the front of the room and held up her hand for silence. "If I could get everyone's attention?" When the conversation quieted, she smiled. "Welcome to *In the Kitchen*. Tonight's menu is in the center of your workspace. We'll be getting started with the Prosciutto-wrapped asparagus appetizer in just a moment. For now, please be sure to stow your belongings on the hooks under the counter at the end of each row and take a minute to wash your hands. The servers will be around shortly to get your drink orders."

Allison tucked her purse and coat under the counter and looked at Marcus. "Are we cooking?"

"It sounded like fun."

Laughing, she stepped to the sink. "I'm not sure you know what you've gotten yourself into. I've burned macaroni and cheese." She glanced at him over her shoulder. "In the microwave." Drying her hands, she stepped out of the way so he could reach the sink. "But I'll give it a shot. Presumably they won't let us poison ourselves, right?"

"That's the theory." He dried his hands and slid the first recipe off the stack. "I'm willing to risk it if you are."

The hostess turned out to be the chef/owner. She guided the class through the preparation of the four-course meal. As they slid the dessert into the oven and sat down to enjoy their entrée, the lights dimmed. "From here out, you're on your own. Servers will be around to check on you. But when those timers go off, be sure to take out your soufflés. Bon appétit, and thank you for coming." There was a smattering of applause before conversations picked up at each of the seating areas.

"This was a great idea. And," Allison took a bite, "it's delicious. Which is surprising since I made it and it's not grilled cheese."

"I'm glad you don't mind. I worried about it a bit this week, wondering if you'd be game to make your own dinner. I hoped you wouldn't be irritated by it."

"Not when it turns out this tasty. You should bring Lindsey sometime. I imagine this would be a great father-daughter activity."

"You think she'd go for this much time with her old man?"

*Here goes nothing. But he really needs to know. Even if I'd just as soon not ruin my chances.* "I do. In fact, I need to confess that I called her this afternoon."

"Why is that a confession? You've been helping her—both of us, really—I know she values your friendship."

"It's because of that, really, that I called. I wanted to be sure she was okay with this." With her fork, she indicated the two of them and their dinners.

Marcus frowned. "Why wouldn't she be?"

"Because you're her father. And I'm not her mother." How could he miss something so straightforward? "She has reservations about you dating in general, though she likes me well enough. Have you talked to her about this at all?"

"No. I…haven't really been able to figure out how to bring it up. And with the pregnancy and Ben dumping her, and my less than stellar reaction to all of that…our talks seem to turn into shouting matches before I realize what's happened. I'll talk to her. Tonight if she's still up, otherwise tomorrow."

Allison patted his hand, letting her fingers rest on his for a moment before resuming her dinner. "Good. She needs you right now."

The buzzers on the ovens signaled around the room. She stood to check theirs and carefully pulled out two fluffy chocolate soufflés. She eased them onto the dessert plates and brought them over.

"I wish I thought I'd be able to replicate this. But for now," she dug her cell phone from her pocket and snapped a photo, "At least I have documented proof."

After they finished eating, they walked down to the waterfront and strolled along the Potomac River for a block, enjoying the view, even as the wind knifed through their jackets. Unable to stand the cold any longer, they hurried back to the car.

Back at her apartment, Allison unlocked her door and turned. "I had a lovely time. Thank you, Marcus."

He leaned forward and pressed his cheek to hers, turning to kiss her cheek as he pulled back. "Me too. Have a good night."

She shut and locked the door behind her. Why had he kissed her? More to the point, why hadn't she enjoyed it?

Phil pushed the last of his poker chips into the center of the table. "All in."

Grant studied Phil from across the table. The two other men in their weekly poker game had already folded, leaving the last hand to Phil and Grant. Finally, he shrugged and pushed a matching stack of chips in as well. "Why not. Let's see 'em."

Phil flipped over the seven and eight of hearts and nodded to the six, nine, and ten in the center. "Straight."

"Man." Grant shook his head and flipped over his two nines. "Three of a kind. You got lucky with the ten in the river."

Phil laughed and collected the chips. "Sorry to break your winning streak."

"No you're not." Grant tapped the cards back into a pile and shuffled them twice before standing. "Game's over, guys. Phil managed to sneak a win."

Amidst congratulations and playful ribbing, the four men sorted and stacked the chips and cleared up the table. Phil took the eight dollars that comprised his winnings with a grin. "Guess the chips and dip are on me next week."

"Don't forget the salsa like Grant always does."

"You can always bring salsa, Jim, if you're worried I'm going to forget."

"Thanks for hosting again, Terry." Phil checked his watch. *What now?* The Friday night game had ended much more quickly than usual. He didn't want to go home and putter around. That left the door open for too much thinking about Allison. He was pretty sure he'd used up his quota for that this week.

Grant and Jim also said their goodbyes and headed out. Since Grant was parked behind Phil, they walked together, rehashing some of the game's high points.

With his hand on the car door Phil paused. "Any news on Brandi?"

Grant shook his head. "So far as I know she hasn't posted bail. Between violating the restraining order and breaking and entering, especially with the handful of drunk and disorderly and possession pops, she's probably looking at a few years in jail at least. Why do you ask?"

Phil shrugged. "Mostly curious. I know it was the right thing to call the police, but I feel bad."

Grant clapped him on the shoulder. "You know consequences catch up to everyone eventually."

"Yeah, I know. Hey...you up for a movie or something? Seems slightly lame to be headed home by eight on a Friday night."

"Sure. You ever get that big TV you were talking about?"

Phil grinned. "Eighty inches of viewing delight."

"I'll be right over."

Terry's house was less than twenty minutes from Phil's. The southbound traffic on the Interstate had cleared out enough that it was an easy drive.

Phil kicked off his shoes and laid his laptop on the kitchen table. "Make yourself at home. There's soda in the fridge. I can probably manage popcorn if you're hungry. *Scarface?*"

"It's a classic for a reason." Grant sat on the stairs and untied his shoes. He grabbed a soda from the fridge before sprawling in a recliner in front of the TV. "We haven't hung out in a while. Why is that?"

Phil glanced up from setting up the BluRay. "Busy, I guess. And they say never hire your friend as your divorce attorney...I guess it was awkward for a while."

"Who says that?"

"I don't know, the ubiquitous 'they.'" Phil took the remote and settled in the other recliner in the room. "You didn't think it was awkward?"

"Maybe a little." Grant held his fingers up with a teeny space between them. "Still, in my opinion Brandi did you a favor."

Phil hit pause on the opening credits. "You ever think about dating again?"

"Not you, too."

"Just asking." He hit the play button.

As Al Pacino's Tony began to be questioned by INS agents, Grant looked over. "What's her name."

"Never mind."

"Hey, you brought it up."

"Can we just move on?"

Grant laughed. "No."

Why had he said anything? Phil groaned and hit pause. "Allison."

"Allison from your firm, Allison?"

"Yeah."

"I thought she just started dating someone?" Grant's look was calculating. "Someone not you."

Phil muttered, "Two dates. They've been on two dates." He punched play.

"If you think I won't talk over the movie, you don't know me very well." Grant watched the screen for a moment then turned back to Phil. "Don't you want to know how I, who does not work at your firm, knows about Allison and her dating habits?"

"Not really." Resolutely, Phil kept his face turned toward the movie, though his eyes flicked in Grant's direction. Curiosity gnawed at him.

Grant simply sat, watching him.

"Oh fine." Phil hit pause again. "How do you know?"

A grin split Grant's face as he began to hum *It's a Small World.*

"Thanks. Now that's going to be stuck in my head all night. Just tell me, okay?"

"Touchy." Grant smirked. "Lilly," his voice softened on her name and he cleared his throat before continuing, "Lilly and Therese Bowers worked together. So when Therese and her husband decided to have wills made, Lilly recommended her favorite family lawyer." He pointed to himself. "Lil and Therese both passed away around the same time. I know Marcus and have, in fact, been consulting with him myself recently. Personal things come up when you talk to your attorney...as you well know."

"So they do." He hit play and watched the action on the screen unfold for several minutes. Why was Marcus consulting with Grant? And what did it mean that he'd mentioned his dates with Allison? You didn't mention casual dates to your attorney. Did you? "You think I should just give up, then?"

"Didn't say that." Grant kept his eyes glued to the movie. "Not knowing Allison personally, I can't really comment from that perspective. But she sounds like a nice person, and if you think you're in a place where you can date again, and you want to, I don't see why you shouldn't ask her out."

"Hypothetically...if I already told her something semi-moronic about how I was never getting remarried, does that change your opinion?"

"No, just makes your job considerably harder." He turned to look at Phil. "Why on earth did you do that?"

"Got spooked. Plus…I guess I'm still not sure about remarrying, from a Biblical standpoint."

"I get that. I've had similar questions now and again. Even though I lost Lilly to cancer, not divorce." Grant smiled wistfully then shook his head. "Are we going to paint our toes next or can we get on with the movie?"

CRBN

Phil woke early on Saturday and lay in bed looking out at the Occoquan River. On the dock, a thick layer of frost sparkled in the early morning light. Grant had made some compelling arguments the night before. The conviction that he could never remarry was rapidly draining away. He'd started to understand how many of the reasons he'd been clinging to were driven by fear of messing up again. *And getting hurt.* The end of his marriage had hurt more than anything he'd ever experienced before or since. And he never wanted to go through something like that again.

He pushed himself out of bed and dragged on sweats. The thermometer on his balcony showed the temperature hovering in the mid-thirties. He looked at the river. It'd be cold. But that's what they made Gore-Tex for. He pulled on his sneakers and windbreaker before heading down to the garage to get out his kayak.

The lack of wind on the river kept the temperature bearable. Phil paddled, ignoring the scenery. He rowed down into Belmont Bay and circled the loop of water before beginning the paddle back upriver toward home. His muscles were singing by the time he made it under the interstate but his mind was blissfully blank. He slowed. Even in winter there was beauty on the river.

Back at the dock, Phil hefted the kayak out of the water and stowed it in his garage. He hadn't arrived at any definite conclusions, but he had more peace than he'd had in a long time. Breathing a prayer of thanks, he headed for the shower, pausing to start the coffee brewing on his way up the stairs.

Clad in jeans and a sweatshirt, Phil tucked a pair of socks in his back pocket and went down to the kitchen. He sat at the kitchen table with his mug of coffee and Bible and continued his study of First Corinthians, pausing when he landed in chapter seven. It was startling to see his own situation discussed by the Apostle Paul. *Of course, I'm not the first person to come to Christ after I was married.* How had he missed this before? He was meeting with Pastor Brown later today. He'd have to bring it up. He had no qualms about having misinterpreted whether or not he *could* remarry. Should he remarry was a whole other question.

*And you're getting a little ahead of yourself anyway...first you have to work up the nerve to ask her out.*

☙❧

Allison arrived at Tae Kwon Do just as the class was starting. She stretched hurriedly and joined the Saturday group on the mat. Sarah spotted her and grinned, tapping her watch. The next time she caught Sarah's eye, Allison stuck out her tongue.

After class, sweaty and exhausted, Allison leaned against the back wall and chugged from her water bottle. Sarah nudged her and flopped on the mat.

"Before you ask, no."

"No, what?"

"No dessert. I need honest to goodness food today. And I'd prefer something that actually grew out of the ground." Sarah rested her water bottle on her forehead and sighed. "I know it's cold outside, but right now, cool feels good."

"Brown and Green?"

"That sounds perfect. Healthy, tasty, real food. Pricey. But nothing's perfect." Sarah propped herself up on her elbows. "And then we can go next door and get a cupcake. There's a new bakery in that shopping center I've been wanting to try."

"So much for no dessert. But deal. Meet you there?" She glanced down at her workout clothes. "Or do we need to shower and change first? I didn't bring anything with me."

"Nah. You're fine. We should be early enough to beat the rush."

Allison jerked her head at the door. "Let's go before we get roped into another class. I've missed too many classes lately to live through that."

The chic organic restaurant wasn't far from the dojang. It was a newer establishment, owned and operated by an older couple recently transplanted from Portland. Allison had never figured out what made them move across the country, but she was glad they had. She was often tired of eating out at the sea of chain restaurants, but good unique places were hard to find

"Welcome to Brown and Green. Sit wherever you like, I'll be over with menus in just a second." The owner smiled and slipped into the back.

Allison pointed to a booth in the front window.

Sarah nodded her assent and they settled in.

"This way we can watch the world go by."

Sarah laughed. "Are you taking up people watching?"

"I've always enjoyed it; just never make the time to do much. After the craziness at work lately, I'm all for something low key." Allison took the menu the owner delivered. Her eyes widened as she deposited a plate of homemade hummus and pita on the table. Shifting her attention to the owner, she said, "Please tell me business isn't bad. You absolutely can't go under."

The woman laughed and shook her head. "We're good. Just trying a few new things out. Now, you take a look at those menus and let me know when you're ready."

Sarah dipped a triangle of pita into the hummus. "Oooh, it's got a little kick at the end. Yum." She redunked the pita.

Allison wrinkled her nose. "You're lucky I like you. That's disgusting."

"What?" Sarah halted mid-bite. "Oh…did I double dip? I'm bad about that, sorry."

Both women jolted at the sound of pounding on the window.

Allison beamed when she saw Lydia and Laura waving madly from outside. She gestured for them to come in. "You mind company?"

Sarah shook her head. "You know me, the more the merrier."

"What are you doing over here?" Laura leaned on the side of the booth.

"Tae Kwon Do is just down the street a bit. This is my friend Sarah, I know I've mentioned her. Sarah, Laura and behind her, lurking in the background, is Lydia. Want to join us for lunch?"

Laura glanced at Lydia questioningly.

Lydia shrugged. "Why not?"

Sarah scooted out and slid into the booth next to Allison. Laura and Lydia slid into the side she'd vacated. When everyone was settled and two more menus and glasses of water had been delivered, Allison looked across at Laura and Lydia. "What brings you two out this way?"

"We were heading next door. That's the bakery Kevin and I decided on. I wanted to get another opinion or two on the cake. Since you didn't answer when I called last night, we decided to come without you." Lydia grinned. "I was going to make you come another time, thus securing yet another sample for myself."

Allison laughed. "And then we'd have to hear you moan about how your wedding dress was going to have to be a size bigger than you normally wear. It's good you ran into us." She glanced at Sarah. "Is that the place we were going for cupcakes after lunch?"

"Yep. Their stuff is to die for. If I ever get married, they are totally doing my cake." Sarah looked at Allison. "I like your friends, they have good taste."

The ladies all laughed.

"You didn't answer Lydia's call last night, nor did you answer mine." Sarah looked at Allison with speculation. "Where were you?"

"My thoughts exactly." Lydia sipped her water. "I'm guessing second date, so it sounds like you have some details to share."

"Date? What?" Laura wrinkled her forehead. "I thought Phil said he wasn't going to date anyone. What changed?"

Sarah nodded. "I have only the sketchiest details, as she's been rather cagey about the whole thing. I'm half convinced she's been skipping Tae Kwon Do for the sole purpose of not filling me in about her mystery man."

"All right, all right." Allison told them about Marcus and the two dates they'd been on.

"Oooh, I've heard about *In The Kitchen*. I've been hinting to Kevin that we should go sometime, but he doesn't seem to have picked up on it." Lydia drummed her fingers on the table. "Maybe you could mention that you've been and how wonderful it was."

"I can do that. Though that probably means I'm going to have to rehash my date yet again...and it honestly isn't all that big a boost to my self-esteem. I'm flattered that Marcus is interested. And he's attractive and fun to be around. But I think his priority right now, and mine, honestly, should be Lindsey. And unless I've completely misinterpreted her, she's not terribly keen on her father dating again. Add to that the fact that I'm still more interested in Phil, despite his fairly clear rejection...I think I'd just as soon go back to the way it was a month ago."

"What? Pining for my fiancé?" Lydia winked. "Yeah, Kevin mentioned it."

"He wasn't your fiancé when I was pining. Besides, one date pretty much proved it was just delusion on my part." But oh how she wished it hadn't been. Kevin was pretty much ideal. Too bad for her that they were better off as friends.

Sarah laughed. "I remember you telling me about that fiasco. Though it was good to clear the air, right?"

"What is this? Does no one talk to the married woman anymore?" Laura frowned, clearly irritated. "Honestly, how did I miss this?"

Lydia glanced at Laura. "Kevin told you and Matt about it before me."

"Really?" Laura poked at her food then shrugged. "Well, I have no memory of that. I'm calling it pregnancy brain and moving on." She fixed Allison in her gaze. "What are you going to do?"

"I told Marcus he needed to talk to Lindsey before I'd go out with him again. Hopefully that will make the situation a little more clear to both of us. It occurred to me that with Marcus, I could end up as an instant mother *and* grandmother. Not sure how I feel about that, to be honest, no matter how much I love Lindsey. And Phil?" She lifted a shoulder. "I don't know. Just keep praying, I guess."

Allison's phone was ringing when she walked in the door. She dropped her things and ran to grab it before it went to voicemail. "Hello?"

"Allison? It's Lindsey...is it okay that I called you?"

"Of course. What's up?" All she really wanted was to take a shower. Maybe a nap. She sat on the edge of the couch to untie her sneakers.

"My dad talked to me this morning. And he actually listened for a change instead of flying off the handle. I wanted to say thanks for making him understand I needed it."

"No thanks required, but you're welcome. He seems like a good man, and a good dad. You've both been through a lot recently...I imagine a few hiccups in communication are to be expected."

"Um. I guess I kind of also wanted to apologize."

Allison furrowed her brow. "For what?"

Lindsey cleared her throat. "I think I kind of talked my dad out of asking you out again. And it's not that I wouldn't be totally psyched, normally, about him dating you. Well, if I was going to be psyched about him dating anyone. I feel awful," her voice broke and she sniffled, "but I just really need him for myself right now."

"Oh honey, of course you do. It's all right." Allison sat on the edge of her bed and tossed her sneakers toward her closet. Something she hadn't realized was caught in her chest loosened. At least now she didn't have to worry about choosing between Phil and Marcus. Still no blinking arrow, but the sense of relief had to mean something. Didn't it? Not that there was really anyone to choose between. Based on Phil's comments she'd be better off disregarding any mixed signals he might have thrown off. Leaving her with no dating prospects on the horizon. *Right back where I started. Lord, if I'm not ever going to get married, could you please make it so I don't want to so badly? Please?*

"You should absolutely be your dad's main focus right now. Well, you and the baby. You've got a lot of preparation to work on."

"That's the other thing that I wanted to talk to you about. I…I'm going to place the baby for adoption. Dad gets it…and I kind of think he's relieved on some levels…it's just…the more I started trying to plan for parenting, even with all the help Dad was offering. I can't do it."

What did you say to that? It was a hard choice to make, and Allison couldn't imagine making it herself. On the other hand, she couldn't really imagine making any of the decisions Lindsey was facing. This way, at least, the baby would have two loving parents from the start and Lindsey would get a chance to finish being a child herself. "Sounds like you've found the option that makes the most sense for you and for the baby."

"Thanks." She took a shuddering breath. "So…would you maybe be willing to go to the adoption agency with me on Monday? Dad can't get the time off. He's been using a lot of leave lately and they're getting annoyed. I know it's a lot to ask…"

Allison didn't have court Monday but there was still a lot to do to prepare for court dates later in the week. If she pushed herself though, she could probably do most of it tonight and tomorrow. And Lindsey deserved to have someone with her. "What time?"

"They open at ten. I can go whenever."

"If we can get there right at ten, I can make it work. Want me to pick you up?"

"Would you?"

"Sure thing." Allison grabbed the notepad off her nightstand and scribbled some notes about the schedule juggling she'd need to do when she got off the phone. "Will you be at church tomorrow?"

"Probably not. My grandma found out about the pregnancy and is threatening to come to town. We may have to go get her at the airport. You could say a prayer for us…she's hard to deal with even when things are good. Dad's already stressed and he just found out about her plan to visit an hour ago."

"I'll definitely pray. And I'll see you Monday morning. Can you text or email me the address so I can figure out what time I should pick you up?"

"Sure. Thanks, Allison."

"No problem, kiddo. Bye." Allison dropped the phone on her bed and peeled off her sweaty clothes. Tossing them in the hamper, she turned the shower on as hot as it would go and waited for steam to billow from the top. Carefully avoiding the spray, she reached in to lower the temperature before stepping in. She rested her forehead against the cool tile while the hot water beat down on her.

Her thoughts were spinning. Marcus was out of the picture. How did she feel? She was pleased he was taking care of Lindsey. She was more invested in the daughter than the dad, wasn't she? It was like Kevin all over again. A nice, good looking man, just the type of man she hoped to marry. But ultimately not *the* man.

She wasn't even that disappointed that he was out of the picture romantically. Sure, she'd miss having plans on the weekend. But she could always start hanging out with Laura and Matt again. And if Kevin and Lydia were there too, well, there was nothing wrong with being a fifth wheel. It was better than being stuck at home all the time. And on the rare instances that Sarah was between one of her six-date only relationships they could have a girl's night. In the mean time, she'd be able to focus on helping Lindsey the best she could.

⟨ೞ⟩

Phil stood in the crowded foyer. What was he doing? He liked his church...why was he trying someplace new? He threaded through the people toward the sanctuary. Sometimes ruts were comfortable for a reason.

He chose a pew and sat, nodding hello to the people near him, and flipped through the bulletin.

"Phil?"

He looked up at the familiar voice and smiled. "Hey, Kevin. Thought I'd come and see if Pastor Brown is as good with sermons as he is one-on-one."

Kevin chuckled and sat, leaving a comfortable space between them. "Better, I'd say. And not just because he's my future father-in-law. Honestly, if things hadn't worked out with Lydia, I'm not sure I would've been able to make myself find another church, no matter how awkward it got."

"That's a lovely recommendation. I'll have to pass that one on next time I need something from him." Lydia slid next to Kevin and leaned forward to peek around him. "Morning, Phil."

"Good morning."

The prelude began. It was nice of Kevin and Lydia to sit with him. He hadn't expected it. *Why is that?*

*Maybe because they're friends of Allison's, not mine?* Allison. What was he supposed to do about her? *Lord...help me out here. Please?*

The service was good. There was a perfect mix of hymns and contemporary music during the worship time. And Kevin was right; Pastor Brown was an even better preacher than counselor, which was saying something. Should he try out a small group today, too? Was there anything for single folks who weren't into the more typical college-aged single-mingle?

Kevin tapped his shoulder. "Want to come to our small group?"

"Are you a mind reader now?"

"Nope, just a good recruiter."

"Give me a snapshot in thirty words or less. Include demographics."

"We're a group of older singles, some couples. Really, anyone who isn't actively using church as a place to find a mate." Kevin frowned. "I lost count, but I think that's under thirty words."

"Close enough." It was too early to get lunch, so if he left he'd be stuck heading home. And his refrigerator was pretty bare, meaning home would entail a trip to the grocery store. While that would be a very good idea, he was definitely not in the mood to deal with it right now.

"I'll sweeten the pot." Lydia's eyes sparkled with mischief. "Come with us and then you can join us for lunch and cast your vote on our wedding cake selection."

Kevin groaned. "How many people are you going to ask before you just order it?"

"The more people I ask, the more samples I get, too. There's a method to my madness." She turned her attention back to Phil. "What do you think?"

"Cake is always persuasive. Lead the way."

The group was small and not afraid to mix humor in with serious Bible study. They'd been in First Corinthians a little over a month and had just made it to chapter seven. The same passage he'd been reading in his own quiet times. The one that he'd spent a good portion of counseling time discussing with Pastor Brown. He might be slow, but with enough hammering, he did finally understand when he was getting hit in the head. Now his only excuse for not dating was cowardice. That didn't sit very well.

The entire group headed to lunch together. It, too, was a noisy and fun event. It was refreshing to see Christians not scared to make the occasional sarcastic comment. At his home church, sarcasm was considered a sure sign that you had issues in your walk with God. While it could certainly be taken too far, Phil's dry sense of humor had always relied heavily on friendly sarcasm. Doing without it had been a struggle.

When the last of the group left, Lydia rubbed her hands together. "Cake time."

"I'm surprised you didn't invite everyone." Kevin grabbed Lydia's coat from the back of her chair.

"Thought about it for a minute, then worried there wouldn't be enough and, as I've already had some, I would have to do the polite thing and let someone else have my share."

Phil snickered. "Where is this bakery?"

Lydia gave him directions and they agreed to meet up in a half hour to give Phil time to get gas in his car.

☙❧

Kevin and Lydia were already seated at one of the wrought iron tables when Phil arrived. A third person had joined them, but it wasn't until he was pulling out his chair that he realized it was Allison. Sweat broke out on his palms. "Hey."

Surprise registered on Allison's face. "Hey, Phil. What brings you here?"

He pointed at Kevin and Lydia. "They do. Well, that and the promise of cake." He eyed the bare table. "Did you eat it already?"

Kevin shook his head. "They've apparently been getting lots of requests for our preferred flavor lately," he shot Lydia a significant look, "so they were out. They've got a batch of cupcakes almost ready, so we're waiting."

"I haven't told that many people." The pink stain across Lydia's cheeks belied her vigorous objection.

Allison angled her head to one side. "Yeah, but how many people have the people you've told told?"

"That's not my fault." Lydia pouted.

"Can I get anyone some coffee while we wait?" He needed something to do with his hands. And an excuse to get away from the table to slow his heart rate. Phil laughed when everyone's hand went up. "Four coffees coming up."

"Need any help?" Kevin stood.

Phil shrugged. "Sure."

The two men got in line. Phil glanced over and saw Lydia and Allison's heads bent together at the table. "Do I even want to know what they're talking about?"

Kevin followed Phil's gaze. "Probably not. I imagine it's one of us. Most likely you." He frowned and looked at Phil before adding on, "From what I hear, at least."

"What's that mean?"

Kevin looked over his shoulder at the women deep in conversation at their table. "Allison seems to be developing a friendship with Lydia. I'm actually pretty happy about that. Allison's good people and Lydia lost the majority of her so-called friends last year." He shuffled forward as the line started moving. "Anyway, she and Allison and Laura...have you met Matt and Laura?"

"Don't think so."

"Hmm, we need to fix that. You'd like them. The three of them have been getting together now and then. I suspect at Laura's urging. She knew Allison in college as well."

"Okay, so they've hung out." They were next in line. Phil gestured for Kevin to wait while he ordered and paid. They scooted to the coffee pick up area and Phil continued. "I guess I don't see what that has to do with me."

Kevin chuckled. "Let's just say your name has been brought up. As has a certain event they refer to as," he made air quotes, "the Cake Incident."

Phil closed his eyes and fought back a groan. So much for the brief hope he'd entertained that the whole thing in the park would fade from memory.

Kevin slapped his back. "Try and look at the bright side. She hasn't written you off."

Phil didn't see where he got that idea. If she was spending time discussing it with friends and making fun, didn't that pretty much guarantee he'd been written off? Wasn't that what he wanted, anyway? *Who am I kidding? I don't want to be written off. Not by Allison.* He grabbed two of the coffees, nodding to Kevin to get the others. If Kevin was right and she hadn't completely written him off…that was definitely one for the bright side. A tiny flicker of hope lit in his heart.

They got back to the table just as a server brought out a plate with four cupcakes.

"Perfect timing, I see." Phil gawked the pale pink frosting over dark chocolate cake. "Why are they pink?"

Allison scooted one of the cupcakes onto a napkin in front of her. "That's black cherry icing. There's black cherry filling in the middle, too. Don't let the color put you off."

Kevin took a bite. "I don't understand why you haven't ordered yet. We're never going to find anything better. Do you not remember our torturous day of bakeries and tasting?"

"He's right, these are heaven. If this is your wedding cake, I want an invite." Phil licked icing off his fingers.

"Just for the cake?" Lydia laughed.

Phil nodded. "Absolutely."

"All right, that settles it. I'll place the order today. Though," she glanced at Kevin, "I guess that means we ought to officially firm up a date."

"Which we can't do sitting here. So we'll order this week. Which means we can also order a number of other things, like invitations." Kevin sighed. "And that means you're going to make me go blind looking through books of invitations again, aren't you?"

Phil chuckled. "Kevin, repeat after me. 'Yes, dear.'"

Kevin grinned.

Lydia swatted Phil's arm. "I need real opinions, thank you. Though I guess I could just have Allison help me choose everything."

"Uh-uh. I've already told you I'm not part of your wedding. I've been a bridesmaid twice, that's my limit, since I do actually want to get married myself some day." Allison shoved the last bite of cupcake in her mouth and stood. "I should run. I've got a lot of work waiting for me at home. I only snuck out of my self-imposed prison for a chocolate fix."

"See you tomorrow." Phil lifted his coffee in a goodbye salute. *I wish she wouldn't run off.* He hadn't realized how much he missed her. *Has she been avoiding me?*

"Probably not. I have an appointment in the morning and then court prep. Looking like another crazy week. Call me when you have the date settled, Lydia, so I can mark my calendar." With a final wave, Allison whisked out the door.

Phil finished his cupcake. Allison didn't act like she was still interested in him. In fact, she hadn't been acting like someone who was interested since she'd gone out with Marcus. *I hope I haven't missed my chance.* What was he supposed to do now? *It's been so long since I had to worry about dating, I think I've lost what meager skill I had.*

Allison found a parking spot in the crowded lot surrounding the town houses that served as a collection of offices. She glanced at Lindsey, noting how tightly she was clutching the strap of her backpack. "You okay?"

Lindsey nodded and swallowed. "Just nervous, I guess." She rubbed her belly and pulled her lower lip between her teeth. "Do you think this is the right thing?"

"I think it's a brave thing. And a hard thing. And a noble thing." Allison squeezed Lindsey's hand. "And I know you've put a lot of thought and prayer into the decision. I don't think any choice is going to be easy though."

"Yeah. You're probably right." Lindsey took a steadying breath. "Let's go before I chicken out."

As they crossed the lot, Allison scanned the sign between two rows of the buildings indicating which offices were where. She pointed to the left. "I think we're heading this way. Do you remember the name of the woman we're meeting?"

"Faith. Um. I can't remember her last name, but hopefully they don't have too many people named Faith."

With a chuckle, Allison pulled open the door to the unit. There were two closed doors on either side of a wide stairwell. Both doors had brass plaques displaying doctor names. A small sign at the landing half way up the stairs displayed the adoption agency's name and an arrow indicating the office was upstairs. She gestured to the sign. Must be upstairs. "After you."

Lindsey hesitated. "Could you go up first?"

Allison slipped her arm around Lindsey's shoulders. "Come on, we'll go up together."

At the top of the stairs was a long hallway. Allison frowned. Where was the office? It wasn't the most welcoming start to the space. Shouldn't there be a receptionist somewhere? A door on the left stood open, revealing a room consumed by a long table. There was a small refrigerator in one corner and a coffee maker on a table jammed into another corner. That must not be it. *Are we even in the right place?*

They continued down the hall, looking in the next two rooms. Both were empty offices. Finally, they emerged in a large open space. A desk formed an extension of the interior hallway wall. It held a small brass sign indicating it was the receptionist's desk. It, too, stood empty. At least they were in the right office. But where was the receptionist? Allison checked her watch. "You said ten, right?"

Lindsey nodded. Her face had lost its color and her breathing was ragged.

"Hello?" Allison crossed the room to peer through another door. This room held two sofas and several bookcases. It looked warm and friendly, like the den in someone's home. But it was also empty.

"Hello?" She made her voice a little louder and shot a confused look at Lindsey.

The door at the far side of the room opened, revealing four women seated around a small table. A fifth woman, slim with silver hair, slipped through the door and pulled it shut behind her. "Good morning. I'm so sorry, we're running a bit late with our morning meeting. I'm Faith." She looked at Allison then shifted her gaze to Lindsey. "You must be Lindsey?"

"Yeah. Hi."

Faith turned to Allison. "Are you her mother?"

"No, just a friend. Allison Vasak. She asked if I'd come along."

"Nice to meet you." Faith gestured to the room with the sofas. "Why don't you two get comfortable in here and I'll be just a minute. I'll go grab my paperwork and so forth. Can I get you something to drink? Water? Coffee?"

"I'd like some water, please." Lindsey shuffled toward the door, still clutching her backpack.

"That'd be great for me as well." Allison followed behind Lindsey and gave her shoulder an encouraging pat. Things weren't off to an auspicious start, but at least Faith seemed friendly. Lindsey sat on the sofa facing the door. Allison glanced around the room. "Where do you want me? I'll be as involved or uninvolved as you need."

"Could you sit next to me?" Lindsey moved her backpack onto her lap. "I'm starting to freak out a little bit."

"Absolutely. I think freaking out is perfectly understandable given the situation. This is a big step, a big decision. And like I said, it's not going to be easy just because you're convinced it's the right thing."

"That is so true." Faith pushed the door shut with her foot and carefully slid a stack of folders onto the coffee table between the sofas. She offered each of them a bottle of water before sipping from her own steaming coffee mug. "It sounds like you're getting some good counsel already. But one of the things we really do recommend is that you meet with a professional counselor. Someone who has training and experience specifically with birth parents. Is that something you think you'd be interested in?"

Lindsey gave a vigorous nod.

Faith smiled as she set her mug down and dug through the pile of folders for a sheet of paper. "This has a list of the counselors we recommend. You may want to see if your health insurance will cover the sessions. Most of the people on the list work with the larger insurers, so you probably can minimize the cost. Even if you can't, see what you can work out. I strongly recommend the counseling."

"Can you give us a picture of what they talk about?" Allison hoped it was all right for her to jump in with questions.

Lindsey shot her a grateful look.

"They won't try to talk you out of your decision, if that's what you're worried about. Mostly they want to be sure that you've thought things through, and then they start helping you process the grief. Because there is a lot of grief involved in placing a baby for adoption. Even when you're convinced you're doing the best thing for the child and for yourself, it's a loss. It's essential to recognize that and face it head on."

Lindsey nodded again.

Why wasn't she saying anything? Allison could understand feeling overwhelmed, but if this was the path Lindsey was choosing, she needed to be more involved. She leaned over to whisper in her ear. "You okay?"

"Yeah. Just taking it in, you know?" She smiled weakly and looked at Faith. "Sorry."

"Don't be. If it makes you feel any better, we actually prefer birth mothers who are concerned. It means you've been thinking through what you're doing and that you already care about the baby. Believe it or not, having a good bond with the baby before you make the placement will help both of you in the long run. So don't be afraid of that." Faith sifted through the paperwork again and opened another folder before passing it to

Lindsey. "Now, this has our basic policies and intake forms. Let me walk you through them."

They spent the next two hours going through paperwork and having the ins and outs of the legal process explained in detail. When it became apparent that Lindsey was doing all she could to simply listen, Allison started taking notes so Lindsey would have something to refer back to in the coming weeks. They ended their talk looking through profile books of potential adoptive parents so Lindsey could see the type of information they provided.

"Now," Faith stacked the folders back into a neat pile and stood, "spend some time thinking and praying about what you want in an adoptive family. Make lists on paper, don't rely on your memory. When you think you've got a good idea, you can call me or email me and I'll pull some profiles together for you to come in and look at. We'll go through as many as it takes to find the couple that you're happy with, though I try to keep it to small batches. Otherwise it's easy to get overwhelmed."

Allison and Lindsey followed Faith from the room. "Thank you. This was very thorough. I think, once she's had some time to process it all, Lindsey will realize just how much information she has."

"Once I recover from information overload, you mean?" Lindsey's smile was closer to a grimace.

"Any last questions?"

"One, I guess...what do I do about Ben? The father."

"We'll have to get his consent. It's easiest if you can talk to him and get him to come sign the releases. If that isn't successful, then we'll need to make an appointment with one of the attorneys we work with to evaluate the other options." Faith tilted her head. "Is talking to him going to be a problem?"

"No...just awkward. But since he made it clear he didn't want anything to do with me or the baby...I can't see him raising a fuss."

"Well, let me know if I can be of any help. We're here for you as much as you need." Faith smiled and shook their hands again before walking them to the stairway.

Back in the car, Lindsey leaned her head back and closed her eyes.

"Still anxious?" Allison started the drive back to Lindsey's house.

"Some...though I'm more peaceful about it than before." She turned and watched Allison. "Thanks for the notes. I was just having a hard time focusing."

"No problem. To an attorney, note taking is like breathing. Let's get you home. You look like you could use a nap."

Lindsey rubbed her belly. "I could always use a nap lately. Thanks, Allison. For everything."

"My pleasure." Surprised at how much she meant it, Allison patted Lindsey's knee. "You're a good kid, Linds. I'm glad to know you."

 CASEO

Phil peeked in Allison's empty office for the sixth time that morning. Where was she? *I hope she's okay.* When she'd said she had an appointment in the morning, he'd assumed she meant with a client here in the office. He'd been hoping to catch her during a break. Maybe convince her to get some fresh air and coffee across the street. That would be a good start back to the easy friendship they'd had before he'd made a mess of things. Now, hyped up on too much bad coffee from the break room, he was rethinking his strategy. Maybe he needed to be more direct.

"She's out for the day."

Phil flinched and turned to see the receptionist, Sam, walking by with a fresh cup of coffee. "What?"

"Allison's out for the day. Then in court for probably the whole day tomorrow." Sam narrowed her eyes. "Something I can help you with?"

Phil shook his head, feeling ridiculous. "No. Just thought I'd see how her weekend was." He shrugged, hoping it looked nonchalant. "Back to the salt mine."

Sam fixed him with a long look. Saying nothing, she wandered back to her desk.

Phil watched Sam. He had the sinking feeling she wasn't buying his story. How long before it got back to Allison that he'd been skulking outside her office?

He chastised himself all the way back to his own office and shut the door. He was not leaving the room again until it was time to go home, no matter how much he was tempted. The last thing he wanted was to be caught outside her office again.

C3&80

Allison checked the text on her phone. Usually Sam only texted when something major was wrong. That woman had her finger on the pulse of everything that happened in the office. Why hadn't she ever finished law school and joined them on the other side of the building? Sam insisted she was content. Allison supposed that was really all that mattered.

*Phil's stalking your office. You owe him money or something?*

Allison drew her eyebrows together. Why would he be down that way? He could get to the break room much more quickly down the other hall. To go past her office required he go considerably out of his way.

*No idea. He say anything?*

Allison waited for the reply. Had he left something in her office? But Phil hadn't been down for one of his drop-in visits since the Cake Incident. If he'd left something before that and not missed it until now, it was hardly worth repeated trips past her office today. Besides, she never locked the door. He could just go in and get it.

*Wanted to know about your weekend. Something I should know?*

She frowned. He'd seen her yesterday. Sure, she'd been a tad preoccupied, but she thought all the pertinent polite chit chat had been exchanged. Weird.

*Nothing I can think of.*

Allison shook her head. She didn't have time to worry about Phil and his randomness right now. The more time she spent with this client's file, the more worried she got that she was headed toward a major defeat in court tomorrow. While she understood that you didn't always win, she didn't represent just anyone. Some criminal defense attorneys would take anyone who could pay. Not her. She continued to be grateful that the partners allowed her to be choosy. She suspected her record was part of the reason they did. Hopefully there wouldn't be too much fallout if she lost this case.

It was lunchtime on Friday before Allison came up for air. She had only just managed to defend both clients this week. The attorneys in the case from Tuesday were already making noises about an appeal. She wasn't sure what grounds they'd try to use. With a bit of luck, the appellate court would uphold the acquittal. *That's a worry for another day.*

The weather was beginning to feel like spring. It was probably just a short-lived relief from the winter, but she decided to embrace it and make the three-block trek to her favorite sandwich shop. Then she could walk an extra block to the Smithsonian Mall, sit on a bench, and watch the tourists. Maybe she'd even buy a roll to feed the squirrels and pigeons. *Just the break I need.*

The air was fresh. Maybe a bit cooler in the shadows than she'd expected, but she could already feel her spirits lifting. Getting out was a good plan. Did anyone else feel like they could smell spring's arrival? The groundhog would rule tomorrow, but she didn't have much faith in the predictions of a tunneling rodent. Still, she hoped the little thing would see its shadow. Or was it not supposed to? She never could keep that straight. Regardless, she was praying for whichever outcome called for an early spring.

It seemed that the majority of the D.C. workforce had also decided to embrace the spring-like weather. The line at "her" sandwich shop was out the door by the time she got there. She stepped behind the last person and checked her watch. They were usually good about moving the line through. If they stuck to that, she shouldn't have to take her lunch back to her desk. *Fingers crossed.*

Fifteen minutes later, she found an empty bench near the Air and Space Museum and settled in with her roast beef and avocado sub. The joggers were out in force, trotting up one side of the Mall and down the other. Allison took a bite of her sandwich. What exactly was the point of running when no one was chasing you? She swigged her bottled iced tea and watched one of the joggers headed her way. He looked like he was enjoying himself. *To each his own.* She tipped her head to one side, his build was familiar. Did she know someone who actually enjoyed running?

Digging through the deli's bag for a napkin, she felt a shadow fall on her and glanced up. "Phil?" She took in his sweat drenched t-shirt and blue running pants and had to concentrate to keep her heart from racing. "You jog?"

Phil laughed. "You ask that as if it's the next worst thing to clubbing baby seals."

She shrugged a shoulder. "Not my thing."

"Fair enough." He nodded to the empty space on the bench next to her. "Mind?"

She shook her head, pulling the detritus of her lunch closer to make more space.

He sat and leaned back with a groan. "I actually prefer to get out on the river with my kayak. I have some weights and such at home as well. But sometimes a run is what fits best into my day. Plus, it was too nice to just sit inside and eat."

"You could have brought your lunch out. Like a normal person." She pulled open her bag of Cheetos.

Phil dipped his hand in and pulled out a handful of the cheesy orange puffs.

"Hey." She swatted at his hand but he dodged with a grin.

"Thanks. And you're right, I could have." He licked the cheese off his fingers. "But then I probably wouldn't have had a chance to steal some of yours."

When he grinned again, Allison's breath caught. Why did he have to be so handsome? And fun to be around? *He's not interested. He made that clear. So this is not flirting. He's just being friendly.* Probably better to just change the subject. Work should be safe. "Anything new in the office? I feel out of the loop after the week I've had."

He shook his head. "Same old. Though I did hear from Marcus."

She felt him watching her and kept her expression bland. "Oh? Did he say how Lindsey's doing? I haven't talked to her since Monday when I went to the adoption agency with her."

"He mentioned that she was making an adoption plan. It sounded like a pretty well thought-out decision. He's still upset though, especially since it appears the father of the baby is hesitant to sign the relinquishment papers."

"Oh no." Allison's shoulders sagged. That jerk. Allison had never met Ben, but she disliked him, and every time she heard more about him, that dislike grew. Lindsey deserved so much better. "Lindsey seemed so sure it wouldn't be a problem. Did Marcus say what happened?"

"Not really. Just that the boy doesn't want her, in his words, 'giving away his baby.' Even though he doesn't want either of them and has made it clear he has no intention of paying child support." Phil scowled. "He sounds like a real piece of work. So Marcus is back to filing a civil suit."

"What? Poor Lindsey."

"Actually, this time it was her idea. She seems to think that they can leverage it into signed papers, which is really all they want." He shrugged. "I've seen the gambit work before. I'm not really sure it's the best way to go about things, but…"

Might work. "She's a clever girl, I'll give her that. I hope it'll help him realize that he can't have it both ways. If it works, it's brilliant."

Phil studied her for a moment before inclining his head. "I suppose. Anyway," he glanced down at his watch, "he should be served sometime in the next hour or two. We'll see how it goes from there."

"I'll have to give Lindsey a call tomorrow and see if she's heard anything." Allison balled up her sandwich wrapper and empty Cheetos bag and stuffed them and her empty tea bottle back into the brown paper sack from the deli. "I guess it's time to get back to work. You heading to the office or finishing your run?"

"The office. I was basically done when I saw you and came over this way." He stood and stretched his arms over his head. "Can I walk with you?"

"Sure." She stood and checked the area for any stray garbage. *Be calm. He's just trying to get back to being friends.* She wasn't sure she wanted to be just friends. It was hard to act like everything was normal when her pulse skyrocketed. *How am I supposed to move on when he's always around reminding me of what I really want?*

As they walked, Phil kept up a stream of casual conversation, as if the whole Cake Incident had never taken place.

*How can he be so normal? Of course, he's not the one who made a food of themselves. Why would he be struggling? It's not as if he's half in love...that's my problem.* She forced her attention back to the conversation. "Sorry, what?"

Phil cleared his throat. "I asked if you had plans tonight."

"Um. No, actually." *Wait.* What had she missed? "Why?"

"I was wondering…hoping, uh, thinking…" He paused and raked his hands through his hair. "This is harder than I remember it being. Would you like to have dinner with me?"

She stopped and turned, planting her hands on her hips as she stared at him. Did he seriously just ask her that? Of course she wanted to. Unless he meant just as friends. Friends hanging out was not something she was ready for. If they were just going to be friends, she needed a little more space to get her emotions under control. But what if he'd changed his mind? She blurted out, "In what capacity?"

Phil blinked. "I'm not sure what you mean."

She let out an exasperated sigh and threw her hands in the air. "People say women are confusing. Would this be a working dinner, where two coworkers consult on a case? Or is it more like two friends with nothing else to do hanging out on a Friday night? Or are you asking me out on a date, Phil?" She held up her hand when he opened his mouth. "Think carefully before you answer, because you get exactly one shot at this, and if you don't choose correctly, you don't get to try again."

"A date." He stopped and drew in a deep breath before fixing his eyes on hers. "Allison, I'm asking you out on a date."

She looked at him. The red stain on his cheeks was adorable. Why was he embarrassed? She felt the corners of her lips tug upward as she watched him struggle to figure out what to do with his arms. He crossed and uncrossed them then clasped his hands behind his back. Finally, he seemed to give up and just let them dangle at his sides, shoulders slightly slumped.

*This is absurd.* Allison snickered, leaning over as her mirth morphed into a full out laugh. When she caught her breath, she wiped her eyes and cleared her throat to quiet the last chuckles that shook her shoulders. "Then I'd love to have dinner with you." She tilted her head to the side. "If you think you can manage to look happy about the idea."

"You're a frustrating woman, Allison."

She turned and continued walking. "So I've been told." She glanced over at him as he kept pace beside her. "You can pick me up at seven."

## 23

Allison looked at Lydia and jerked her thumb at Kevin. "Why'd you bring him? I need wardrobe help, not computer advice."

"He's actually quite good with fashion." Lydia shot him a look that had him shaking his head. "Sorry, inside joke."

"Well, ha ha then. Can we focus, please?" This shouldn't be so hard. She got dressed every day. *Not for a first date with Phil.* That was the crux of the issue. She needed this to be perfect. There was too much at stake.

Allison hooked a hanger holding a pair of jeans and a dark green sweater into the collar of the shirt she was wearing. Grabbing the other two hangers holding outfits she held them aloft. "On the left, we have khakis and dark pink." She extended that outfit briefly. "Here in the middle, jeans and green. And finally on the right, black jeans and a black and white top. All sweaters because it's probably going to be cool tonight and I have no idea what we're doing. Plus they're flattering."

"He didn't give you any idea where you're going?" Lydia frowned as she looked between the outfits.

"No. Though to be fair, I didn't really give him much of a chance." *I was too busy trying to act casual...and keep myself from hyperventilating.*

Kevin chuckled. "There's the Allison I know and love." He pointed to the outfit in the middle. "Pitch the blue jeans. If you end up at a nicer restaurant you'll feel under dressed and self conscious the whole time."

Allison glanced at Lydia who nodded agreement. She unhooked that outfit and draped it over the armchair before holding out the other two outfits. "Which one?"

Lydia frowned and pulled the green sweater off the discarded hanger. "Put this with the khakis."

Allison rearranged the outfit as directed and held it up.

"That's the one. Why wasn't that one of the options to begin with?"

Allison shrugged. "I don't know. I never wear this sweater with khakis." She collected the outfits and pointed at her friends. "Stay there, I'll be right back." She disappeared down the hallway. After several minutes, she emerged dressed in the khakis and green sweater holding three pairs of shoes.

Kevin sighed. "Really? You can't pick out your own shoes?" He glanced at his watch. "It's nearly six thirty and I did actually have a date with my fiancée planned this evening."

"Shush. This won't take that much longer." Allison waved the shoes. The outfit was a winner. She'd need to remember it. The green sweater really did go well with these pants. She probably could choose the shoes on her own, but at this point, why risk it?

Lydia pointed to a pair of low-heeled tan suede boots.

Allison grinned. "That was my pick, but I wasn't sure if they were too casual." She dropped the other shoes before pulling on the boots and striking a pose.

"You look fine. Can we go now?" Kevin stood and held out his hand to Lydia.

Laughing, Lydia took his hand and grinned at Allison. "You do look great. Let me know how it goes." She grabbed her purse from the foyer table as Kevin tugged her out the door. "Oh, and Laura wants an update, too."

"Thanks, guys." Allison chuckled and shut the door. She blew out a breath and glanced around her apartment. She took the rejected shoes back to her bedroom closet then looked around the main area once more. She rubbed her stomach. Only thirty minutes until she found out if a date with Phil was as great as she'd so often imagined it would be.

*Lord, please don't let the traffic be bad.* Phil had left work early so he could get home, clean up his car, and change before picking up Allison. There was nothing wrong with the black slacks and dress shirt he'd worn to work for a new client meeting, but he'd wanted to be a little more casual. The dark green sweater and khakis he'd changed into were comfortable and not something he'd wear to work. *Why am I so worried about what I'm wearing? Must be nerves…it's been a long time since I went on a date.*

He sang along to the radio as he zipped north, careful to keep his speed less than five miles over the limit. He was grateful that Allison lived in Arlington. Avoiding the Beltway was always a good idea. The traffic heading back toward the city was heavy, but it was moving well. They should have no trouble making their dinner reservation. As the song changed, Phil launched into the first verse. *How long has it been since I've sung in the car?*

He pulled in front of Allison's building and snagged the last visitor spot. The red brick building was a recent addition to the area. Within the last five years, certainly. He'd toyed with moving this direction when Brandi had kicked him out. Being within walking distance of the Metro definitely had its advantages. But when he'd seen the Victorian-styled townhouses on the Occoquan, he'd known he had to have one. He didn't even mind the extra time commuting. The city was great for work, but he enjoyed being able to get away at the end of the day.

He slipped in behind a resident, bypassing the buzzer. The key was to look like you belonged. With a smile and brief nod, he pressed the button for Allison's floor. The inside was more luxurious than he'd anticipated. *Wonder what it costs to live here.*

Allison pulled open the door, confusion written on her face.

"I followed someone in." He grinned mischievously. "Surprise."

Allison shook her head. "We're not supposed to let that happen. I do it all the time too." She glanced at her watch. "Right on time…" she trailed off as she looked at him.

"What?" Phil glanced down. "Did I spill something already?"

Allison began to laugh. "Do you want to come in while I go change?"

Perplexed, he frowned. Why did she need to change? "You look great. Why…" He followed her gaze. Green sweater and khakis. *What are the odds?* "Great minds. You sure you don't want to just be twins?"

"Not on your life. Come on in, it won't take long." She opened the door wide and stepped aside so he could enter, closing it behind him. "Have a seat. I'll be right back." She darted down the hallway.

Phil looked around. He never would have thought to pair aqua and dark purple together, but it worked. The riot of colors on the area rug somehow managed to add to the sense of fun rather than make the room gaudy. Tucking his hands in his pockets, he walked through the room, peering more closely at the photographs she had on display. *Those have to be her parents.* He could see bits of her in each of them.

"All right, now I'm ready."

"That dark pink suits you. And it's definitely not something I'll ever copy, so a safe choice for the future, too." He checked his watch. "We should still make our reservation easily. Unless traffic has dramatically changed in the last ten minutes."

"Around here you never know, but we'll hope." Allison grabbed her purse and opened the door. "After you, I want to be sure the lock catches. It's been acting up. After that, I'll let you get the doors. Promise."

Phil took back-roads south to Shirlington, an eclectic strip of boutiques and restaurants. The street parking was already full, but he managed to snag a spot in one of the garages without too much looping around. The streetlights and trees twinkled with little white lights, adding a festive glow to the sidewalks and median garden areas.

"Do you get down here much? When I lived closer to the city, I used to come here to browse and people watch all the time."

"Not often. I always mean to, but never do." Allison glanced in a restaurant window. "That's supposed to be great Thai food."

"It is. We'll have to come back another time. I wasn't sure if you'd go for that, so I made reservations here." He stopped under a black and white striped awning advertising an upscale American bistro.

"Aren't we under dressed?"

Shaking his head, Phil pulled open the door. "You can get away with anything from a tux to nice jeans in here. They're fairly unpretentious. And the food is incredible." He let the host know they had a reservation. Between the flickering candles and white linen draped tables against the dark wood floor, the atmosphere exuded romance.

The host indicated that they should follow him as he made his way up two steps to the raised portion of the restaurant. They continued to the far corner and a table for two that provided a great view out onto the main boulevard but still gave the feeling of seclusion. Phil pulled out a chair for Allison and slid it in as she sat before taking his own seat.

Allison looked across the table, her hand resting on the closed menu. "What do you recommend?"

Phil flipped his menu open and scanned the two pages. "The filet mignon is always fantastic. But really, you can't go wrong here. At least I never have." He looked up and caught her gaze. "What are you in the mood for?"

She opened her menu and glanced at it before snapping it shut. "Filet it is. If you say it's good, I'll take your word for it."

"You're going to make ordering easy."

As if summoned, their server appeared. Phil took Allison's menu and handed them over as he ordered for both of them. "So tell me about your week."

"Really? That's your opening conversational gambit?" Allison rolled her eyes. "Let's try this, you tell me about my week. I'll tell you how close you got."

He paused to sip his water. "All right. Let's see. You were out most of Monday. You said you were helping Lindsey in the morning. Then…" The week of an attorney was pretty straightforward. Even though they didn't practice the same kind of law, Phil was confident he could get close enough. "You went home to finish court prep with fewer distractions. Tuesday and Wednesday were court, with late nights both nights?"

Allison nodded.

"Thursday you took the day off and went to the spa."

"Bzzzt. I wish. And you were doing so well. Thursday ended up being more court. I very nearly got my head handed to me on that case. It was only due to my expertise in juggling baby geese while tap dancing that I managed to triumph in the end." She blew on her fingertips before dusting them on her collar.

"That would make today wrap-up day."

"You got it. Look at you, well versed in the ever-so-exciting week of an attorney." She chuckled. "Since I'm guessing your week was simply a variation on the theme, why don't you tell me about your weekend? I know you had cake Sunday after church…how did you hook up with Kevin and Lydia though? I didn't realize you knew them."

"I didn't, actually. I met Kevin at the Christmas party, obviously." The spurt of jealousy he'd experienced when he saw Allison and Kevin at the party had kicked off the introspection that brought them here. Should he mention that? Probably not. There had been hints before then that she might be interested, but he'd never been sure. *I wonder if Kevin's comment was deliberate. Not that it matters. We're here now.*

"Maybe I should start over." Phil waited as their food arrived and the server ground fresh black pepper over the gorgonzola-crusted filets. He reached across the table and took Allison's hand before bowing his head and offering a short but heartfelt prayer for the food and their time together. He gave her fingers a quick squeeze before releasing them and slicing into the thick steak. "I guess the best place to start is when I was married. Brandi, that's my ex-wife, and I had a hard-partying lifestyle. I stayed sober during the workday, mostly, but otherwise that was our hobby. My friend, Grant, worked at the same firm I did. He was constantly covering for me and trying to get me to come to church with him. He finally convinced me to go to a regional men's weekend sponsored by several area churches."

Phil searched Allison's face, looking for something that would tell him her reaction to the story. Most of it was common knowledge within the Bible study group at work, but he'd never told her directly. Would she be able to see beyond his past? "I ended up asking

Jesus into my heart and getting hit over the head with conviction about things I needed to change in my life. I started going to church and to Alcoholics Anonymous. I realized all the things I needed to do to be a better man and a better husband. The problem was Brandi didn't want a better anything. She was happy with the way things were, and my changes started impacting her fun."

"That's all she could see?" Allison shook salt onto her green beans.

Phil nodded. "When I realized the changes I'd made were hurting our marriage, I decided to get some counseling. One of the speakers at the men's event was Paul Brown."

"Lydia's dad?"

"Yeah. I'd thought he seemed approachable. I didn't want to tell anyone at my new church what was going on, so finding someone I didn't know seemed like a good idea. I worked with him for the better part of a year while my marriage was falling apart. I'd hoped Brandi would come, too." Her refusal still gnawed at his gut. Could he have done something, anything, differently? Was there something else he should have tried? He set down his fork and knife. "She made it clear that wasn't going to happen. Then she kicked me out. Paul helped me through that, too."

"So that explains how you know Lydia's dad. What about Kevin and Lydia?"

"Brandi pops up every now and then when she's having trouble with her current boyfriend or husband, sometimes both at the same time. This time it feels different. So I went to see Paul. He invited me to dinner and Kevin and Lydia were joining them." He pushed aside the reminder of Allison's date with Marcus and drained the last of his water. "Then I ran into them at church on Sunday. I decided to see how Paul was in the pulpit."

"And they suckered you into tasting their cake for another outside opinion." Allison chuckled. "Everyone who goes to the wedding is going to have had at least one cupcake in their chosen flavor before the big day."

"I have to admit, it wasn't hard to convince me to go. I have a pretty serious sweet tooth."

"You don't look like it."

He laughed. "I jog."

"Touché." Allison scooted her chair back and excused herself.

He scooted his empty plate away and watched as she disappeared into the back hall where the restrooms were. She was so easy to talk to. Though he didn't need to monopolize the entire date. That wasn't likely to result in a second date. *And I really want there to be a second date.* He'd turn the tables during dessert. He didn't want her thinking he was a narcissist. He signaled the server that he was ready for the check and was signing the receipt when Allison returned.

"All that talk about a sweet tooth and no dessert?"

"There's a great little bakery down the promenade. They have a German chocolate cupcake that's divine. Though actually, I might go for the salted caramel this time." He stood and offered her his elbow. "Then we can take a little stroll down the other side of the street and get some coffee. If it hasn't gotten too chilly."

Allison slipped her arm through his. "Sounds nice."

They stepped out into the moonlit night. There was a light breeze, but the temperature still hovered in the mid-50s. "Will you be cold?"

Allison shook her head.

"Great." He started down the street at a relaxed pace. "What are the top ten things I should know about Allison Vasak that I haven't already figured out?"

Tossing her head back, Allison laughed.

They chatted amiably on their way to the bakery. After some discussion, they agreed to split two cupcakes so they could each taste the other. Rather than eating in the crowded bakery, they crossed the street, stopping here and there to peek in a store window when something caught their eye. Finally, they found a coffee shop. It was also crowded, but the outside seating was empty.

Allison pointed to one of the small wrought iron tables. "I'm game if you are."

"All right. Have a seat, I'll be right back with something to keep us warm." He disappeared into the shop. As he waited in line, Phil watched her pull her cell phone out of her purse. He resisted the urge to check his own email. Anything from work could wait, and he'd just as soon not worry about anything personal at this point. Finally at the front of the line, he ordered two coffees and headed back to Allison. "Anything good?" He nodded at her phone.

"Not really. Got a text from Lindsey, so I'll check in with her tomorrow. That kind of thing." She shrugged before wrapping her hands around the hot paper cup.

"If it's too cold, we can have a car picnic."

"I'm okay so far, but if that breeze kicks up too much more I might take you up on that." She sipped and let out a little moan of pleasure. "They know how to make coffee here."

"That they do." Phil got out the cupcakes and cut them neatly down the middle with a plastic knife he pulled from the bag. He set two halves in front of Allison on a napkin, putting the other halves in front of himself.

Allison's phone began to ring almost at the same time as Phil's. Frowning, he checked the caller ID. "It's Marcus."

"Mine's Lindsey." Allison chewed on her lower lip as she answered.

When they hung up, Phil collected the cupcakes and dropped them back into the bag. "Marcus is calling the police, but I told him we were on our way."

"All right. Let's go."

## 24

Allison had her door open as soon as Phil parked beside the police car in the Bowers' driveway. She wanted to run to the door to make sure Lindsey was okay but waited for Phil to come around the car and join her on the sidewalk. They walked up together and she knocked on the frame of the open door.

Marcus sat on the sofa with his head in his hands. He glanced up at the knock and gestured for them to come in.

"Where's Lindsey?"

Marcus pointed to the stairs.

Allison touched Phil's arm lightly before hurrying up the staircase. *Please Lord, let her be okay.*

"Lindsey?" Allison poked her head in the first bedroom.

Lindsey sat on the floor with her knees drawn up as much as her pregnant belly would allow. Her elbows rested on her knees and her head was in her hands.

Allison sat beside her and slid an arm around her shoulder. "Tell me what happened."

Lindsey looked up. Tears coursed down her cheeks. She swiped at them impatiently. "Ben came over. I thought he was going to agree to the adoption. He doesn't want me," her voice hitched, "or the baby. I don't understand why he won't just do this."

"I take it he isn't worried about the civil suit?"

"He says his dad's lawyer is convinced they'll be able to get it thrown out. Can they do that?"

"I don't know all the details, but that's a possibility with any kind of lawsuit. I wouldn't think so in this case, but..." Allison shrugged. "So why did he come over?"

"To try and buy me off. He says if I don't want the baby that he'll pay for me to go to Kansas and have a late term abortion. Then," anger blazed in her eyes, "he says, 'Since neither of us want the baby, that's a better alternative.'" Lindsey glared at Allison. "How is that a better option? I don't want to kill my baby. I want to give it a better life than I can provide on my own."

"Oh, Lindsey." Allison rubbed Lindsey's shoulder. How did anyone convince themselves that an abortion was the better choice for all concerned? Lydia flashed into her mind. *Okay, that's unfair. People do things they'd never imagine when they don't think they have a choice.* But how was it any different for Ben to terminate his parental rights instead of forcing Lindsey to terminate the baby?

"I started screaming at that point." Her cheeks turned pink. "I know I shouldn't have, but he just made me so mad. I explained to him that an abortion wasn't happening. Then he hit me."

"What? Where?" Allison leaned back searching for telltale signs.

Lindsey lifted her shirt revealing a purpling knot on her abdomen.

Allison's eyes widened. "We need to get you to the doctor, get you and the baby checked out."

Lindsey swallowed. "I just wanted to wait for you. Dad's…in a state. The other policeman man took Ben. I'm pressing charges for assault this time."

"He's hit you before?"

She nodded reluctantly. "Don't tell my dad, all right?"

Allison's lips thinned as she studied the girl. "I'm not promising. It'll help make a stronger case to show a repeating pattern."

The blood drained from Lindsey's face.

Allison held up a hand. "Let's not worry about that right now. First things first, you need to get checked out." She helped Lindsey to her feet. "I'll go down and tell your dad where we're going. Take a minute to get yourself together before you come."

Allison found Marcus and Phil involved in an intense conversation with the remaining police officer. They paused when she came in.

"Lindsey needs to be seen by a doctor to make sure everything's okay. I really don't think she should wait until tomorrow."

Phil nodded. "We'd just come to that conclusion. I thought you and I could drive Lindsey, and Marcus could meet us at the Emergency Room when he's finished giving his report here. He'll need to be there since he's her parent, but we can get the process started."

"Okay. She'll be down in a minute."

The police officer finished up just as Lindsey came downstairs. Allison caught several looks from Marcus as they got ready to leave for the Emergency Room. Had he realized she and Phil were on a date? Most likely. How awkward was this going to be? She wanted to continue to help Lindsey as much as she could. The girl had wormed her way into Allison's heart with her clear thinking and bravery in making such a difficult choice.

When they explained the situation at the ER check-in desk, the staff whisked Lindsey into the back quickly. Since neither Phil or Allison were family, they couldn't do anything beyond wait for Marcus to arrive. When he did, they pointed him to the correct nurse and looked for a place to wait.

Allison knotted her fingers together in her lap. "I hope the baby's all right. Lindsey's finally at peace with the situation and making plans for both of them to have a good, solid future." She glanced up at Phil, her eyes brimming with tears. "She just doesn't deserve this."

Phil took one of her hands and clasped it between his. "It's going to be okay."

Allison leaned over to rest her head on Phil's shoulder. Even as worried as she was about Lindsey and the baby, the contact brought a tiny thrill.

An hour later, Marcus came out looking tired and worn. "They're going to keep her overnight. Everything looks fine, but they want to be cautious since the bruise and swelling on her abdomen are right around where the baby's head is positioned." He closed his eyes and took a deep breath. "So far she's not having any contractions or anything else that would lead them to think she'll miscarry or need to deliver early."

"That's such good news." Allison tugged her hand from Phil's. "Do you want us to stay?"

"No. There's nothing you can do. I'm going to be here with her." Marcus offered a faint smile. "She said I could as long as I didn't freak out. So I'm trying. Even though I'd really like to…"

"Please don't threaten someone's life in front of two attorneys." Phil stood with a wry smile and offered Marcus his hand. "I'm glad you called us. Keep us posted, all right? We'll be praying for both of you." He glanced at Allison. "Ready to go home?"

Allison stood and collected her purse from the floor. "Tell Lindsey to call me if there's anything I can do. That goes for you, too."

"I'll go get the car. Why don't you wait here? It's gotten colder out there." Phil strode out into the parking lot, tucking his hands in his pockets to ward off the chill.

"So...you were on a date?"

Heat rushed across Allison's cheeks. "Yeah. I..."

Marcus shook his head. "You don't need to explain. The timing is wrong for me right now. Especially with this new situation. Lindsey comes first, for you, too, I think."

Allison nodded. "She wasn't really keen on it, you know."

"I know. I think she would've come around. But..." Marcus shrugged and offered a wistful smile. "If things don't work out down the road...keep my number, okay?"

"I will. Please don't forget to keep me updated."

Marcus nodded once before he headed back to Lindsey. Allison moved to the glass doors to watch for Phil. Marcus understood. As much as she'd enjoyed the conversations she'd had with Marcus, there'd never been anywhere near the connection she felt with Phil. Of course, that might have come with time. Really, it was best for everyone. *Why do I feel bad, then?*

CRISTO

Allison flipped the deadbolt then peeked through the peephole to watch Phil stride back down the hallway. She could still feel the tingles in her fingers from holding his hand at the hospital. Why hadn't he kissed her good night? Frowning, she pushed the thought away. There were plenty of good reasons; it being their first date was certainly at the top of the list. Normally, if her date had tried to kiss her this early it would mark the end of that relationship. Why should her rules be any different with Phil? Looking down at the cupcake bag he'd insisted she take, Allison pursed her lips. *I think a late night snack is in order.*

In the kitchen, she put half of each cupcake on a paper towel and poured a large glass of milk. She made sure the bag was closed so the other pieces wouldn't get stale and set it on the counter. She knew what she was having for breakfast tomorrow. Which one should she try first? *Salted caramel or German chocolate? Decisions, decisions.* They both were delicious. *Just what I needed in my life, another awesome bakery within easy distance. Maybe I should take up running.* With Phil by her side, it might not be *that* terrible.

25

Phil frowned from his kitchen window as Grant parked in front of his house. It wasn't like Grant to drop by, which meant something was up. He pushed away from the table and opened the door as Grant took the front steps two at a time.

"Good morning."

"You might want to remove the first part of that." Grant shrugged out of his coat and hooked it on the antique hallstand. "Tell me you have coffee."

Phil closed the door and ushered Grant into the kitchen. He watched as Grant filled a mug and dropped into a seat at the kitchen table. Phil topped off his own mug before joining him. "What's going on?"

"Brandi made bail."

"What? How?"

"Apparently her latest husband isn't quite as done with her as she claimed. Or they've reconciled. Or something. He put up the money for her and listed their condo as her residence."

Phil scrubbed his hands over his face. "Have they set a trial date?"

"You're probably looking at six months. And that's if they don't make a deal. Realistically speaking, the DA is going to try and do that rather than take up their time. No one was hurt, and Brandi's a woman."

"So?"

"Come on, Phil. Do you really think anyone is going to look at her and then look at you and think that you're the one in any danger?"

"Which was exactly my point in the first place." Just great. He looked around the kitchen. "Guess it's time to move again. And just not tell my mom my new address. Though I think maybe she understands now that Brandi isn't the daughter-in-law she wants to try and get back."

"Let's not do anything drastic, all right? I don't know for sure she won't go to trial. I'm just guessing. But even so, you've got the restraining order. Which they wouldn't have granted if they didn't also see the potential for trouble. And that was *my* point in the first place. Anyway, maybe now that she realizes you're serious about it, she'll leave you alone."

Phil scoffed. Brandi didn't do anything the way most people would. And taking a hint was definitely not something she was good at.

"Okay, fine. That's semi-unlikely. But maybe the husband will do a better job of keeping her in check now that they're at least on speaking terms again. She usually leaves you alone when she's with someone, doesn't she?"

"Yeah. Yeah, she does. You're right." Phil pushed his chair back so it was balancing on the back legs. Would Marshall be able to keep her in line? Did he even want to, or had he posted bail for some other reason? No way to know. The hard part was to not wonder about it. "I'm just so tired of dealing with her…I went out with Allison last night."

"Wow. You move fast. How'd that go?"

"Really well, actually. Right up to the point we had to take someone to the ER."

Grant laughed. "This is a story I have to hear."

Phil filled his friend in on the details of the evening. "I'm curious what Marcus had to say after I left, but he was gone when I got back with the car, so…" He shrugged.

"I imagine that's between the two of them. She went out with you, held your hand, and seemed interested in doing it again. I'm guessing the other guy's not really in the picture."

"Yeah. Having been out of practice for awhile it's a little harder to keep perspective."

"So what's your plan?" Grant drained his mug and crossed the room to the coffee pot.

"Plan?"

Grant jiggled the carafe. "You mind if I finish this?"

"Go for it."

Grant poured the last of the coffee into his mug and returned to the table. "Your plan for how to continue. Next date, whatever."

"I figured I'd call her this afternoon and see what her schedule's going to be like this week."

"You really are out of practice. You need to give her some space, see if..."

"Nuh-uh. I'm too old for games. And frankly, Allison's too important." Phil drummed on the edge of the table. "I may have been hiding behind the idea that divorced people shouldn't date, but that doesn't mean I wasn't paying attention and wishing it wasn't the case. I'm more sure about Allison than I've ever been about anyone. Including Brandi."

"So what changed your mind?"

"Some of it was our conversation last weekend. But I also spent some more time talking with Pastor Brown. He's a pretty straight shooter on stuff like this, and he's been through enough in his life that he's not one of those preachers who sits in the pulpit and never gets his hands dirty, you know?"

Grant chuckled. "Know the type. Hmm. Maybe I should check out his church sometime."

"I went last week and enjoyed it. I think I may make the switch permanent. Anyway, we talked a lot about First Corinthians chapter seven. The Apostle Paul's been talking about how divorced people are guilty of adultery if they remarry, but then he goes on to say that if the unbelieving spouse wants the divorce, the believer is free from any condemnation should they remarry. So if I chose to date and potentially remarry, given my circumstances with Brandi, I could."

Phil rocked forward, letting the chair rest back on all four legs. "Pastor Brown went on about how some scholars look at the words that were actually used in the other verses to make an argument that when Paul says they're guilty of adultery, it's because they were just separating and then remarrying, without actually going through the whole divorce process. I'll admit to getting a little lost on that score."

"But it's not as relevant to what you're dealing with anyway." Grant spun his mug on the table. "So you were really convinced that you would be sinning if you dated again?"

Phil nodded. "I essentially chose Jesus over my wife and our years together. I wanted— still do want— to be sure that I make the most of that relationship every day. Letting Brandi have a divorce was hard, man. Even before I became a Christian I was adamant that I wasn't going to contribute to the fifty percent statistic. With my mom's habits growing up...we'll just say I was determined to make marriage a commitment that mattered."

"So should I be reserving a date in June?"

Phil balled up a napkin and threw it across the table, hitting Grant in the eye.

"What? You said you were serious about her." Grant laughed and tossed the missile back.

"I'll keep you posted, okay?" Phil leaned back, stretching his arms over his head until his shoulders popped. "So other than bringing news of Brandi over here, what are you up to today?"

"Nothing planned."

"Wanna hit the river?"

⚬⚬⚬

At seven-thirty, Allison finally gave up trying to sleep in. Pippin had been making a nuisance of himself since before six. Not that she'd been sleeping that well anyway. She couldn't stop worrying about Lindsey and the baby. Gathering Pippin up, she scratched between his ears as she made her way into the kitchen. *Why didn't I take the three minutes and set the coffee up last night?* She deposited the cat on the kitchen table with a can of wet food as a special treat, and dug out some coffee beans.

Pippin devoured the food and watched her as she puttered around in the kitchen. Allison dropped a few treats into his bowl. "Don't get used to this, now. You tend toward chubby. You and I both know that. And I get tired of hearing about it from the vet." She gave his ears another scratch before running her hand down his back, laughing as he arched his back and swished his tail in pleasure.

With coffee and half of a cupcake, Allison checked the time as she sat at the table. It was probably late enough. She punched in Marcus' cell number and waited.

"Marcus Bowers." His voice was thick with sleep.

Allison cringed. "Morning. Is it too early? This is Allison, by the way."

"No, it's fine. Hang on." There was quiet shuffling and the click of a door on the other end of the phone. "Linds just got to sleep, so I didn't want to disturb her. Hospitals are not the place to be if you want to rest."

"How is she?"

"Shaken. Exhausted, though that's mostly from someone coming in every time she finally managed to sleep." He let out a weary sigh. "She had a few contractions, but nothing major. They didn't need any drugs to stop them. I'm hoping we'll be headed home later today."

"That's wonderful. And a relief. Any news on Ben?" Allison shooed Pippin away from her cupcake then caved and tore a piece off for him.

"Nothing yet. The officer said he'd keep in touch. At this point I'll just wait and see what happens. With it being the weekend, I can't imagine anything will go quickly. And I'm more focused on Lindsey right now anyway."

"Which is absolutely as it should be. Let me know if there's anything I can do though, okay?"

"I will. I appreciate it."

"Will you tell her I called to check in?"

"Sure."

"Thanks…and Marcus? I'm sorry. About Phil?" Maybe she hadn't needed to bring it up. He hadn't seemed to find it awkward. But she had. *And now I've mashed a perfectly good cupcake.*

"There's no reason for that. You're a lovely woman, Allison. Inside and out. Anyone would be lucky to date you. I think I hear someone else going in…if they wake her up, heads are going to roll. I'll have her call you when she's awake. Thanks for checking on us."

The phone clicked in her ear. Maybe she really was the only one who found it awkward. *He's there for Lindsey right now, and really doesn't need your neuroses.* She shouldn't have said anything. Now she felt stupid, along with awkward. Allison frowned and scooped up a handful of crumbs, smashing them into a ball. Catching Pippin eyeing her, she popped it into her mouth. "What? It's my breakfast."

With a feline snort of derision, Pippin turned his back and began his morning grooming regime.

*Back to bed or early Tae Kwon Do?* She'd miss Sarah if she hit the early class. Which wasn't entirely bad. She didn't want to rehash her date quite yet. The grin that split her face was involuntary. Phil had asked her out. *Finally.* She could still feel his hand wrapped around her own. There hadn't been fireworks, but there had been a sense of rightness, almost like being wrapped in a cozy cocoon. That didn't really do it justice. It hadn't been boring, or friendly. There was definitely a spark. But it wasn't the rocket's red glare she'd always expected based on movies and friends. Were they just exaggerating? Or was Phil *not* the one for her after all?

She was on her way back to the bedroom, her mind still not completely made up about whether or not she was headed back to bed, when the phone rang. "Hello?"

"Hey, it's Laura and Lydia. Can you buzz us up? It's a dire emergency."

The giggling she heard in the background calmed any worry before it fully had a chance to form. "Hang on." She threw on some clothes and dragged brush through her hair. *Good enough.*

Neither Laura or Lydia looked like they were experiencing any sort of emergency. Allison waved them toward the couch then sat and tucked her feet under her. "What's the emergency?"

Laura shot Lydia an amused glance. "You tell her."

Clearly frustrated, Lydia ran a hand through her hair. "You remember how I realized on Sunday that we'd have to firm up our wedding date before I could order the cake?"

Allison nodded and looked at Lydia expectantly.

"Well, it turns out, Kevin is in some sort of all-fired hurry to get married." Lydia huffed out a breath. "I thought we had basically decided on the September or October timeframe. Though I was open to Christmas or New Year's, too. We have so many reasons to wait. I mean really, I haven't even been sober a year yet. I'm still doing all sorts of counseling and while, sure, okay, I'm doing well. It just seems like we ought to be sure that I'm going to keep on track."

Allison looked over at Laura. "She's already said this to me."

Laura chuckled. "She has to build up to it. Wait, it's worth the back story."

"All right, keep going." Allison settled back in her chair.

Lydia shot both of them a disgusted look. "Leaving the bakery Sunday, Kevin says, 'What about April sixth?' Then he has the audacity to look at me all innocently when I, very reasonably, could do nothing but shriek."

"That's like," Allison paused and looked up at the ceiling as she counted, "nine weeks away."

"Exactly!" Lydia threw herself off the couch and started pacing around the room. "He's all 'it's supposed to be the peak of the cherry blossoms' and 'it's after Easter so your dad won't be too busy' and on and on." She narrowed her eyes at Laura. "Almost as if he's been plotting and discussing this date with people for a while."

Laura held up her hands defensively. "Don't look at me. Though I can't tell you what he and Matt talk about when a game's on. That's my time to hang with Jennie since Matt loves to hold the baby and introduce her to the sport. Half the time I have to pry Jennie loose, as she's already well on her way to being sports crazy. Plus, when Uncle Kevin's around," she shrugged, "I might as well be chopped liver."

Lydia turned her gaze on Allison, eyebrows raised.

"Oh no. Uh-uh." Allison shook her head vigorously. "I've barely even talked to Kevin without you in ear shot since you got engaged. Look, why don't you just talk to your folks. Surely they'll throw up a road block about it being so fast. With your two older sisters already married, they've planned enough weddings to understand that's quick."

"Oh, I had that exact same thought. So when I got home I tried to talk to my mom about how ridiculous it was and she called the church to see if the sanctuary was free." She stopped pacing and threw her arms up in the air. "And it was. It's not now, because apparently I'm getting married on April sixth."

Allison gamely tried to choke back her laugh. She made the mistake of catching Laura's eye and both of them collapsed into giggles.

"It's not funny." Lydia whined as she flopped onto the couch. "I now have two weeks, possibly three, to get invitations mailed. I did, just barely, manage to squeak in my cake order since they require an eight-week lead-time. But I have no dress. My bridesmaids have no dresses. I don't even know what colors I want to use, for crying out loud."

"Didn't you have a career in PR? Isn't half of that event planning of some sort?" Allison took deep breaths to stop her laughter.

Lydia glared.

Allison crossed the room, squeezed onto the couch next to Lydia, and patted her knee. *Try and think from her perspective. This is fast. Still hilarious.* "It's going to be all right. Breathe deeply. Banish your inner Bridezilla. And let's focus." She rubbed her hands together. "I'm going to go get some paper. Laura, would you get us something to drink? It's probably just water or coffee, but I'm good with either. Or whatever you find in there."

Pippin padded in from the kitchen. Allison scooped him up and dropped him in Lydia's lap. "You snuggle him and calm down."

Within minutes, each one had a cold glass of iced tea from the pitcher Laura had found in the back of the fridge and Allison had a legal pad and collection of pens.

"How old is this tea?" Laura sipped cautiously and wrinkled her nose. "It smelled okay, and seems to taste okay, but I just want to know if it's going to kill us."

Allison lifted a shoulder. "No idea. I have a vague recollection of making tea in the last two weeks, but things have been so crazy it could have been last night or it could have been two Sundays ago."

"That doesn't inspire confidence." Lydia eyed her glass and set it on the coffee table. "Speaking of last night…"

"Nope. We'll talk about that later. We're dealing with the wedding right now. There's nothing I love better than an organization project. So," she clicked her pen, "let's start with the invitations."

It was nearly noon when Allison set down her pen and flexed her fingers. "Feeling better?"

Lydia nodded and looked at the dozens of sheets of yellow paper that had been sorted into piles. "Much. If you ever decide to give up the law, you'd make a pretty awesome wedding planner."

"No thank you. Besides, this," Allison gestured to the messy array of paper, "is really the same as getting organized for trial. Just a lot happier." She glanced at her watch and stretched. "I don't know about you two, but I'm starved."

"I could eat." Laura rubbed her stomach. "But having explored the inside of your fridge, I recommend we eat out."

"Ha ha. I've been busy." Allison made a face. "But eating out's not a bad idea. And then afterward we could stop by the one dress shop we haven't made it to and look there."

Laura groaned and Lydia sighed.

"What? You don't think that mere organization magically gets things done, do you? We now have to actually act on each list." Allison shook her head. "You two are pathetic. Figure out where we're eating that's not too far from the shop. I'm going to run through the shower and put on clothes that didn't sit in an emergency room for several hours."

"Wait. What? What emergency room?" Laura looked concerned.

Allison laughed. "Interesting date last night. I'll fill you both in over lunch."

26

Phil settled into the same pew he'd sat in the previous week. He hoped Grant would join him. It had seemed like he was interested when he left after a day paddling on the river and an early supper at a local seafood place. On the other hand, if Grant was half as sore as Phil was, he might just stay home. Only the knowledge that Grant might be looking for him had gotten Phil up and out the door.

Kevin plopped down next to Phil. "Back again?"

"Yeah. I'm pretty sure this is a permanent switch." Phil looked at Kevin and frowned. "Something wrong?"

Kevin glanced around before speaking. "Lydia has finally kicked the wedding planning into high gear. Could be my fault since I talked her into a date that's not too far off, but unfortunately, she feels the need to share just about every final decision with me. I thought women were supposed to want total control over their wedding?"

Phil chuckled. "Welcome to the mysterious world of women."

"She and Laura and Allison spent nearly all day yesterday doing wedding stuff. Then Lyd spent our entire date last night giving me the blow-by-blow."

"There are going to be some blows if you don't watch it, McGregor." Lydia shoved him playfully. "Good to see you again, Phil." She smiled at Kevin. "We didn't talk wedding the whole time. I did get to hear about Allison's fascinating date on Friday with this guy." She pointed at Phil.

"Do I even want to know?" Phil hunched his shoulders.

Lydia chuckled. "She had a marvelous time. Even if you did end up at the ER."

"That sounds promising." Kevin frowned as the organ started the prelude. "You'll have to fill me in after the service."

Phil shook his head. The way Lydia said it had made it sound much more interesting than the truth. Allison had had a good time. She'd said as much, but he was always a little skeptical, thinking people were just humoring him. But if she'd told her girlfriends, well, that had to mean she'd meant it. And she'd been out yesterday when he tried to call, not ignoring him. *Paranoid much?*

When the service was over, Kevin turned to Phil. "So, Emergency Room? Is that the happening new place for dates these days?"

"Thankfully, no." Phil briefly explained the situation. "I didn't hear from Marcus yesterday. I hope that means all is well and they're back at home. I wonder if I should have checked in on them?" He'd check in on them this afternoon, too.

"Or you could see if Allison's heard from them." Lydia poked her head over Kevin's shoulder and grinned. "Two birds, one stone."

"Stop meddling, Lyd." Kevin's look was stern.

"What? She helped me a lot yesterday. I owe her one."

"I was already thinking that same thing. So no harm done." Watching Kevin and Lydia was fun. Allison had good taste in friends. "I probably shouldn't say anything, as I imagine it's going to go straight back to Allison, but now that I've got my head on straight I'm happy to admit how serious I am about her."

Kevin clapped Phil's shoulder. "That's great. Allison deserves a good man." He glanced at Lydia. "And we can keep it to ourselves and let the two of you figure things out. Right, hon?"

Lydia rolled her eyes. "Of course. Though if she asks, I'm not lying."

"Fair enough." Phil glanced at his watch. "I think I'm going to bail on small group. I've got some phone calls to make."

"What do you mean he's divorced?"

Allison shifted uncomfortably beneath her mother's steely gaze. "I'm not really sure what the question is, Mom. He was married, she divorced him."

"How old is he?"

"Thirty. They got married young. He became a Christian, turned his life around, and she decided she didn't like the new Phil." Allison struggled to remain matter-of-fact. There was no point in speaking any of the snide remarks dancing on her tongue. They'd only make the situation worse. Besides, despite how she came across, her mom really was trying to look out for her. Even if it was unnecessary. Biting back a sigh, she added, "It's been close to five years now, I think."

Her mother stared at her and drummed her fingers on the arm of the Louis XIV style armchair. Allison waited. Interrupting her mother while she was thinking was never a good idea. She let her eyes drift around the room. When did her mother turn into someone so stiff and formal? And when had all the décor shifted to reflect that? Even the colors felt formal. The one piece of furniture that wasn't some form of taupe or pale green was done in a taupe and green damask. *Relax*. At twenty-seven, she shouldn't feel like she was trespassing in an adults-only zone.

"And he thinks that a divorced person should be able to date someone who is not divorced?"

"Apparently, since we went out on Friday. And I'm hoping that he'll ask me out again." Allison frowned at her mother. "Can't you be a little happy for me, Mom? Phil's a great guy. I've worked with him for almost four years and we've been good friends for three of those. Honestly," she fought the urge to throw her hands in the air and ended up making a ridiculous version of jazz hands in her lap, "the fact that he's divorced wasn't something I figured would matter to you in the slightest."

"Honey." Her mother's face softened. "Your dad and I just want the best for you. I have a hard time understanding how being someone's second wife can possibly fit that description. It might be another story if you were also divorced. But you're not."

"So, what?" Allison stood and paced behind the settee. This was ridiculous. And not a conversation she'd imagined having. "He's damaged goods because Jesus changed his life and the woman he thought loved him decided that change wasn't something she wanted to live with? Should he have turned his back on God to keep his marriage intact?"

"No, of course not." Her mother's lips thinned. "Sit down, you'll make a path in the rug. You know how expensive it was."

Allison resumed her seat. *Will she always be able to make me feel like a disobedient child?*

"It's wonderful that Paul..."

"Phil."

Her mom waved her hands dismissively. "Phillip, then, came to Christ. Obviously that's something we want for everyone. But that doesn't make him husband material."

Allison pressed her fingers into her eyes and slowly counted to twenty. When she thought she could speak without screaming, she met her mother's gaze. "Did I say anything about getting married? We've gone out once."

"At your age, dear, every date could lead to marriage. And you should keep that in mind. You're not getting any younger."

"Mom. I'm twenty-seven. That's hardly an old maid."

"But you'll be thirty-five before you realize it, Allison. Having children at that age can be difficult. You need to think these things through more carefully."

Allison's stomach sank. Yet again, she'd proven a disappointment to her mother.

"I wonder what's keeping your father?"

Dad knew perfectly well how this interview would go and had made himself scarce to avoid the ugliness. Allison stood. "Why don't I go look for him? Then we can see if lunch is ready."

"Oh, there you are Thomas."

Despite the tension in the room, Allison grinned as her dad strode in. She flung herself into his hug and squeezed.

"There's my girl." He tipped his head back so he could see her without relaxing his grip. "You look lovelier every day. Just like your mother."

Irene colored prettily at the compliment.

As much as her own interactions with her mother were strained and uncomfortable, her parents loved each other. Allison didn't always understand their relationship, but it worked for them.

"Daddy. Where were you hiding?"

His robust chuckle filled the room as he crossed to the sofa and sat, tugging Allison along with him. "Ah, I got caught up. I've discovered a new author. His thrillers leave you breathless from the first page to the last. Thankfully he's several books into the series already, so I can pick up the new one as soon as I finish the first. I'll send the one I've finished home with you. I think you'll enjoy it."

Her mother looked up at the ceiling.

Thomas whispered conspiratorially to Allison. "Your mother never has appreciated fine literature."

"Fine literature? I appreciate fine literature perfectly well, thank you." Irene sniffed and gestured to the shelves surrounding the fireplace, each lined with leather-bound volumes of classic literature that ranged from boring to deadly.

"Ha. Got ya, Irene." Thomas hefted himself to his feet. Though he wasn't a heavy man, he was tall and broad. Everyone always assumed he'd played football and it pained him to admit that he didn't even have a firm grasp on all the rules.

"Allison has a new beau."

"Oh?" Thomas smiled. "Any young man would be lucky to have you, baby. You should bring him to dinner so we can meet him."

"Like I told Mom, we've only been on one date." Allison hated the defensive tone she heard in her voice and took a breath.

"Well, bring him around anyway. You don't date all that often. It'll be nice to meet him." Thomas caught Irene's disapproving grimace and frowned, looking between the two women in confusion. "Won't it?"

"He's simply not suitable, dear. He's divorced." She said the word as if it conveyed some sort of deadly disease.

Thomas held her gaze steadily. "Mm. Is he a believer? Able to provide for a wife? An upstanding member of society?" Irene nodded stiffly in answer to each question. He shrugged and smiled at Allison. "Bring him around. I'd love to meet him."

Irene excused herself, pleading a headache.

"He's a nice man, Daddy. I like him a lot."

"Don't worry about your mother. She'll come around. She has some very specific opinions…about everything," he grinned, "as well you know. I'll work on her."

CR& 

The tension headache that had been brewing since she first mentioned Phil to her mother exploded as Allison closed the door to her apartment. Why couldn't her mother just be happy for her for once? Wouldn't she ever be good enough? She shook four pain relievers into her hand and swallowed them dry before falling face first onto her bed. Pippin jumped up and bumped her ear with his nose. At least somebody loved her. She grunted. Pippin gave a soft prrrrrow and walked down her back before curling into a ball on her rump.

When the phone began to ring she whimpered. "Go away, go away, go away." After several rings, it stopped. Then her cell phone started up. *Can't people just leave me alone?* She rolled over, eliciting an alarmed yowl from Pippin before he stalked off. She shuffled down the hall to dig through her purse hoping to just find the thing and make the noise stop.

"Hello?" Irritation and fatigue mixed in her voice.

"Hi, Allison. It's Phil. Is this a bad time?"

"No." She headed back to the darkness of her bedroom. Flopping back onto the bed she wedged the phone between the mattress and her ear. "Just have a headache. What's up?"

"I can let you go. Sorry."

"No…" she exhaled noisily. "It's okay. If I'm talking to you, at least the ringing stops."

Phil's chuckle echoed across the line. "Glad to help. I had two purposes in calling. First, I was wondering if you'd talked to Lindsey or Marcus?"

Even with the head pain, Allison decided he sounded cute when he turned all brisk and business-like. "Mmmm, yeah, I called yesterday morning. Marcus was hoping she'd be released later. But Lindsey was supposed to call and never did. It's on my list to check in with them again, but I had my standing monthly lunch with my parents after church and just got home."

"I take it from your tone that didn't go so well?"

*Understatement of the century.* She rolled over and laid an arm across her eyes. "I always love seeing my dad. But my mom and I...we're either too different or too similar. I can never decide."

"I've had friendships like that. Never family. Sorry."

"It's fine. Just the conversation was particularly wearing today." Should she mention that he was the topic of conversation? No, that was probably better done in person. If ever. "You said two purposes for calling?"

"Ah. Well...I was wondering if you were free this Friday, or Saturday is fine too. To go out again. With me, obviously."

Some of the tension in her head eased. "As it turns out, I am free both days, and I would like to go out with you again. Very much."

"Is one day better than the other?"

"Wanna say Friday? I've got another crazy week at the office this week. It might be a nice way to decompress. And hanging out with you is never stressful."

"Sounds like a plan. Though I do want to clarify something."

Allison's heart sank. "Okay?"

"We're going out, not hanging out." Phil cleared his throat. "I just don't want there to be any confusion. I like you, Allison. As a friend, absolutely. But more than that, too. I'm hoping we're on the same page?"

The knot in her stomach loosened and her lips curved into a grin. "Yeah. We are."

"Cool. So, I guess I'll see you at work tomorrow?"

"Yep. Thanks for calling, Phil."

"Thanks for answering." He chuckled. "Go rest so your headache goes away."

The smile stayed on her lips as she ended the call and rolled to her side. Pippin hopped back on the bed, nosed her ear again, then curled up behind her knees. This time, Allison let herself drift off to sleep, images of Phil swirling through her dreams.

Phil sat on his deck watching the river as twilight seeped into the sky. *All that worry about how Allison would react for nothing.* She was still interested. This was one aspect of dating he hadn't missed. He didn't like feeling insecure or unsure of his next step. He probably shouldn't have been as blunt about liking her, but he didn't want to play games.

What should they do on Friday? He wanted to do something fun, maybe something with a little more interaction than just dinner and dessert. Maybe play miniature golf? Are the courses open yet? *Pretty sure they don't open until after Easter.* Maybe bowling? All the smoke though. And beer. Plus, some people just didn't like to bowl.

The phone rang.

"Hello?"

"Who's the chick, Phil?" Brandi's voice was slurred and shrill.

Phil could hear people talking loudly in the background as well as country music blaring from an audio system that had several blown out speakers.

"I'm not sure what you're talking about, but I'm also not having this conversation, Brandi. I have a restraining order, remember?" He should have checked the caller ID before he answered.

"Yeah. We need to talk about that, too. First things first though, what's her name?"

"Goodbye, Brandi. Don't call again." Phil started to hang up but brought the phone back to his ear as she shouted something. "What was that?"

"I said I'd find out on my own. You don't get to cheat on me."

*That's classic.* He'd found out after their divorce was final that she'd been cheating on him for at least the last year of their marriage. *Don't dwell on it.* "We're divorced, Brandi. Have been for a while. It's not cheating. Leave me, and everyone I know, alone. Goodbye." This time he clicked the phone off over her shouted objections. He'd get his numbers changed in the morning. *I probably have to give the new number to Mom. Maybe she'll keep it to herself this time.*

## 27

Allison tapped on the frame of Phil's office door. "Happy Monday."

"It's Monday, that's for sure." Phil grimaced and waved her in. "You seem chipper. Head all better?"

"Yes, thanks. I pretty much went straight to bed after we hung up. Sleep is always a good thing." She didn't need to mention that meant she'd slept in her clothes, diagonally across the bed on top of the covers.

"What's up?" He slipped the wire frame reading glasses off his nose and tucked them in his shirt pocket. How had she never noticed them before? Or how cute they made him look. What would it take to get him to put them back on?

"Just got off the phone with Lindsey. She's home. They're pretty sure the baby is fine and she's in no danger of early delivery or miscarriage. So far as they can tell at least. So that's good news. She wanted me to pass along her thanks for your help with her dad."

"Glad to hear that. Had they heard anything more about Ben?"

Allison shook her head. "Not yet. I think Marcus was going to follow up today. Lindsey is going to see if Ben would be willing to sign the adoption papers in exchange for Marcus dropping the charges. I'm not sure the police would agree to that, but since the assault charge carries a pretty heavy penalty, he might be more inclined to cooperate now than with the threat of a civil suit."

Phil gave a wry chuckle. "Sounds like I'm down a case again, most likely."

"Sorry."

He shook his head. "It's good. This is one case I'll be happy to let go."

Allison eased back a few steps. "I'll let you get back to it. Just thought I'd pass along the news."

Phil was already putting his glasses back on, his attention focused on his monitor as she backed out of the office.

Allison stopped for a bottle of water on her way back to her office. Something about the situation with Lindsey and Ben was bothering her, but she couldn't quite put her finger on what it was. Maybe Faith at the adoption agency would be able to help her figure out what. Would she even talk to Allison about anything specific? Unlikely. She was just a friend with no legal standing in the situation. Lindsey was going to have to handle it, but she needed to make sure she did it all the right way. Allison texted Lindsey to suggest she call the agency and keep them apprised of the situation with Ben. Hopefully they'd have some good advice.

∽◈∾

After a quick stop to drop her laptop bag and some files in her car, Allison headed to the Metro. As she rode the escalator down, she quickly checked the email she'd gotten from Lydia to be sure she got on the right train. She was rapidly coming to consider Lydia a good friend. For so many years she'd been envious of Kevin's affection for the woman. Last year, that envy had transformed to pity and, if she was honest with herself, a tiny bit of smug disgust. But as she got to know Lydia, Allison started to understand what Kevin saw in her. And now? Now she was on her way to meet Lydia at a vintage clothing store to look at a wedding dress.

She pushed through the crowded train, making it out the doors at her stop just as they started to slide shut. *Why can't people remember to leave a path to the door?* Allison adjusted her purse and hurried to the street exit. She was a little more than five minutes behind schedule. She hated being late.

Lydia leaned on a lamppost at the top of the escalator. "Hey there. I was starting to wonder if you were bailing on me."

"No. I wouldn't do that. Probably." She grinned. "What you need to know is that I am eternally five to ten minutes behind. No matter how hard I try or how much I hate it."

"So noted. Though to be fair, I only just got here. Seems we're two of a kind on that score." Lydia nodded down the block. "It's just down here. They sent me a photo, but I want to see your reaction without any preconceptions. Plus, things often look different in a picture."

Allison had to lengthen her stride to keep up with Lydia. "Are we speed walking, too? 'Cause I didn't wear the right shoes for exercise."

"Sorry." Lydia slowed. "I'm really excited. The whole dress-shopping thing has been a bigger nightmare than I'd expected. You watch these TV shows and they make it seem like you just know when you see the right dress. Like the skies open and rainbows dance around while the angels sing."

"And that's exactly how it works when you're spending the gross national product of an African country on your dress." Allison scoffed. "You, I am glad to say, have a much more realistic price point."

"There's that." Lydia's eyes sparkled as she tugged open the shop door. "Let's hope this is the winner."

Allison followed behind, trailing her fingers over the silky dresses that draped from the mannequins on either side of the main aisle as Lydia headed straight for the counter. They had some lovely things on display.

"Hi. I'm Lydia Brown. You're holding a dress for me?"

The clerk nodded while she looked Lydia over from head to toe. "I think you're going to love it. And I don't say that to everyone. Come this way, I'll get you set up in a changing room."

"Wait here, Allison, okay? I want to make a grand entrance." Lydia grinned over her shoulder.

Allison laughed and stroked a peacock blue cocktail dress. The plain silk dress with elbow sleeves and a scooped neck featured a delicate lace overlay. A slim belt adorned the waist and marked the difference between a fitted bodice and a fuller pleated skirt. Peeking under, she saw that there was, in fact, a crinoline adding to the puffiness at the hem. It was very 1950. And also incredibly gorgeous. Casually, Allison flipped the unassuming white tag over. In addition to having a button closure up the back of the dress, it had a very reasonable price. She wasn't sure what she needed it for. But did you really need an excuse to buy a gorgeous dress? She chewed on her lower lip and glanced toward the fitting rooms.

She knocked on the door of the room she'd seen Lydia disappear into. "How's it going?"

"Just one more minute."

"Okay." Allison caught the clerk's eye and gestured to the blue dress. "Can I try this on after she's finished?"

After giving Allison a quick once-over, the clerk nodded and began to remove the dress from the display form. Would she refuse to let someone try something on if she didn't feel it was a good fit? Allison watched the woman lovingly handle the dress. *Yeah…she probably would. Glad I passed.*

"All right. Drum roll, please." Lydia opened the fitting room door and stepped out, gently holding the skirt of the dress in her hand. When she'd cleared the door, she let the skirt fall and did a half turn. "What do you think?"

Allison let out an involuntary gasp. The creamy white chiffon dress with a fitted bodice looked as if it had been designed for Lydia. Though the under dress was sleeveless, it was topped with a sheer overlay decorated with sparkling ropes of crystals that made swoops like delicate bunting ending in crystal rosettes. The overlay draped below the collarbone and fanned out into a fluttery sleeve that fell just below her elbows. In the back, it plunged to a shallow vee to meet the sash at her waist. The skirt was full and flowing with the barest hint of a train. "It's gorgeous." She walked around Lydia, marveling at the details. "Deco era?"

Radiant, Lydia nodded. "This is it, isn't it?"

"I think so. It's certainly more you than anything I've seen yet. And you've dragged me to look at more dresses than I care to count."

"You enjoy it. Admit it."

Allison laughed and held up her hands. "All right, all right. Maybe it's fun. And now," she looked over at the clerk who had the blue dress draped over her arm, "it's my turn."

"Oooh. Pretty blue." Lydia looked at the clerk. "This is going home with me. I'll go change."

The clerk smiled and showed Allison to a second fitting room. Allison ducked inside and quickly shed her work clothes. She slid into the dress, grateful that the dressmaker had put a zipper in underneath the buttons. Button-up dresses weren't made for single women without maids. Smoothing the lace down, she admired herself in the mirror. "I believe I've found what I'm wearing to your wedding, Lydia. You ready?"

"Yep, let's see it."

Allison emerged from her fitting room at the same time as Lydia.

"Oh, Allison. It's like it was made for you. Good thing I found the perfect dress, or you'd outshine the bride. You have to get it."

"Yeah, I do."

The clerk beamed at them before nodding to Lydia. "I'll ring you up while your friend changes."

Allison hurried back into the changing room. She stroked the dress as she slipped it off, carefully arranged it on a hanger, and put her work clothes back on. She didn't need another dress, but it was too lovely to pass up. And maybe now that she and Phil were dating, she'd have more opportunities to wear something nice. Carrying the dress with her, she joined Lydia at the register to pay.

As they left, each with a dress bag draped over their shoulder, Allison grinned at Lydia. "It's too bad Laura couldn't make it. She's going to love the dress."

"Both of them. Hmm…I wonder if I should drag her back so we can find her dress for the wedding."

"Not a bad idea." Allison stopped at the metro and gave Lydia a quick hug. "Thanks for inviting me. I think you would've been fine without an extra pair of eyes, but I'm glad I got to see it. And find this." She patted her dress.

"I'm parked just down the block. Want me to give you a ride back to your car?"

"Would you? That'd keep the dress from getting squashed on the train before I have a chance to wear it."

CRELED

Her cell phone started ringing as she unlocked the door to her apartment. Allison glanced at the caller ID and frowned. The same number had called four times now. It wasn't one she recognized. With a sigh, she answered as she started toward her bedroom to hang up her new dress. "Hello?"

"Allison? It's Phil. Are you okay?"

"Phil?" She pulled the phone away from her ear to double check the number. "Yeah, I'm fine. I just didn't recognize the number. Where are you calling from?" Allison hung the garment bag in her closet. Unable to resist, she unzipped it and caressed the fabric.

"New number. That's actually part of why I'm calling, to make sure you had this number and my new land line as well."

She zipped up the garment bag and settled into the armchair by the window, scratching Pippin's head when he jumped into her lap. "You changed both of your numbers? Why?"

Phil's sigh clearly conveyed annoyance. "Long story. Though I guess you really ought to know what's going on." There was a long pause over the line before he relayed the incidents with Brandi that had taken place over the last several weeks. "I don't think you need to worry. She's full of bluster, and I've never suspected it would ever go beyond that...still, I understand if you'd rather not go out with me. I...I have a lot of baggage."

Allison hugged Pippin. How did someone justify being so vindictive when they were the one who wanted the divorce in the first place? She'd seen plenty of cases where the person not in favor of the divorce went a little crazy. But not the one who determined the course. Or so long after the fact. It didn't change anything anyway. There still hadn't been a big flashing arrow, but the way things were transpiring showed God's hand pretty clearly.

"No. If you say not to worry, then I'm not going to worry. You've always been very up front about your baggage, and I appreciate that. But...I've got some of my own, actually. And they want to meet you."

Phil's attempt to cover a snicker was unsuccessful. "I heard that. You won't be laughing long, pal."

"Sorry." He cleared his throat. "Should I ask?"

"No. You should run. Run far away. Screaming is optional, but recommended." Allison set Pippin down on the floor, much to his annoyance, and stood so she could pace. "My dad's not so bad. Though he hasn't really changed his intimidation tactics since I was seventeen and had just started dating. Still, with him, you can tell it comes from love. But my mom..." She rubbed the back of her neck and paused to stand at the window. "I don't even know where to start with my mom."

"Parents love me. Or, at least, they always have in the past. I'm not worried."

"You say that now. In the interest of full disclosure, they know you're divorced. Mom is not in favor."

"Hmm...still not worried. Like I said, parents love me."

"All right." *You have no idea what you're getting into.* "If you're willing to meet them, I'll set something up. But please don't say I didn't warn you."

"Fair enough. Same goes with Brandi. The worst I can see her doing is finding out your phone number and making a few crank calls. But since I already know you ignore numbers you don't recognize, that shouldn't bother you."

"If it does, I'll let you know. You said you changed your land line too?"

Phil rattled off that new number and Allison scribbled it on her hand to program into her phone later. They chatted for a few more minutes before hanging up.

Allison plugged her phone into the charger, double checked the lock on her front door, and crawled into bed with a book. Life was excellent right now. She had a new, close friend in Lydia and a boyfriend. Boyfriend. Maybe her mother was on to something with her use of the word 'beau', it certainly had a nicer ring. Word association brought visions of rings and dresses to mind. *Let's not jump the gun here. We've been out once, with another date planned. It's perhaps a tad early to be pricing reception halls.* Peace and warmth spread through her. *Thank you, Jesus. Forgive me for doubting your love.*

## 28

Allison brought a change of clothes to work with her on Friday. She and Phil had agreed to leave for dinner from the office to be sure they made their reservation. He hadn't been willing to share any other details, just that they were doing something he'd not done before either and that he thought it sounded like a lot of fun. He did, finally, concede that she should probably dress up a little, but still be comfortable. Since she enjoyed the one day a week she was allowed to wear jeans to the office, and she didn't have court to overrule that outfit choice, the slacks and light sweater for their date came along in a bag. To avoid having to plan car logistics, she braved the morning rush hour crowds on the Metro.

*I've been out with him once already...why am I so nervous?*

Near the end of the day, a tap on her doorframe startled her out of her daydreams.

Lindsey stood in the doorway looking amused. "Hey. Bad time?"

"No, sorry." Allison gestured for Lindsey to come in. "I've been on edge all day. What brings you into D.C. today?"

"Dad's meeting with Maureen at the Center. I didn't have anything I needed to talk about with Catherine, so I had him drop me here. I'll walk over when I'm done." She crossed the room and sat, folding her hands over her belly. "I wanted to thank you for your help last week and for nudging me to get in touch with Faith at the adoption agency. She had some good ideas about getting Ben to sign the consent forms without coercing him."

Coercion. *That's* what had been bothering her. "That's excellent. Does that mean it's all signed? You're ready to choose a set of parents?"

"Not quite. But I did convince Ben to meet with an independent adoption attorney. She seemed really nice when I explained the situation on the phone. So she's going to sit down with him, tonight actually, and go through the legal repercussions of him not allowing me to place the baby." A smile tugged at the corner of her mouth. "Apparently she has a spreadsheet with all the costs of a child for eighteen years. Plus she'll discuss what happens if he wants to marry someone or when I do. Custody issues, and all that." Lindsey shifted in her seat with a wince. "Probably similar to the information they gave me at the Center that started me thinking seriously about adoption in the first place. What's great is that if he realizes how serious this is, she has all the paperwork right there and since she's not connected to me in any way, his signature on the paper will be completely voluntary and verifiable as such."

"Sounds great. Can you send me the attorney's information? That seems like someone I should cultivate as a contact. You never know when you'll need someone with adoption law experience, as I'm now finding out. Honestly, I tried to do some research this week," Allison shook her head. "Adoption law is a whole different animal than what I'm used to."

"Yeah, absolutely." Lindsey wiggled her phone from the pocket of her snug pants and fiddled for a moment. "There. Should be in your email soon."

"Thanks. Definitely keep me posted on how things end up with Ben."

"I will." Lindsey shifted in her seat. "I've also been meeting with the counselor Faith recommended. She's been helping me work through a lot and make sure that I'm not choosing adoption out of some sense of penance."

"I hadn't thought about that as a possibility. Do you think you are?"

Lindsey shook her head. "No. I mean, there's no question that sin brought me here, I get that. And I'm sorry for it. But I also really feel forgiven, you know?"

"That's great, Lindsey."

"I still question the decision sometimes though. That's one of the reasons I'm still going to the counselor.

I mean…how do you really *know* you're making the right choice? What if he, or she, grows up to hate me because of this? Or…well…there's a lot for me to pray about."

"I'm praying for you too. It's good that you're thinking about the big picture though. I'm proud of you, Lindsey. I'm not sure I could do what you're doing."

"Thanks." Lindsey glanced at her watch and pushed herself out of the chair. "Anyway, I should probably get going." She turned back at the doorway. "One more thing? I wanted to say I'm sorry…about you and my dad? I wish…"

"Stop there. You have nothing to be sorry about. If anyone should apologize, it's me. I'm just glad that he stopped and really considered your feelings before too many dates. I thought he had already, or I would never have gone out with him in the first place. I hope you know that."

"I do. I'm glad the baby," she rubbed her hand over her stomach again and looked up shyly, "introduced me to you. I'm really hoping you'll still be my friend when he or she isn't in the picture anymore."

"You're not the only one who's glad. You sure you're all right to walk to the Center? You've winced several times since you got here."

"They told me they're Braxton-Hicks contractions and totally normal. They're just disconcerting. Walking shouldn't be a problem."

Allison studied Lindsey for a moment before nodding. "Okay. Be careful, all right? Stop by anytime."

Lindsey waved as she turned.

Allison leaned her head back and closed her eyes. She rolled her neck along the top of her chair. The muscles stretched and several vertebrae popped. She was grateful Faith had known just what to do. The last thing Lindsey needed was for the adoption to end up having legal complications down the line. Really, that's the last thing anyone needed. Allison couldn't imagine what the adoptive parents would go through if it turned out the baby's father hadn't legally surrendered his rights.

"Was that Lindsey I saw leaving?" Phil poked his head in her office.

Allison opened her eyes, smiling involuntarily when she looked at him. "Yeah. She stopped by to tell me they may have a fully legal way to convince Ben to sign the papers." She filled him in on the plan for a little reality therapy for the man.

Phil chuckled. "I like that plan better than either of the other two solutions we'd considered. And, that also means they can still pursue the assault charge. I hope they do." He narrowed his eyes. "What kind of scum hits a pregnant woman?"

"No argument." Allison flicked her eyes to the computer monitor and noticed the time. "Gosh. It's basically time to go, isn't it?"

"That was why I popped by. I need to make two more calls, want to say twenty minutes? That should still give us plenty of time to get there."

"I'll be ready."

ᚼᚼ

"Do I get to know where we're headed now?"

"All in good time, my dear. All in good time." Phil shot her a quick grin before checking his mirrors and zipping into the middle lane so they could make the exit to I-395.

She kept quiet as he navigated through the traffic and onto the George Washington Parkway, where traffic finally settled into a constant stream of moving cars. "Old Town?"

Phil nodded and navigated onto the main thoroughfare. "Any thoughts on street parking versus a lot or garage?"

"I'm a garage girl, myself. I figure that way you don't run the risk of getting towed because you forgot to read a sign or feed a meter."

"Reasonable. Garage it is."

She watched him scan the street. "There's one just up ahead on the left."

"Got it. Thanks." They parked and walked to the corner. Phil slipped his hand in Allison's and gave a light tug. "I think it's this way."

Allison smiled at the warmth of his hand enclosing hers. "There are so many good restaurants down this way…"

"Nope. It's a surprise. Hm. I should have brought a blindfold…Aha. Here we go."

They turned the corner and Allison smothered a laugh with a cough. The sign for *In the Kitchen* swung gently above its door.

Phil stopped and pulled the door open. "I've been wanting an excuse to come here since they opened. They teach you to cook the meal, then you get to eat. The chef, and her recipes, are supposed to be fantastic."

Allison went in ahead of Phil.

The chef glanced up from the hostess station and grinned. "Back already?"

Phil stopped, the door clipping his heels as it swung closed. He looked at Allison, clearly confused.

Her shoulders slumped. She'd been hoping to find a way to stall this revelation until after supper. "Marcus brought me." She turned and rested her hand on his arm. "It's so wonderful though, I'm really very excited to come here again. Especially with you." Was it possible for him to understand how much she preferred being anywhere with him?

Slowly, Phil smiled. "Well then...Reid, party of two."

The chef laughed. "Just through there. You're in the back row, far right. The menu's different tonight, so it'll be a whole new experience."

They made the dessert first, as the chocolate mousse needed to set up while they created and ate the rest of the meal. It was delightful that Phil actually seemed to want to participate and learn. Marcus had left the bulk of the cooking to her. She wasn't sure if that was an attempt to let her have the fun or because he had no interest or, if she were going to be uncharitable, an expression of his thoughts on roles in a relationship. It hardly mattered since Marcus was firmly out of the picture.

When dinner was ready, they took the rack of lamb, roasted new potatoes and French green beans over to the dining table at the end of their workspace. The chef had them plate the food family style, so they arranged the three serving dishes where they were easily within reach.

Phil held Allison's chair as she sat then took his own. "Why don't we say the blessing before we serve?"

"All right." When Phil took her hand, she smiled and bowed her head. She missed most of the prayer. Very few of the Christian men she'd dated in the past had bothered to even suggest praying on their dates. Let alone simply assume that they would.

After murmuring "Amen," Phil reached for the rack of lamb and carved three chops. He carefully transferred them to Allison's plate before offering her the roasted potatoes and green beans. Only after she'd taken what she wanted did he fill his plate.

"I have to say I'm a little disappointed that someone beat me to the punch with coming here. I was hoping for some big points for creativity."

"You still get them. Not everyone would think something like this could be fun. And, if you want me to be honest?"

He nodded, fork paused on the way to his mouth.

"You actually seemed to enjoy the whole process. That didn't seem to be the case when I was here before."

"So tactful." Phil shook his head. "I know you went out with Marcus a few times. And it's fine. It's not like I hadn't essentially told you to not bother looking my way." He speared a new potato.

Allison concentrated on eating for a moment. She took a deep breath and glanced at him out of the corner of her eye. "Can I ask what changed your mind? I'm glad you did, don't get me wrong, but you seemed so sure in the park."

He set his silverware down on the edge of his plate and turned his chair so he was looking at her more directly. "There were a number of things, starting with you, actually." He reached over and took her hand. "You're the first woman I've been interested in since the divorce. So it was easy to just say I was done, because there didn't seem to be a reason not to be. Then, over the course of the past two years as we became friends, it was a lot more difficult to deal with the fact that I could never be the man for you." He gave her fingers a light squeeze. "After the cake thing, I started really praying about it. Then you went out with Marcus and I'll admit I wasn't happy about it. My sister helped me realize there was a strong possibility that I was being stupid."

Allison laughed. "I need to meet your sister. I already like her."

"Yeah, well. She's pretty smart for a baby sister. So I prayed some more, and God kind of hit me over the head. Paul Brown reinforced the idea. And before I could wuss out, I made sure I'd run into you so I could ask you out." He grinned. "I hadn't planned on jogging the Mall that Friday, but I saw you headed that way and figured it was a golden opportunity."

She squeezed his hand then gently pulled her hand away so she could resume eating. "Well. I'm glad you did." She remembered what Laura had said when she was bemoaning the state of things in January. "It takes courage to change."

When the meal was finished and the dessert bowls all but licked clean, they headed back out into the clear, moonlit night. "Up for a walk, or would you rather call it a night? I know you've had a busy week."

Allison patted her full belly. "A little stroll is probably just the thing." She smiled and slipped her hand into his as they made their way down the charming street. The shops were all closed, but the front windows held delightful displays. As they walked, they peered at the treasures behind the glass.

When they reached the end of the block, Phil tugged her hand. "Let's go see the river. The moon's bright enough that it should be lovely."

They hurried across the street then zigged into a park that bordered the Potomac River. A paved path led through the grassy expanse. Allison pointed to a bench that looked out over the gently rippling water. The air was still, so the early February evening was just on the cool side of pleasant.

Phil slid his arm around Allison's shoulders when they sat.

"It gets a little colder when you sit." She wriggled closer to him.

He chuckled and rubbed her arm. "We don't have to stay. I just love seeing the water. It's my favorite thing to do at home...sit out on my balcony and watch the Occoquan River. Even when it's snowing outside, I'll bundle up and stay out as long as I can handle it. There's something peaceful about a river."

Allison peeked at Phil, admiring his profile in the moonlight as he watched the water.

He turned his face toward her, his voice dropping to a husky murmur. "If we count cake in the park, and lunch on the Mall, this is our fourth date." He held her gaze. "Would that make it all right for me to kiss you?"

Her breath caught in her throat and her eyes widened. The corners of her lips tilted up and she gave a slight nod.

Watching her steadily, Phil lowered his lips to hers, his hand coming up to cradle her cheek. Time seemed to slow, then stop as their lips met.

Reluctantly, he eased back. "I've wanted to do that since September."

"September?" Her brain was fuzzy and overloaded with sensation. Those were definitely fireworks. Maybe her friends hadn't exaggerated after all. "What happened in September?"

"I'm not sure. I just remember you came running into the office after lunch, dripping wet and laughing.

And I couldn't catch my breath. It was like I finally saw you."

"I remember that day. It was one of those random storms that crop up in the fall. There was a woman out walking her dog and when the skies opened, she popped up this umbrella that she took out of her purse and held it over the pup. She was getting drenched, but the pampered dog was prancing daintily along, dry as could be." Allison chuckled. "It was the funniest thing I'd seen in a while. I laughed the whole elevator ride up." She frowned. "I don't remember seeing you though."

"You wouldn't have. I ducked into the copy room. I was so confused...I didn't think I'd ever feel that kind of attraction again. I certainly didn't want to. But you." He looked back out over the river. "I still have a hard time believing that you're willing to be with me. There's enough memory of who I used to be that I can't imagine deserving someone like you."

"Phil." Allison took his chin and turned his face back toward hers. "I've been in one relationship since law school and only on a handful of dates beyond that. Do you want to know why?"

Phil nodded.

"Because the majority of single, Christian men my age don't seem to have any interest in being different from the single, non-Christian men my age. It's as if the fact that they didn't find their spouse in college has freed them from having to live by the standards God set up. I'm not interested in that. I want to get married and start a family with a Christian man who loves me. As I've gotten older, I've realized it's unlikely that I'm going to find someone who doesn't have some sort of baggage from prior relationships. And I'm okay with that. Everyone has a past. But not everyone is you. And you're who I want to be with."

He pressed his lips to hers. "You're amazing. Thank you."

## 29

Over the next two weeks, Allison was swamped at work and spent most of her time at home buried in research and preparation for her ongoing cases. In addition to dinner out on Friday nights, she and Phil tried to have lunch together every day except Wednesday when they went to the office Bible study. As the weather improved, they often walked out to the park in front of the building or down the few blocks to the Smithsonian Mall. They never seemed to lack for conversation. And Phil didn't mind holding her hand in public. Her only other truly serious boyfriend had been a stickler about public displays of affection being a no-no, including holding hands. The brain fizzing kisses Phil snuck in when he could? Those would definitely not have met with Daniel's approval. Her mother had been crushed when she and Daniel broke up. Her father had sent her a congratulatory gift.

Mom's campaign to meet Phil had taken on a new tenor. Allison wasn't going to be able to put it off for much longer. The idea of her mom grilling Phil about his divorce and why he would dare to think himself worthy of her daughter left her feeling sick. Phil insisted he was looking forward to meeting her parents. But he didn't have any idea what he was getting into. Even so, it was likely that he'd get his wish today. Against her better judgment, Allison had agreed to go to church with Phil.

She'd grown up in a big church. When she went to college, she'd enjoyed trying smaller churches and discovered a real preference for congregations where all the faces were, at a minimum, familiar. After moving back to the D.C. area, she'd tried to return to what she'd always considered her home church, but it had grown so large she could never get comfortable. Kevin had invited her to his church many times, but since it was even larger, she'd never felt any desire to give it a try. The fact that her parents went there didn't help. Somewhere along the line, she and her mother had grown apart. Suddenly nothing she did was ever quite proper enough, or good enough. Growing up, she'd known what was expected and had strived to meet those expectations. Had she ever measured up? She wasn't sure. But she'd never felt the heaping coals of disappointment she now experienced with every visit to her parent's house.

Allison smoothed the sides of her black pencil skirt and checked to see that her amethyst blouse was tucked in all the way around. Her mother had given her this outfit, which meant it ought to meet with her approval. *What am I doing?* She looked longingly at the jeans she would normally wear to church. *Grow up.* Besides, wearing heels was a small price to pay for seeing Phil.

With Pippin padding hopefully along beside her, she went into the kitchen. The phone rang as she reached for the coffee. *Maybe Phil's calling to cancel.* She wanted to see him, but it would get her out of seeing her parents. *Stop it. It's going to be fine.*

"Hello?"

"He signed them, Allison."

*Who signed...oh!* Allison grinned and setting the coffee down on the counter. "Oh Lindsey, that's excellent. I'm so glad. When?"

"Just last night. Ben came over to let me know. Dad almost slugged him, and he wasn't allowed in the house—and really I'm okay with that. I'm just grateful that the papers are signed and he's now completely out of the picture. For good."

"Have you been looking at profiles? I've been meaning to call you and check in, but it's been just crazy at work."

"Don't worry about it. That's kind of what I figured. But no...that's the other reason I was calling, actually." Lindsey cleared her throat. "Do you think you could go with me again? Any time. I'll work around your schedule. I'd just really like your opinions."

"You're sure you want me? Not your dad or...I don't know, someone?"

"You don't have to, if you don't want to…" She sounded heartbroken.

"It's not that at all, Lindsey. I'm happy to go with you, I'm just surprised, I guess, that you don't have someone else you'd rather take." She paused and thought through her schedule for the week ahead. "I've actually got a little breather this week and next as far as work goes. You make an appointment with Faith and let me know when it is, and I'll be there. I can pick you up, or whatever."

"Really?"

"Really. Just let me know."

"You're the best. Thank you."

After hanging up, Allison checked her watch again and frowned. She tossed a few treats in Pippin's bowl, dumped her coffee into a travel mug, and hurried out the door.

CS80

Phil scanned the crowded foyer. He thought he was where Allison said she'd meet him, but he was still learning the names people used to describe places in the building. He'd never imagined going to a church this large, but he was making some connections and gradually feeling more at home. And you couldn't beat the preaching. The spiritual insights he'd been gleaning over the past weeks made getting lost in the building totally worthwhile. It was wonderful to feel like he was actually growing in Christ instead of floating along. He caught a flash of purple in the corner of his eye and turned. Something about the way the person was moving...he grinned and raised his hand to catch Allison's eye.

"I was beginning to worry you were skating out on me. Kevin and Lydia are saving us a spot."

"Sorry. Lindsey called just as I was getting ready to leave."

"Everything okay?"

"Actually, everything is better than okay. Ben signed the papers to terminate his parental rights. So she's now completely free to place the baby." Allison murmured apologies as she stepped over the people who had filled in the pew, making her way to the open seats next to Kevin and Lydia.

"That's great."

"What's great?" Kevin glanced over as the worship team took their places on the stage and the music started.

"Tell you later." Allison focused her attention on the front, smiling when Phil slipped his hand in hers.

At the end of the service, Phil bumped her shoulder with his. "Penny for your thoughts?"

Allison jolted. "Just ruminating on how some big churches manage to feel like small ones and wondering why they can't all be that way. Sorry."

"I've had that thought a few times myself." Phil grinned. "Whatever it is Pastor Brown does, it's a good thing." He stood and tugged her to her feet. "Since we came to the worship service instead of going to a small group, can I entice you into lunch?"

"Yeah. Pretty easily, actually."

"How about we go in my car and I'll bring you back here afterward?"

She smiled. "Sounds good. Which side are you parked on?"

Phil nodded toward the far exit and took her hand in his.

They stopped to chat with a few people on their way to his car.

"You're either more outgoing than I realized, or the people here are really friendly."

"Maybe a little of both." Phil grinned.

Phil blinked in the bright sunlight as they pushed through the doors into the parking lot. Allison dug in her purse, she emerged with sunglasses. "Where'd you park?" She put on the sunglasses and turned to Phil. "Hey, what's wrong?"

His lips thinned into a grim line and he strode off at an angle into the parking lot.

Phil stopped in front of a car that had clearly seen better days. The windows were a mess of spider-webbed cracks. All the lights were smashed and massive dents covered the majority of the car's body. All four tires were flat. Gaping flaps of rubber left no doubt that they'd been slashed. Red writing covered the whole thing. After he unraveled what one of the scrawls said, Phil stopped trying.

"This can't be your car. I mean, it's the same make, but…Phil…what happened?"

Phil groaned before turning his back on the wreck to look her in the eyes. "Brandi. It had to be Brandi."

"Yoo-hoo! Allison?"

Phil looked around then back at Allison. Something was wrong. All the blood had drained out of her face and she was wearing what he recognized as her forced smile. He turned to follow her gaze across the lot.

Allison lifted her hand in greeting. "Mom."

Her mother closed the distance between them and brushed delicate air kisses near her cheek. Her dad brought up the rear with an apologetic look for both of them.

"See, dear?" She flicked a look over her shoulder at her husband. "I told you that was Allison. I'd recognize this outfit anywhere. It's so perfect for you, honey." She smiled at Allison, her eyes flitting to take in Phil and the car. The tiniest wrinkle formed in the center of her forehead. "Who's your friend?"

Allison stepped back to stand beside Phil. "Mom, Dad. This is Phil Reid. Phil, my parents."

Could the timing be any worse? Phil slipped his arm around Allison and offered his hand to her parents. "It's a delight to meet you Mr. and Mrs. Vasak."

Her father returned the handshake and winked at Allison. Phil felt some of the tension in Allison's shoulders lessen under his arm. At least it seemed like her father was pleased.

"Were you heading out to lunch?" Irene's gaze flicked from Allison to Phil.

"That was the plan. But it seems my car's out of commission." Phil frowned and turned to Allison. "Sorry, I'm going to have to take care of this."

Her mother's eyebrows shot up. "Oh dear. This is your car? What on earth happened?"

Phil shrugged. *Great first impression. But better than trying to hide it. Right?* "I'm not sure, actually, Mrs. Vasak. I can only guess my ex-wife had something to do with it."

Irene let out an imperious sniff and shot a meaningful look in Allison's direction. She smiled politely at Phil. "Well then, why don't we leave you to that. Allison, dear, why don't you join us for lunch?"

"Oh no, I'll stay and help here. I've got my car. Phil might need a ride."

"Nonsense." Her mother's tone brooked no argument. "He's certainly capable of taking care of this himself. And we have some things we need to discuss."

Allison sighed. "Mother..."

"It's okay, Allison." *Someone ought to get a good meal. And Phil really didn't want Allison to stick around long enough to decipher Brandi's writing.* "I'll call my attorney and a tow truck."

"You're sure? I'm happy to stay."

"I'm sure." *It was clear she didn't want to go to lunch with her parents. And Phil understood somewhat, he'd caught the look her mother had given her. But she didn't need to be here, either. He'd do anything he could* to keep Brandi's venom away from Allison. He pressed a quick kiss to her mouth. "I'll call you later this afternoon." He smiled warmly at Allison's parents. "It was a pleasure to meet you."

Allison's shoulders slumped. "I'll take my own car and meet you. Where are you headed?"

Phil watched as Allison and her parents veered off in separate directions. He'd hoped to meet them under better circumstances. It was clear that as first impressions went, he'd just bombed. He dialed Grant and explained the situation. After some discussion, Phil agreed to wait before calling a tow truck. Grant was on his way with a camera.

After a half hour, Grant pulled his car into the nearly empty lot and parked behind Phil's mess of a car. Stuffing his hands in his pockets, he let out a low whistle. "Wow, man."

"Yeah." Phil pushed himself off the curb where he'd been waiting and dusted off his pants. "I've had time to decipher her scrawl, too. I kind of wish I hadn't."

Grant studied some of the writing, his eyes widening. "Vindictive little thing, isn't she?" He frowned. "You need to call the police. Photos are good, but really, you need to file a report."

"I know." Phil sighed heavily. "I already called them. They should be here soon."

"So, other than that, how's your day?" Grant grinned.

Phil snorted. "It was nice having Allison come to church with me. Right up until we discovered this on our way out to lunch. And then her parents came over and saw it."

"Oooh. Not good."

"Not really, no. Her mom is already predisposed not to like me because of the divorce. Having a malicious ex isn't going to help."

"Do you have any idea why Brandi's doing this?"

Phil scratched his head. "She called and made some noises about how she'd heard I was dating someone. Typical Brandi. I blew her off, though I did change my numbers. All I can think is word got back to her that I'm pretty serious about Allison." He looked up at the wisps of cloud hanging in the sky. "'Cause I am."

"Why didn't you mention this?"

"I'm having a hard time reconciling the threats and this behavior with the person I was married to. I guess I was hoping it was just a phase and I didn't need to take it seriously."

"You've never needed a restraining order before, Phil. She's never broken into your house before. She's never destroyed your personal property before." Grant gestured to Phil's car. "Use your head, man. This is not the work of someone in a phase that will eventually go away. Something's knocked her completely off her rocker."

"We can't prove it was her."

"No." Grant stared at Phil. "But you know it, and I know it. If the police can't find some evidence to get her bail revoked, you're going to need to figure out how to keep Allison out of her sights."

30

"Ready?" Allison looked over at Lindsey. The girl was pale and had twisted the strap of her purse into a tight spiral.

Lindsey shook her head slightly, eyes wide. "I don't know if I can do this."

"You don't have to know for sure right now." Allison reached over to touch the girl's hand. *Lord, give me the right words here, please.* "But...at this point, you think this is the right thing to do. So let's go and look. You don't have to choose anyone today, or tomorrow, or next week. There's still plenty of time. When are you due?"

"April twenty-seventh."

"See? It's not even March yet. Let's go in and look, and if you want to leave in ten minutes, then that's what we'll do. We'll come back another day. Or we'll start looking at cribs and the stuff that you'll need at your dad's house for a baby."

Lindsey sucked in her breath sharply. "I can't raise a baby." She stared at Allison before offering a weak smile. "Thanks. You're right. I don't have to choose today." She rubbed her hand over her belly and let out a breath. "It's like shopping. I'm just scoping out the store." She winced. "That sounds terrible."

Allison laughed. "A little. But you're not wrong. It's just a bit more important than finding the right pair of jeans." She angled her head. "But if that helps you get out of the car, then let's go with it."

Lindsey released her seatbelt. "I'm being a chicken. I don't know why this is so hard."

Allison opened her car door. "Hmm, let's see. You're choosing to do what's best for you and your baby, despite the fact that it's probably the most selfless thing you'll ever do. Clearly, it should be easy." She rolled her eyes and jerked her head toward the adoption agency's building. "Come on, let's go shopping."

Lindsey slipped her hand into Allison's, her fingers clinging in a desperate grip, as they climbed the stairs. They found the receptionist at the front desk this time and waited while she finished a phone call. She looked expectantly at Lindsey. Clearing her throat, Lindsey tried to speak but managed only a nervous squeak.

"We have an appointment with Faith. Lindsey Bowers and Allison Vasak." Allison squeezed Lindsey's hand. "Remember, you don't have to decide anything today. Keep that in mind, okay?"

Faith popped her head out of her office and smiled. "Go on into that room," she gestured to the room with sofas where they'd met previously, "I'll be right there."

Woodenly, Lindsey crossed the open area into the homey meeting space and perched on the edge of the sofa nearest the door. Allison set her bag down. "I'll be right back." She found the receptionist at the copy machine. "Could I get something for her to drink? Maybe a Sprite?"

"Oh, sure. Of course. There should be some in the fridge over there."

Allison scanned the contents and settled on ginger ale. Taking two cans, she headed back toward Lindsey. She met Faith in the open area just outside the door.

"How's she doing?" Faith shifted the stack of what looked like high-school reports in their neat vinyl covers.

"Nervous, bordering on freaked out." Allison frowned. "I tried to remind her she doesn't have to choose right now, but I almost wonder if she'll feel better once she's made that decision."

"Sounds like she's perfectly normal." Faith smiled. "Let's get started and see if even taking that first step doesn't help calm her nerves some."

Allison followed Faith into the room and popped the top of one of the sodas before handing it to Lindsey. Faith set the stack down on the coffee table and settled into a chair.

"I brought just a handful of portfolios based on the criteria you mentioned on the phone and your answers in the paperwork you filled out. If you don't see a match here, I have many more to draw from, and we'll keep looking until we find the family you're comfortable with. Take your time." Faith leaned forward slightly and waited until Lindsey met her eyes. "And try not to worry. You'll find just the right people to parent your baby."

Lindsey offered a weak smile.

"Now, I can stay if you want, or go. Totally up to you."

"Would it be okay if I looked with just Allison for a little bit?"

"Absolutely." Faith rose. "I'll be in my office if you need me." She pulled the door closed as she left and they heard her murmur to the receptionist.

Allison glanced at the multi-hued pile of portfolios. Where did you even start with something like this? If she didn't know, Lindsey was probably even more overwhelmed. Time to take decisive action. "What's your favorite color?"

"Purple."

Pursing her lips, Allison fanned the stack out on the table and found a portfolio cover that was a blueish-purple. "Then let's start with this one."

They spent an hour going through the small stack Faith had left with them. By the end, Lindsey had two set aside for further consideration, but had decided she wanted to see a few more. While Lindsey went to the restroom, Allison tracked down Faith to give back the portfolios of those Lindsey had ruled out and ask for another stack. With a second, smaller, pile in hand, she went back into the room and waited for Lindsey to return.

Another hour passed as Lindsey weighed the pros and cons of each possible adoptive family. Finally, she had a front runner. With that portfolio in her hands, Lindsey looked at Allison, a tear slipping down her cheek. "I feel so bad for the other couples. I want to choose them, but they just don't feel right…and I feel mean for being picky."

"I get that. I do. I know it's not the same, but there are clients I can't, well, won't take on. And though I always feel bad, I have to go with what I know is right. If I'm not the best attorney for someone, it's not right for me to take them on. And if you don't feel one hundred and ten percent comfortable with a particular family as the parents for your baby, then you need to keep looking until you are."

Lindsey sniffled and nodded. "Okay. I'm not being selfish?"

"No. You're being a good mom."

Her words brought on a flood of tears. Allison pulled Lindsey into her arms and rubbed her back as the girl wept. Gradually, the sobs subsided into hiccups and Lindsey pulled away, swiping at her eyes. She smoothed the damp and slightly wrinkled cover of the portfolio in her lap. "This is them. It's the right choice."

Allison stood, stopping to rest her head on Lindsey's briefly before going to the door. "I'll go get Faith."

CustomGlyph

Allison dropped Lindsey, armed with a copy of her chosen family's portfolio, back at her house. Should she go into work? She had plenty she needed to do, but the throbbing behind her left eye had returned now that she didn't have Lindsey's problems to distract her. She rested her head on the steering wheel. *Don't be a baby.* When the light turned, she pointed the car downtown.

Phil was sitting in her office when she got there. Allison pushed away the flare of resentment. She just wanted ten, maybe twenty, minutes to settle her mind. She'd spent the drive reliving the lunchtime chastisement her mother had provided, despite the looks they got from nearby tables, the day before. Her dad had shot surreptitious sympathetic looks, but he wouldn't back her up against her mom. He might go around her mom's back to help when he thought it was right, but even that was rare. Mostly Allison got silent moral support, which in the overall scheme of things never felt all that useful.

"Hey." Allison tried for a smile, though she was pretty sure it ended up a grimace.

Phil wrinkled his forehead, concern evident. "You okay?"

"I will be. What's up?"

"The car yesterday. It's pretty certain that Brandi's behind it. The police found a few fingerprints, and thankfully she's in the system, so maybe there's a chance to actually do something about her. But," Phil frowned, "I thought you should know that it seems her behavior is escalating. And…I'll understand if that makes you want to rethink things."

Allison flopped into her desk chair, trying to ignore the sinking feeling in her stomach. "Is that what you want?"

"No." He shook his head vigorously. "But I want you to be safe." He rose and shut the office door before walking around the desk. Swiveling her chair, he rested his forehead on hers and ran his hands up her arms before twining his fingers into her hair. "I couldn't live with myself if something happened to you because of my past."

"Phil…"

He pressed his lips to hers then leaned back. "Just be careful. For me?"

Dazed, heart racing, Allison nodded. She stared blankly at her computer for several minutes after he left. How did he affect her so deeply? Trying to push worries about Lindsey, Brandi, Phil, and her mother out of her mind, she opened her email and got to work.

Phil got home to find Grant parked in front of his house. He pulled into the garage but, rather than going upstairs from there, he backtracked and knocked on Grant's window.

Jumping, Grant looked up from his e-reader and sighed. He pushed the door open. "'Bout time you got home."

"I didn't know I had company." Phil peered in the back window. "I don't see dinner in there."

Laughing, Grant pushed the door shut with a click and pressed lock on his key fob. "Why would I bring takeout when you have some of the better local restaurants just a short stroll away?"

"So if you didn't bring takeout, what did you bring?"

Grant shook his head as they walked down the brick sidewalk and considered their dining options. "Bad news, actually." He paused by a restaurant's outdoor menu and scanned the offerings. "This place any good?"

Phil shrugged. "It's fine. Not the best, but a good meal for a decent price. Haven't been in a while."

"Let's see if it's better than you remember."

They opted for a table on the deck in back where they had a view of the river. It was warm enough, even without the standing heaters the restaurant had placed strategically around the patio, but the extra heat was welcome when the breeze kicked up. Since it was Monday night, there were very few customers, and everyone else had chosen to eat inside.

When they'd placed their orders, Phil sipped his water. "Let's have it."

Grant sighed and focused on precisely aligning his fork and knife before he spoke. "They matched the fingerprints to Brandi. But when they went to talk to her about it, the condo was empty. It looks like she and the guy split town. Probably on Sunday, right after the vandalism."

Phil rubbed his neck. "Or they're hiding out. I don't think she's done, Grant. I'm not sure why she's so ticked. She left me. But the point is, she's not safely locked away where I don't have to worry about her."

"Sorry."

"Yeah." Phil glared out at the water. How long did you have to pay for a mistake? And what right did he have to drag Allison into his mess? She deserved better. "Any idea how Romans 8:28 works into this?"

"Not right now, no." Grant paused as the server brought their meals and refreshed their drinks. "But maybe we'll see it down the road. Or not. I think sometimes you just have to trust that God, in His sovereignty, knows what He's doing. It's not easy to do, but after a while, I was able to see that even with losing Lilly."

Phil watched his friend's eyes cloud with sorrow. He wanted that kind of love. One that lasted long after the other person died.

Giving his head a shake, Grant offered a wan smile. "Anyway. At some point, I think you have to move past wanting clear explanations and reasons for everything that happens. God is God, not us. You can argue the problem of evil for days on end and never get closer to a solution until you sit back and accept that we're not called to understand, we're called to trust."

"When did you get so smart?"

Grant laughed. "Always have been, you were just too stupid to see it."

They talked about lighter subjects for the remainder of the meal. Phil recounted his dates with Allison. Grant, in turn, reported the news from the poker group and promised to give Phil's new church a try before too much longer.

After waving goodbye, Phil climbed the front steps and unlocked the door to his house, glad to be home. A twinge of worry nagged at the back of his mind as he thought about Brandi going after Allison. Locking up, he headed to the top floor and out to the deck. Before he could talk himself out of it, he punched in Allison's number.

"Hello?"

"Hey. It's Phil…were you asleep?" It was just minutes after eight.

"Nearly. Long day." She yawned and he heard a muffled feline protest in the background. "How about you?"

"Long probably covers it. I just wanted to hear your voice. I won't keep you."

"No, it's okay. If I go to bed now, I'll be up at three a.m. anyway."

Phil chuckled and propped his feet on the deck railing as he watched a vee of geese flying overhead. "Tell me about your day, then."

He listened as she described her morning with Lindsey. He was amazed at her strength, and Lindsey's. When the chill in the air got to be too much, he stepped back inside, being sure to lock the balcony door. It was something he'd never taken much care to do in the past. But with Brandi on a rampage…he wouldn't put it past her to find a way to climb up.

"I had dinner with Grant tonight."

"Oh?"

"You remember Grant? My friend…and attorney?"

"Of course. He lives up this way doesn't he? It's nice that he came all that way on a Monday."

"Yeah. Mostly it was to let me know that they matched fingerprints on my car to Brandi, but they can't find her. Allison…" Phil wasn't sure what was legitimate worry and what was him being protective of someone he cared about. "Just be careful. I know I said that already today…but I don't want anything to happen to you."

"I know. I appreciate it." She yawned loudly.

Phil smiled at the sound. They'd been on the phone for an hour. "I'll let you go. It's probably not too early for bed now, right?"

"Right." He could hear the tired smile in her voice. "I'll see you tomorrow, Phil. I love you."

The phone clicked in his ear. Phil sat on the edge of his bed, frozen until the cranky fast busy buzz interrupted his daze. He clicked off the phone and set it next to him. He heard Allison's voice in his head telling him she loved him and his heart soared. Then it crashed to the pit of his stomach. Had she meant it? She was tired at the end of a long day. Maybe she'd forgotten who she was talking to? Maybe he shouldn't read too much into it. That would be the smart thing. Smart or not, he wanted the words to have been meant for him. What would Brandi do with that little tidbit if she found it out?

## 31

Friday morning, Allison's phone rang just as her alarm started beeping. She rolled onto her back and hugged her pillow, groaning. Pippin, clearly annoyed by the noise, seated himself on her chest and batted at her chin. She rumpled his ears, then patted around on the nightstand for her alarm, finally managing to silence it. The phone rang once more. Pippin let out a curious meow and Allison pushed the pillow half off her face and looked at her cat. "I don't know, Pip. But thankfully..." The phone started up again. Grumbling, she wiggled to a sitting position and grabbed the handset. "What?"

"Okay. So you're not a morning person. I apologize, but it's an emergency." Lydia's voice was frantic on the other end of the line. "Please tell me you can call in sick today. The wedding is exactly six weeks from tomorrow and I don't have a reception hall. I haven't mailed the invitations, though they are currently stacked in boxes on my kitchen table. The bridesmaids, and yes, I know you're not one, have no dresses. You have to help me."

"Wait. What?" Allison scrubbed a hand over her face and tried to get her brain functioning. Throwing her legs over the side of the bed, she headed toward the kitchen. "Why aren't your bridesmaids helping with this?"

"Because they're my sisters and they're all who-knows-where, doing who-knows-what and will only be here for the rehearsal dinner and the actual wedding. Since I have three sisters and don't want to have a monster wedding party, I couldn't ask any friends to be in the wedding too." Her voice had taken on the pleading whine of a small child.

"All right. Take a breath and let me think." Allison poured a mug of steaming coffee and was thankful she had taken the time to set it up the night before. She filled Pippin's bowl with his breakfast and considered the day ahead. "I've had a long week in court. Today was supposed to be my catch up day in the office. And I think I have plans with Phil tonight, if I can bring myself to face him." She winced, recalling her parting words on the phone Monday night. She'd been grateful more than once this week that she'd spent most of her time out of the office and had only managed to see him for a few seconds here and there. It was clear he had questions, but he had the sense not to bring it up at work.

"What's going on with Phil? Never mind, you can tell me that while we're out today. Please say you'll help me."

Allison leaned against the kitchen counter and took a long drink from her mug. "Yeah, I can probably swing a day off. Gracious knows I've got the time accrued. Tell me what you're hoping to get done again."

"Invitations need to go in the mail and I need to choose bridesmaids dresses and book a reception location." Hope filled Lydia's voice. "Totally doable, right?"

"Have you at least started addressing the invitations?"

There was a long silence on the other end of the line.

"So…that's a no. You have a list of addresses, right?"

"That I do have."

"Do you have a moral objection to using the computer to address the envelopes? Because if you do, I'm not your girl. My handwriting dictated that I either go into computers, medicine, or law."

Lydia sighed. "At this point, no. I don't love it, but it would take us all day to write them out by hand. Can we at least use a font that looks hand written?"

"That I can help you with. And, depending on the envelopes you've got, maybe we can print right on them and not use labels." Allison refilled her coffee and checked the time on the coffee maker. "Why don't you load up the invitations and head over here. Bring something approximating breakfast. We should do the invites first."

Lydia squealed into the phone. "You're a lifesaver. I'll be there as fast as I can."

The phone clicked in Allison's ear and she frowned. "No hurry." She set the handset down and looked at Pippin. "Guess we're having company today." She set up her laptop in the living room and sent a quick email to her supervisor letting him know she'd be out. She included Sam on the carbon copy, since the receptionist was really the one who needed to know. Then she dug out her cell phone and texted Phil.

*Helping Lydia with wedding stuff 2day. Won't be in. Probably need rain check on 2nite?*

She headed to the bedroom to run through the shower before Lydia showed up. When she was dressed, she saw a text had come in from Phil.

*Save 2morrow 4 me. Need to talk to you!*

Uh oh. Allison chewed her lip as she quickly texted back. *Everything okay?*

*Am fine but have been trying to catch you all week. Plus I miss u.*

She smiled. Even as mortified as she'd been when she realized what she said, she'd missed him as well. And, if she was honest with herself, she'd meant the words. She just hadn't intended to be the first one to say them.

*Miss u2. 2morrow 4 sure.*

There was a knock on her door. Honestly. People needed to stop letting other people follow them into the building. Lydia had a small rolling suitcase propped next to her as well as an overstuffed tote bag slung over her shoulder.

Allison reached for the handle of the suitcase. "How many invitations are we addressing?"

"It's not as bad as it looks." Lydia dropped the tote bag just inside the door and rolled her shoulders. "They haven't been stuffed yet. So there's the invitations, the reply cards and envelopes, the inside envelope, and finally the outside envelope. Plus the stamps and," she patted the pockets of her jeans before pulling out a flash drive, "the guest list. I think the last time I added anyone we were right at two hundred."

Allison shook her head. "Two hundred? Good grief."

Lydia shrugged. "Did you forget my dad's the pastor of a large church? I can't invite just who I want to come. There are a whole bunch of people who have to be invited or they're going to feel slighted and it'll cause general unrest blah, blah, blah." She rolled her eyes. "I tried to get away without asking the entire world, but the only alternative we could come up with that might have worked—and I stress might—was a family-only wedding. It was tempting, but not really tempting enough."

"Where's the food?"

Laughing, Lydia grabbed a box of donut holes from the top of the pile of boxes in the tote bag. "You said you weren't picky. This was on the way...and a drive through."

"Fair enough. Coffee's in the kitchen. Could you refill my mug while you're in there? It's by the pot." She took the donut box and the flash drive. "I'll get us set up. Which box has the outer envelopes in it?"

"No idea. I think they're in the suitcase." Lydia headed into the kitchen, stopping to lean over and scratch Pippin who watched from the doorway.

There was no way Allison was digging through those boxes. Lydia could find the envelopes when she got back with coffee. She plugged the flash drive into her laptop and opened the file on it. The neatly organized spreadsheet suggested Kevin's involvement. At least it would be easy to make a mail merge. She looked up and took the coffee Lydia held out. "Find me the outside envelopes, would you? I need to set up the size and then we can fiddle with alignment and font."

Lydia dug through the boxes, finally emerging with a pale pink envelope.

Allison let out a quiet whistle when she felt the paper. "These are nice."

"They're a discontinued design. I got them for seventy percent off. I was just glad they had as many as I needed. In fact, I have about fifty extra. I had to agree to buy whatever they had in stock. It still saved us a bundle." Lydia perched on the couch next to Allison, looking over her shoulder. "I'm trying to spend as little as possible to have some padding for the reception. If we can swing it, I'd really love to do a river cruise of the monuments. Just not sure if that's realistic at all with the time and money constraints we're dealing with."

"Let's get this started then we can talk budget." Allison cocked her head to the side. "Have you done any research?"

Lydia held her fingers an inch apart. "I thought I had 'til September. Or later."

With a chuckle, Allison sent the envelope through the printer as a test run. They made a few tweaks and ran a second test. Satisfied, Allison queued up the rest of the list and positioned Lydia by the printer with stacks of envelopes. When those were piled neatly and they'd taken a quick break for a new pot of coffee, they started on the interior and response card envelopes.

"Who thought up having three envelopes for these things?" Allison watched as her printer continued to churn out pink envelopes.

Lydia shrugged. "No clue." She paused in the process of carefully applying stamps to the finished envelopes and reached into a box and held up a white embossed card with a pink and chocolate brown damask print surrounding an oval filled with calligraphy. "What do you think?"

Allison looked at the invitation and grinned. "They're lovely." She tapped her fingers on her knee. "And I think I know just the bridesmaid dress...I just have to remember where I saw it." She handed back the invitation and crossed to the pass through where she kept her mail piled. Gingerly pulling out the stack of catalogs, she returned to the couch and flipped through them. In the second to last one, she finally found it. Folding the catalog over, she tapped the photo of a pale pink crepe-over-silk dress that fell in soft ripples to just below the model's knees. It had a sweetheart neckline and split butterfly sleeves that floated just above the elbow. A chocolate sash tied around the empire waistline.

"Ohhh." Lydia flipped to the front to see what catalog it was before looking again. "It's perfect. And they're reasonable, too. I won't pretend that my sisters will have another use for them, but they could wear them to the theater or something if they wanted to." She pushed herself off the floor and grabbed Allison in a hug. "I might actually get this wedding planned, thanks to you."

Allison laughed. "You chose the colors, I just happened to remember seeing something pretty." The printer spit out its final envelope and whirred to a stop. "Now, let's get these things stuffed and ready for mailing." She glanced at her watch. "We can grab lunch after we go to the post office."

When they'd finished hauling the boxes of wedding invitations into the post office, Allison and Lydia decided to find lunch in Old Town Alexandria. Two of the possible reception locations were there, so they could park, grab lunch at one of the little cafes, and then see about the rest on foot.

Once the server took their orders and dropped off iced tea for both of them, Allison pulled out a legal pad and pen. "Okay. Talk to me about budget."

"Not just yet. I keep waiting for you to mention Phil and, so far? Nothing. I hereby decree no more wedding talk until dessert. So, spill."

Allison tapped her pen against the paper and frowned. She continued fiddling with the pen as she spoke. "Things are actually going really well. Other than a few hiccups with his ex-wife being loony tunes and my mom being completely anti-everything to do with him because he has an ex-wife."

Lydia's face registered sympathy.

Allison charged on. "Oh, and I blurted out that I loved him and then hung up and we haven't really had a chance to talk since. Partly because I'm a huge chicken and partly because work has been insane. It's clearly been eating at him, if his texts this morning were any indication."

Lydia pointed to Allison's iced tea. "Take a breath, then take a drink. I'll spend that time trying to figure out how any of that goes along with things going really well."

Allison chuckled weakly. "I've always been an optimist?"

"Where to start." Lydia pursed her lips. "How about with: are you really in love with him or did you just blurt out something before thinking?"

"At the time it probably was a blurting situation. You know how you say 'I love you' when you get off the phone with family? But having been unable to think about much else all week…I've realized it's true." Allison rubbed her chest. "Is that supposed to make it hard to breathe?"

"Absolutely."

"I'm not sure if that's comforting."

"That's normal, too." Lydia grinned. "I've pretended to be in love enough that now that I've found the real thing I can see the difference pretty clearly. That said…do you think he's in love with you?"

Allison lifted a shoulder. "Not sure. I hope so, obviously. But…like I said, we haven't really had a chance to talk." She took a long swallow of tea. "He's already said that 'we need to talk' tomorrow."

"Ominous."

"Yeah. 'We need to talk' is never a good phrase."

"Unless it is." Lydia shrugged. "Still. If it turns out that he returns the feeling, then I don't think I'd worry too much about the other stuff. If he's the one God has for you? He'll work things out."

"I get that it happened for you. And I totally believe that God takes an active role in people's lives. I just can't say I've ever seen Him overly interested in mine."

Lydia reached across the table and patted her hand. "Wait and see then."

"Do you know how frustrating that is?"

"Did you forget who you're talking to?" Lydia laughed. "And I will also point out that not waiting is never the best idea. I can vouch for the fact that learning the hard way is best avoided." She cocked her head to one side. "What else is going on?"

Allison tapped her fingers on the side of her glass. "What if he's not the one God has for me? What if I've somehow manufactured this whole thing simply because I found him attractive and wanted to be in a relationship? To actually have a chance at getting married before I'm old and gray?"

"That seems unlikely, given that he was completely uninterested in dating anyone just a few weeks ago. His change of heart? I can't see how that's anything other than God working in his life."

Allison inclined her head. "That's fair."

"Now, enough about you, let's talk about me some more."

Allison laughed. "I wondered if you'd be able to make it to dessert." She picked up the pen. "Let's talk numbers."

## 32

Phil battled nerves all day Saturday. Neither working out in his gym nor a long row on the river helped. Should he call Karin? She'd probably have some good advice, or at least something encouraging to say. But she also had her own life to worry about. Besides, he'd changed his mind about what to do with Allison tonight so many times he felt ridiculous, and she'd surely wrangle that fact out of him. He'd finally settled on throwing some steaks on the grill and whipping up a salad. They could sit on the lower deck if it stayed nice. And it was a more private place to talk than a restaurant. He prepped the salad and set it in the fridge beside the steaks that were marinating and glanced at his watch. He'd offered to drive up and get her, but Allison had declined, saying it was silly for him to make that drive twice.

Peering out the kitchen window, he saw her car and wiped his hands on his jeans. He caught sight of his bare feet. Should he run up and get shoes? *Enough. It's fine.*

He laughed at himself as he pulled open the door and leaned in the frame, watching Allison as she climbed the stairs to his porch.

"Find it okay?" He reached for the covered dish she carried and gave her a peck on the cheek.

A smile bloomed on her face. "I did. I'll admit to having wondered what these town homes looked like inside. I've noticed them the few times I've come down for the craft fair and thought how charming they were." She craned her neck to look around him.

"Come on in. I'll set this in the kitchen and give you the grand tour."

Allison toed off her shoes and left them by the door before following Phil into the kitchen. He watched as she looked around curiously. "Does it pass?"

Pink faintly tinged her cheeks. "It's lovely. I was actually trying to squash just the tiniest bit of jealousy."

He chuckled and set her dish down on the black and beige speckled granite. "Come on, I'll show you the rest, then we can throw the steaks on the grill." He showed her into the open dining room and great room that finished off the main floor. "You'll see the balcony in a few minutes, so we can skip it for now."

As he showed her the house, he tried to imagine what it looked like through her eyes. It didn't seem too much the home of a bachelor, though the double recliners and massive TV in the great room did cause an internal wince. "I've thought about making one of the bedrooms upstairs into a media room, but then I wouldn't have a guest room. Not that I've ever actually had a guest, but there's always the possibility, right?"

"It's always nice to have space for someone to visit. This," she tapped the back of one of the recliners, "looks comfy."

"Come on, I'll show you the upstairs." He pulled open what looked like a closet door and revealed the elevator with a flourish. "I hardly ever use the thing, but it's good to give it some exercise. Might as well see the place in style." He pushed the button for the second floor then grabbed Allison's hand and pulled her against him, touching his lips to hers before murmuring, "Besides, I can't kiss you on the stairs."

Allison's eyes widened with surprise and she eased back as the doors slid open. He unwillingly let her go.

"To the left is the smallest room, I use it for my office." He pointed out the guest bath as they passed it. The office was a tiny space, completely filled by an L-shaped desk.

"This is supposed to be a bedroom?"

"That's what the floor plan said." Phil grinned. "You can see why it's the office. At the other end of the hall is the guest room. Technically it's supposed to be the master bedroom, but," he shrugged, "I like the top floor better."

He followed behind as she explored the guest room. "Nice choices on the furnishings."

"That would be Karin, my sister."

"That makes more sense." Allison gave him a teasing grin.

"We can take the stairs this time." Phil gestured for her to precede him. The stairs opened directly into one large room that he used as the master bedroom. The bathroom and walk-in closet used the space beside the stairs. He crossed to the balcony and opened the door. "This is my favorite spot." He held out his hand for her, watched as she hesitatingly crossed the room, and tugged her out on to the deck.

"I'm not sure about..." Allison turned and looked out across the river. "Oooh. No wonder you love it out here."

"Yeah. The views from the other balconies are nice, but up here on the top? You can't beat it. It's why I went ahead and splurged a little for the back row of the complex. I didn't want anyone or anything to interrupt the view."

Allison turned to meet his gaze. "Phil. About the other night."

A smile played at the corner of his mouth. "Before you say anything, I just want to ask. Did you mean it?"

She closed her eyes and nodded once.

Phil pulled her into his arms and rested his cheek on hers. With his lips barely brushing against her ear, he whispered, "I love you too."

Pulling back, Allison's eyes roamed over his face, her expression serious. "You're not just saying that?"

He shook his head and met her eyes. "Love is a big word. It's much too serious to just say. I love you,

Allison." He lightly kissed the tip of her nose. "Why don't we go get those steaks started?"

❧

As Allison neared her exit on the Interstate, her cell phone rang. Frowning as she glanced at the time, she connected her Bluetooth headset.

"Hello?"

"Allison? It's Lindsey."

"What's wrong, Linds?" Allison double-checked her mirror and squeezed into the right lane. "Are you all right?"

"Yeah. I'm fine. It's my grandmother. She fell and isn't doing very well. My dad's in a panic, but he won't leave me here alone, and I'm not allowed to fly anymore."

"Why can't you…the baby." Allison turned down the street that went by her building and pulled into a parking spot on the street. "How long would he need to be gone?"

"I'm not sure. I only heard his half of the conversation with my aunt, but it doesn't sound good. Even though we live on the other side of the country, he's really close to his family. I don't want to be the one keeping him from going."

"You're his family, too, Lindsey."

"I know that. I do. But if grandma dies and he's not there…I don't know how he'll take it."

Allison rubbed her temples and tried to think. The fuzzy warmth she'd been enjoying after her dinner with Phil was rapidly slipping away. "What can I do?"

Lindsey's words came out in a rush. "I was wondering if, well, could I maybe stay with you for a little bit? Then dad would be free to go. He'd trust you to be in charge of things and I wouldn't be a bother, I promise."

She liked Lindsey and wanted to help…but this was more than an appointment or two. On the other hand, Marcus wasn't going to be any use to Lindsey if he was preoccupied with his mom. "Is your dad still up?"

"Yeah."

"All right. I'm on my way over. Let him know I'm coming, and why, and we'll talk about it. You've mentioned the idea to him already, right?"

Lindsey cleared her throat. "Kinda."

"Do better than that by the time I get there, okay?"

"Okay. Thanks, Allison."

"I'm not promising anything, Lindsey. Just that I'll talk to your dad." She disconnected the call and blew out a breath before pulling back out into the street. *Lord, give me wisdom.* As she navigated the streets, she called Phil.

"You home?" Phil's voice sent a flood of warmth through her.

"Not quite. There's been a little development." Allison filled him in on her brief conversation with Lindsey. "I'm not sure what the right answer is. I was hoping, actually, that you'd pray with me about it?"

She could hear the grin in his voice when he said, "I'd love that." While Allison drove, Phil prayed for guidance and clarity of mind as well as protection for Marcus, his mother, Lindsey, the baby, and the adoptive parents.

Allison felt a sense of peace flow over her. "Thanks."

"My pleasure…let me know how it goes. I'll keep praying for you."

The idea that someone loved her enough to pray with and for her was new to Allison. She whispered a quiet prayer of thanks as she parked in front of Lindsey's house.

After Sunday morning services at her usual church, Allison begged out of lunch with her small group and hurried back to her apartment. She had, somewhat reluctantly, agreed to let Lindsey live with her for about a month while Marcus took a leave of absence and went to be with his mom. It was possible he'd be home sooner, depending on how his mother was doing. Under the theory that it was better to plan worst case, Allison prepared for a month.

The one bedroom condo had always been plenty for her. She didn't have guests, generally, and if family came to town, they usually stayed at her parent's house. Should she ask her parents to put Lindsey up instead? No. Definitely not. Her parents would, inevitably, be the picture of politeness, but what trauma her mother would inflict in the guise of being helpful?

"No, Pippin. We're the better choice. Though I'm still surprised Marcus didn't have closer friends she could stay with." She squatted to scratch behind his ears. "I guess he really has isolated himself since his wife's death." Straightening, she clicked her tongue and got started on the rearrangements needed to accommodate a houseguest.

When the doorbell rang at just after four in the afternoon, the living room had been transformed into a semi-private area, thanks to some string and extra bed sheets. It would serve well enough as a bedroom. Allison opened the door and smiled at Lindsey. "Who'd you follow in?" She was going to send an email to the management company about enforcing the building security regulations. This had gone far past occasional and verged on defeating the purpose of a secure building.

Lindsey and Marcus shrugged in unison as they came in, each lugging a suitcase and a smaller bag.

"Where do you want these?" Marcus looked around.

Allison pointed down the hall. "Linds, you get the bedroom. After trying out the sleeper sofa, there's no way I'm putting a pregnant woman on it."

"Oh, I can't…"

"Yes, you can." She nodded down the hall again. "Take your things that way." As she watched the luggage go, she added, "You know we have laundry in the building, right, Lindsey?"

Marcus laughed as he reemerged carrying a manila envelope that he handed to Allison. "That's all the official paperwork in case anything goes wrong while I'm out of town. I tried to convince her she over-packed. If you can believe it, this is actually pared down quite a bit."

Lindsey settled on the arm of a chair that was poking out of the makeshift room divider. "I like to have options. Half of what I brought probably doesn't fit, but I couldn't stop myself."

"Well, there's plenty of room in there for you to spread out, so it's not a big deal either way."

"Thank you, Allison." Marcus took Allison's hand and patted it. "I hate to leave Lindsey right now…and I feel like I'm being a terrible parent. But if I don't go, I'm going to feel like I'm a terrible son."

With a gentle smile, Allison pulled her hand free. "Don't worry about it. We're going to have a grand time. She'll be safe and sound and you can be both a great father and the perfect son."

Marcus' eyebrows raised. "Not sure that I'd go that far, but I appreciate the sentiment." He turned to Lindsey. "You're sure you're okay with this?"

She nodded. "Go, Dad. I'll be fine."

"Be a good guest. Help out around the house, pick up after yourself."

Lindsey rolled her eyes.

Marcus looked at her sternly. "I'm serious."

"I know, Dad. Don't worry about me, I know how to behave." She crossed to her father and wrapped him in a tight hug. "I'll miss you, but this is the right thing. Give Grandma a big hug and kiss from me."

"I will." He looked at Allison over Lindsey's head and mouthed 'thank you' one more time. Pressing a kiss to his daughter's head, he eased out of her embrace and checked his watch. "I should be off to the airport. I'll call when I get to your grandmother's."

"Have a safe flight." Allison waved.

"Bye Dad. Love you." Lindsey watched until her dad turned the corner in the hall then shut the door. "I really appreciate this, Allison."

"Not a problem. Come on, let's get you settled."

Over Lindsey's objections, Allison left a set of car keys. Even though Lindsey was doing her schoolwork online until after the baby was born, she felt better knowing that if Lindsey needed to get somewhere, she could. Driving to work was a luxury that she justified to herself, despite living a block from the Metro. It just made things easier. But she could deal with commuting being a little harder for a while if it meant peace of mind about Lindsey.

Only about ten minutes behind her usual schedule, Allison waved to Sam at the front desk and turned toward Phil's office. Nerves did somersaults in her stomach as she thought through what she needed to talk to him about.

"Good morning." Just the sight of Phil brought a broad smile to Allison's face. "Got a minute?"

"Sure, come on in." He returned her grin and scooted his chair so the computer monitor wasn't in his way. "What's up?"

Allison closed the door and settled in his guest chair before clearing her throat. "I want to preface this by just telling you that I'm sorry."

"What? Why?"

"I'm getting there." She rubbed her temples as a headache began to form and let out a measured breath. *This shouldn't be so hard.* "My parents want you to come to dinner on Saturday. This Saturday...and it's kind of not optional."

His eyebrows shot up.

"Obviously you can say no, but that's just going to make it worse eventually. Oh man." Allison pressed her hand to her stomach. "Like I said, I'm sorry."

Chuckling, Phil leaned back in his chair. "It just so happens that I'm free Saturday. So I would love to have dinner with my girlfriend and her parents."

Hearing the word 'girlfriend' shot a thrill through her, despite a pang of anxiety. "Okay. I'd say I'll tell them, but, well, I already kind of agreed because I knew they weren't really open to discussion."

"Are they mass murderers or some sort of social deviants?"

"No. Of course not. Why would you even ask that?"

"Just trying to understand why you're so nervous about this." He shrugged, hands outstretched. "If they're normal people like you and me, how bad can it be, really?"

Allison hunched her shoulders. "Ooohhh, I wish you hadn't said that."

Phil laughed and shooed her with his fingers. "Get to work. It's going to be fine."

"You don't know my parents."

Shaking her head, Allison started down the hall to her own office. The last time she'd talked with her mother about Phil she'd been treated to a barrage of devilishly barbed comments covered in silk. The uncomfortable conversation flitted through her mind no matter how she tried to focus her thoughts elsewhere. *Too bad Doctor Who's not real...he could just zap me ahead to next Monday and save me the grief...And that's about as likely as dinner going well.*

34

Outside her parent's house, Allison looked at Phil and forced a smile. "I appreciate how optimistic you've been about this all week. But I'm still sorry." She glanced at the flowers nestled in the back seat. "Those are a nice touch...but I really doubt they're going to help."

"Let's wait and see if you end up owing me that apology." He flashed a grin and got out of his new car, hurrying around to get her door. Tucking her hand in his arm, he gently led her up the path. "Nice house."

"Yeah. I never know how to warn people...I always think just mentioning that they live in Great Falls should be enough. But..." Allison shrugged. "I'm afraid I come from money."

Phil chuckled. "I love you anyway."

Allison smiled and leaned forward to press the doorbell. After a minute, they heard footsteps approaching and the door swung open.

"You made it." Allison's father checked over his shoulder then gathered Allison into a fierce hug, whispering in her ear. "Your mother's on a tear tonight. I hope you warned your young man." Pulling back, he extended his hand to Phil. "Nice to see you again, Phil. We weren't properly introduced the other day. I'm Tom, Allie's dad." His eyes flicked back over his shoulder. "Best keep it to Thomas around Irene though, she hates nicknames. Now, come on in. I believe we're having hors d'oeuvers in the living room."

Allison paused to set her purse and sweater on the antique oak hall stand. She smoothed the skirt of her dress and took a deep breath before retaking Phil's arm and following her dad down the hallway.

Irene was posed in her favored armchair, reading glasses artfully resting on the tip of her nose as she flipped the pages of book. She looked up with a serene smile as they entered. "Allison, dear." She flicked her eyes down to the slim gold watch on her wrist. "Right on time."

"Mother." Allison leaned down and kissed her cheek. "You remember Phil?"

"Phillip, lovely to see you again." Irene remained seated but extended her hand.

Phil pressed her fingertips and smiled. "The pleasure is all mine. These," he offered the dozen roses he'd brought, "are for you. Thank you so much for having me in your beautiful home."

Irene's eyes widened slightly as she took the flowers and a faint but real smile flickered across her face. "They're lovely. Thank you. Won't you two sit? Lottie should be on her way with a tray shortly."

As she finished speaking, an older woman dressed in a simple black skirt and white blouse entered the room carrying a silver tray. She set the tray on the coffee table without a word and took the roses that Irene held out.

"Evening, Lottie." Allison looked at the tray. "Those look delicious, thank you."

A tiny smile graced Lottie's lips and she bobbed awkwardly before hurrying from the room.

Phil looked at Allison with questions visible in his eyes.

Irene huffed out a breath. "Honestly, Allison. I don't understand why you insist on chatting with her when guests are present."

"Because she's been a part of the family for as long as I have, or longer. And because Phil isn't simply a guest, he's my boyfriend, and I brought him here to get to know my whole family." Allison reached for one of the stuffed mushrooms.

Irene's eyes narrowed before she turned the full force of her attention on Phil. "Allison tells me you're divorced. Do you have children?"

"Mother." Was she really going to start in without any sort of preamble? This was going to be worse than she'd imagined.

"No, it's fine." Phil laid his hand on Allison's knee as she started to rise. "Yes, ma'am, I'm divorced.

And no, we didn't have any children. That, at least, is a blessing. I've seen first-hand the pain divorce can cause when children are involved."

Irene sniffed. "Your parents are divorced, then, too?"

"Yes, ma'am. Dad walked out on us when I was five and my sister three."

Silence filled the room.

Allison cleared her throat. "He's also a successful attorney, heads up the Bible study in our office, and was involved in men's ministry at his previous church." She shifted to include Phil in the conversation. "Do you think you'll do something similar now that you've made the switch to Pastor Brown's church?"

Phil opened his mouth to speak but Irene cut him off. "I think perhaps I should make myself clear."

Allison swiveled to frown at her mother and shake her head in warning.

Irene barreled on. "I don't approve of divorce. I certainly don't approve of a divorced man courting my daughter. I don't believe it's something the church should encourage or, frankly, allow."

"Now, Irene." Thomas sent his wife a warning look.

"Daddy, just don't." Allison stood and glared at her mother. "I expected more from you, Mom. You're the first one to talk about how all sin is equal at the foot of the cross and how once that sin has been confessed, it's been forgiven and we're no longer to hold it against our brothers in Christ. Well, Phil's divorce doesn't even qualify in that same discussion. His wife left him even after he did everything he could to save the marriage. Phil didn't sin." She flung her arms out with exasperation. "Even if he had, are you going to sit there and tell me that somehow you get to pick and choose what to forgive when Jesus doesn't?" She glanced at her father and nodded stiffly. "Excuse us please, Daddy. I find I'm not feeling well and would like Phil to take me home." She stalked from the room, pulse pounding in her ears. Allison grabbed her things from the hall stand and yanked open the door, nearly hitting Phil in the face.

"Hey. Allison." Phil rested his hand on her shoulder. "Slow down, take a breath."

Crossing her arms, Allison turned, her head shaking. "I'm sorry. She had no right to behave that way." She rubbed her temples. "Neither did I. I'm sorry…could you just take me home?"

Phil looked at Allison then glanced down the hall toward the sitting room with a frown. Pulling the door shut behind him, he wrapped his arm around her shoulders and led her back to the car.

CSEO

Phil pulled up in front of his sister's house. The fact that lights were on made it likely she was home, and still awake. He grabbed the pizza off the passenger seat and knocked on her front door. Karin pulled the door open and blinked.

"Did I wake you?"

"Almost. I just got home from a double and was working my way in that direction." She sniffed the air, her mouth curving into a smile. "Pizza?"

"Yeah, but I can just take it home."

Karin shook her head, opening the door wider so he could get through. "I could do with pizza. I don't think I got lunch today." She frowned. "Maybe that was yesterday. Either way, I can eat." She shut the door and shuffled behind him to the kitchen table. "So what brings you here on a Saturday night? I thought you had that big 'meet the parents' date going on."

Phil grimaced. "Oh, I did. It could have gone better." As he got out plates and served each of them a large slice of the deep-dish pizza loaded with every kind of meat imaginable, he related the abbreviated meeting with Allison's parents, the near silent drive back to Allison's apartment, and her firm insistence that she'd talk to him later.

"Wow. Sounds like her family's almost as messed up as ours." Karin wiped the sauce that was dripping down her chin.

"It didn't actually feel that way. Under it all, you could tell they love each other. They just have some communication difficulties."

"There's an understatement."

"Yeah, probably." Phil sighed. "Still, I think Allison was more hurt by her mom than angry. And embarrassed. I tried to explain that it wasn't that big a deal. But...she doesn't seem to want to believe me."

"So what now?"

"I'm not sure, Kar." Phil picked a piece of sausage off the slice of pizza and ate it. "I'm in love with her. I was really hoping this would go better than she thought it would..."

"Wait, she knew it was going to be bad? And she still made you go?"

"She tried to talk me out of it. I made her go, if anything. I don't think I fully appreciated what she was trying to tell me." He pushed his plate away. "Anyway, I wanted to have a chance to get to know them. For them to get to know me."

Karin scooted back from the table and went to the fridge. She grabbed two bottles of water, setting one down in front of Phil before resuming her spot. "That's tough. Though it's not as if you've been dating all that long. What is it, six weeks now?"

"About that, yeah. But I've known her a lot longer, don't forget. We've been coworkers and friends for several years."

Karin studied him across the table. "You really are in love with her, aren't you?"

Phil nodded. "I want to marry her."

"Whoa." She shook her head. "Did I not just remind you that it's only been six weeks? Add in the fact that, apparently, her parents despise you...don't you think you're being a tad premature?"

"It's just her mother. Her dad seems to like me just because I make Allison happy. As for the six weeks thing, didn't I just remind you that we've known each other much longer? And it's not like I want to marry her next week. We could be engaged for a year or so, if that's what she wants."

Karin drained her water and set the empty bottle back down on the table. "No proposals until I meet her."

Phil grinned. "I'd like you to meet her. I think you'll love her, she's really great. Hey, I know, you could come to church with me tomorrow."

Laughing, she shook her head. "Nice try, but no thanks. I'll go get my schedule and we can pick a Friday."

## 35

Phil stuck his head in Allison's office at noon on Monday. "Come on."

"Hang on a second." Allison typed several more words before looking up. Pink stained her cheeks. "Oh. Hi, Phil."

"Oh. Hi, Allison." He mimicked her chagrined tone and rolled his eyes. "Come on. It's lunch time."

"I've got stuff…"

He crossed the room and glanced at her monitor. Using the mouse, he saved her document and pressed his lips together. "It'll keep thirty minutes. I gave you some space yesterday, but today we're going to talk." He watched the blood drain from her face and shook his head. "It's not ominous. Come on." Grabbing her hand, he pulled her out of the chair and toward the door.

"At least let me get my purse."

"Nope, I'm buying. You're set."

Still holding on to her hand, he tugged her through the reception area, ignoring the look of obvious speculation on Sam's face as he pulled Allison into the elevator. Once they were outside in the sunshine, Phil saw her relax.

"That's better. It's always good to get away from your desk for a little bit." He glanced at her out of the side of his eye and decided she wasn't quite ready to talk about Saturday. Or meeting Karin this Friday. "How's the roomie working out?"

"Lindsey?" Allison's voice conveyed her surprise at the conversational topic as well as warmth for the girl. "She's great. Honestly, if I wasn't sleeping on the sofa bed, I'd never know she was there. I think my apartment's cleaner now than it was when I moved in. She gets her schoolwork done first thing, and has been doing chores before moving on to anything else."

He chuckled. "Sounds ideal. Any word from Marcus?"

"From what I gather from Lindsey, Grandma is hanging in, mostly, but still in pretty serious condition. So it's good he's there, though he's also apparently taking some guff about Lindsey's situation." She shrugged. "Lindsey's a little skimpy with details. I think she's trying to be as unobtrusive as she can be, plus, I wonder if she's just avoiding dealing with it. She's pretty comfortable with her plan. In fact," Allison glanced at her watch, "I need to call her when we're back and see if she's heard from Faith about a meeting time."

"Who's Faith?"

"The social worker at the adoption agency. She's setting up a meeting with the adoptive parents Lindsey selected. Lindsey wants to meet them, just for an hour or so, before everything gets moving. But she's changed her mind about that so many times, I'm kind of on call."

Phil squeezed her hand. "You're amazing."

"She gets to me. I'm not sure what it is, but she's this incredibly brave young woman in so many ways and a frightened child in others. I just want to do what I can to help."

Phil stopped in front of a food truck offering Afghan fare. "What are you in the mood for?"

Allison looked back the three blocks they'd traveled. "We passed four different Gyro trucks."

"Ah…but you've never had one from here, have you? These are the real thing." Phil grinned and stepped to the window, chatting amiably with the man in the truck before ordering two Gyro combos. He handed the sodas to Allison and carried a box lid with two foil wrapped paper plates. "Let's grab a bench over in that park." He nodded across the street to a small green area outside a group of buildings.

When they were settled and Allison had taken a bite, Phil cleared his throat. "Best ever, yes?"

"Yeah, you were right. These are better than I expected." She dabbed at the juice dripping down her chin. "How'd you find them?"

"I kept walking past the last one I tried. When I found him, I knew I was done looking." He glanced over at her. "Seems to be a theme in my life these days." He watched Allison swallow and smothered a chuckle at her obvious consternation. "Which leads me to Saturday."

"Phil…"

"Allison. It's fine." He held her gaze until he was reasonably sure she believed he meant it. "We'll try again another time. Maybe if we invite them down to dinner at my house, where I have the home court advantage, things'll go better."

"She's still going to be obnoxious."

He laughed. "Did you forget I'm a lawyer too? I eat obnoxious for breakfast. Plus, I suspect your dad's working on her. You didn't see his face when you stormed out."

"I didn't storm out."

"Oh honey, you did." He patted her hand. "And I appreciate you standing up for me, but it really wasn't necessary. I know where she stands. I knew that beforehand. She'll come around. It's clear she loves you. We just need to convince her that I'm right for you. I am, right?"

"Of course you are. Why do you think I was so upset?"

"I worried, just a little, that you were embarrassed of me."

"Oh, Phil. I'm sorry. That was never my intention." She rubbed her fingers on a napkin before taking his hand. "It didn't even occur to me that you might get that impression. Forgive me?"

"Absolutely…on one condition." He grinned. "Come to dinner at my sister's house next Friday. She's the only real family I have besides my mom. You'll meet her at some point, but if you thought your relationship with your mother was fraught…"

Allison laughed. "I'd love to. And I'd even like to meet your mom."

"Well, generally Karin and mom won't be in the same room together. So we'll do two separate dinners." At her curious look, Phil frowned. "Long story. I'll fill you in another time. As it is, we're very close to the end of the thirty minutes I promised you, so we probably should hurry back."

They crammed their trash into an already over-full can and hurried through the crowds of office workers filling the sidewalks. At the door to their building, Allison grabbed Phil's elbow to stop him from going in. "You're sure you're not mad about Saturday?"

"Not in the slightest." He kissed the tip of her nose. "I love you, Allison. It's going to take more than a semi-hostile mother to scare me away."

## 36

Allison got back to her desk after a long client meeting and flopped into her chair. It continued to amaze her how some people could desperately need a criminal defense attorney and not understand why. Or maybe they just didn't want to admit it, even to themselves? She rubbed her eyes as she frowned at the blinking message light on her office phone. Putting off those calls for another minute or two, she checked her cell phone. The voicemail symbol was lit on it, too. After punching in her passcode, she listened to the messages on her cell while scrolling through the Caller ID on her office phone.

"Allison?" Lindsey's recorded voice was a whisper and held a trace of worry. "I think someone's in the apartment. I'm not sure what to do. Call me back. If you don't, then I guess I'll call the police? Call me back."

Alarmed, Allison skipped to the next message. The content was similar, but the frantic tone of Lindsey's voice had increased. In the background, she could hear things crashing and breaking. She didn't need to hear any more. Throwing her laptop into its bag, she grabbed her purse, and hurried to the door.

"I'm heading home if anyone needs me." Allison tossed the words at the receptionist as she flew through the lobby.

"Wait, what?" Sam hurried after her into the elevator area.

"Something's happened. Not sure what yet, but I'm heading home. I should be back in tomorrow." The elevator came and Allison jabbed the button for the parking garage before she was fully inside. She was half-way to her usual parking space when she remembered she'd been leaving the car for Lindsey. She dialed Phil.

"Phil Reid."

"Phil, it's Allison. I need you."

"What's up?"

"Could you drive me home? I'll explain on the way, but I think I need to get there faster than the Metro."

"Sure. Meet you out front?"

"Thanks." Allison headed up the stairs to the building's main lobby. She hadn't been waiting long when Phil stepped out of an elevator.

"Hey. What's going on?" Phil jingled his keys as he held the door for her and nodded toward the parking garage he used.

"I've got some frantic voice mails from Lindsey. It sounds like someone broke into my apartment...I've been trying to get a hold of her but she's not picking up."

Phil increased his pace. "Did she call the police?"

"She said she was going to. So maybe they're there and that's why she's not answering. I don't know...I'm worried."

Phil unlocked the car and held her door while she got in. After hurrying around to his side, he squeezed her hand briefly before backing out of his spot and pointing the car toward her place.

Traffic was lighter in the middle of the day and they made good time. Phil let Allison out at the front entrance of her building and she rushed through the lobby doors. When she made it to her floor, she saw a small collection of uniformed police standing outside her door. She exhaled, a sense of relief flooding her. There were no stretchers or ambulance personnel visible, so hopefully Lindsey was all right.

"Excuse me?" Allison addressed the nearest officer. "I'm Allison Vasak. This is my apartment. Is Lindsey all right?"

"Allison?" Lindsey rushed through the door carrying Pippin and flung her free arm around Allison.

Allison returned the hug before leaning back, her eyes roaming over Lindsey's face. "You're okay?"

Lindsey nodded.

"What happened?"

"Ma'am." The officer cleared his throat. "We received a call about a suspected break in from this young lady. She said she's staying with you while her dad's out of town?"

"That's correct. I have temporary guardianship papers inside if you need to see them?"

"I don't think we do at this time." He scribbled something on the clipboard he was carrying before returning his attention to Allison. "We responded and found the mess, but the suspect had fled moments prior to our arrival. This young lady indicated she believed the suspect is a female. Probably heard the sirens or looked out the window and saw the flashing lights, and decided it was time to leave."

"Thank you, officer." Allison kept her arm around Lindsey's shoulders and turned to look through the door. Her eyes stung when she saw the damage. Every picture had been ripped from the wall, glass smashed. There were several jagged slices in each piece of furniture and the stuffing was boiling out of them. Her laser printer had been tipped on its side and appeared dented. Shards of glass and torn papers littered the floor in every direction.

"I'm sorry, Allison. I should have done something…"

Swallowing back a combination of tears and rage, Allison squeezed the girl's shoulders. "No. You did exactly the right thing. This is just stuff." She took a steadying breath. "I'm glad you're not hurt."

Phil hurried down the hallway. "Sorry that took so long, parking around here is awful during the day." He peered through the door and gasped.

"Yeah. That's about right." Allison rubbed her forehead and turned to the policeman. "When can I start cleaning up?"

"We should be finished in another half hour or so. We're looking for prints and anything else that might help us identify the suspect."

"You didn't see the person?" Phil looked at Lindsey who shook her head.

"Not really. I heard her screaming and swearing...so I grabbed the cat and hid." She turned her pale face up to Allison. "I'm so sorry."

"Stop apologizing. You did exactly right." Allison rubbed her hand up and down on Lindsey's arm.

"Her?" Phil glanced at the officer. "I have an idea who it was."

Allison turned to Phil. "Who?"

"Brandi." Phil pulled out his phone and looked up the most recent information Grant had sent him about her whereabouts. "I can forward this to you, officer...but it's probably already in the system since she's wanted for questioning in another investigation." He kneaded the back of his neck and looked back inside Allison's apartment. "I feel like this is my fault."

"No." Allison linked the fingers of her free hand with his. "If it was her, she did this all on her own. And we don't know for sure that it was her...though I guess I can't really imagine who else it would have been. For now, I'm grateful no one was hurt, though I suppose we ought to find another place to stay until I can get things cleaned up." She closed her eyes and made a strangled laugh. "I'll call my parents. Won't that be fun to explain?"

Phil ducked his head. "There's probably not a better choice, is there?"

"Not really. They've got the room and they'll love you, Lindsey." She waited for the officer to finish talking with another of his people then asked, "Is it all right if we go in and just pack up a few things?"

"Yeah, that should be fine. Just make sure you check in with me before you go."

Allison sent Phil back to the office. He was reluctant, but finally agreed to do as she asked. She and Lindsey got their necessities put together, herded Pippin into his carrier, double checked that the police were okay with them leaving, and headed to Allison's parents' house.

When they pulled up alongside the curb, Lindsey's eyes widened. "Shouldn't we have called?"

"I think it's better to explain once we're in and settled. Mom won't say no in person, and with the way I ended our last conversation, it's very likely she'd say no on the phone just on principle." *Especially if I explained the whole situation.* Allison sighed. "Sorry to involve you in all my family drama."

Lindsey chuckled. "Seems fair to me. You've had your share of ours."

With a wan smile, Allison got out of the car. "Come on. Leave the bags for now, I'll get them once we've chatted a while." She headed toward the front door with Lindsey following behind.

"You ring the bell at your parent's house?" Lindsey tilted her head. "Can't you just go in?"

Allison scoffed. "Right."

Tom opened the door and grinned. "Allison. What a nice surprise. Your mother's actually out with the ladies still, their lunch ran long."

"Even better." Allison gave her dad a hug then gestured to Lindsey. "This is my friend Lindsey. She's been staying with me while her dad's out of town for a family emergency."

"Pleasure to meet you." Tom's eyes flicked down to her belly but he didn't say anything. "Where are my manners. Come in, come in. We might have some pie still. Anyone up for pie?"

"Pie is always a good idea, Dad, you know that." Allison followed her dad toward the kitchen. She checked over her shoulder to be sure Lindsey was following. The girl looked awestruck. She hung back until Lindsey caught up. "Not hungry for pie?"

"Oh…pie is good. But this house…" Lindsey blinked. "You grew up here?"

"Not the whole time. We moved here when I started high school. Dad had some investments that he timed just right." She shrugged. "This is all my mother. If it was up to Dad, we'd still be in our old, normal sized house. But this makes her happy, so we go with it."

They entered the kitchen and found Tom seated at the island with a piece of pie in front of him and two slices in front of the stools to his left. "So, what brings you over in the middle of a work day, Allie?"

Hopping onto the stool, Allison grinned at the nickname. "Mmm. No one makes chocolate pie like Lottie." She sighed happily before relating the news of the break in and the possibility of Phil's ex-wife being involved. She watched as her father's face paled then turned a dark red.

Clenching his fork, Tom stabbed his pie and looked at Lindsey. "You're sure you're all right? And the baby?"

"Yes sir. I hid." Lindsey hunched her shoulders.

Tom nodded vigorously. "Just the right thing to do. Never know with the crazies today." He turned a piercing stare at Allison. "I thought you had to be buzzed into the building. That was one of the things I liked about your place."

"Lots of the tenants let people follow them through. You just have to look like you know what you're doing." Allison frowned. "I hope this might make people a bit more vigilant. And yes, the manager is going to look through the lobby security tapes with the police to see if they can figure out who let Brandi in."

"You'll stay here until your place is put back together." Tom nodded to punctuate his words.

"Dad, I don't want to put you out. Besides, Mom might have something to say about it."

Tom waved away her objections. "Your mother will agree with me. She's not irritated with you, no matter what you think." He smiled. "In fact, she rather likes your young man. It'll just take her a bit to be willing to admit it to anyone."

"Starting with herself?" This wasn't a conversation she wanted to have right now. Possibly ever. Allison pushed her empty plate away.

Tom laughed, a deep, throaty sound. "You know your mother. Now," he tapped a finger against his lips, "I think you should take the Jack and Jill guest suite. That way you can both have your own room but share the en suite. Save you from having to go up and down the hall at night, should you need the restroom."

"Thanks, Dad."

"Yes. Thank you, Mr. Vasak."

"Tom, please. Or Thomas if Irene's around. She's always hated nicknames. Though I guess if you grow up being called 'Re-re' you're entitled." He stood and offered his hand to Lindsey. "Let me show you to your rooms, and then I'll go out and get your bags."

Allison handed him her car keys. She could always count on her dad. And he'd smooth things over with mom. It was good to have people to rely on, even when you didn't always understand them. "I know the way. You can just go get the bags now and save yourself a few steps. Pip's in his carrier in there, too."

## 37

Phil called Grant on his way back to the office. Grant agreed to contact the police officer in charge of the car vandalism case and make sure that he was aware of the new investigation. Since the crimes had occurred in different counties, it was a good idea to make sure everyone was on the same page. Maybe that would help speed up the process of finding Brandi and getting her behind bars.

Maybe there was some truth to the idea that divorced people ought not to remarry. His heart sank as he considered the danger he'd inadvertently put Allison in. And Lindsey. A chill ran through him. What if Allison had been working from home? He didn't know what had happened to unhinge Brandi, but her behavior had bounded past vindictive and hurdled straight into crazy.

Phil didn't feel like going home. He'd managed to finish out the work day, but the thought of an evening at home left him restless. After some debate, he decided to see what the Wednesday night offerings were like at his new church. Maybe he'd be able to talk to Paul for a few minutes. *Unlikely, since it's a work night for him.*

When he walked into the foyer, he saw Kevin leaning against a wall, talking to a couple. The woman was holding a baby who appeared to be asleep and a little girl was dancing in circles around their group.

Kevin spotted him and waved. "Phil. Come meet the Stephensons."

Phil crossed the foyer and extended his hand. "Hi. Phil Reid."

"Matt and Laura, this is Phil." Kevin's eyes sparkled with humor.

"Oh, wow. Phil." Laura grasped his hand and shook it as she looked him over. "Really nice to meet you."

Matt shook his hand and grinned. "We've heard a lot about you. Good to finally meet you." He nodded to the little girl dancing. "That's Jennie, and this is Grace."

Phil peeked at the peacefully sleeping baby and smiled. "They're both lovely. Congratulations." He cleared his throat. "So, I guess you're friends of Allison's?"

Matt clutched his heart and made an exaggerated expression of hurt. "What? She hasn't told you all about us? I'm crushed."

"She might have mentioned you." Phil pretended to think then shook his head. "No, just Laura, actually."

Laura laughed as Matt said, "Ow."

Kevin grinned at Matt and Laura. "Told you."

"You're right." Laura shifted Grace and looked at Phil. "Kevin mentioned that you'd fit into our group perfectly. Anyone who gets Matt's bizarre sense of humor is always welcome to hang out."

"So." Phil glanced around the still empty hallway. "I'm either incredibly early or I didn't pay attention to what time things get going around here on Wednesdays."

"Most of the activities start around seven." Kevin glanced at his watch. "So you're only about thirty minutes late. No one else in our class showed up, so we're just waiting on Lydia and then we're going to go get a late dinner. Want to join us?"

"Yeah. I'd like that. You're sure?"

"Of course. Why don't we swing by and see if Allison wants to come, too?" Laura turned and shot her daughter a look that instantly calmed the dancing to a more manageable level.

"She's at her folks for a while." Something had to be done about Brandi. He'd never considered himself especially prone to violence before, but he was beginning to understand how people got there. He summarized the situation.

Lydia arrived as Phil related the end of the story. "She's okay? And Lindsey?"

"Yeah, they're both fine. But there was a lot of property damage."

Kevin twined his fingers through Lydia's as he watched Phil. "You know this isn't your fault, right?"

"Yeah, I guess. Though you have to admit, I'm somewhat responsible. If I wasn't in the picture, Brandi would never have targeted her."

"Dude." Matt frowned. "Don't be ridiculous." The others chimed in with their agreement.

Phil appreciated the thought, but couldn't quite bring himself to believe it. His past—his mistakes—had put two innocent women in danger. If not for him, none of this would have happened.

## 38

Allison woke Thursday morning feeling fuzzy and confused. She scowled at the unfamiliar room. The events of the previous day came flooding back. She threw her feet over the side of the bed and tip-toed into the bathroom. Peeking through the door into Lindsey's adjoining bedroom, she smiled to see the girl still sleeping soundly, Pippin curled up at the foot of her bed. She pulled the door closed and locked it before turning the shower as hot as it would go.

Dressed in jeans and a long sleeved shirt, she went to the kitchen and slid onto a stool to watch Lottie fix breakfast. "Morning, Lottie."

"Miss Allison." The older woman turned with a big smile. "It's nice to have you here with us, even under the circumstances. You still take your breakfast the same way?"

"That'd be great, thanks." Allison poured a mug of coffee from the carafe that sat on the counter in front of her. "I thought Mom and Dad said you were semi-retired? Getting here for breakfast doesn't really seem like retirement to me."

Lottie laughed. "Normally your folks are on their own with a bowl of cereal or whatever they can scare up. But your dad called me last night to see if I would come to make breakfast." She shrugged and expertly flipped a pancake. "I'm not going to let my favorite girl go without a good start to the day. And a mother-to-be needs more than cereal, too." She tilted her head appraisingly. "She still sleeping?"

Allison nodded over the top of her coffee. "I thought I'd let her rest as long as she needed. I don't want her to try and help with the clean up, and she would. She'll be safer, here."

Tom came in looking chipper. He kissed Allison's cheek and settled on a stool next to her. "Morning, sweetheart."

"Morning, Dad." She looked beyond him to the hall. "Where's Mom?"

He chuckled. "She's still primping. With a guest in the house, she wasn't satisfied with her normal breakfast attire."

"Lindsey's still sleeping…or did she mean me?"

Lottie turned, hands on her hips. "Miss Allison."

Lottie had never needed many words to put Allison in her place. She hunched her shoulders and mumbled, "Sorry."

Tom nodded. "She's right, you know. Your mother loves you. She just has a hard time relating to you as a grown woman sometimes. She's had a completely different life than you've had, but she's proud as can be of you."

"She has an odd way of showing it." Allison sipped her coffee. "I know, Dad. I do. I just get tired of always having to be the one who's wrong, even when I'm not. And Dad? Phil's not going away. She needs to get used to him."

Tom patted her shoulder. "I'm working on her. Just give her some time to come around." His eyes flicked to the hallway. "And maybe keep the whole ex-wife connection out of any talk about your apartment? Because that's not going to help things."

"Already figured that one out, thanks Dad."

Irene came in, patting at the back of her perfectly arranged hair. When she saw Allison she smiled and crossed the room for a perfunctory kiss. "Good morning, dear. Where's your friend?"

"Still sleeping." Allison poured another mug of coffee and offered it to her mother. "I thought it'd be better for her to rest."

Irritation flickered across Irene's face before she schooled her features into a serene smile. "Of course. Lottie? We'll not hold breakfast. Just keep something warm for her."

"Certainly." Lottie watched Irene head through the door into the dining room and rolled her eyes.

Allison smothered a snicker.

"You two might as well go on and get settled. Seems like a leisurely breakfast in the kitchen isn't on the menu today. I'll be right out with the platters."

"Can I help?" Allison stood and reached for the stack of plates and silverware.

Lottie shooed her away. "You know your mother won't have that. Even if your guest is asleep. Now, both of you, go sit so everyone gets fresh pancakes."

Tom scooped up the plates anyway and gestured for Allison to get his coffee cup and lead the way.

C3 80

Standing in the doorway of her apartment, Allison swallowed back tears. It really was a disaster. She had almost talked herself through the door when her cell phone rang.

"Hello?"

"Hey. Where are you?"

Despite the chaos in front of her, Allison smiled. "Hey, Phil. I'm standing in the doorway to my apartment trying to convince myself to go in and start cleaning."

"Ugh. If there's more to do this weekend, I can help, but I've got court in," he paused and Allison heard shuffling papers in the background, "forty minutes."

"Don't worry about it. I took the rest of the week off, and I may end up taking next week, depending on how things go."

"Are you sure you want to do it yourself? I'd be happy to pay for someone…"

"It's not your fault, Phil. You didn't cause this."

"Neither did you."

Allison sighed. "I know. But it's my place. I appreciate the thought, I really do, but it's okay."

"All right. If you change your mind, just say the word."

She chuckled. "Good luck in court. I love you."

"I love you, too. Call you tonight?"

"You'd better." She hung up smiling and pushed herself through the door and into the wreckage.

Where should she start? She might as well be methodical about it. Allison went into the kitchen. She'd get one room completely finished before worrying about the next. She had all the broken dishes swept up and double bagged and a load of pots and pans in the dishwasher when the intercom for the front door buzzed. Wary, she pressed the button. "Yes?"

"It's Lydia, can I come up?"

Allison pressed the door release and frowned at the rubble as she walked to the door.

"Wow. Phil wasn't exaggerating." Lydia came in and set her purse by the door before giving Allison a hug. "I came to offer my services in exchange for floral help."

"Floral help?" Allison closed the door and gestured to the kitchen. "I'm starting in here, figured I'd work my way through one room at a time."

"Flowers. Floral. Wedding?" Lydia blew out a breath as she surveyed the kitchen. "Point me in the right direction."

"Pick a cabinet. Sort through what's in there and see what was mangled and what can be saved. It's neurotic, I realize, but I'm going to sanitize everything before putting it away again."

Lydia nodded sympathetically. "Believe me, I understand the need to wash things." She pulled open a lower cabinet, winced at the jumbled mess inside, and sat on the floor to start sorting. "So. I don't want to just do roses. I want something unique...but that's where my inspiration ends."

Allison boosted herself onto the counter and chuckled as she opened a cupboard, barely dodging a vase that fell out and shattered on the floor as the door swung wide. She hopped down and grabbed the broom and dustpan to take care of the new shards on the floor. "Well, it's spring and you're using pink." She paused in her sweeping. "Can florists get cherry blossoms?"

⁂

Other than the contents of cupboards waiting in line by the sink, they had the kitchen put back to rights and the dishwasher wooshing away on its third load by lunchtime.

"I need food." Lydia groaned dramatically and melted over the arm of the sofa.

Laughing, Allison checked her watch. "Seems reasonable." She stretched and felt several vertebrae pop as they adjusted back into place. "I could use a break from the chaos myself. There's a nice deli down the street about a block. Feel like a walk?"

"As long as there's food at the end, I'm in." Lydia bounced off the couch and headed for the door. "Let's go, pokey."

Making sure to lock the door, Allison followed behind. "Mind if I call and check on Lindsey real fast?"

Lindsey was laughing when she answered. "Hello?"

"Hey, it's Allison. I just wanted to check in and make sure you're doing all right."

"I'm great. Your mom is fun."

Allison blinked. *My mom?* "Um. Okay?" Quiet chatter she couldn't quite make out continued in the background. "Do you need anything?"

"Nope, but thanks. Irene already took me out for a few things I didn't think to grab when I packed. Oh, actually, yes. Do you think you could grab the rest of my stuff when you come back tonight? Since it's so crowded at your place, even after it's all put together, Irene's convinced me to just stay here 'til Dad's back."

"Really? Are you in the right house?"

Lindsey laughed. "Do you want to talk to your mom?"

"Yeah. That'd be good." Allison pointed across the street as they waited at the light.

"Hello, dear." Irene came on the line. "Did you need something?"

"Mom. You don't have to put Lindsey up more than a few days. I'll have things back together by the weekend."

"Pish posh. And don't roll your eyes at me."

Her mother knew her too well. She'd been about to do just that.

"You know I love that expression. Anyway, in this case it fits. Lindsey's delightful and we have more than enough room. Her father already said it was all right with him."

"You talked to Marcus already?"

"Of course. I'm not asking someone's daughter to stay at my home without talking to her father. You know that. Now, just toss the rest of her things in your car when you head home tonight and I'll make sure they get cleaned as needed."

"If you're sure."

"Have I ever not been? It's fine. We're about to start another round of backgammon, so I'm going to run. Have a great day, honey."

Allison frowned at the phone before tucking it into her pocket.

"Something wrong?" Lydia paused with her hand on the door to the deli then stepped aside as another group headed in.

Hoping she didn't look as dazed as she felt, Allison shook her head. "No. Well, maybe. My mother invited Lindsey to stay with them until her dad is back. It's like she doesn't realize the girl's pregnant. And not married. And sixteen."

"Your mother can't be that bad."

"No...she's worse." There was simply no way to reconcile the mother she knew with her actions toward Lindsey. "She's up in arms that I'm dating someone who's divorced. Like it's the worst sin a person can commit. And it's not like I didn't have a moment or two of doubt, because I do take marriage seriously. I get where she's coming from, kind of. But he didn't leave his wife, she left him."

"From what I've gathered, which is very little and only gleaned through years of listening to what's not being said, Phil tried very hard to keep the marriage together, long after the ex made it clear she had no interest. Have you told your mom all that?"

"I thought I had." Allison shrugged. "Let's get a sandwich. I haven't figured my mother out in the last twenty-seven years. It's probably not going to happen in the next five minutes."

Lydia slung her arm around Allison's shoulders. "My treat, then. And afterward maybe we can hunt up some ice cream."

39

Allison woke earlier than usual on Friday and went in search of her dad. She found him, as she'd expected, in the room that was originally intended to be an office that he'd converted into his library. He was stretched out in a dark leather arm chair, his stocking clad feet propped on the matching ottoman. Reading glasses perched at the end of his nose.

He looked up over the half moon lenses when she came in and smiled, setting aside his paperback. "Allie-cat, you're up early."

"You haven't called me that since I was ten." Allison gave him a fierce hug before flopping into a matching chair next to his.

"What's on your mind?" Tom took off his reading glasses and folded them, setting them on top of his book.

"I'm not really sure how to start." She clasped her hands together in her lap and stared at them for a moment before looking up to meet her father's eyes. "Does Mom even like me?"

"Of course she does. She adores you." He cocked his head to one side. "Why in Heaven's name would you even ask?"

Allison shrugged, feeling sheepish and small. "I just don't feel like she ever takes anything I do seriously." She twisted her fingers together. She knew this conversation wasn't going to be easy, but she hadn't been able to shake the idea that it needed to happen. And she knew her dad would be honest. "She was so upset when I chose computer science for my major in college. Do you remember?"

Tom nodded.

"And then, when it turned out that in many ways she was right, and I wasn't cut out for programming as a career…she never said 'I told you so,' but she oozed smugness."

"Are you sure you weren't just imagining it? From what I heard and saw, she was only supportive. Sure, she was a bit upset that you'd spent all your time in college in a computer lab, but that was more because the one thing she wanted you to leave college with…"

"Was an engagement ring. I know." Allison sighed. "Just one more way I'm a colossal disappointment."

"Allie. Neither of us is disappointed in you. How could we be?" The concern on her father's face was evident.

The hurt in her heart she thought she'd buried deep flared up. "Then why can't she ever say something positive? I did well at law school. I'm a *good* lawyer. I help people, and I'm picky about who I represent even though, as understanding as they are, my firm wishes I'd be less choosy." Focusing on her breathing, Allison worked hard to swallow her tears. "And Phil…he's a good Christian man…I love him, Daddy."

"Oh, baby." Tom held out his hand and waited until she took it. He gently pulled her out of the chair and into his lap.

She buried her face in his shoulder and he wrapped his arms around her.

"Your mother loves you and only wants the best for you. Beside that? She's so proud of you she can hardly keep buttons on her blouses. Don't shake your head, it's true. We're a family of outspoken individuals and we butt heads, but I don't think it ever occurred to your mother, or to me, that you'd think that meant we didn't love you. Both of us appreciate you for the woman you've become." He sighed and rested his cheek on her hair. "Do you want to know what I'm proudest of right now?"

"Sure." Allison sniffled.

"Despite how hurt you feel, you've kept us in your life and never let on that we'd done that to you. So many families would have let something like that rip them apart. But you've forgiven and continued to be in our lives. It's a beautiful gift, Allie." He sat for a moment. "I'll talk to your mother. It's harder, as you age, to change the way you think and act. But once she knows how she's hurt you, I have no doubt that your mother will make the effort. What about you?"

Allison nodded.

"There's my girl." Tom gave her a squeeze before nudging her off his lap. "What do you say we go see what Lottie's got planned for breakfast today?" He gave her a conspiratorial smile. "I tried to plant the seed last night that French toast wouldn't be unwelcome."

Laughing, Allison wiped residual moisture from her eyes. "You're angling for all the things Mom's put on the never-eat list, aren't you?"

Tom feigned innocence. "Not at all. I just want our guest to be well fed." With a grin, he sauntered from the room.

Lighter at heart, Allison followed.

&#x3053;&#x3056;&#x3057;

Phil, Kevin, and Lydia showed up at Allison's apartment at lunch time. Phil carried several bags of food and placed them on the kitchen counter. There was an enticing variety of smells emanating from them. Kevin and Lydia followed, each carrying an armful of flattened storage boxes.

"You guys are the best." Allison threw her arms around each of them as they came in. "Just drop the boxes against the wall. The kitchen is put back together, let's eat in there. I'm starved. Any news on finding Brandi?" Allison looked at Phil.

He shook his head and distributed lunches around the small table. "Not that I've heard. I was hoping the officer in charge of your case might have been in touch." Phil frowned. "I know it's going to take some time, but I'm anxious to get this settled. I'm sorry this has bled into your life."

Allison waved away his apology. "I've been looking for the bright side in all of this and I realized that I've been meaning to do a good Spring Cleaning for three years now." With a grin, she gestured to a neatly stacked pile in the corner of the kitchen. "Now I've made the time to go through what I have. And honestly, I don't even know where some of this stuff came from. So we'll pack it up and hopefully someone at the Salvation Army can use it."

Kevin chuckled, taking a big bite of burger. "That explains the boxes you asked for. I was wondering why you needed them when all you were doing was tidying up. Though having seen the living room, the damage is more extensive than I first imagined."

"That's after some significant work, too." Lydia shuddered. "You should've seen it yesterday. We did the kitchen and then got started in there. If it was Brandi? She's got a serious mean streak."

"Yeah. Chalk that up to something I didn't know when we were married." Phil balled up his trash. "Where do you want me to start?"

Everyone else quickly finished their lunch and Allison pointed out the various areas that needed to be addressed. Without further comment, they got to work. By dinnertime, the living room and bathroom were back to normal. All the boxes had been filled and loaded into Phil's car. The Salvation Army was an easy detour for him on the way home, so he volunteered to drop them off. The clothes and linens that didn't need dry cleaning were all packed up for Allison to wash at her parent's house. Lydia had a pile of suits to drop off at the dry cleaner.

"Thanks again, guys. This actually feels doable now. I shouldn't have any issue finishing up over the weekend. Hopefully the maintenance man will be by to change the locks tomorrow."

"If he isn't, let me know and I'll come take care of it." Phil patted his pocket to make sure he had his car key. "You're sure you don't want to go out for dinner?"

"I'd love to." Allison stretched up to kiss his cheek.

"Awwww." Kevin laughed while Lydia swatted him.

"But," Allison glared at Kevin, "I should get back to my folk's house and start on the mountain of laundry and spend some time with Lindsey. Surprisingly, she seems to be having a grand time with my mom, but I just think I ought to be around, in case Linds needs a break."

"Will we see you at church?" Lydia adjusted her grip on the basket of dry cleaning.

Blowing out a breath, Allison nodded. "Yeah. I think it's probably time to admit that I'm changing churches." She glanced at Phil from the corner of her eye. "Just makes sense to be where my friends are."

Kevin slapped Phil on the back. "You've now accomplished what I've been trying to do for years. Congrats, man." He grinned at Allison. "About time. Come on, Lyd. If we're going to get those dropped off and still make your mother's wedding planning dinner, we should get going." He cast a mock-desperate glance over his shoulder as they headed for the door. "Unless someone needs me?"

Allison laughed. "Nope, have fun. And thanks for dropping those off."

Phil shut the door behind Kevin and Lydia and held out his arms. Allison walked into them, resting her head on his shoulder. "Thanks for taking a half day to help. I know you had stuff at work you had to rearrange. This has hit me harder than I realized."

"It's tough to have a place you thought was safe made vulnerable." Phil ran his hands down her arms. "I'm glad I was able to help even a little."

Allison tilted her head up when he stopped talking and watched him. "What's going on?"

He turned to face her, his expression pained. "I don't want Brandi to taint what we have, but I feel like her stain is always going to be there. It doesn't seem fair to you."

"I appreciate that. I do." She reached up to cup his cheek. "But I'm not worried about fair." Allison pursed her lips and searched his face. "Just before the Christmas party, Kevin asked me if I minded about your divorce and all that implied."

"Before the Christmas party?" Phil looked at her, confused.

"Long story, involving a harebrained idea to try and make you jealous which, thankfully, Kevin talked me out of." She waved that away. "Anyway, what I told him was true then and it's even truer now. I get that you have a past. But I do too. It's not the same as yours, sure, but we're both sinners, saved by grace. And that's enough for me. You're enough for me."

He rested his forehead on hers, his arms circling her waist. "You're an amazing woman, Allison."

"I love you, too."

40

Phil tapped his foot and glanced at his watch. Karin was running late, as usual. He turned to look at the sparkling displays that filled the jewelry store's window. He could just go in by himself...but he knew he'd be overwhelmed in a minute if he did.

The small jewelry store just off Occoquan's quaint main street had caught his eye the first time he'd seen it. Thinking he'd find a Christmas gift for his mom and sister, he'd gone in. And promptly turned right back around. The lavish displays that surrounded the room had made his head spin and turned something as simple as finding a pair of earrings into an affair more nerve wracking than his first court appearance.

"Hi. I'm late. Sorry." Karin ran the last few steps and stopped, panting. "I had to park down under the bridge. I thought for sure there'd be street parking free on a week night."

"You could've parked in my driveway and walked over."

Karin closed her eyes. "Yeah, if I hadn't been so distracted by being late, I might have thought of that." She laughed. "Are you sure you want someone as ditzy as your sister helping with this?" Sobering, she studied his face. "Are you sure you're ready to be doing this?"

"Yes to both." Phil hooked his arm through hers.

"All right. But promise me you're not giving this to her until I have a chance to bestow a seal of approval."

"No pressure though, right?" Phil opened the door and gestured for her to go first. "Besides, you'll get to meet her Friday. That's just three short days away." He paused on the threshold, the door closing and bumping his heels. His palms got sweaty just looking around at the glittering display cases. "How do we start?"

"I've died and gone to heaven." She turned to Phil, beaming. "I'm glad I didn't know this was here, I'd be visiting you a lot more often. As for starting, are you going traditional?"

Phil shrugged.

"Phil." Karin sighed, shaking her head. "Have you put any thought into this yet?"

Phil hunched his shoulders.

"Okay. We'll start with traditional and if none of that grabs you, we'll move on." She frowned at her brother. "This would be easier if I knew her too, then I could provide suggestions." She took two steps down into the main part of the room and glanced in each case as she made her way around the perimeter. She stopped on the far side of the room and turned, gesturing for Phil to join her. "How big are her hands?"

Phil tugged a ring out of his pocket. "This fits the right finger."

"Good to know, but not really what I meant. How'd you get that without her knowing?" She discretely waved off a sales lady. "Never mind, not important. Does she have big hands? Small hands? Meaty hands?"

Phil laughed and grabbed Karin's hand, frowning and examining it from various angles. "They're about the same size as yours, actually."

"Yeah? Then she can handle a slightly bigger stone. Good for her, maybe not as good for you." She looked down at the rings. "Answer without thinking, okay? Just blurt out the first thing that comes to mind."

"Okay?" She had good taste, that's why he wanted her here. But what was she up to?

"Favorite fruit?"

"Apple."

"Favorite sport?"

"Baseball, I guess. You know I don't love sports." Phil drew his eyebrows together. "How does this help?"

"Zip it. Last one, have you ever cried because you're happy?"

Phil gawked at his sister. "Are you serious? I'm a guy. I would never admit to crying because I was bleeding to death internally, let alone because I was happy."

Karin rolled her eyes. "Fine, we'll leave teardrop as a maybe. But given your other answers," she glanced at the sales woman and nodded for her to come over, tapping the case, "could we see this one, this one, and these two, please?"

The woman smiled and unlocked the case, removing each ring and placing them on a black velvet pad. "Those are all lovely choices." She glanced between Phil and Karin before addressing Karin. "Not for you, I take it?"

"Ha. No, I'm his sister. Though of course if he wants to buy me something while I'm here, I'm not going to say no. Just probably not a diamond. Come closer, man. You can't choose an engagement ring from half way across the room. She won't bite. Right?"

"Right." The saleswoman picked up the ring with the largest stone and gestured for Karin to slide it on. "This is an ideal cut, which basically means it has the maximum sparkle, one carat round solitaire. It's colorless, rated E, and internally flawless. The setting is platinum."

"This is gorgeous. What do you think?" Karin admired the ring on her hand and flashed it at Phil.

"The setting seems a little plain. Should it have more going on?" Phil sighed. "This is why I brought you, Karin."

"To me, no. The engagement ring should be fairly simple, you can jazz it up with the wedding band you choose later." Karin glanced down at the four rings she'd selected. "All of these have a fairly straightforward setting, with only minor differences in the height of the prongs. But that may just be my preference." She slid the ring off and set it down, picking up the next and putting it on.

The sales woman repeated her spiel. This diamond was slightly less expensive, but still very highly rated.

Phil looked at it on his sister's hand and shook his head. "Not that one. I'm not sure what I don't like, but something about that one isn't right."

"Fair enough." Karin took it off.

The sales woman replaced it in the case while Karin put the next one on.

Phil shook his head and looked down into the case. He tapped above a different ring. "Could we see this one?"

Karin put on the new ring and held it out for Phil to see. The sales woman smiled. "This is one of my favorites. The white gold setting is a little more ornate with eighteen channel set princess cut diamonds, totaling a half carat, and pave diamonds along the outsides as well. The center stone is in what we call a cathedral setting, that's what makes room for the scrollwork on the side. The stone itself is roughly equivalent to the first ring you looked at."

"That's the one." Phil looked at Karin. "Do you like it?"

"Uh, yeah." Karin held up her hand and admired the flashing of the diamond. "Who wouldn't." She looked at Phil. "You didn't need me at all, did you?" She slid the ring off and handed it to the sales woman. They confirmed the sizing and the sales woman headed off to have the ring cleaned and boxed.

"I really did. I'm fairly certain I wouldn't have made it all the way through the door. I've been looking online. I know you don't get nearly as good an idea of what you're looking at, but I couldn't make my feet go into a store to look in person."

When he'd paid and tucked the ring into his pocket, they strolled down the quaint street. "Can I buy you some ice cream before you head home?"

"Absolutely."

CUSTO

Every night that week, Phil found himself looking at the ring imagining a future with Allison by his side. He hoped she'd be willing to move into his town house after they were married. He loved everything about it, and while he would readily agree some of the furnishings and décor could use a woman's touch, the house itself would be ideal for a new couple. He'd even bought a second chair for the upstairs balcony. Now when he sat out there, he pictured Allison sitting with him, watching the river.

Though she'd taken the Metro to work, Allison had asked him to pick her up at her apartment before their dinner with Karin. He'd watched her leave thirty minutes ago. With a final glance out his office window,

Phil packed up for the weekend and headed down to his car. He wasn't nervous, really. But he was hoping Karin would see what he did in Allison. He'd gone against both her and his mother's warnings with Brandi. Though neither had ever said "I told you so," he wanted to be sure that this time they agreed he was using his head. Before he got too down on himself, he paused to remember that most of his choices went against both Karin and his mother's advice at that stage of his life. Marrying Brandi was just one more little rebellion. He was so glad to be done with that, and so amazed and thankful that Jesus had forgiven him, as had his family. He prayed that somewhere down the line his mom and sister would also find Christ.

Pulling his thoughts back to the evening, he parked in the twenty-minute spot outside Allison's building and, going against years of training, called to let her know he was waiting out front as she'd asked. He saw her exit a few minutes later and got out of the car to wave. Opening her car door, he kissed her cheek as she got in.

"You know it goes against everything in me to not come get you at your door, right?"

"Sorry. They're trying to figure out what to do about visitors after the break in, so they've disabled the remote door system. Now to let a visitor in you have to meet them in the lobby. If I was going to do that anyway..."

"That makes sense. Though it's not like Brandi got buzzed in, right? She just followed someone with a key?"

"They're not sure now. It looks like she might have followed a visitor in after they were buzzed up. None of it makes sense to me, honestly. I get that these things happen. This is a populated area, there's going to be crime. But you just never think it'll happen to you."

Guilt gnawed at Phil. Was he doing the right thing? Would Allison be safer if he broke things off? He'd never forgive himself if she got hurt because of his baggage.

"Anyway. Where are we meeting your sister? Karin, right?"

"Right. She wanted to cook, so we're going to her house. Is that okay?"

"Sounds great. I'll admit to being spoiled at my folk's house. Even though it was just a few days, there's nothing like a homemade meal that you didn't make. I've thought about dropping by a few times since I got back into the apartment, but I left my car there for Lindsey, just in case. I can get to everything I need on foot or the Metro, other than to see my parents...and really it'd be more for the awesome food."

"Next time you want to go, let me know and I'll take you. Anytime, honestly."

"Thanks." She looked out the window as they pulled into Karin's neighborhood. "I almost bought a town house in here. I might've ended up neighbors with your sister."

"That's a fun thought." Phil chuckled as he parked in a visitor spot. "She could have totally ruined my chances before I realized what I'd be missing."

Slipping her hand in his as they walked to Karin's door, Allison laughed. "Or she could have sped up the process because she'd met someone she liked so well."

Karin threw open the door before Phil could ring the bell. "Right on time." She stuck out her hand. "I'm Karin, you're Allison and I'm so glad I finally get to meet you."

Allison shook her hand and winked at Phil over her shoulder as she went in. "I'm glad to meet you, too."

The two women chatted amiably as Allison helped set the table. Phil hovered around the edges. He'd known his sister would like Allison, but he hadn't been sure they'd hit it off immediately. Several times he caught Karin's eye and grinned at her surreptitious thumbs up.

Dinner was a cheerful extension of the conversation that started when they arrived. Karin had outdone herself with the food, leaving Phil verging on overly full. As they settled in the living room with coffee, he watched Allison observe his sister.

"You can't possibly eat like this every day. But if I could cook like that, I think I'd have to."

Karin laughed. "I love to cook for other people. When it's just me?" She shrugged and plopped into a chair across from the loveseat Allison and Phil occupied.

"I sometimes manage to actually microwave a meal. But I eat a lot of PB&J."

"What is it with you two and peanut butter?" Allison stuck out her tongue.

"Wait, what?" Karin looked at Phil, frowning. "I was all set to tell you what great taste you had and then...blasphemy. Who doesn't like peanut butter and jelly? That's...un-American."

Phil shook his head. "It's her one flaw."

"Bleh. Not eating wall paper paste and overly sweetened processed fruit products smeared on perfectly harmless bread is not a flaw. If anything, this peanut butter fixation is a genetic flaw that *I* am overlooking in you." Allison grinned at Karin. "Both of you, for that matter."

"Well." Karin sipped her coffee. "I guess that rules out dessert, for you at least."

"You didn't." Phil's mouth watered at the possibility of peanut butter pie.

"I did."

"You're the best sister in the world."

"I know. And hey, more for us."

"Okay, I'll bite. More what?" Allison looked between the siblings.

"Peanut butter pie with grape jelly glaze." Phil smacked his lips together. "The one thing our mom could make that consistently tasted good."

Allison shuddered. "That doesn't even sound appetizing. I'll stick to coffee."

Karin huffed out a breath. "You don't know what you're missing. Ready for some now, Phil?"

"Definitely." When Karin disappeared into the kitchen Phil stole a quick kiss. "You have to at least taste it. You might change your mind."

"I really don't see that happening."

"Trust me." Phil looked up at Karin as she emerged with two plates. He took his and offered a tiny bite to Allison. "Don't be a chicken."

"What are you, ten?" Allison frowned but took the bite. She chewed with a thoughtful expression on her face and washed it down with a swallow of coffee.

"Want your own slice?" Karin took a bite of her own.

"I'll pass. But I appreciate the experience."

Phil and Karin laughed in unison and continued eating. When the dishes were cleared away and the coffee pot empty, Allison and Phil took their leave. Karin gave Allison a firm hug goodbye, mouthing her approval to Phil over Allison's shoulder.

As she snapped her seatbelt buckle, Allison looked at Phil. "I hope I passed. Your sister is lovely."

"She's great, isn't she?" He started the car and slowly backed out of the parking spot. "I'd say you passed with almost flying colors. The PB&J thing is going to count against you for a while, but I imagine she, and Mom, will get over it with time."

Allison snickered. "If that's the only hurdle I have to manage, I can deal with it. Heck, if I have to, I can choke down a sandwich or two to keep the peace."

Phil patted her knee. "I don't think it'll come to that." He stopped at the red light that joined his sister's neighborhood to a major road. "Now, do you want me to drop you at your parents' house or your apartment?"

41

Allison puttered around in the kitchen after Phil dropped her back at her apartment. She'd toyed with the idea of going to her parents' house, but she'd already arranged for her dad to pick her up Saturday morning. She'd spend the weekend there, riding into work with her dad Monday morning. Two nights under her mother's thumb was more than enough. *That's not fair. Or nice.* Her dad's words in the study were the reason she was spending the weekend there, but the saying about old habits was proving true. *Baby steps.*

The timer on the oven buzzed. Allison opened the door and pulled out a pan of dark chocolate brownies. This was her idea of dessert. Not a peanut in sight. Just rich, gooey chocolate brownies with the thinnest ribbon of marshmallow worked through. She cut a large chunk and dropped it on a plate. She licked the chocolate off her fingers then ran them under cool water to ease the sting from the still-too-hot treat.

The phone rang. Frowning slightly at the blocked number and the time, Allison answered. "Hello?" Silence greeted her. "Hello?"

*Probably a telemarketer whose robo-dialer clock got messed up.* She clicked the phone off and took her brownie into the living room and flipped on the TV. Time to break in the new furniture with some vegging. The phone rang again.

"Hello?" This time there were faint scraping sounds and breathing audible in the background. "Did you know this is a class three misdemeanor? I'm hanging up. Stop calling. Or I'll press charges." *So much for it being a telemarketer. Probably kids who think they're funny.*

She clicked the phone off again and flipped the channel. When the phone started ringing a third time, she ignored it. After several rings, the caller either gave up or her voicemail answered. Allison didn't care either way as long as the ringing stopped. She found a movie on the classic movie channel and settled in for a little relaxation.

Five minutes later, the phone rang again. Checking the Caller ID revealed a blocked number. Allison turned the ringer off and returned to her movie. But the phone kept ringing, lighting up the display, every five minutes for the first hour of the show. *This is ridiculous. Where are these people's parents?* Allison's dad had once told her about a special whistle you could blow into the phone and then call the police so they could stake out hospitals for people with shattered eardrums. Wouldn't it be nice to have one of those? *Maybe that's a little harsh for kids who think they're clever. But honestly, it's getting late.* Tapping her fingers on her knee, she watched the phone. *What if it's not kids? After the break-in…what if it's her?* When it started to ring again, Allison jumped. She answered and hung up again without speaking. Then she dialed Phil.

"Hello?" He sounded groggy.

"Please tell me I didn't wake you."

"Not quite, no. What's wrong?"

"Someone keeps calling from a blocked number. I've answered a few times. Ignored it. Hung up on them…they just keep calling and I'm not sure what to do. Honestly, I'm getting a little spooked."

"You could try the call back, what is it star something?" There was a pause and muffled scratching sound. "Hang on, let me get my laptop."

"I can look it up. I'm not sure why I didn't think of it myself. Thanks, honey. I'm sorry to bug you." Her call waiting beeped. She glanced down and saw that the call was blocked. Swallowing the fingers of fear that worked their way up her throat, she said, "Here they are again."

"Try star fifty-seven. Though I'm not sure that'll work while we're talking. Call me back, okay?"

"Okay." She hung up. The phone began ringing. Allison waited until it stopped then, hands shaking slightly, dialed *57. After a short pause, she got a confirmation that the trace had been saved. Unsure what to do, she used her cell phone to call Phil. After explaining the situation, he recommended she call the police officer in charge of her vandalism case and promised to pass on the information to his case officer as well.

Where had she put his number? She dug through three pairs of pants and two purses before she found the officer's card. Flipping it over, she saw he'd written his cell number on the back. She chewed her lip. Should she wait and call in the morning? It was entirely possible she was overreacting and it really was just kids. Or a goofed up telemarketer. When the phone began ringing again, she grabbed her cell and dialed.

◌ଌ୫◌

Allison was groggy when her alarm went off Saturday morning. The phone calls had continued for most of the night. Even with the ringers off the digital display lit up every time a call came in. She'd tried to block the light, but knowing that it was happening kept her from getting to sleep. Allison had tried to take comfort in the fact that the police were aware of things, but it hadn't made much difference.

A long, blistering shower and three cups of coffee helped her feel somewhat more awake. When the display on her phone lit for the first time that morning with a blocked call, Allison headed into her closet and pulled out her suitcase. She packed what she'd need for a week. She could always swing by for more things if she needed to. Her parents would be glad to have her, even if she didn't explain the situation. Maybe things weren't as bad between them as she'd thought.

The display lit up again. Allison zipped up the suitcase, checked to make sure everything was turned off and locked, collected her laptop bag, and headed downstairs to wait in the lobby where she wouldn't have to see the phone.

When Tom arrived he looked started by the number of bags at her feet but said nothing. Instead, he grabbed the luggage and worked it into the trunk of his sports car. As they turned on to the Interstate, he cleared his throat. "What's going on?"

"Crank calls." Allison twisted her fingers in her lap. "Or harassing calls. However you want to classify them." She leaned her head back and closed her eyes. "Even with the ringer off, I barely slept."

"Did you call the police?"

"Yeah. They're looking into it. They figure it's tied to the break in. I imagine they're right."

"Is he worth it?"

Allison didn't even have to think about her answer. "Yeah, Daddy. He really is."

Tom studied her face then nodded once. "Pippin and Lindsey will be glad to have you back. Even though she and your mom get along well, the generation gap is starting to show just a bit." He smiled slightly. "Though your mother left me a note the other day that used texting abbreviations."

"Mom texted you?"

"Oh no, nothing that drastic. She just used the lingo on a note that she put on the refrigerator."

Allison laughed. "Thanks, Dad."

He signaled a lane change. "It's going to be okay, baby."

## 42

"Hey." Allison poked her head through the doorway into Lindsey's room.

Lindsey looked up from the childbirth book she was reading and smiled. "You're home." With considerable effort, she pushed herself into a sitting position on the bed.

"Where are Mom and Dad?"

"Irene said something about a weekly dinner. It sounded like she thought you'd know what she meant." Lindsey closed the book and set it aside. "Dinner's in the oven on warm when you're ready."

Allison pulled the straight-backed chair out from the desk and sat, tapping her fingers against her knee. "Weekly dinner? Oh, duh." She shook her head. "Monday night. It's their small group from church. I'm not hungry yet. You?"

Lindsey shook her head. "Not really."

"We'll wait a bit then. What'd you do today?" She nodded toward the book. "Other than research, of course."

"Did some school. And I called Faith, like you suggested. She said the nerves are normal. Also like you said." Lindsey's chubby cheeks broke into a grin. "I've got several appointments lined up for additional counseling. Dad said he was happy to pay for them. But he thinks his insurance might cover it anyway. Faith also talked to Brian and Olivia, and they said they'd pay for it if I needed them to."

*Brian and Olivia? Oh, right. The couple Lindsey chose.* "That's great. When do you start?"

"Tomorrow, if it's really okay for me to keep your car?"

"Yep. If Dad's not heading downtown, I can take the train or Phil said he'd pick me up, but it's completely out of his way, so I'm keeping that as a last resort." She shifted and propped one foot up on the desk. "Everything else okay?"

Lindsey's answer was cut off by the doorbell.

Allison frowned as she rose. "I'll go see who it is. I can't imagine Mom and Dad were expecting someone, but maybe it's a package. Be right back." She hurried to the front door and peered through the side window. Surprised, she pulled open the door. "Lydia? What are you doing here?"

"Wedding crisis. What else?" Lydia peeked in the house. "Can I come in?"

Allison stepped aside. "Of course. But you remember I'm not in this wedding, right?"

Lydia laughed, but the sound had a hollow ring. "Yeah. About that…"

"No." Allison shut the door and pointed down the hallway. "Lindsey and I are hanging out in the guest suite. Come on back."

Allison let Lydia have the chair and settled on the floor, leaning against the wall. When introductions had been made she pointed at Lydia. "What's the emergency now? You've got a dress, venues, and cake. The invitations are sent and, from what Kevin's emailed now and again, guests are actually replying in good time…what else is there?"

"Music." Lydia dug through the oversized bag she carried as a purse and emerged with a fat notebook. After flipping through several sections, she set it on her knee and tapped the open page. "We've been working on the service, because we're pushing it for ordering programs at this point. I'd hoped to have them at the printer last week. Do you know how many places you need music in a wedding?"

"Not off the top of my head, no." Allison shook her head and glanced at Lindsey.

Lindsey rolled her eyes. "For all I thought Ben and I would get married and live happily ever after, the wedding part was never all that fully formed. I kinda figured we'd just hit the courthouse. Fast is good when you've got this going on." She rubbed her belly.

"I wish I'd thought of that...though I don't think my sisters or my parents would have forgiven me if we eloped." Lydia sighed. "Anyway, I have the processional music mostly set. But there are all these places for special music." Her voice took on the slightest hint of wheedling. "Kevin says you have a lovely voice?"

Allison rubbed her forehead. "You want me to sing. Two weeks out, and you're asking me to sing." She should say no. There was entirely too much going on in her life right now. Between Phil, her caseload, and Brandi's antics. Throw in trying to be around as much as possible for Lindsey...there just wasn't time. Allison looked at Lydia. *Why does she have to look so hopeful?* "Of course, if you waited for Kevin to ask, I'd probably have two days...do you have a song picked out?"

Lydia wiggled happily in her seat, tugged sheet music out of the notebook, and offered it to Allison.

"At least it's something I know. All right. Fine. But I'm wearing my blue dress." *What happened to no? I'm such a sucker.*

"That's perfect. And you don't even have to be visible if you don't want to. You can stand over near the piano. There'll be a big flower arrangement to hide behind."

"That'll work."

"I'll send you an email with the pianist's information so you can get together to practice." Lydia shoved the wedding notebook back into her bag and smiled at Lindsey. "When are you due?"

"Late April or early May."

"Do you know if it's a boy or girl yet?"

Lindsey shook her head. "I decided not to find out. Since I'm placing him or her for adoption, I didn't want to get too attached and start thinking up names. Faith, she's the social worker at the adoption agency, says that bonding with the baby is good for everyone involved, but," she swallowed and flicked her eyes over at Allison, "I just don't know. It's already so hard."

Lydia nodded. "I can imagine. Though some of the other choices that seem easier end up being just as hard, maybe harder. Just in different ways."

*Wow. She's come a long way in the last year. I never would have thought she'd be so open about her abortion and the mess it started.*

Lindsey mouth turned down at the corners. "I guess. I worry that I'm going to live the rest of my life wondering where he or she is and how they're doing...and not know the answer. I know the agency promises me letters and pictures, and I guess I could have said I wanted to have visits and phone calls, but that really limited my choices for adoptive parents. Plus, I'm just not sure how fair that is to the baby. I want him, or her, to know who mom and dad are, without any confusion. Maybe we could make it work...but I guess I don't really want that level of involvement. Still, with only asking for pictures and updates, once the paperwork is signed it'll be easy for the couple to conveniently forget. It's not like I'll have any way to make them do it."

"It's a risk." Lydia leaned forward and held Lindsey's gaze. "But it's better than the choice I made. I know where my baby is, and it haunts me, because while heaven is a wonderful place, no one should end up there because his mother was selfish." She flashed a tight smile. "I should get going."

Allison pushed herself to her feet. "I'll walk you out." She looked at Lindsey. "Want me to bring dinner back with me?"

Lindsey nodded and picked up her book.

When they reached the door, Lydia looked back down the hall. "Should I not have said that? I was trying to be encouraging, but I worry that it came across…hateful."

"I didn't see hateful. I'm not sure it helped right now, but maybe in the long run it'll help with her anxiety and second guessing. She's seeing a therapist again starting tomorrow – she did the initial birth parent counseling, but felt like she needed more. Hopefully continuing on will help her with the grief and whatever else goes into a decision like this." There had to be so much to process. Could you ever really get to a place where you didn't question your decision now and then? "I honestly can't imagine. I'm so incredibly proud of her, and amazed by her maturity in the face of this, but I couldn't promise that I'd be able to do the same."

"I don't think anyone has an idea until they get there." Lydia made a stern face. "Which you'd better never do, missy. You and Kevin give me hope for future generations of Christian singles."

"How so?"

"You've stayed committed to abstinence, despite the odds. And neither of you are ugly agoraphobics who don't leave the house. You're out there, living, being normal single adults, minus the sex. That can't be easy, either."

Allison shrugged. "Never thought about it that way, really."

"Well, you should." Lydia stepped out into the cool spring night. "Make sure you tell Phil that you'll have to sit up front at the wedding. He can sit up there with you, obviously, but he'll need to come early, too, if that's what he wants to do." She started toward her car without waiting for a response.

Allison closed the door and frowned. She hadn't actually asked Phil if he'd go with her to the wedding. He hadn't mentioned it either. Did he not want to go? Did he think he wasn't invited? She didn't remember seeing his name on the guest list. Kevin and Lydia probably assumed he'd be her plus one. She'd talk to him about it when he called tonight.

Other than the extended commute, staying at her parent's house didn't impact Allison's week. Her client load was under control with nothing major on the immediate horizon. She'd been able to help Lydia and Kevin with still more wedding matters and Lindsey had raved about her sessions with the birth parent counselor. The only serious disappointment was that the police didn't have anything new to tell her about the break in or the phone calls. Though the number of recorded hang-ups on her voice mail indicated they'd continued for the next two days, the police could only track the call to a pre-paid mobile. Since those didn't require anything other than enough cash to purchase, it was a dead end. Allison had heard the "pursuing every avenue" speech enough as an attorney to know it basically meant the cops were stymied and ready to move on to something more pressing that they had a chance of solving. She didn't really blame them.

Since the calls had stopped, she had Phil drop her off at her apartment after their date on Friday night. It was good to get back into her own space, though she and her mom had had several pleasant conversations while she was at their house. Thinking about that made her warm inside. Even if it didn't completely banish the nagging feeling that nothing she did would ever really be enough. It was clear her mom wasn't thrilled with her career and dating choices. But now she seemed somewhat willing to trust Allison to be the adult she raised her to be. It was progress.

Saturday morning, Allison met with the accompanist for Kevin and Lydia's wedding. They spent several hours perfecting the music for the wedding. The one song she'd agreed to sing had morphed into three. It was good to discover her voice wasn't overly rusty from disuse. Saturday night, she and Phil had gone out with Kevin and Lydia and Matt and Laura. That had been more fun than Allison had imagined it would be. She'd been close friends with Kevin, Matt, and Laura since college. Phil and Lydia fit in seamlessly. She hoped the six of them would be getting together for a long time to come.

Early Sunday morning, the calls started again. Allison yanked the cord out of the wall and used her cell phone to notify Officer Neil, not caring that she clearly roused him from bed. If she was going to be tormented at 2 a.m., he could be too. He promised to look into it. *Not that he can do anything. They've done what they could…I'll just have to get my number changed.* She stared at the ceiling until the pink fingers of sunrise finally made their way through her bedroom window.

Allison drank nearly the entire pot of coffee before church. What did it mean that she was only slightly jumpy and still exhausted after all that caffeine? *Exhausted. It means you're exhausted.* She saw Phil standing with her parents and Lindsey just inside the foyer. *Uh-oh.* She pasted on a smile and headed toward the group.

"Good morning." Phil took a minute to study her. "You don't look like you slept very well."

"Gee, thanks." Allison made a face at him while her parents and Lindsey laughed.

Irene placed her hand on Phil's arm and shook her head reprovingly. "Phillip, dear, don't you know better than to say that to a woman?" She smiled at her daughter. "You look lovely, honey."

"Thanks, Mom." Had her mother really just called Phil 'dear'? Maybe there was hope after all. She'd have to think about that later. "To address the issue of the circles under my eyes, and yes, I know they're there because I couldn't find my concealer this morning, I was up most of the night after the crank calls started up again around two."

Phil's face clouded, anger sparking visibly in his eyes. "Why didn't you call me? I would have come and picked you up…did you call Officer Neil?"

"Yeah, for all the good it does." Allison shrugged. "I pulled the cord out of the wall and I'll get my number changed tomorrow. What I want to know, and really it's something Officer Neil wanted to know that I hadn't thought of, is if she's watching my apartment. The calls stopped after I left. Now that I'm back, they've started up again. It seems obvious. And creepy. And that's why I was up most of the night."

Phil put his arm around her shoulder and rubbed her arm. "Are they going to look into it?"

"Officer Neil said they would. So, I know I shouldn't worry about it, but that's a tough order to follow." *Time to change the subject.* "How is everyone else this morning?"

Lindsey shrugged. "Pretty good. Though I'd wanted to ask a favor and now I'm not sure if I should."

"There's no question...you should." Allison reached out to squeeze Lindsey's hand. "What's up?"

"After meeting with Diane, my counselor, again yesterday, she said she thought I might benefit from meeting Brian and Olivia before the baby's born. I've been on the fence about it since Faith asked, but...I think maybe I want to. But I was wondering if you'd come too?"

"I can do that. When?"

"Tomorrow night? Faith suggested getting coffee, so that we're meeting somewhere public and it's less awkward. I think it's going to be awkward regardless."

"Faith didn't want to be there?"

Lindsey's shoulder lifted. "She offered. But I think I'll be more comfortable with you. You really don't mind?"

"Not at all. You'll have to pick me up though, since you've still got my car."

Lindsey smiled. "Thanks."

Phil tugged Allison's arm. "Let's go get a seat, sounds like the service is getting ready to start."

⚙️

At Phil's prompting, Allison called the phone company after church. It took entirely too long to get through to a live person. *No wonder you can't figure out what's going on, they don't actually have people to help you.*

The woman at the phone company suggested Allison simply add the anonymous call block service to her plan since the calls all came from a blocked number. This was an easy thing to do and, as soon as she hung up, she had her dad try it out, using *67 to turn on per-call blocking on his number before dialing. The phone didn't ring. She called back to check that he'd called and, since he insisted he had, she considered the matter solved and settled in for a quiet afternoon of catching up on work.

Monday dawned with the promise of a beautiful spring day. Allison hummed to herself as she made breakfast. Pippin twined between her ankles, seeming to share her good mood and pleasure at being back at home. With a chuckle, she gave him an extra scoop of wet food as a treat. It had been a blissfully call-free night. She was caught up on her work and optimistic about the day ahead. Even the slight anxiety about going with Lindsey to meet Brian and Olivia couldn't dampen her enthusiasm.

By the time she got home from work, there was just enough time for her to make a sandwich and change before Lindsey called to let her know she was downstairs.

Allison hurried down to the lobby, smiling when she saw her car. She ran her hand down the hood as she opened the passenger door. "Missed you, baby."

Lindsey laughed. "Do you need her back? I really don't drive all that often, and I'm sure your mom would take me if I needed to go somewhere."

"Him." Allison grinned. "Georges, if you must know, and no, I'm doing fine riding the Metro in to work. Honestly, I've frequently thought about driving less, so this is a nice chance to see if it's really feasible."

"And is it?"

Allison shrugged. "From a 'can it be done' perspective? Sure. From a 'do I like it' perspective? Nope. I'm a car girl."

Lindsey pulled into the parking lot at the coffee shop and took a deep breath. "Here we are."

Allison patted her knee. "It's going to be fine." She opened her door. "I should also point out that having you pick me up is evidence that I drive too much. We're what, five blocks from my apartment?"

Lindsey laughed.

*That's better.* Nerves were one thing, but the utter terror she'd glimpsed on Lindsey's face had worried her.

Even if she didn't know how she'd feel if the situation was reversed.

The coffee shop was empty. Allison wasn't terribly surprised. Monday nights weren't typically hang-out nights, even in this trendy Arlington neighborhood. While Lindsey staked out a grouping of comfortable chairs, Allison ordered their drinks.

"Oh, thanks." Lindsey took the cup and sniffed it.

"Hot chocolate. I didn't figure you should have coffee. But I also figured you'd want something to do with your hands."

Lindsey sipped. "Mmm. Plus, chocolate."

"There's that." Allison looked over as the bells on the door tinkled happily.

A couple, probably in their early thirties, walked through the door and glanced around, visibly nervous. The woman nudged the man with her elbow and nodded toward where Allison and Lindsey were sitting.

"I think maybe they're here." *They look nice. Like people I'd be friends with.*

Lindsey looked up and drew the corners of her mouth into a smile as she waved. "Brian and Olivia, we're over here."

The couple crossed to the chairs. Brian glanced at the counter then at Olivia. "Would you like a coffee?"

"Sure. Something small and vanilla." Olivia sat, dropping her purse to the floor by her feet. "Decaf." Obviously intrigued, she looked up at Lindsey through her dark lashes.

"Hi. I'm Allison, a friend of Lindsey's." Allison extended her hand across the coffee table to Olivia.

"Hi." Olivia took the offered hand, turned to Lindsey, and smiled. "And you're Lindsey. Obviously I'm Olivia. And that's my husband Brian."

Brian lifted his cup in a salute as he returned to the seats. He handed Olivia a steaming cup and glanced inquisitively at Allison.

"Allison, hi. Lindsey's friend."

"Pleasure to meet you. And you, Lindsey."

"Thanks for agreeing to meet me." Lindsey cleared her throat and set her hot chocolate down. "I'm not thinking of changing my mind, or anything like that."

Brian and Olivia visibly relaxed.

"I thought I should get that out of the way." Lindsey paused and picked up her drink again. "I guess I'm starting to process this whole thing and it seemed like meeting you might help. Or at least the therapist I'm seeing thought it might." She chuckled weakly.

"I don't know if it helps, but I'm guessing we're just as nervous as you are." Olivia leaned forward in her seat. "You're doing something so incredible for us, and we've been waiting for a baby for so long…you have no idea how grateful we are."

Brian grabbed Olivia's hand. "Do you have any questions you'd like to ask us? About anything?"

Phil waited until he saw Lindsey drive off to her meeting with the adoptive parents before pulling alongside the curb at the Vasak's house. *God, give me the words. Please, let this go well.* He should probably have brought flowers or some kind of gift to help smooth the way. *Too late now.*

Tom opened the door with an inquisitive smile. "Good evening, Phil."

"Hi, Mr. Vasak." Phil cleared his throat. "I wondered if I might be able to speak to you and Mrs. Vasak for a few minutes?"

Tom's simply nodded and opened the door wider to allow Phil to come in. "We're in the den watching some TV. Irene has a penchant for police procedurals, though she'll deny it to your face if you ask. She says she watches them for me, never noticing that I just sit and read while they're on."

"Her secret's safe with me."

"Can I get you a soda or some iced tea?" Tom paused by the kitchen door.

"No, thanks."

Tom gestured for Phil to precede him into the den. "Honey, Phil's stopped by."

Irene looked up, a slight frown creasing her forehead. It was quickly replaced by a polite smile as she reached for the remote. The action on the screen froze. "Phillip, how lovely to see you again. Can I offer you a drink?"

"Already did, dear." Tom crossed to his recliner and moved the book from the seat, carefully marking his place before setting it aside. "Please sit, won't you Phil?"

Phil considered his options. There was a chair just inside the door. Would that be too standoffish? It was awfully far away from the other seats. The other option, though, was the sofa with Irene. He opted for the chair, perching on the edge of the seat.

"So what brings you out this way this evening?" Irene shifted so her attention was focused on Phil and not the paused television.

Phil took a deep breath. The speech he'd prepared on the way over vanished as his mind blanked. He blurted out the first words that came to mind. "I'm in love with your daughter."

Tom and Irene both flinched.

Phil cleared his throat. "Um. Maybe I'm not going about this the right way." He huffed out a breath. "I came by tonight because I knew Allison would be out and I wanted to ask your permission to ask her to marry me."

Silence stretched across the room.

Irene's face paled and she turned to look at Tom, eyes wide. Tom blinked and stared at Phil before he started to chuckle.

Why was he laughing? Phil had imagined many reactions, but laughter wasn't among them. He smiled tentatively.

Tom's chuckle turned into a guffaw.

"April Fool's, right?" Tom slapped the arm of his recliner. "That's a good one. You had me going there for a moment."

Irene's shoulders relaxed and she smiled. "It is April first, isn't it?" She shook her head and leaned back into the sofa. "Clever. I can't recall the last time someone's done an April Fool on us, can you, dear?" She looked at Tom who shook his head as his chuckles continued.

Why would they immediately jump to the conclusion that it was a prank? Was that more to do with him? Or Allison? Why hadn't he thought to check the date?

"Actually," Phil waited until the chuckles quieted, "I hadn't realized it was April Fool's day. I'm serious. I love Allison, and I believe she loves me. I'd like her to be my wife."

"Your *second* wife." Irene corrected him with a disapproving glare.

Phil acknowledged her with a nod. "True. I have been married previously. And that marriage ended despite my best efforts. I'd be happy to release Pastor Brown from any confidentiality if you'd like to talk to him. I spent months in counseling with him trying to find a way to save my marriage to Brandi, not to mention the months I spent after the divorce trying to come to grips with what I perceived as my failure to do so." He paused and rubbed the back of his neck. "I can understand where you're coming from. I don't know if, at first glance, I would want someone like me for my own daughter. But I hope that I'd trust my adult child enough to realize that she wouldn't choose someone who didn't meet the standards I'd worked so hard to instill in her."

Irene's mouth turned down in a frown.

Tom reached over to lay his hand on her arm. "Allison has a good head on her shoulders, Irene." He sighed. "And she's told me enough about Phil and her feelings for him that I suspect she'll be overjoyed."

Irene gaped. "But they've hardly been dating at all. What's it been?" She pinned Phil with a glare.

"About eight weeks."

"Two months, Tom." Irene shook her head. "Two months is not long enough to get to know someone well enough to even think you're in love. Let alone consider marriage. There's no need to be hasty, and if track records mean anything, lots of reasons to take things slow."

Her barb struck home.

Blood pounded in Phil's ears and he stood with a curt nod. "I see. I appreciate your time, and apologize for interrupting your evening. I can see myself out." Stiffly, he turned from the room and stalked down the hall to the front door. He wanted to slam it. It would serve them right if something fell off the wall and shattered. *Be a bigger person.* Using every ounce of self-control he could muster, he let the door click softly behind him before running to the car. Gunning the engine, he took off down the street.

Allison was looking forward to lunch with Phil. The meeting with Brian and Olivia the night before had gone incredibly well. For the first time since she made the decision to place the baby for adoption, Lindsey seemed completely relaxed. And Brian and Olivia were delightful. They'd made it so easy for everyone to talk and, after the initial awkwardness, the evening had continued as if they were old friends. Even though she was on the outskirts of the whole situation, Allison was thrilled and was looking forward to sharing the details with Phil.

At eleven thirty, she went in search of Phil. She studied him for a moment from outside his office door, enjoying the way his reading glasses perched on his nose and the little wrinkle in his brow from deep concentration. Smiling, she knocked on the doorframe.

Phil looked up with a frown. Rather than turning into a smile, as Allison expected, the frown deepened.

"What do you need?"

Allison blinked. Was something wrong? Maybe he was having a bad day? "Um. I was hoping you might be up for an early lunch? But if you're busy, I can wait."

"Don't wait if you're hungry. I'm buried right now, probably won't bother with anything more than the granola bar I keep in my desk." He turned his attention back to his computer.

Allison hovered in the doorway another minute. Something was definitely wrong. Should she push for details or just leave it alone? *If he wanted to talk about it, he'd say something. Right?* Had she done something wrong? *You haven't talked to him since church. Everything was fine then...this isn't about you. Probably.* Better to get back to work and worry about it later. *Yeah, right.*

C33&

Phil waited until Allison left before pulling off his glasses and pinching the bridge of his nose. He knew it was unreasonable, but he was still angry with her parents and it seemed to be trickling over into irritation with her. He hadn't meant to be short with her, but he'd not been able to stop the words before they came out.

He leaned his head back and stared at the ceiling. What was he supposed to do now? There was an engagement ring sitting on his dresser at home, one he desperately wanted to give to the woman he'd just brushed off. Asking for her parents' permission was simply something he'd thought would be a good idea. Phil hadn't entertained the idea that they might say no, or laugh hilariously, and then make it clear the answer was no. He scowled at the slightly water-stained ceiling tile by the window. Was he just being old fashioned? He knew Allison had a good relationship with her parents, and he didn't want to do anything that might come between them. On the other hand…he stopped that line of thought. He'd been raised with the firm understanding that you didn't propose without a parental blessing. He sighed and returned his gaze to his work. Things had been a lot simpler when he'd been determined to stay single for the rest of his life.

ಛಶಜ

　　Allison walked by Phil's office several times throughout the rest of the day. Though she was reasonably certain she caught his eye, he never acknowledged her beyond a curt nod. What was going on? She packed up early and headed home to finish the day. *At least that way I don't have to keep getting the cold shoulder.*

　　Her cell rang as she walked out into the street on her way to the Metro.

　　"Hello?"

　　"Hey, it's Lydia. You busy?"

"Not really, no. I'm on my way to the metro, actually. Things in the office are weird, so I figured I'd finish the day up at home. What's going on?"

"Laura's gotten it into her head that I need a bachelorette party. Tonight."

Allison laughed. "Wasn't yesterday April Fool's Day?"

"No, I'm serious."

"Okay, what exactly does a bachelorette party for people who, at least to my knowledge, don't drink, smoke, gamble, or go to strip clubs entail?"

"Movie night at a friend's house. Lots of bad-for-you food, staying up 'til all hours."

Allison checked the traffic and darted across the street in the middle of the block. "Sounds fun, but I have to work tomorrow."

"Okay, so we could cut back on the up 'til all hours part," Lydia wheedled.

Sighing, Allison stopped at the top of the escalator. "Someone's going to have to pick me up, Lindsey still has my car."

"Actually…"

"What?"

"So…I live in my parents' basement and Laura has two small kids and a husband…"

Allison groaned. She just wanted to go home and…*and what? Pout?* "Fine. But you're helping clean up afterward. I just put my place back together."

Lydia squealed. "You're the best. We'll be there around six with food and movies. Don't worry about a thing."

Allison looked at the silent phone and shook her head. "Yeah, right." Tucking the phone into her purse, she descended into the Metro station. Now she had to spend time that she should be working tidying up. Then, with people coming over, there was no way she'd get her work finished. Sometimes people were more trouble than they were worth.

By the time Laura and Lydia arrived, Allison had done the minimum amount of work she could get away with and had tidied up slightly. She eyed the box of pizza and the overloaded grocery bag and pointed at the kitchen. "Let's take that all in there. Can we eat first? I missed lunch."

Laura shot her a confused look. "How does someone miss a meal? And don't tell me you weren't hungry, that's a physical impossibility."

Lydia laughed. "Don't mind her. She's grumpy because the 'baby weight' hasn't magically disappeared this time."

Allison looked at Laura. "What baby weight?"

"Exactly." Lydia grinned triumphantly at Laura. "Now come on, let's eat."

"I thought you had lunch with Phil most days. Was he out today?" Laura plopped a slice of pizza onto one of the paper plates they'd brought along.

Allison watched Lydia try to jam two half gallons of ice cream into her already full freezer before taking a slice of pizza for herself and settling at the kitchen table. "No, he was there. And I went to see if he wanted to eat early because I was actually very hungry."

"So what happened?" Lydia finally succeeded in shoving the ice cream into the freezer and shut the door. "Be careful opening that, the ice cream's going to fall on you."

"I wish I knew. He acted like I was solely responsible for world hunger, or malaria or something." She picked the bell peppers off her slice of pizza and pushed them into a pile on the side of her plate. "After that, I kind of lost my appetite. I spent the rest of the afternoon trying not to worry about what was going on and got very little actual work done. Which is why Lydia was able to catch me and talk me into this."

"Perfect therapy." Laura helped herself to another slice of pizza while Allison looked on, amused. "What?"

"Nothing. I have nothing to say." Allison lowered her gaze to her own pizza, fighting laughter.

Laura narrowed her eyes and poked a finger at both of them. "When you're nursing a baby and burning all those extra calories, you'll understand. Until then, zip it."

Lydia mimed drawing a zipper closed across her mouth, her eyes sparkling with mirth as she glanced at Allison.

"So, back to me." Allison started pulling the mushrooms off her pizza. "What do I do about Phil?"

"First, tell me this." Laura frowned and looked at Allison's plate. "Does he know about your pizza problem?"

"What?" Allison looked down at the neat piles of toppings on her plate. "Look. I like cheese pizza. Plain old boring cheese. But I let people put whatever they want on it and then pick it off. Ignoring any of the flavor tainting that goes on. I think it's very accommodating of me. So, to quote a good friend, zip it."

Lydia laughed. "She's got you there. And hey," she reached over and slid the piles off Allison's plate onto her own, "more toppings for us. You want any, Laura?"

Allison waited until the toppings had been divvied up. "So, suggestions? Thoughts?"

"Well, did you think of anything that you might have done? Have you had an argument?" Laura folded her slice in half to keep the extra toppings from falling off as she took a bite.

"Not that I'm aware of, no. We had a good time at his sister's house, she seemed to like me...oh no. Do you suppose she told him I wasn't right for him?"

"I guess it's a possibility...but how anyone could not like you is beyond me." Laura wiped her fingers on a paper towel and glanced at the freezer. "How long do we have to wait for ice cream?"

Lydia burst into gales of laughter. "It's for during the movies. Eat another slice of pizza if you're that hungry. I promise not to say anything."

Laura stuck out her tongue. "I'll wait." She turned to consider Allison. "Seriously, though, Allison? You're an adult. He's an adult. You need to talk to him. There's no point in all this speculation. Maybe he was just having a bad day."

"Yeah, I know." Allison sighed. "I really hate confrontation like that though."

"Quick, write that down, Laura. A lawyer who doesn't like confrontation." Lydia started to giggle. Laura quickly joined in. After a moment, Allison joined in as well.

છ80

Phil poked his sister's doorbell a second time and shifted the grocery bag to his other hand.

"Little late, isn't it?"

Phil jumped as Karin came up behind him and nudged him out of the way so she could unlock the door.

"You're just getting home." Phil did his best to look contrite. "I can go."

"Don't worry about it. I'm not as tired as I usually am; I lost count after my fifth cup of coffee today. Plus," she eyed his grocery bag, "I'm guessing that has ice cream in it. That sounds about perfect for dinner." She jerked her head toward the kitchen. "Come on."

Phil shut the door and tugged the Rocky Road ice cream out of the bag as he made his way to the kitchen. Karin already had out two spoons. "Did you want a bowl?"

He reached for a spoon. "This is fine."

Karin pried the lid off the tub and set it on the counter. "Couch. I *am* too tired to bother with the table." Once they were settled, Karin spooned up a huge scoop and nibbled at it. "So, spill it."

Phil dug a smaller spoonful out. "I went to ask Allison's parents for permission to marry last night."

"You weren't expecting it to be a fantastic conversation. I take it that's an understatement?"

"You could say that." He dug out another spoonful. "They said no."

Karin blinked and stared at Phil. "What?"

"Yeah. Pretty much."

"I...but...wha..." Karin licked a drop of ice cream off the end of her spoon before it could fall. "How is that even an option?"

"I'd never considered that it was, to tell the truth...so what do I do now?"

Pursing her lips, Karin dug out another bite of ice cream. "I don't know. I'm stunned." She frowned at her spoon for a moment. "Did they say why?"

"I get the impression it's mostly to do with being divorced. Though Brandi hasn't helped matters. Between destroying her apartment and the crank calls she's been making to Allison lately...she may have managed to ruin things." He stuck his spoon in the carton and leaned back. "I've kind of got it boiled down to two options. I can ask her anyway, despite her parents' disapproval, and hope they'll come around. Or I can break up with her...which I *really* don't want to do."

"Or you could wait, keep things the way they are, and see if they come around. That's the more logical thought…why didn't it make your list?"

"Because I don't want to wait."

"Why not?"

"I'm worried if I wait, she'll realize she can do so much better. That she'll find someone who doesn't have the past I do…who's worked as hard as she has to keep pure."

"She didn't strike me as stupid, Phil."

"What's that mean?"

Karin sighed. "Give her some credit. If she wanted that, she'd be dating that. Seems to me, she wants you." She leaned forward and set the ice cream carton on the coffee table. "You should be talking to her, not me."

"When did you get so smart?"

Karin stood and took the ice cream back into the kitchen. "I'm keeping this as my counseling fee."

"Fair enough. Thanks, kid." Phil gave his sister a tight hug before heading out to his car. How could he bring up the subject with Allison without giving away his plan to propose?

45

Allison spent most of Wednesday morning in a haze of exhaustion. Lydia and Laura hadn't left until nearly two a.m. And even then, Allison had trouble falling asleep after all the sugar she'd consumed. She forced herself to get up when her alarm sounded, in part because Pippin was insistent about being fed and also because she had a filing deadline she needed to meet in the afternoon.

At work, she kept her door shut and chugged more coffee than was probably wise, but she met her deadline with an hour to spare. With the motion now working its way through the system, she leaned back in her chair and closed her eyes. And nearly fell asleep. She stood and paced around the office to get her blood moving. There was no way she'd get any more work done. She was too tired. And too wired from the coffee to go home and nap. She checked her watch and started packing up. She'd hit the afternoon Tae Kwon Do class and then work some more this evening. And she'd be able to legitimately avoid Phil. Or at least somewhat legitimately.

Annoyed at herself, Phil, and the whole situation, she waved to Sam on her way out to the elevators. It wasn't until she was on the metro to her apartment that she realized she had no way to get to the dojang. She punched in Sarah's number as she rode the escalator up from the station.

"Heya, stranger."

Allison winced. "I know, I know. I'm a terrible friend. Can you forgive me?"

Sarah's laugh made Allison smile. "Of course. I've actually been busy, too. So I probably would've been ditching you the past several weeks anyway. What's up? Shouldn't you still have your nose to the grindstone?"

"I should, but I'm going to work tonight. I'm having trouble focusing and thought I'd hit the afternoon class."

"That's do-able. Dinner after?"

"Definitely. My treat, even."

"Uh oh. I feel a favor coming on."

Allison chuckled. "You know me too well. I loaned my car to someone and need a ride."

"That's it? That I can do. Give me half an hour to tie up some loose ends here and I'll swing by for you."

"You're the best, Sarah." Allison unlocked the entry to her apartment building and tugged open the door.

"You said it, not me."

Laughing, Allison tucked her phone away and punched the button for the elevator. She caught a flash of movement at the front doors and turned. As her gaze locked with the skeletal woman with stringy brown hair who was trying to jam something between the front doors, the woman paled and ran. Allison pressed the speed dial for Officer Neil and sprinted to the doors. She was trying to spot the woman in the crowds coming up out of the Metro when the policeman answered his phone. She explained the situation and he assured her someone would be out to look, but advised her to put it out of her mind. It was possible the events were completely unrelated.

☙❧

Sweaty and pleasantly tired, Allison leaned back in the chair on the patio of *Brown & Green* and waited for Sarah to get back from the restroom. Since it was a lovely spring evening, they'd decided to sit outside despite the intermittent breeze that brought a little chill with it. They also thought it increased their chances of not offending the other diners with their workout clothes.

"I went ahead and ordered while I was in there. Apparently we just beat the rush. The main room is packed now." Sarah sat down across from Allison. "I figured we were both going to get our usual anyway."

Allison chuckled. "I should say I was planning on branching out, just to be obnoxious, but you're right." She set the menu aside. "So what's new?"

"Well, the big news," Sarah paused dramatically before whipping out her left hand and wiggling it under Allison's nose, "is that I'm engaged."

Allison snatched Sarah's hand and tugged it close to eye the ring. "What? When did this happen?"

"Last night." Sarah grinned and tugged her hand back. "I was going to call you today anyway."

"Congratulations! That's so great...but, well, to prove I'm apparently completely out of the loop on your life, to whom are you engaged?"

"Dillon."

"Dillon. As in Mr. I-love-you-but-won't-commit-we-should-date-other-people Dillon? As in stomped on your heart two years ago and walked out of your life, Dillon? As in..."

"I know, I know. That's why I didn't tell you when we started going out again at the beginning of January. First, I wasn't sure where things were going, and I was really hurt still, too. But you know I never was able to get over him. And then, I was worried you'd be angry with me."

"I'm not angry with you. At least not now that he's come to his senses. But I do wish you'd given me the opportunity to knock some of that sense into him. And if he hurts you again, make sure he knows I'll come after him with everything I can muster."

Sarah grinned and looked over Allison's shoulder.

"So noted." Dillon leaned in and kissed Allison's cheek. "Will you forgive me? I know I treated Sarah badly. And I know I hurt you in the process, too."

Allison watched as he linked his fingers with Sarah and scooted his chair as close to hers as he could. They looked good together. Right, somehow. Would she ever have something like that? She'd thought she was headed there with Phil. But now? She didn't know. *Worry about that later…just be happy for Sarah. Somehow.* "Since she has, I will." She shook her head and pointed at Sarah. "You're going to make me an old maid, aren't you?"

"Well," Sarah drawled, "I was hoping you'd be my Maid of Honor. Though I know how you feel about that third time."

Allison huffed out a breath. "For you, I'll risk it." *Not like I've got wife potential anyway at this point. That seems pretty clear.* "I believe the two of you owe me some details, since apparently," she sent a mock glare across the table, "there are three months of secrets between us."

It was good to see her friend happy. And Dillon, for all his issues in the past, seemed to have gotten it together. Even if it did mean she'd have to be a bridesmaid yet again. Allison paused to collect her mail in the lobby of her building on her way up to her condo.

The "Mission: Impossible" theme song poured out of her purse.

"Hi, Daddy."

"Allie, can you get to the hospital? I know your car's at our house, but we've just taken Lindsey to the ER. I know she'd want you here, plus you're her legal guardian now, we probably need you."

"I'll get a cab. Which hospital?"

As soon as she disconnected with her father, Allison called a taxi. Her dad had made her program a cab company into her phone when she'd been in college. The habit had stayed with her and had proved useful more times than she could count. Once she was on her way to the hospital, she left a message for Marcus and another for Phil letting them know as much information as she had and promising to call again as soon as she had details.

The ride to the hospital was short. Allison didn't have much time to worry before she found her mom and dad in the waiting room of the ER.

"They have Lindsey in the back, but since we're not family, they wouldn't let us go with her." Irene clutched the straps of her purse, an unusual display of anxiety.

Allison pulled a file folder from her own purse. "Wait here, I should be able to get us back there." She marched over to the admitting desk, gently but firmly interrupting the conversation the nurse was having with another person. She quickly explained the situation and showed the nurse the notarized paperwork Marcus had signed before leaving town. After several minutes of conferring between the admitting nurse and other staff, Allison waved to her parents, gesturing for them to join her as they were escorted back to Lindsey's room.

"Hey, Linds." Lindsey's pale, strained face and the IV in her arm had Allison's pulse skyrocketing. *Panic isn't going to help.* She made her voice light and teasing. "Not enough excitement for you at my folks' house?"

Lindsey winced. "Apparently not." Her gaze flitted to Irene and Tom. "I'm so sorry."

"Good grief, don't be ridiculous." Irene stood at the foot of the bed and patted Lindsey's leg. Despite her no-nonsense tone, she showed signs of strain around her eyes. "What have they said?"

"Not just Braxton-Hicks like I was hoping. But they're pretty sure they'll be able to stop the contractions. That's what this is supposed to do." She gingerly wiggled the arm hooked up to an IV. "They told me what it was, but I didn't really catch most of it." Her worried gaze sought Allison's.

"I'll get more details when the doctor comes back." Allison squeezed Lindsey's hand.

"Did they have any idea why this happened?" Tom hovered at the edge of the door, clearly uncomfortable. "You're young and healthy. It doesn't make sense."

"I can answer that. Excuse me." A harried looking young man in scrubs squeezed past Tom and checked the machines at Lindsey's head. After a few questions about how she was feeling and whether she needed anything, the doctor addressed the rest of the room. "I'm Doctor Jason Garcia." He flashed a smile. "It's looking like we've slowed the contractions. I expect they'll stop within another hour. Another hour or two with no recurrence and we'll release her. As for why, it seems counterintuitive, but often extremely young mothers experience pre-term labor. Lindsey's on the upper edge of that classification, but still vulnerable. She was also clearly underweight prior to becoming pregnant. That's another risk factor and since this wasn't a planned pregnancy, the fact that she didn't get early prenatal care might have contributed. Still, the baby appears healthy and active, but not distressed, and the contractions are easing." The doctor offered a perfunctory smile. "I don't see this being more than a little hiccup in the overall scheme of things. You can follow up with your regular OB tomorrow." With that, he bustled from the room and they heard him introducing himself to the patient next door.

"Well." Allison rested a hip on the edge of Lindsey's bed. "I guess we just wait then."

"Could you call my dad?" Propped against the sterile hospital pillows, Lindsey looked even more like a child than usual.

"Absolutely. I'll go do that now and be right back."

Lindsey wasn't released from the emergency room until after two in the morning. Allison rode home with her parents and Lindsey and crashed at their house. She overslept and woke to the sun streaming in the top of the guest room windows. It was nearly noon. She got the keys to her car, promising Lindsey she'd be able to use it the next day for her counseling appointment, and rushed back to her apartment to change for work.

Allison caught Sam's disapproving frown as she rushed in just before one thirty. She had a client due to arrive any minute and was completely unprepared. She'd do fine once the meeting was underway. *I wish I'd had the morning to prepare. Like I planned.* She dropped her laptop into its dock and started it booting while she arranged the files she'd need for the meeting.

"Afternoon." Phil poked his head through the door. "Got a minute?"

"Not really." Allison didn't even look up. "I've got a client due any second and things with Lindsey last night threw me totally off schedule." *And I wouldn't have been behind in the first place if not for you.* The words almost left her mouth, but there was no need to be petty. Probably.

Phil frowned. "Okay. Are you free tomorrow night?"

She shook her head. "Rehearsal dinner." Allison glanced up and eyed him warily. Might as well get it asked and over with. "You're still going to the wedding with me on Saturday, right?"

Phil hesitated before nodding.

There it was. He was finished with her. She could at least try and make this as easy on herself as possible. "You don't have to…"

"No. I said I'd take you. I just…" he glanced down the hall as Sam's cheerful voice echoed in their direction. "We need to talk."

Sam appeared with Allison's new client in tow and smiled brightly as she made introductions.

Phil nodded politely and headed back to his office.

Allison fought off a wave of nausea. He was going to dump her. There was nothing to do but to put on a professional smile and get through the day. *Fake it til you make it. Or until you get home and can break down in privacy.*

CR&BD

*Idiot.* Phil knew better than to say those foreboding words and then walk away. And even if he hadn't known, the look of pure panic that flashed across Allison's face would've clued him in. He sighed and jostled his mouse to wake his computer.

He walked by her office several times over the course of the afternoon, but her door was closed. Client meetings often ran for several hours. Why couldn't this one have been an exception? At six thirty, he made one last trip down that part of the hall and found her door open. But her light was off and she had clearly left for the day. He went back to his office to pack up for the night and head home.

Should he drop by her apartment? No. It would probably be better to wait until after the wedding. If she was still speaking to him by then. He left several voice mails for her on the drive home, but either her battery was dead or she wasn't picking up when she realized it was him. What now?

He'd just settled out on his deck with a tall glass of iced tea when his phone rang. He answered after the first ring, not bothering to check the Caller ID. "Allison?"

"No, it's not your little slut, Phil. It's your wife."

"She's not a slut and you're my ex-wife, Brandi." Phil sighed and rubbed his temples. When would he learn to always check the readout before answering? And why couldn't he just hang up? "You're married to Marshall now, remember?"

"Not for long."

*Not taking that bait. I don't even want to know.* "How'd you get this number, Brandi?"

She cackled. "It's amazing how cooperative they are at the phone company when you show a little skin. Just have to figure out who to approach."

Whatever desperate worker she'd conned into giving out his new, supposedly unlisted number deserved to get fired. Though Brandi could be persuasive when she wanted to be. Even charming, if the stakes were high enough. He'd learned that the hard way himself. Time to make it clear that this needed to end. "You've got twenty seconds and then I'm hanging up. So say your piece. Fast."

"Who do you think you are? You can't talk to me like that."

"Fifteen seconds."

"It was good between us." Brandi's voice took on a pleading whine.

Phil recognized the slight slur that indicated she was drunker than she'd admit.

"Don't you miss us?"

"Ten seconds."

"You jerk. We'll see if you change your mind when the ho's out of the picture."

The phone clicked in his ear. Phil called Grant and the police officer in charge of his case against Brandi.

They both promised to do what they could and assured him that it was unlikely Allison was in any immediate danger. Though Brandi had escalated her behavior with her vandalism of Allison's apartment, as soon as she'd realized someone was at home, she'd fled. Phil tried to take comfort in that, but left another voice mail for Allison, just to be safe. Beaten down, he unplugged the phone from the wall. It would be just like Brandi to keep calling all night. He wasn't in the mood to deal with it.

Allison listened to the latest voice mail from Phil and her jaw unclenched. Her insides still twisted when she remembered his parting words, but he was clearly concerned that Brandi might try something. At least he was willing to warn her. That had to be positive, right? As she got ready for bed, she called him back. They were adults. Adults who clearly needed to have a serious conversation, even though she was dreading the outcome of it. Better to get it over with. When both of Phil's numbers went to voicemail, Allison stopped trying. Maybe his message wasn't as positive as she'd hoped after all.

Pippin was also annoyed with her. What was it with the men in her life right now? Allison fought a smile as she watched the cat stare at her over his shoulder before deliberately turning to look out the window. The end of his tail twitched. She didn't really blame him. She'd been very busy the past several weeks and Pippin was used to being her primary focus, not the afterthought he'd become.

"I'm sorry, Pip." Allison shook the cat treat can enticingly. She saw his ear twitch, though he didn't look her way. She opened the top to the can and shook them again. "Mmm. Salmon flavor."

Shaking two treats into her palm, she walked to the window and ran a hand down his back. He purred quietly before turning to regard her regally. She offered the treats. He sniffed them, glanced at her again, then daintily took them between his teeth before hopping down from the window sill and settling himself on the sofa to eat.

Allison closed the can. "I wish people were as quick to forgive." She sat by Pippin and scratched behind his ears while he crunched.

Somewhere between three and four in the morning, Allison decided to take the next day off. She wasn't getting any sleep and between going to the counselor with Lindsey in the afternoon and needing to get to Kevin and Lydia's rehearsal by five, the day was going to be too busy to run on fumes. Plus it got her out of running into Phil at the office and having him tell her again, in deep, ominous tones, that they needed to talk.

"So I'm a chicken." She gave Pippin a final rub behind the ears before heading into the kitchen for some coffee. While she was in there, she filled his food bowl and freshened his water. Since Lindsey wasn't due to pick her up until noon, Allison decided to splurge and laid out the ingredients for coffee cake.

ॐ

Allison made it home just after three. Her dad had picked Lindsey up at the counselor's office so Allison could have the car for the rehearsal. When she was finished, she'd drive to her parent's house, get Lindsey, and go back to her apartment. Lindsey would take the car back to her parent's house so she'd have it for another meeting with the adoptive parents and Faith that was scheduled for Saturday morning. The rigmarole was getting irritating, but Allison did her best to paste on a smile and roll with it. For now, she was happy to have her car parked in its spot in the underground garage of her building.

She'd barely settled in with a book when her phone rang. Sighing, she checked the readout. "Hey, Lydia. Why aren't you too busy to be on the phone?"

"Allison. I need help. I can't do this."

Frowning at the fear she heard in her friend's voice, Allison spoke quietly. "Can't do what?"

"Marry Kevin. This is insane. I don't know what I was thinking. Oh, gosh…what I am going to do?"

"The first thing you're going to do is calm down and tell me where you are. Then, before you talk to anyone else, you're going to wait 'til I get there. Okay?"

"Okay. I'm at home." Lydia rattled off the address and directions to the entrance into the basement apartment.

"Give me twenty minutes." Allison looked mournfully at her book then set it aside. One of these days she was going to have time to read more than two pages and possibly figure out who the FBI's mole was. Her dad had made too many veiled hints lately. If she didn't get it read soon, he'd spill the beans. Thankfully it wouldn't ruin the story for her, but she liked to see if she could guess. With a last scratch for Pippin, she slid on her shoes and headed for the door, grateful she had her car.

જ્જ

Lydia threw open the door when she knocked. *Whoa.* She'd never seen Lydia look this rough. Her blonde hair was sticking up in the back and frizzed around her face. Smeared mascara streaked down her cheeks.

Alarmed by her friend's sorry state, Allison stepped in and pulled Lydia into a hug. "What's going on?"

Lydia crossed the room and flopped onto the couch, gesturing for Allison to sit. "I can't do this. I woke up this morning and realized that I don't think Kevin knows what he's getting into. Tomorrow night..." she cast a panicked look at Allison. "He deserves to have a bride who can legitimately wear white." Lydia buried her face in her hands.

"So…sex is the problem?" Allison squirmed. This was absolutely not a conversation she wanted to have. With anyone. "Are you sure I'm the right person to be talking to about this? I don't have any useful experience."

"That's just the point!" Lydia threw her hands in the air. "How would you feel if you got to your wedding night, a night you'd been saving yourself for and anticipating as something pure and holy, the union of two people in a covenant with God, and remembered that the other person was a sullied, broken mess when it came to holding up her end of the bargain?"

Allison cleared her throat. "Um. You've met Phil, the man I've fallen in love with, right? Or perhaps I should say the *divorced* man I've fallen in love with. I could be wrong, but I'm assuming he and his ex-wife had sex. And given that he wasn't a Christian when he got married, I'm kind of assuming it happened before they were married." She shifted in her seat. She really didn't want to be here. She liked Lydia, but friendship had its limits. Or it should. "Haven't you and Kevin talked about this?"

"Of course we have. And he just keeps saying he knows I have a past and that it's covered by Jesus' blood and on and on." Lydia met Allison's eyes. "But I don't think he really gets it. And…I'm scared that the memories are going to ruin things for both of us."

"Aha." Allison pursed her lips. "I'm guessing maybe that last part is the biggest issue." *Now what, Lord?*

*You got me here, You need to get me through it.* "I don't know, obviously, what it's going to be like, Lydia. But what I do know is that it's not okay to cling to any past sins once you've confessed them and been forgiven. If you put the thoughts out of your mind and ask God to free you from them, He will."

A tear sipped down Lydia's cheek. "Do you really think so?"

Allison nodded. .

Lydia swiped at her cheek. "That's what I've been praying for ever since Kevin forced my hand on committing to a date. And I think it's a large part of what was holding me back in the first place. So much of my time in rehab was spent processing the addiction and the reasons I ended up there. But even with that and seeing God's grace in my life, I haven't been sure He would really forgive so much...and I felt like I had to choose what to continue to carry. The sex seemed like less of a burden to hold onto than the abortion."

"Oh, Lydia." Allison moved to sit next to her. "You know better than that. Don't you listen when your dad preaches?"

Lydia laughed, clearly surprised. "Yeah, I do...but I always figure he means people who haven't sinned as badly as I did."

"I guarantee you there are people in the pews who have done just as much, or more, than you. We're all sinners, Lydia. And thankfully it's a true or false situation, not something with a ranking. We're either forgiven and set free, or we're not."

Lydia nodded slowly as the words seemed to sink in.

"And that ends my ability to preach."

"I'll have to suggest you to my dad next time he needs a fill-in. We'd be out well before the lunch crowds." Lydia smiled and threw her arm around Allison's shoulders. "Thanks. I didn't know who else to call. Rachel, my friend from rehab, is out of the country for work right now. Laura's so busy with the girls, and Matt and Kevin are, well, Matt and Kevin."

"And your parents?"

"Would've told me to stop being an idiot. Which is what you did, but you were a lot nicer about it."

*Thank you, Jesus. That was easier than I expected.* "You should probably consider a shower."

"What time is it?"

"Quarter after four."

Lydia jumped to her feet. "What? How? Oh, gosh."

Laughing, Allison stood as well. "I'll see you in a bit. And don't worry, I think it's considered normal for the bride to arrive fashionably late."

Allison walked out to her car. Once inside, she drummed her fingers on the steering wheel. There wasn't really time to go home and change, or she'd be late to the rehearsal as well. She didn't really need to change, though she'd planned to throw a blazer over the top of the jeans and blouse she'd worn to the counseling appointment with Lindsey. With a shrug, she started the engine. There were probably already people at the church setting up. Maybe they needed some help.

Should she say something to Kevin about Lydia's nervousness? How would that conversation go, exactly? She'd just let Lydia handle that one on her own. Besides, once the wedding was over, she suspected the worry and doubt would disappear.

She backed to the end of the driveway and checked her mirrors. She spotted another car pull away from the curb, then hesitate. She waved for the driver to go on, but the car just sat there. *Fine. Who cares about right of way? If you're going to let me go, I'm going.* She finished backing out and headed toward the church. After driving a few miles she noticed the same car traveling behind her. It was odd, though not all that unusual. She often saw the same cars on her way to work. Over time, she'd dubbed them her commuting buddies and started looking for them, enjoying the various foibles of her fellow travelers.

It wasn't far from Lydia's house to the church. After Allison locked her car, she tried to toss her keys in her purse and missed, sending them flying to the ground. She bent to retrieve them and noticed the same car from Lydia's neighborhood pull into the church lot, flip a tight U, and peel back out into traffic. *That was weird. I wonder…* Before she could finish the thought she heard her name called from across the parking lot.

"Allison." Kevin waved for her to join Matt and him.

She crossed the parking lot and nodded to the potted tree that sat on the pavement between them. "What's this?"

Matt jabbed a finger in her direction. "Your fault."

"What? How is this my fault?"

Kevin brushed his hands off on the sides of his legs. "I believe you are, in fact, the one who suggested cherry blossoms for the flowers. So in this case, Matt is right. This," he gestured to the tree, "is a cherry tree."

"Where are the blossoms?" Allison squinted at the tree's bare branches.

"That's the million dollar question now, isn't it?" Matt scratched the side of his jaw.

Both he and Kevin laughed as the blood rushed from Allison's face. "So what are you doing for flowers?" She closed her eyes. "Lydia's going to be so upset."

A look passed between Kevin and Matt.

"Are they all like this?"

Kevin jerked his head toward the sanctuary. "Why don't you go see."

*What have I done? You can't have a wedding with no flowers...and you can't get flowers the night before the wedding.* Allison tugged open the door into the foyer and hurried to the first sanctuary entrance. She peeked through the window and gasped. Potted cherry trees, each about eight feet tall, covered in a dazzling display of pink and white blossoms lined the center aisle. Four slightly taller trees formed a bower on the podium, the table holding the unity candle centered beneath their limbs.

"Nice call." Kevin came up behind her.

"It's gorgeous. And you're evil for making me think my idea had backfired so miserably. What's planted at the base of the pots?"

Kevin shrugged. "Something purple."

Allison rolled her eyes and looked back at the simple but gorgeous room of blooming trees. "I can't even fathom what this cost."

"That's the great thing." Matt strode up, dusting off his hands. "I got the dud loaded back up in the truck. These are all on loan."

What did he mean? Allison shot Kevin an expectant look.

"Matt's dad has a friend who owns a garden center. So long as none of them are damaged, we can return them on Sunday. Matt and a few other guys volunteered to pack them up tomorrow night after the reception so they don't get knocked over during services on Sunday. We would have left them, like people usually do with their floral arrangements, but decided it wasn't worth the potential cost."

"That's incredible. I'd expected a few twigs here and there. But this is…" Allison shook her head, "…unbelievable."

"It was a good idea." Kevin bumped her shoulder with his. "Now let's go find Mary and see what else she needs done. Everyone else should be showing up before too much longer."

Pleasantly full of the manicotti and garlic bread the women in the church had provided for the rehearsal dinner, Allison waved goodbye to the stragglers in the wedding party and headed to her car. She dialed her voicemail as she walked.

"Hi...it's Phil. Look, I'm sorry...for a host of things, but I think we probably should rewind to me being obnoxious on Tuesday and go forward from there. Please call me. I love you."

He still loved her. Lightheaded, Allison hit the return call button as she pulled out into traffic.

"Hey. You called back. I wasn't sure you would."

"I'm sorry too. I wasn't sure if I should pry on Tuesday...and then I got hurt and pouty. I'll admit that's a besetting sin of mine. And then you did the whole 'we need to talk' bit and I froze up inside."

"I know. I kicked myself pretty hard for that the rest of the day. I tried to stop by and explain, but you'd left...I really love you, Allison, are we okay?"

Were they? She didn't want to be without him. The past few days when she'd thought he was finished with her had been horrible. "Yeah. Yeah, we are. I love you, too, Phil."

"You have no idea how happy that makes me."

"I probably have some idea, seeing as how I feel the same when you say it." She stopped talking for a moment as she squeezed between two cars so she was in the correct lane for the next turn. "Is everything all right? Whatever was bugging you on Tuesday?"

Phil hesitated. "I had a run in with some people that went worse than I expected and just didn't handle it well, you know? But it'll be okay."

Allison jumped at the blare of horns behind her and lightly pressed her brake as the car in front of her slowed. The car behind her careened toward her back bumper, barely stopping in time.

"Aren't new clients grand? Hey, let me call you back. Apparently we've more than our share of idiots on the road tonight and I'd like to make it home safe and sound. I'll call you when I'm home, okay?"

"Sounds good. Drive carefully."

Allison dropped the phone into a cup holder and sped up, trying to get the car behind her off her tail. It seemed like each time she accelerated, they did too, keeping their bright headlights aimed perfectly into her mirrors, making it a challenge to see. She was glad she knew the road to her parent's house well. It was a hilly, curvy affair that still managed to have two lanes of traffic in either direction. The posted speed limit was consistently ignored. Between the darkness in front and the blinding lights of her tailgater behind, Allison kept a strangle hold on the wheel until she turned into her parent's neighborhood. Switching off the engine in the driveway, she lowered her head and waited for her hands to stop shaking before getting out.

Lindsey pulled open the door before Allison made it all the way to the porch. "I'm ready if you are."

"Everything okay?" Allison paused and looked toward the house. She really didn't want to get back in the car just yet.

Lindsey shrugged. "Sure. Just feeling a little cooped up. Your folks went to a play, so I've been hanging out in my room. And that's nice, but I'm ready to get out."

Allison handed Lindsey the keys. "Why don't you drive? That way we don't have to park when we get to my building, you can just drop me at the front door and be on your way." *And I don't have to deal with the crazies any more tonight.*

"Works for me." Lindsey grinned. "Let's go."

Lindsey backed out of the driveway after the briefest look over her shoulder. Allison drew in a breath. *Don't be a nervous Nelly.* She'd ridden with Lindsey before and while she definitely drove with the exuberance of youth, she wasn't reckless.

The car zipped back toward Allison's apartment.

"This road cracks me up. You think you're in the ritzy suburbs of D.C., then you get off the Interstate and all of the sudden, here's a windy country road." Lindsey took a blind curve at a speed that had Allison rethinking her decision to let the girl drive.

"Um. Yeah. Let's keep that in mind, okay? Maybe do what we can to get back to my place in one piece?"

Lindsey chuckled and eased off the accelerator. "Sorry. There was some doofus riding my tail. I thought if I sped up a little they'd back off."

*Surely it's not the same car.* Allison turned to look over her shoulder, but all she saw was headlights about four car lengths behind them. "Looks like it worked."

Lindsey signaled then turned into the cloverleaf onto the highway. "This part is less of a joy. I don't understand why they keep all these left-lane merges around here."

Allison swiveled and checked out the lane they needed to merge into. "You're clear if you speed up just a tad."

Lindsey accelerated and glanced over her shoulder. Just as she was pulling into the lane, the car behind them accelerated as well.

"Watch out."

Lindsey tapped the brakes. The other car zipped into the lane and pulled alongside their car, hovering with the front end even with the rear tire, so the headlights hit the side mirror.

"What is wrong with them?" Lindsey frowned and moved her head around. "I can't see. The light's reflecting right into my eyes."

Allison lowered the window and pulled the mirror so it folded in. "Is that better?"

"Light-wise, yes. But now I can't see to change lanes."

Allison glanced over her shoulder. "They're still there. And there are at least four cars behind them, so you can't just hang out until they pass. Gun it."

Lindsey pushed the gas pedal to the floor. For a moment, it looked like they would be able to make it. Then the car next to them swerved back into the merge lane, smashing into Allison's door and pushing the car into the concrete barrier. Glass shattered and metal squealed as the car skittered against the concrete before coming to a rest. Horns blared as cars continued to zip past.

Allison tried to reach up to swipe at her forehead, but her arm protested, the pain working its way through her shock. Carefully she turned her head. "Lindsey?"

The girl groaned.

Allison gritted her teeth and reached into the cup holder for her cell phone. It had been thrown by the impact. She tried to feel around on the floor with her feet to no avail. *Jesus, help us. Keep Lindsey and the baby safe. And please…have someone call 911.*

The tapping on her shoulder and strobing lights disoriented her. How much time had passed? Allison wasn't positive she'd remained conscious.

"Miss? Miss? Are you all right?"

"Mostly." Allison turned her head and managed a weak smile for the EMT. "Please check on Lindsey, the driver, she's pregnant."

"They're taking care of her. Are you feeling dizzy or disoriented?" He flicked the beam of a flashlight into, then back out of, her vision.

"Not really." Now that someone was talking to her, she felt more focused. Except she hurt. "Is she okay? Is the baby okay?"

The EMT studied her then straightened. "I'll go ask. You stay put, no moving." He pointed a finger at her. "I'm serious."

Allison watched as he strode off to confer with another EMT at the front of the car. Lindsey was on a gurney, already loaded into an ambulance. Allison saw them slam the doors shut and winced as the siren flipped on, adding its voice to the flashing lights before moving out into traffic.

The EMT returned. "She's banged up, maybe a little worse than you, though I think your arm is going to be a while healing. They're concerned her water broke, so they're rushing her in now. You'll follow as soon as another ambulance arrives."

Tears welled in Allison's eyes as the pain in her arm, head and shoulder increased. She closed her eyes and focused on breathing while the EMT finished checking her out for transport. She needed someone to call Phil. And Marcus. But she couldn't get the words out.

## 48

Phil was reading in bed, waiting for Allison to call back. What was taking so long? Should he call her back instead? No. She'd had a big day. Maybe she'd ended up being too tired to talk. Wouldn't she have at least called to tell him that? A yawn interrupted any further thought. Phil slipped a bookmark between the pages of the latest spy thriller he'd checked out of the library and clicked off the bedside lamp. He'd see her tomorrow at the wedding. He'd just gotten settled when the phone rang.

*Figures.* Phil rolled over and fumbled for the phone. "Hello?"

"Is this Phil Reid?"

He didn't recognize the voice. "Yes?"

"Phil, it's Tom. Vasak. Allison's father?"

"Is she all right?" Something had to be wrong. There was no other reason for Tom to be calling him. His heartbeat kicked into high gear.

"Yes. Well, mostly. A car pushed them into the concrete median on the Beltway. Hit and run at this point, though they might have a license plate from the traffic cameras."

"How hurt is she? Where'd they take her?" Phil pushed the covers off and threw his legs over the side of the bed. "I'll be there as soon as I can."

"She's asleep right now. She's got a broken arm and some bruising, it's really not that serious. They gave her something for the pain that's knocked her out. There's nothing you can do."

Phil frowned. "Did you say 'them'? Who else was in the car?"

"Lindsey was driving. She needed Allison's car tomorrow, well, today."

"Is she all right?"

"For the most part, though the trauma of the accident seems to have started labor again and last I heard, her water might have broken. If that's the case, she'll have to deliver."

"And Allison?"

"I promise you, she's going to be all right. Phil, why don't you get some sleep and come tomorrow morning, first thing."

"I don't want her to be alone all night."

"She won't be. I'm going to stay."

Phil rubbed the back of his neck. What was the right thing? He didn't want to stay here—he needed to be with Allison. But her parents already didn't' like him. If he showed up after they told him to stay away was there any chance they'd change their minds about him? *Doesn't matter. I need to be there. The accident...that had to have been Brandi. My fault. She's hurt and it's my fault.*

"I need to be there. Even if they'll only let one person in her room and you're claiming that spot...I just need to be there."

"Phil...I won't stop you, but I think you'd be better off getting a good night's sleep."

Phil let out a harsh laugh. "That's not happening either way. Sir, I need to come."

Silence stretched across the line for several heartbeats before Tom spoke again. "I'll see you when you get here then. And, Phil...for what it's worth, the conversation on Monday? I would've liked a chance to get to know you better beforehand, but it's clear, to me at least, that you're good for my little girl. Make her happy. Irene'll come around."

Phil opened his mouth but no words came. He cleared his throat and tried again. "Thank you, sir. I'll be there as fast as I can."

CROWD

Tom was sitting beside the bed, holding Allison's hand when she opened her eyes Saturday morning. Memories of the previous night came flooding back. They hadn't been able to find her cell phone before taking her to the hospital, so the EMT who'd been talking to her had used his own phone to call her parents when she rattled off the number. She'd tried to get them to go to Labor and Delivery to be with Lindsey, but they'd been adamant that someone would come and be with her. Allison had already been admitted for observation when her dad arrived.

"Have you heard from Mom? How's Lindsey?"

Tom gave her a weary smile. "She's in labor. Last I heard she hadn't delivered, but it's been a couple hours. Your mother did manage to get a hold of Marcus and he's on his way back. She also wanted you to know that she wants to be here with you more than she can say, but just didn't feel like she should leave Lindsey alone."

"She's right. It's good that she's there with Lindsey...and I'm glad Marcus is on his way back." Lindsey was safe. With that worry taken care of, she wanted Phil. Allison squeezed Tom's hand. "Daddy? Could you call Phil? Please?"

"I already did, honey." His eyes flicked to the doorway. "But don't tell your mother." He rolled his eyes. "He's been here all night, too. He just stepped out to get some air and call his sister. He said something about her maybe having an inside scoop on Lindsey. But I didn't quite understand that."

"Karin works in the NICU. At least I know one pair of hands over there is good."

"It's the best NICU in the area, Allie, I'm pretty sure all the hands are good. But I understand what you're saying." He scooted his chair closer and reached up to brush her hair out of her face. "I should probably tell you…"

A nurse bustled into the room. "Good morning." She checked all the monitors and smiled at Allison. "How are you feeling?"

"Okay." If you didn't count aching all over. Allison adjusted herself to a more upright position. "When can I go home?"

The nurse chuckled. "From the way things look, I'm guessing as soon as the doctor makes his rounds. That should be another hour or two. They get a slightly later start on Saturdays." She nodded at the temporary cast encasing Allison's left arm. "Have you had one of those before?"

Allison nodded. "Sadly, yes."

"All right. We'll send you home with care instructions, and some pain medication, but otherwise, you've just got some scratches and a big bump on your head that should fade with rest and time. Though I'm sure you feel that's plenty. Still, no concussion, which is good." She checked her watch and nodded briskly. "Call if you need anything."

She didn't want to wait. She wanted to go home. Now. "What should you tell me?"

"Knock knock?" Phil poked his head in the door. "I saw the nurse leaving and hoped that meant you were awake." He produced a bouquet of flowers from behind his back and offered them to Allison with a flourish.

Her heart leapt and the throbbing of her aches faded. She buried her nose in the arrangement of mixed blooms and inhaled. "They're lovely. Thank you." She glanced at her dad and saw him shift in his seat.

"Morning, sir." Phil nodded to Tom with a strained smile.

Tom returned the nod and stood. "I think I'll stretch my legs since you won't be alone now, baby." He leaned over and pressed a kiss to her forehead, just below the black and blue lump where her head hit the car door.

Allison watched her dad leave before looking at Phil. "Sorry I didn't call you back."

"Well, you have a good excuse this time. Just don't let it happen again." He kissed her head just beside the spot her father had kissed before settling into the chair at her bedside. "I mean it. Don't ever let this happen again. I don't think my heart could take it. How are you feeling?"

"Achy, but better now that you're here. I know it'll be worse later today or tomorrow when everything starts catching up with me."

" Have they said when you can go home?"

"Not officially, but the nurse sounded optimistic that it'd be soon. Until I know for sure that I can't make the wedding, nothing is getting said to Lydia or Kevin." She really didn't want to leave her friends high and dry. Nothing was wrong with her voice. If she could get out of here, she could still sing. "Got it?"

Phil held up his hands and mimed a zipper across his lips. "Mum's the word... Any news on Lindsey?"

She shook her head. "I was kind of hoping you'd have some."

"I haven't been able to do more than leave a message for Karin. That's pretty typical when she's at work though." He squeezed her hand. "I'm sure she's okay. Did they get in touch with Marcus?"

"Yeah, he's on his way back."

"Good." Phil watched her for several seconds. "I talked to Grant this morning before I came. He's been following up with the police about Brandi. They're pretty confident this was her. They've tracked down the car and are hopeful it's just a matter of time 'til they catch her at this point." He took her hand in his and squeezed gently. "I'm so sorry. I feel like I brought this on you. All of it."

One corner of Allison's mouth twitched up. "You're worth it."

Tom cleared his throat from the doorway. "I brought coffee..."

Phil leaned back, though he didn't release Allison's hand. "Just what the doctor ordered."

It was after two when Allison, aided by Phil, finally made it back to her apartment. She was aching all over and desperately wanted to lie down and go back to sleep. But she couldn't bail on the wedding. Her voice was fine. She just needed a shower and some aspirin. She wanted the pain killers that had been sent home, but they made her too sleepy. Aspirin would have to be enough.

"Could you get a trash bag from under the sink for me?"

Phil frowned. "Can't the trash wait?"

"It's for my arm," she gestured to her cast, "I've got to take a shower, if only to get the hospital off me."

"Got it." He disappeared into the kitchen as the phone began to ring.

Making her way slowly to where the phone sat on the coffee table, Allison lowered herself to the sofa before answering. "Hello?"

"Allison? It's Mom."

"Hey, Mom. How's Lindsey?"

"Physically, she's fine. But she wanted to talk to you, hang on a second."

There was shuffling, then Lindsey came on the line. "Allison? He's here, and so perfect."

Allison grinned and felt a tear slip down her cheek. "Oh, Lindsey, that's wonderful. How do you feel? Did you call Faith? Have Brian and Olivia come?"

"I called Faith this morning, she was going to wait to hear from me before letting Brian and Olivia know. Allison, he's so precious...I don't know if I can do this."

She leaned back into the sofa and closed her eyes. Now her heart hurt too. "Lindsey, sweetie. Do you remember the reasons you didn't think parenting was the right choice for you or your baby?"

"Yes, but..."

"Have any of them changed?" This was hard. But what Lindsey needed to hear was the truth.

Silence stretched across the line before Lindsey finally spoke, a pout in her tone. "No."

"I can't imagine how hard this is going to be. But you need to make sure you do what's best for you and for him. Yesterday, you thought placing him with Brian and Olivia was best for both of you. Today, seeing him, I get that it's real...but you need to pray about what's best and do that." Allison chewed on her lip. "Do you want me to come and stay with you?"

Phil came back with a trash bag and sat next to her on the couch. He looked at her quizzically.

Allison mouthed "Lindsey" and rested her hand on his knee.

Lindsey sighed. "No...you're right. I'll call Faith and have them come. Maybe it'll be a little easier when I see them together."

"I love you, Lindsey. You're an amazing, incredible young woman."

"Pray for me, Allison. Please? This is harder than I thought it'd be."

Irene came back on the line. "How are you, dear?"

"Sore. Stiff. Running late."

"I won't keep you, then. I spoke with your father...tell your young man I appreciate him taking such good care of you."

Allison gave the phone a surprised look before hanging it up. She turned to Phil. "My mom says she appreciates your help with me. You might want to write that down in a journal or something."

Phil chuckled. "I might just do that." He handed her the trash bag. "Now, as much as I'd love to stay, well," pink stole across his cheeks, "I'm not actually all that comfortable being in your apartment alone while you're in the shower. Plus I need to get home and change if I'm going to be presentable at the wedding."

The look he gave her sent warm tingles down to her toes. "When you put it that way…"

Phil's phone rang. After a brief conversation, he hung up. "How do I buzz someone in?"

Allison pointed to the security pad by the door. "Who are we letting in?"

"My pinch hitter." Phil strode to the door to watch for their guest. "There she is. You remember Karin?"

Karin came in with a hesitant smile. "Is this okay? Phil thought you might need help with your hair and makeup, and that kind of thing, and didn't think he was the right man for the job."

"Bless you both. I've been trying to figure out how I was going to get ready since we left the hospital. I can manage the shower, I think, but beyond that." Allison shrugged. "I was going to just make do." She crossed to Phil and kissed him. "You're the sweetest man on the planet."

"Sweet?" Phil frowned as Karin pushed him out the door. "How about something more manly?"

"We'll figure out adjectives while she gets ready." Karin appraised his outfit. "Go home and change. I'll get her to the church in time." She shut the door and turned to Allison. "All right, let's get this show on the road."

## 49

Allison squeaked into her seat just before the ushers began bringing in guests. She wilted under the disapproving glare of the wedding planner who tapped her watch and made a notation on her clipboard. What was she going to do, blacklist her from weddings at the church? She glanced over her shoulder. Where was Phil? He was cutting it even closer than she had.

When the mothers were seated, Allison slipped her phone from her purse and checked to be sure it was on vibrate. It was. She also had a text from Lindsey. Opening it, she saw Lindsey propped up in a hospital bed, surrounded by Irene, Brian and Olivia, who was holding a tightly wrapped bundle that could only be the baby. A tear slipped down her cheek. *Jesus, thank you for that new family. Heal Lindsey's heart. Give her confidence and peace in her decision.* She saved the photo and scrolled through her call log. Nothing new from Phil.

When Lydia stepped through the doors at the back of the sanctuary, it was as if everyone took a breath at once. She was a gorgeous bride. Her progress down the tree-lined aisle made it seem like they'd transported the sanctuary to a secluded glen somewhere. When Lydia and Kevin joined hands under the arched bows, Allison felt her heart constrict. Though she was overjoyed for her friends, she wanted that happiness for herself…and she wanted Phil to be part of it. Where was he?

The ceremony proceeded quickly, and before she realized it, Allison was finished singing and back in her seat, watching her friends, now husband and wife, walk joyfully down the aisle hand in hand.

Allison waited until the sanctuary had cleared out before making her way to the foyer. There were still several clumps of people mingling, though the wedding party had been whisked off somewhere. She spotted Matt and Laura and their two girls and headed that way.

"That was lovely, wasn't it?" Allison squatted down to their older daughter's level. "You made a beautiful bride, Jennie."

"I wasn't the bride. I threw flowers!" Jennie giggled and twirled, causing her skirt to billow out.

"Ohhh." Allison smiled at the girl's exuberance. "Well, you were a star." She straightened and chewed her lip. "Do you think I could catch a ride to the reception with you? My date appears to be AWOL."

Laura glanced around the foyer. "Phil's not here?" In the process of looking, her eyes lit on the cast on Allison's arm. "What happened?"

"Long story, probably not fit for little ears. The short version is that Lindsey and I were in a car accident yesterday. But it's all tied in to the rest of the drama, I think."

Concern clouded Matt's face. "How's Lindsey?"

"She had the baby this morning. The trauma induced labor. But everyone seems healthy from what I've been able to gather. I haven't had much time to really check on things. They kept me overnight and by the time I got home it was a rush to get here. Maybe I should just call a cab and go see Lindsey, skip the reception."

"No. Come with us." Laura grabbed Allison's good arm. "It's going to be fun, and I know Kevin and Lydia would both miss you. Who knows, maybe Phil will join us there."

"Yeah, maybe." Why hadn't he made it to the wedding? Or at least texted to say he got held up? If he wasn't coming, she really didn't want to go to the reception. She was tired and achy and starting to think she'd misread his attentions at the hospital. "I'm going to step outside and call my mom to check in on things. She's staying with Lindsey. Even though Marcus made it back early this morning, Mom wouldn't leave her side. But we can go whenever...I appreciate the ride." She wandered through the foyer, stopping to say hi to several people. When she finally made it outside, she sat on the bench placed in the garden to the side of the main doors and pulled out her phone. Still no messages from Phil.

∞

When Phil arrived home, he found an unmarked police car sitting in his driveway. Resisting the urge to drive past, he pulled into the garage and parked. The detective was already getting out of his car when Phil stepped out into the driveway.

"Good afternoon. Mr. Reid?"

"Yeah." Phil hooked his thumbs in his back pockets. "Can I help you?"

"I hope so. I'm Detective Gomez, I've been trying to coordinate the recent cases involving your ex-wife, one Brandi Jenks. There was another incident last night, I believe?"

"That's the assumption. Would you like to come in?"

"Sure."

Phil led the detective up the inside stairs from the garage and into the kitchen. "Can I offer you something to drink?"

"Just some water."

While Phil filled two glasses with ice and water from the in-door dispenser of the fridge, the detective rattled off the facts of the various incidents with Brandi.

"Is that correct?"

Phil sat one glass in front of Detective Gomez and sat opposite him at the kitchen table. "Sounds right." He scrubbed a hand over his face. "Have they found her yet? If she rammed Allison's car into the concrete barrier, wouldn't she have been injured, too?"

"We're watching emergency rooms." The detective gave Phil a long look. "Sir, have you had any contact with Ms. Jenks since the break-in at Allison Vasak's apartment?"

"She's called a few times. I reported each one to my attorney, who I believe passed that information on to the police. But I haven't seen her." *Thank goodness. I'm not sure I could keep from throttling her at this point.*

The detective sighed and drained his glass. "All right. If she contacts you, please call me as well as your attorney." He pulled a card from his breast pocket and slid it across the table.

"Absolutely. Thank you." Phil stood and offered his hand before showing the police man back down to his car.

Running up the stairs, Phil glanced at his watch. He was going to be a few minutes late, but if he hurried, he could still probably make the majority of the wedding.

Dressed in his black pinstriped suit with a cobalt blue shirt and a blue and silver tie, Phil patted his pants pocket nervously. The boxed ring made a soft bulge under his hand, but it didn't appear visible from the outside. He wasn't incredibly happy with the idea that Allison's mother would eventually come around, but it beat the outright 'no' he'd been given earlier in the week. He took a deep breath to steady his nerves.

His cell phone rang as he was backing out of the garage. "Hello?"

"Phil, baby." Brandi's voice was slurred and shrieking.

"Brandi." Phil put the car in park and wearily leaned his head on the steering wheel. "Can you please turn yourself in and just be done with all of this? I'm begging you. Just stop."

"I've got a better idea. Meet me at the train bridge. That's what, ten minutes for you? Marshall here hopes you'll hurry, don't you hon?"

Phil heard shouting in the background and felt a stab of worry. What was she doing?

"I'm calling the police, Brandi. I need to go."

"You can bring them, too. Doesn't matter. But don't miss this, Phil. Marshall's depending on you."

Phil sprinted back inside to find Detective Gomez's card. He punched in the numbers as he returned to his car and headed through town toward the train bridge over the Occoquan River.

"We'll be right there. Don't do anything stupid, Mr. Reid. Being a hero's not real worthwhile if you're dead."

"Got it." Phil clicked the phone off and dropped it on the passenger seat. He should text Allison and let her know he was going to be late. He glanced at his watch and winced. Scratch that, he was going to miss the whole thing. He hoped he'd make it to Old Town in time to attend the reception. Should he just let the police deal with it, regardless of what Brandi implied? Marshall's fearful holler in the background echoed in his head. Whatever game Brandi was playing, Phil was going to have to see it through.

He pulled off the road on the south side of the Route One car bridge and hiked through the wild grass to the train bridge a few dozen feet away. He frowned as thorns snagged his pant legs and scuffed his freshly polished dress shoes. Squinting, he saw someone sitting on a lump in the middle of the tracks of the bridge.

"Brandi!"

The form on the bridge stood and waved before weaving its way closer. "Phil, you made it." She turned to look over her shoulder. "Say hi to Marshall."

Phil's eyes flicked to the lump on the tracks then back to Brandi.

"He won't say hi back though, I'm afraid. He got annoying, so I had to hit him with this." She pulled a gun from the waistband of her jeans and leveled it at Phil. "I didn't really want to deal with the dead weight, but he just wasn't cooperating." She narrowed her eyes as she looked over Phil's shoulder. "You stop there. Sounds like your friends are on their way."

The sound of approaching sirens split through the quiet evening.

When Phil started to turn to see how close they were, Brandi waved the gun.

"Nuh-uh. Stop and just be still. I doubt they're going to rush into anything before they figure out what's really going on. Maybe you're not so important after all."

"Never said I was, Brandi." Phil thought of his cell phone on the passenger seat of his car. He should have taken the two seconds to let Allison know where he was. *Please let me get a chance to explain.*

Brandi snorted. "Maybe not in words, but your holier than me attitude made it pretty clear you thought your precious *Jesus*," she spat the word, "made you special. Better than me." She gave him a disgusted look. "You were pretty happy to party with me for five years before you had your little spiritual awakening. Then all of the sudden I'm not good enough? Ha! I showed you then, I'll show you now. And Marshall over there?" She looked over her shoulder with disgust. "He comes to me and says he thinks there's more to life? Then he goes and finds Jesus too?" The crazed expression in her eyes intensified. "All the men I marry turn out to love some dead dude more than me. You think I'm gonna stand for that? No way, no how." She waved the gun in Phil's direction. "So come on, Mr. Goody Two Shoes, whatcha' gonna do now?"

Phil shook his head. His heart was racing, but there was no way he was moving from the relative safety of solid ground. "Brandi, I'm sorry you think it was personal. I wanted you to see the same thing I did. I tried everything I could think of, but remember, you're the one who kicked me out. Even after that, I tried to show you how much better life could be. I prayed you'd find the courage to change."

"I don't need to change. What has all that change done for you? And I have plenty of courage."

Phil thought of Allison. The way her eyes lit up when she saw him. How slipping his hand into hers was like coming home. He thought of the peace he got when he seriously humbled his heart before the Eternal Father and poured out his longings. The richness of life he'd been experiencing ever since he realized the changes he needed to make in his heart. But no amount of explanation would convince Brandi. She'd made up her mind and her heart was hard. So instead, Phil bowed his head and closed his eyes. *Jesus, reveal yourself to her. And if she won't see you, Lord, keep Marshall and me safe.*

A train whistle sounded down the track. Phil's eyes snapped open and he looked beyond Brandi to Marshall who remained unmoving in the middle of the tracks.

Brandi stood frozen until the whistle blew again. She turned and ran back onto the track, her balance off from whatever she'd been consuming that evening. She nearly fell between the ties several times as she made her way out to Marshall.

Phil looked helplessly on as she struggled to haul one of Marshall's arms up. He imagined she was hoping to haul Marshall's unconscious form to safety. Several police officers rushed past him toward the tracks while others hollered into the radio back at the parked cars. The screech of metal on metal filled the air as the freight train tried to stop. Sparks and smoke billowed out from the wheels.

Phil saw Brandi look over her shoulder at the train and leap to her feet, leaving Marshall in a heap. She continued to dart down the tracks away from the police, heading unsteadily across the bridge. She slipped several times before stumbling and falling between two ties. He turned back toward the road and closed his eyes as he heard the unmistakable sound of a body hitting the concrete support column followed by a distant splash. Phil sank slowly to his knees in the wild grass and buried his head in his hands.

50

Allison stood at the gangplank of the Potomac River cruise that Lydia and Kevin had booked for their reception. The last guests had boarded. All that was left was for the wedding party to come aboard and be announced, then the ship would set off. She wasn't sure what to do. She moved to the side of the dock and perched on a bench, pulling out her cell phone for the millionth time to check its battery. Still no word from Phil.

"Hey." Kevin cocked his head to the side and tucked his hands in his pockets. "Why aren't you on board?"

Allison sighed. "Phil didn't make the wedding. He hasn't shown up here...I'm torn between being worried about him and wondering if this is his gentle approach to breaking up."

Kevin frowned. "That doesn't sound like Phil."

"I know. But not calling isn't like him either." *Though who knows how people react when they're done with you? I never thought he'd be one to use the silent treatment, but look at last week.* She forced her lips into a smile. "Congratulations, by the way. The two of you look good together."

A grin split Kevin's face. "You have no idea how happy I am that today is finally here." He glanced over his shoulder as Lydia broke away from the clump of hugging sisters and practically floated toward him.

"I think I can guess." Why couldn't she just be completely happy for them? She was tired of the jealousy. But more, she was tired of always being the last one standing alone on the sideline. She stood and gave him a tight squeeze. "I'm happy for you." It wasn't completely a lie. Allison turned to embrace Lydia as she joined them. "Congratulations."

"Thanks." Lydia peered over Allison's shoulder. "Where's Phil?"

Allison shrugged.

The horn on the boat sounded, long and low. "We should get aboard." Lydia turned to Allison. "Are you coming?"

Allison looked at the bright lights of the boat. Her heart sank and tears pricked her eyes as laughter spilled over the balconies. She shook her head. "No. I think I'll just go home. I love you guys."

Kevin slipped his hand into Lydia's. "Call him, Al. Find out what's going on before you jump to conclusions." With a final hug, he and Lydia followed the wedding party onto the boat.

Allison sat back down on the bench and listened as the DJ announced the wedding party. Laughter, cheers, and applause drifted over the river as the ship moved out into the water to sail past the monuments glowing in the twilight.

When she could no longer hear the revelry, Allison stood and wrapped her good arm around her middle, fighting a chill that sprang from nowhere. She turned and slowly walked back toward the brightly lit streets of Old Town Alexandria. *Why hadn't he come?*

∞

Phil ran down the sidewalk as the low horn sounded from the pier. Talk about missing the boat. *Idiot.* He sprinted around the corner and saw the stern lights of the ship fading down the river. He stopped and stuffed his hands in his pockets. *And that's that.* His fingers closed around the ring box and he swallowed the lump in his throat.

He kicked a rock, watching it bounce and careen in odd directions as it struck cobblestones. What did he do now? He didn't want to go home. Not yet. He followed the rock, kicking it again each time it stopped. When it bounced into the street, Phil paused and looked around. He was back at the park he and Allison had visited on their date. Thinking of her, he dug out his cell phone and frowned. Apparently the battery had died during the drive. He continued down the path toward the water.

Phil's eyes flicked over to the bench where he and Allison had sat. Someone was already there. His shoulders slumped and he continued past the small clearing.

"Phil?"

He spun. "Allison?" He retraced his steps and peered into the dim space. He shrugged out of his jacket. "You look cold. Put this on."

"Thanks." She slid her good arm into the coat and tugged the other half over her shoulder and cast. "Is everything okay?"

There was no way to answer that. Nothing was okay. And yet, with her still here, everything was all right. Phil dropped onto the bench next to her and took her hand in his. "It's a lot better with you here. I saw the boat pulling away and thought you'd be on it."

"I almost was. But I was worried. Maybe a little mad." The corners of her mouth twitched up. "Mostly worried."

"I'm sorry I didn't call. I kept meaning to, then I thought I'd make the wedding, and then..." He took a deep breath and stared out toward the river as he related the confrontation with Brandi. "So...that's a closed chapter. But my heart breaks for her." Was it possible she could understand?

"It's always sad when someone dies, but it's so much worse when we know they weren't a believer."

Phil let out a breath. "Exactly."

"And Marshall?"

"I'm not sure. She clocked him pretty hard, he was still out when the ambulance arrived...but at least he's alive." *And we're all finally free of her.* "What a mess."

Allison leaned her head on his shoulder. "I'm sorry."

They sat for a moment under the clear sky. There were too many lights to see stars, but the quiet swish of the river and the lights from nearby boats were nearly as soothing. Phil licked his lips. "About Tuesday." He needed to explain if there was any chance of a future together. She'd understood about Brandi, would she understand about this, too?

"Phil...it's all right. You're allowed to have a bad day."

"It's not that." *Here we go.* "I was in a bad place because I went to see your parents Monday night."

Confusion clouded Allison's eyes as she looked up at him. "Why on Earth would you do that?"

He reached into his pocket and pulled out the small velvet box. Carefully opening it, he offered it to her. "I wanted to get their blessing before giving you this and asking if you'd do me the incredible honor of being my wife."

Allison froze. Wide eyed, she reached out with one hand and stopped just short of the ring, her gaze snapping up to meet Phil's.

"They said no."

She blinked. A frown creased her forehead. "What?"

He nodded once and swallowed again, fighting nerves. "This morning, I got the impression that they, or, your dad, might have thawed slightly to the idea…still I won't lie." He cleared his throat. "They're not excited about the prospect. But Allison, I love you. I want to spend the rest of my life with you." He slid off the bench onto one knee and took the ring out of the box, sliding it just over the fingernail of her left ring finger. "Will you marry me?"

A slow smile worked its way across Allison's face as she guided the ring onto her finger. Tears spilled out of her eyes as she leaned forward, her lips resting against his as she breathed the words, "Yes, I'll marry you. I love you, too."

*Oh, thank you, Jesus.* Phil stood and gathered her into his arms. "What about your parents?"

"They'll come around."

## Author's Note

Thank you so much for reading Courage to Change! I hope you enjoyed following along as Allison and Phil fell in love. If you did enjoy it, I'd appreciate it so much if you'd leave a review on Amazon, Goodreads, or whatever online retailer you enjoy. Your reviews help other readers find and enjoy my books.

I'm continually grateful to God, my family, and my critique partners for their help in my writing endeavors. None of this would be possible without them.

I'd love to connect with you on my website (http://www.ElizabethMaddrey.com) or my Facebook page (http://www.Facebook.com/ElizabethMaddrey). And if you haven't already signed up for my occasional newsletter, I'd love to share information about new releases and upcoming events with you. You can find a subscription link on my website or Facebook or you can subscribe directly by visiting this link http://bit.ly/2g0AGvf

## About the Author

Elizabeth Maddrey began writing stories as soon as she could form the letters properly and has never looked back. Though her practical nature and love of math and organization steered her into computer science for college and graduate school, she has always had one or more stories in progress to occupy her free time. When she isn't writing, Elizabeth is a voracious consumer of books and has mastered the art of reading while undertaking just about any other activity. She is the co-author of *A is for Airstrip: A Missionary's Jungle Adventure*, a children's book based on the work of a Wycliffe missionary, and is a member of ACFW.

Elizabeth lives in the suburbs of Washington D.C. with her husband and their two incredibly active little boys. She invites you to interact with her at her website www.ElizabethMaddrey.com or on Facebook: www.facebook.com/ElizabethMaddrey